Eleanor de Jong is the daughter of academics and grew up in Europe, America and the UK. She studied history and politics at university, and is now settled in London with her partner. *Delilah* is her first novel.

DELILAH

In the ancient Holy Land, the Israelites and the Philistines are locked in bitter conflict. Samson — a seemingly unbeatable adversary — has come to symbolise Israelite defiance and the dominant Philistines are desperate to uncover the secret of his power. Delilah — desirable, headstrong and reckless — is tired of living the dull life of a demure maiden. She wants more, and tempted by an offer she can't refuse, is persuaded to make a bargain. But this is no easy game of win or lose. Instead, Delilah makes an astonishing discovery, one that she could never have imagined. But a sequence of events have been put in motion and only a miracle can change the course of history . . .

ELEANOR DE JONG

◆

DELILAH

Complete and Unabridged

CHARNWOOD
Leicester

First published in Great Britain in 2011 by
HarperCollins*Publishers*
London

First Charnwood Edition
published 2012
by arrangement with
HarperCollins*Publishers*
London

British Library CIP Data

De Jong, Eleanor.
  Delilah.
  1. Samson (Biblical judge)- -Fiction.
  2. Delilah (Biblical figure)- -Fiction.
  3. Religious fiction.
  4. Large type books.
  I. Title
  823.9′2–dc23

  ISBN 978–1–4448–1009–7

Published by
F. A. Thorpe (Publishing)
Anstey, Leicestershire

Set by Words & Graphics Ltd.
Anstey, Leicestershire
Printed and bound in Great Britain by
T. J. International Ltd., Padstow, Cornwall

This book is printed on acid-free paper

Acknowledgements

Four pillars stop the roof from falling in on my head — you know who you are. Much love and thanks to all of you.

At Working Partners, Michael Ford helped me prune the dead wood from the vine so it would produce better fruit and Charles Nettleton navigated the boat through over-fished waters. My huge thanks to you both.

And a word too for Kate Daubney for her additional research and all the biscuits.

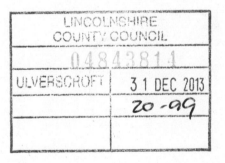

1

'Lilah! Where are you?'

Delilah tucked her feet more tightly beneath her and closed her eyes. She knew she couldn't be seen — that was the magic of her tiny nest between the vines, especially now, with the leaves so broad and green and the clusters of grapes beginning to swell on their stems — but it made sense to keep still and wait for Ekron to pass. Up the slope behind her, the sounds of the wedding party were like the rush of a distant river.

'Delilah? I know you're — ' She heard him break off and clear his throat, growling to himself, trying to keep his voice deep, to give the impression of being the man she knew he longed to be. He sounded so close; he must be in the next row over beside the well.

'I know you're out here, Delilah. You can't keep secrets from me!'

Ekron's last word came out in one painfully high squeak above the rest of the sentence, and Delilah gulped down the giggles that rose inside her. She could hear him wailing to himself as he trudged away along the path. His face would be burning red like the evening sun by now.

The scuffs of her stepbrother's sandals against the dusty earth became quieter as he continued his search further down the slopes. She couldn't understand his hurry to grow up. She'd be happy if she was eight forever, but he had begun

1

marking off the time until his twelfth birthday even though it was at least four moons away.

When he was out of earshot, Delilah untucked herself and sat cross-legged against the trunk of the vine. She ran her fingers along a pair of branches that rose over her shoulder, feeling the bark as it twisted around itself, already brown in the late summer heat. One branch was fatter than the other. Her father had once told her that it was branches like these that should be tied to the supports, for they would provide the frame of a plant year after year. The other branch, weaker and thinner, had coiled along the stronger one, strangling it. Delilah knew that if her father had been here, he would have cut the tendril away, even though it already held the promise of fat fruits.

Thinking about her father made her sad, and she pulled the leaves gently apart to peer up the valley towards the house. There was a strange little hump on this part of the slope that raised these few vines slightly above their neighbours. She'd found the hiding place by accident over a year ago, tripping among the neat rows of vines on her stepfather Achish's estate as she ran headlong from her mother's howls and the ritual laments of the gathered mourners. Tearing her dress had been just another horrible part of that wretched day.

Ekron had come after her then too, like he always did when she was upset, but she'd dodged him and weaved among the vines, faster than him, more desperate to escape than he was to catch her. From the secret nook she'd watched the groundsmen with their spades, repairing the ground that had been broken up to accept her father's body. His burial had been quick, hurried along by the Israelite traditions of which he had been so proud. Later that night, as her mother stitched her dress and Delilah cleaned the dust and tears from her face, she'd all but forgotten Achish's words of comfort by the graveside — not to worry, that he'd take care of her. Until that moment, he'd been just her father's employer, and a man with whom she rarely came into contact. She'd been too young to realise that one day he'd be something more.

Now, fourteen months later, the earth above her father's grave looked as brown and smooth as the earth around it, the only mark of its presence a young olive tree that cast a thin shadow across it. Achish had kept to his promise, and today marked the day that he took Delilah's mother as a wife. They had a new family, a new home, and each night she added the great Philistine god El to her prayers, thanking him for his kindness. Her mother had learned to smile again and Achish had made that happen. Ekron seemed happy enough too, to have Delilah as a stepsister as well as a friend. But Hemin — well, Hemin couldn't smile if you pasted one on that thin face with clay. And Delilah knew Hemin would sooner make herself sick than call Delilah her sister.

' — of course, it will be very difficult for Achish, raising that Israelite child in his own Philistine family — '

Delilah let the leaves fall together again and

3

tilted her head to listen. Over by the well she could see the feet of two women, old wrinkly feet in fussy sandals, their painted leather now dusted with dry earth.

'She is a handful, I'm sorry to say.' That was the voice of Achish's first wife, Ariadnh. She sounded a bit more formal than usual, as though she was trying to impress the woman she was speaking to. 'She has no sense of her place, no sense of how lucky she is.'

'Lucky indeed. I mean to say, her mother Beulah seems a pleasant woman — '

'Pleasant enough for an Israelite — '

'But she has married out of her culture and well above her station. Surely Achish knows how people will see it: the effects of such an association on himself, on his children, on you — '

'It's not merely a question of station, of course. Clearly I couldn't possibly say this to Achish myself — '

'It's not a wife's place to speak frankly to her husband — '

'Although Beulah does speak quite bluntly to Achish, I've heard it — '

Delilah bristled. How dare Ariadnh talk that way about her mother? From a young age, she recognised that there were differences between the two peoples who occupied the land, but it was only now, as the two worlds came together, that she realised the Israelites were a station beneath. One rarely saw Philistines in the fields when the sun was at its hottest, and even in the city there were areas that Philistines wouldn't go

4

to without a chaperone. Among the other workers on Achish's estate, Israelite and Philistine couples didn't mix.

She crawled out of her hiding place. The two women were still chattering on and had turned to walk slowly back up the hill again. Delilah crept along, listening carefully.

'But that's the Israelite way,' the other woman was saying. 'As the senior wife, you will need to take care that little Hemin and Ekron are raised properly, and that Beulah's more casual manners don't infect them. You only have to look at Delilah to know that she lacks breeding and self-control; she has none of the poise of Hemin, no sense of her new father's status in the community — '

'Lilah!'

Delilah looked up to find Ekron standing at the head of the row, waving to her.

'I've been looking everywhere for you. Where have you been? Come back to the party. My father is asking for you specially. He has a honey cake he wants you to try.'

Though she was barely tall enough to see over the vines, Delilah lifted her chin at the now silent women who were peering over the rows at the eavesdropper. She gave a haughty grin to Ariadnh and skipped away up the slope towards Ekron, aware that her hair was springing wildly about her head. This morning, especially for the marriage ceremony, her mother had tied her curls into the neat twist favoured by older girls, and entwined flowers to match her own headdress into her daughter's hair. They'd long

5

since fallen out or been snared on the branches of the hideaway. Delilah didn't care. If Ariadnh and her friend expected her to look like little more than a farm girl, she might as well stop worrying about keeping clean and tidy, and enjoy the day.

Ekron beamed at her, and they set off together, back towards the big house. The guests were starting to thin out now, and several were walking away in groups down the long path to the city road. She couldn't see her mother or Achish among the remaining crowd, and no one paid any attention to the two children approaching the thatched awning that covered one edge of the courtyard.

'Did you not hear me calling for you?' Ekron asked.

'No.' Delilah gave him a big smile and widened her eyes, just the way she'd seen Hemin look at the stable boys when she wanted to be allowed to pet the horses. 'I've been running among the vines.'

'I didn't see you.'

'I run quickly. And quietly.'

'You do.' Ekron started to pat her on the shoulder, then his hand fell away.

'What?'

Ekron looked at his feet. 'Nothing.'

'Can you get me a drink? It's so hot today.'

'What do you want? There's one with rose petals and honey — '

'Lemon. I want lemon.'

Ekron gave her a little bow. 'Don't forget that father — I mean Achish — well, he wants — '

He winced. 'What are you going to call him now?'

'Father, I suppose, even though he is not my proper father — '

'And don't you ever forget it, Delilah,' said a voice behind her.

Hemin was standing with her arms folded, tapping one foot on the ground. She was only a year older than Delilah but her dress was a grown-up's, identical to her mother Ariadnh's. 'I'd never want to be confused with being your sister, Hemin.'

'And I'd sooner pull every vine from this land than be confused with being *your* sister. Except that's your job as the vine-keeper's daughter. Where have you been? Father's been asking for you, but you look like you've been rolling in the dirt. You've got vine suckers in your hair.'

In truth, there was little chance that anyone who saw the two girls together might mistake them for sisters. Hemin had been the same height as Delilah until two years before, but she had recently shot up and was taller than Delilah by half a head. With the spurt, though, she'd lost none of her ungainly youth. While Delilah's hair was black as a raven's wings, such that in some lights it flashed with purple, Hemin's was the brown of the earth. Her eyes were too far apart and prone to squinting, as though frequently suspicious of the world around her. In fact, all her features were a shade too small for her face. Her nose was dainty certainly, but like a child's, and her lips seemed permanently pressed together. Delilah's skin was darker by several

7

shades, her lips fuller, and her eyes tilted up at the corners. Hemin teased that she had some Assyrian blood sullying her ancestry, but Delilah didn't care.

She noticed that Ekron had disappeared from her side. Typical! He'd never stand up to his sister. Hemin smoothed her hands over her still perfectly neat hair, and flicked at her earrings. They were new today, a present from Achish. Her stepsister had missed no opportunity to swing them under Delilah's nose before the ceremony, taunting her that her ears weren't yet pierced.

'A pretty house does not improve a dull landscape,' said Delilah under her breath. She'd no idea what it meant, but she'd overheard Ariadnh say it about her mother during the ceremony.

'What did you say, you little — '

'Hemin?' Delilah heard Ariadnh's cautious voice above her head, and she glanced up with deliberate sweetness. *You may be the first wife, but anyone can see you will never be the favourite, not now.*

In the courtyard, her mother, so pretty and happy, was sitting next to Achish, laughing along with him. Her heart warmed to see her mother looking like that. Even with her father's cold body in the ground some way down the hill behind her, she felt that nothing could really spoil today.

'Fetch Ariadnh a drink of the rose water, Delilah, and one for me too,' said Hemin, moving into her line of sight.

'Get them yourself.'

'Fetch us the drinks, Delilah. We'll be sitting over there.'

Delilah stuck her tongue out at Hemin's back, then turned smartly in the opposite direction, almost colliding with Ekron, who was holding two drinking bowls.

'I brought your lemon drink.'

'Hemin wants water to wash her hands. Can you get it for her?'

'Of course. Take these.' He handed her the two bowls, then hurried off towards the table of refreshments that stood beneath one of the colonnades in the courtyard. Delilah drank slowly from her bowl as she watched him, savouring the tartness of the drink. She suddenly felt hot and tired; tired of Hemin and her meanness, tired even of Ekron with his endless enthusiasm for running around after her.

But there was her mother, smiling across the courtyard at her, and Achish laughing and holding out a plate to draw her attention. Delilah skipped through the guests and cuddled up between them, taking a cake from the plate as her mother's hand slipped around her waist. It was very good cake, and Achish had just begun to explain to her how he'd endured the attentions of the bees while collecting the honey when the smash of crockery against the flagstones interrupted him.

The hubbub of the conversation stopped abruptly. Across the courtyard, Hemin stood over her brother, her arms spread wide. Ekron was shaking as he stared at the wet shards of pottery at his feet.

'What did you do that for, sister?'

'Pah!' shouted Hemin. 'You're no brother of mine if you take your orders from that little Israelite cat.'

Delilah felt her mother's fingers squeeze her waist, and twisting around, she saw Achish's jaw stiffen. This was her father's special day. How could Hemin be so cruel? To cover her embarrassment, she tugged Achish's embroidered sleeve.

'These are lovely cakes,' she said. 'Tell me more about the bees.'

Achish's eyes fell to her and he smiled a little sadly. 'They have a nasty sting, Delilah, but they're just defending their territory.'

2

Six years later

'It's just as well, Delilah, that it was I who had the purse today, and not Achish,' said Beulah, smiling indulgently. 'I've no doubt he'd have let you come away with four dresses, not just two.' Delilah watched the housegirl squeeze through the narrow door into the cool recesses of the house, her arms piled high with cloth-wrapped packages.

'But I really couldn't decide, Mother. The colours were all so pretty.'

'Thank goodness I managed to talk you out of those Egyptian reds, for there would be nothing left to spend on Hemin's dowry if you had bought that particular dress.'

'And the groom must be paid to take her off our hands!'

'Tsk!' Beulah scolded.

Delilah couldn't quite tell if her mother's outrage was genuine or merely a warning, so she gave a neat little curtsey of contrition and tucked her hand into the crook of her mother's arm. The seemingly bottomless well of Hemin's meanness was directed at both of them, but Beulah bore it with an inexhaustible reserve of patience. Delilah snapped back as a rule, through stubbornness now, rather than real irritation.

11

'Well,' murmured Delilah, 'the groom will have to have the courage of the god Ba'al, the wisdom of the goddess Asherah, and allow himself to be blinded by the earthy passions of the goddess Qadeshtu — '

'You're much too young to know of Qadeshtu,' said Beulah primly, her eyes crinkled with amusement.

'I'm nearly fifteen! I'd surely be married already if it weren't for the difficulty of finding a man fool enough to take Hemin.'

'Samson's no fool. He is a catch, Delilah, make no mistake.'

'But only an Israelite catch — '

Beulah pressed her lips together in a look of mild pain. 'Your lack of interest in your culture is nothing to be proud of. Samson's already well regarded. Some say he'll even be leader one day.'

'Leader of what?' Delilah asked. 'A patch of sand which the Philistines can take away at any time.'

Beulah waved a hand. 'Land means nothing. If Samson is made a Judge of the People, he will control their hearts.'

Delilah realised arguing would only drive a wedge between them. A part of her felt guilty too. It was true that since her father's death, she'd enjoyed the life of a Philistine and conveniently forgotten the plight of her father's people, living and working under Philistine rule. It was easy to, within the shady confines of the house. She offered her mother a smile. 'All I'm saying is that it serves Hemin right after all her years of belittling us for being Israelites to have to marry one.'

Beulah pulled away to look soberly at her daughter. 'Achish's example is one we should all follow. None of us is better than the other, and this match is Achish's way of signalling that to his own community as well as to ours. He foresees a time when Israelites pay the same taxes as Philistines, when families can eat and shop together. When we're equals.'

Delilah bit back the easy retort that Hemin's equal could only be found in Lotan, the God of Destruction. She seriously doubted that one marriage would sow the seeds of conciliation, but it was typical of her stepfather's optimism. 'Of course, Mother,' she said.

'Anyway,' murmured Beulah, the corners of her mouth twitching into the slyest of smiles, 'Hemin should be grateful for this match, for Samson is apparently quite without equal in one particular area.'

'What do you mean?'

'Well, I think it's Hemin who will have to pray to Qadeshtu, for Samson is clearly one of her most gifted disciples already.'

'Mother!' squealed Delilah. 'How do you know such things?'

'Samson's reputation goes far and wide — ' Beulah smirked. 'Perhaps that's not quite the right way to put it.'

Delilah began to giggle, and soon mother and daughter were laughing together.

On the floor above, a shutter opened and Ekron peered out into the courtyard. 'What's going on down there? I'm trying to study — Oh, Lilah, it's you.'

Delilah wiped her eyes with the corner of her shawl and pressed her hand on her ribs to calm her breathing. 'We just got back from shopping.'

'Did you manage to choose a dress for the betrothal ceremony?'

'Two, actually,' she said breezily. 'Would you like to see them?'

Ekron leaned further out through the window. 'You'll try them on for me?'

'I suppose so.'

'I'm coming down. Meet me in the hall.'

Delilah shrugged at him but Ekron had already disappeared from the window and she could hear his bare feet on the rush matting upstairs.

'You should be careful of Ekron's feelings,' said her mother.

'A second opinion will be useful!' Delilah replied.

'You have never needed anyone else's opinion. Besides, you know that you look beautiful in both dresses. And Ekron will surely tell you so.'

Delilah ignored the awkward implications of her mother's words and led her into the hallway. The house-girl had left the packages in two neat piles on a table by the stairs and Delilah picked through them, discarding rolls of napkins for the betrothal, and another parcel that they had collected for Ariadnh from the cloth merchant. The betrothal ceremony was to take place a full month before the wedding, as was the Philistine custom. Convenient as well, Delilah thought, in case either party wanted to back out.

Ekron stopped halfway down the stairs and

14

Library: Lincolnshire County Council
Branch : Grantham Staff PC
Drawer : Grantham-Till 1
Receipt: SB126900
Staff : LCC Staff
Date : 31/08/2017 Time: 11:35
Brw No : 1000000741

Overdue item.................. £0.50
04518135
GST...................... £0.00

Overdue item.................. £0.50
04980936
GST...................... £0.00

Overdue item.................. £0.50
04536109
GST...................... £0.00

Overdue item.................. £0.50
04582132
GST...................... £0.00

SUBTOTAL £2.00
ROUNDING £0.00
TOTAL Including GST £2.00

sank down onto a step, his head level with Delilah's.

'Did you have fun, Lilah?'

'I wish you wouldn't call me that.'

Ekron rolled his eyes. '*De*-lilah.'

'As it happens, I did. They have some very beautiful fabrics in town, sailed in from all ports on the Great Sea. Even fancy Phicol would find something to please his vain old head.'

'Don't let him hear you call him that,' said Ekron. 'Besides, if you want me to call you Delilah, then you should call my employer by his proper title too.'

'Fancy *Lord* Phicol, Grand Ruler of the Philistine City of Ashkelon?'

'Lilah!'

Delilah grinned at Ekron and began untying each of the packages. Nominally Phicol was merely the chief of the Philistine lords who administered the city and its immediate vicinity, but over the past years his personal estate seemed to have expanded, with an ever greater retinue of servants. An outsider might think he fancied himself as a king rather than a governor.

From the first package, Delilah pulled out a shift of coarse linen in a vivid burnt orange, which the merchant explained had been coloured with a mixture of red and yellow madder roots imported from a land far to the west. The dress was designed to lie flatteringly low across the shoulders and beneath the neck, but the fabric was still stiff with newness. Three or four careful washes with the launder stone would soften it. She pulled the straps of her own

15

tunic off her shoulders, leaving them bare, and held the dress against her body, turning to the mirror stone in the hallway. Her skin had lost the deep brown of her youth, when she'd spent most of her time in the fields, and now glowed like rich honey. The material worked well against it, and Delilah scooped her long dark hair back over her shoulder. Her tunic slipped a little further down her chest, but Delilah rescued her modesty.

Behind her, she saw Ekron blush and shift on the stair. 'You will look like the falling sun in that,' he said.

She pouted at herself: her face had become thinner these last few years, and she'd lost the dimples in her cheeks. But now her cheekbones were more defined too, angling sharply beneath the dark pools of her eyes.

'Does that mean you like it?'

Ekron swallowed. 'It's beautiful.'

Out of the corner of her eye, Delilah could see Beulah shake her head, so she covered her shoulders again and busied herself unwrapping the second dress. This was of a much finer linen, in a beautiful deep purple, and cut more plainly at the neck. It would need a belt to accentuate her waist, but its skirt was a little longer and fuller than the orange dress. The seller had rattled on about how fashionable the colour was in Egypt, and how the Pharaoh's wife had adorned the neck of a very similar dress with a collar of amethysts. From the moment she stepped into it, Delilah had thought it the loveliest thing she'd ever seen. Even now, she wanted to press it against her face as if breathing it in would somehow make her more beautiful too. She was just about to show it off for Ekron's benefit when she heard the unmistakeably angry slap of sandals crossing the courtyard.

'Oh, it's you,' said Hemin, entering the hallway. The path to womanhood had been generous to Hemin, softening her mean little face with curved cheeks and a neat snub nose. Sadly it had done nothing for the sharpness of her tongue. 'I thought it was the housegirl. Did you collect Ariadnh's things?'

'It's one of these on the floor.' Delilah kicked lightly at the packages, then danced back a step or two as Hemin tried to reach for the skirt of the purple dress.

'What in the name of Anat do you think you are doing with something that colour?'

'Oh, but isn't it beautiful, Hemin? I bought it today.'

'It's *my* betrothal ceremony, Delilah. You were told not to buy anything dark in colour because it would distract from my banquet dress.'

'That plain old blue thing you got last week? Yes, I expect it will.'

'Shame you wasted so much of *my* father's money on it then, because you won't be allowed to wear it.'

'I suppose it wouldn't do to look prettier than the bride, but then that wouldn't be difficult — '

'Can't you two leave it for just a few hours?' sighed Ekron.

Hemin swatted her brother's caution away, and took a step nearer to Delilah. 'You can put

17

cheap vinegar in a fine jar but it won't turn it into wine.'

'I'm surprised you know that much about the family business,' replied Delilah.

Hemin sucked a breath through her teeth. 'You think you're so clever, cosying up to Father, trying to worm your way into the running of the vineyard. But you will always smell of dusty earth and rotten grapes, and you'll always be the concubine's daughter. Even the best dress in the world won't change that.'

Over Hemin's shoulder, Delilah saw her mother sadly lower her head, and her anger swelled. 'At least I know a grape from a grain. What use will you be as the wife of a hill-man, if you can't tell a sheep from a goat? Samson is a man who gets his hands dirty — '

'Delilah!' Ariadnh's sharp voice cut through the row. Hemin glanced with relief across the hallway, then smirked at Delilah. The fight wasn't over yet.

'What's this?' said Ariadnh, reaching for the purple gown as Delilah withdrew it from her reach and folded it away. 'I thought I told your mother to buy you something plain.'

Beulah cleared her throat, but didn't speak.

Ariadnh took the orange dress from Ekron, who had been holding it tenderly in his hands. She shook it out in front of her, then ran her fingers along the stiff neckline. 'Is this the only other dress you bought?'

'For now.'

'Then you can wear this one.'

'But it's not ready to wear yet, it needs

washing and there isn't time — '

'Then you should have thought of that and bought something that was ready to wear. Achish will agree that the purple one is completely inappropriate for the betrothal. So you will have to suffer in the orange one or wear that white one you have on.'

Hemin looked smugly at Delilah. Beulah had warned her in the shop that her choices would cause trouble, but they would all have to live with it. The orange would be unbearable to wear, so she'd just have to find a way to wear the purple instead, and hope not to be spotted until it was too late to be made to change. Anyway, when Achish saw it, he'd surely agree that it suited her perfectly.

'As you wish, Ariadnh,' said Delilah contritely.

'You'll look lovely in the orange one,' said Ekron.

Hemin scowled at him, but Delilah said nothing. She was watching Ariadnh, who had picked up her own package from the floor and was peering between the layers of cloth that bound it, smiling to herself.

'Come with me, Hemin. These are for you. I've some important things to talk to you about.'

Hemin gave Delilah a final farewell sneer, and took Ariadnh's hand, skipping girlishly up the stairs after her. As their whispered laughter floated down into the hallway, Beulah crossed the hall to join her daughter.

'I did warn you.'

'But it was worth it.'

Beulah kissed her daughter's forehead without much affection. 'Was it really?' She picked up the package of napkins and handed them to Delilah. 'Take these to the kitchen.'

'I'll do that,' said Ekron, standing up.

'That would be kind,' said Delilah. She touched the back of his hand as he took the load.

Ekron followed Beulah through the doorway towards the back of the house. Delilah quickly folded her dresses back into their packaging, then slipped off her sandals and quietly ran up the stairs, dropping the dresses onto her sleeping couch before moving swiftly down the corridor towards Hemin's bedroom.

She generally avoided this end of the house, but today her curiosity got the better of her. There was a large window off the hallway through which she could hear the high and low of laughter and whispering between her stepsister and stepmother.

' — so that when he slides his hand around your back, and pulls this ribbon, your nightdress will fall smoothly to the floor — '

The rest was lost in Hemin's gasping laughter. The package must have contained Hemin's clothes for the wedding night, and Ariadnh was clearly giving her the sort of instructions that only a mother could give. Delilah tucked herself in behind the shutters so that she could listen without being seen.

' — for if you are to enjoy the first night with your new husband,' Ariadnh was saying, 'there is much that you will need to know.'

Delilah felt a nauseous mixture of jealousy and

20

dismay swell inside her. She may have the more beautiful dress, but in one respect at least Hemin would shortly be beyond her.

' — and what if I don't please him?' Hemin was asking.

'Bah!' snorted Ariadnh. 'Men are not difficult to please. Even men as renowned as Samson.'

3

Delilah put down the tray of empty drinking bowls, and adjusted the ties of her belt so they fell more attractively against her hip. She'd agreed to serve drinks to the wedding guests only after Achish had promised her new jewellery. Hemin hadn't been privy to the bribe, and had rejoiced to hear that her stepsister would be called upon to look after the guests.

She'd curled her hair for the occasion, and it fell over her bare shoulders in waves of silken ebony. She'd selected her amber necklace, not so much for the colour, but because the pendant nestled at the limits of decency in the shallow valley between her breasts. 'You should be careful,' her mother had muttered. 'I don't want to lose you just yet.'

The crowd of Israelite men who stood in the shade of the porch made no attempt to disguise their interest in Delilah, and muttered in Hebrew to one another. She couldn't stop the smile that came to her lips.

Achish had been very clear that morning that they were to make their guests as welcome as possible. These strangers had a roughness about them though, guzzling their wine as quickly as she could fill their bowls.

Betrothal, she thought, seemed to be about a lot of talking and a lot of waiting around. Achish had been locked away in his study for most of the morning with Hemin's husband-to-be, the man whose name was on everyone's lips, but whom no one had yet seen. The dial in the courtyard had moved on nearly one full mark since the arrival of Samson and his retinue, and the sun was dipping past its zenith. The scents from the flowers in their basins grew ever stronger, mingling with the thick aroma of the unmixed wine.

'More drink!' said one of the Israelites, in clumsy Philistine.

Beulah quickly emptied another third of the jug between the six bowls on Delilah's tray. 'Achish wouldn't approve, but I suppose it's all in the spirit of the occasion.'

'They think I can't understand what they're saying about me,' giggled Delilah. 'They're very coarse.'

'In a pack, men are like foxes,' replied her mother. 'All snarls and bristling hair. Get one on his own and he's a different animal. No doubt one of these fellows is eyeing you for himself and you'll be next.'

Delilah shuddered. 'I'll never marry a hairy Israelite.'

'Your father was a hairy Israelite!'

Delilah laughed and glided back towards the men with the tray of drinks, feeling their eyes follow her as she moved around the room. Of course, the purple dress had quite a bit to do with that, especially the way its richness seemed to light up the blues in her black hair and it clung to the curves of her hips. Not that she

23

wasn't used to a certain amount of attention, although with her mother or Achish by her side she'd learned to deflect it with a graceful, studied shyness.

Delilah and her mother would be sitting on the groom's side of the courtyard for the ceremony. *With their own kind*, Hemin had whispered, none too quietly, to Achish. She smiled inwardly now as she offered drinking bowls to Samson's Israelite friends. Close up, she couldn't help but notice how muscular the men were. They had none of the softness that she saw in the Philistine men of Ashkelon. They looked odd in their clean tunics — like a rustic vintage served in fine drinking bowls. Samson was rumoured to be twice as big as any of these fellows, able to wrestle a bull calf to the ground with nothing but his hands. What *would* her stepsister make of him?

She'd just invited a shy smile from the youngest of the Israelite men — a handsome, curly-haired youth who had done little but stare at her since he arrived — when Ekron appeared, frowning, at her elbow. He'd been hanging around at the bottom of the stairs that morning when she had first come out of her room, and his eyes had been glued almost drunkenly to her as she walked slowly down to meet him. He half-smiled at her now, but he seemed distracted by the Israelites over her shoulder.

'Ekron?'

'Oh — what?'

'Is the ceremony going to start soon?'

'I think so. I came to tell you that Lord Phicol

24

has finally arrived. I want to introduce you to him.'

Delilah followed his gaze to a group who hovered at the rear of the courtyard. Three were slender young men, each of them bare-chested but for the red military sashes that crossed to wide-pleated skirts and aprons. Behind them stood a short, solid man of about forty years, clothed in an embroidered tunic over his leather skirt. His flat face was sliced off at the brow by the base of a tall, elaborate headdress that signified the Philistine aristocracy.

'I suppose that's him at the back,' murmured Delilah.

His presence had drawn some excited whispering and covert stares from other guests — notables of Ashkelon and distant relations.

'When I've completed my scribe's training I'll be given a tunic in that style to wear on formal occasions, so that I can accompany His Lordship. And a headdress too. It won't be that grand, of course — '

'And I hope you won't look that silly either.'

Delilah was surprised to see how cross Ekron suddenly looked. Lately his sense of humour had all but vanished. 'It's a great honour to wear the robes, Delilah, just as it is to work for His Lordship. He is a very clever man, careful about the affairs of our people — '

The Israelites seemed to be making a show of ignoring Lord Phicol and his finery altogether. They talked loudly amongst themselves, as Ariadnh briskly crossed the courtyard to greet each of the guests. The 'old' wife, as Delilah

25

always thought of her, gave Ekron a sharp nod.
Then her eyes travelled up and down Delilah's
body. Her lips pressed together in a tight smile.

'I have to go and collect Hemin now,' said
Ekron. 'She is ready.'

'At last,' muttered Delilah.

'Be kind to her today,' he pleaded. 'This is a
big day for her, and for our family. It was
significant enough that my father married your
mother and accepted you both into our family,
but for Hemin to marry Samson is a very
important step in the relations between our two
peoples.'

'That sounds like a speech right out of Lord
Phicol's mouth.'

Ekron blushed a little. 'Well, he is right.'

Delilah watched him leave, if only to avoid
catching Ariadnh's attention. Too late. She was
bearing down like an angry whirlwind.

'You were supposed to wear the orange dress,
Delilah. You gave me your word yesterday.'

Delilah was about to answer when she noticed
movement inside the house. Hemin was pacing
awkwardly in the half-covered hallway. Ariadnh's
daughter looked pretty enough, and something
clever had been done with her hair, which had
softened her angry mouth. But even though the
betrothal gown was elegant, a pleated shift of
flax-coloured linen, Hemin looked uncomfortable in her own skin, as ill at ease as ever. And as
their eyes met, Delilah was delighted to see that
her stepsister was unable to conceal her raw fear
at being upstaged.

Ariadnh leaned towards Delilah. 'Go and

change your dress immediately, before Hemin enters the courtyard,' she hissed. 'Another few minutes will not make any difference, and if you are too long we'll simply start without you.'

'Excuse me, madam — '

'What is it?' Ariadnh turned on the young man who had appeared at her elbow. 'What do you want?'

'The master wants to see Delilah in his study.'

'What for?'

'He didn't say, madam.'

'Then you can go to your room, Delilah, and change before you go to see him. Achish must not see you like that. He'll be furious.'

I doubt that, thought Delilah, turning her back on Ariadnh, and following the servant past the Israelite men into the house. But by the door to Achish's study, the young man gripped her arm. His fingers were warm and strong against her skin and she didn't pull away, even though he was standing too close to her.

'What are you doing?'

'Don't you recognise me?'

Delilah frowned and looked him over. Dark curls smoothed down, sharply angled jaw, large eyes black as the night —

'Joshua? Is it really you? It's been — '

'Three summers,' he grinned. 'Achish — master — has had me working at the port.'

Had it been so long? Delilah remembered the days when Joshua, Ekron and she would play together among the vines.

'I didn't recognise you without straw in your hair and a barrow of horse muck at your feet.'

27

He wore a spotless white tunic and a wide leather belt as part of his house servant's uniform. The last time she'd seen him was as a skinny youth, half-naked in the stables, clad only in the knee-length Egyptian shorts the stable boys found comfortable for their labours, the rest of him strung with whatever ropes and leathers were required to tack up the horses. Something of Ariadnh's remarks to Hemin yesterday about the mysteries of a man's body came flooding back to mind, and she instinctively took a step back.

'I'm not the only one who cleans up well,' he said.

She blushed, then remembered the summons. 'I shouldn't keep Achish waiting.'

'He doesn't want to see you.'

'What?'

'I made it up. I — well, I thought you needed rescuing.'

Delilah was touched to see his cheeks burn beneath those glorious dark lashes. 'I'm a lady of the house now. I should have you flogged for such insolence.'

'But you won't, will you?' said Joshua, widening his eyes in mock alarm. 'I heard Ariadnh and Hemin moaning about you and it seemed so unfair to make you change your dress. It's not your fault if you're prettier than — '

Before she knew what she was doing, Delilah had stood on her tiptoes and kissed him, full and soft on the mouth. She lingered for a moment, close enough to feel his breath still on her lips, then rocked back, lowering her gaze. But he didn't move and eventually she looked up to find him smiling back at her, lips slightly parted.

The smile fell away. She was aware of someone approaching.

'Don't you have serving duties?' said Ekron to Joshua, slipping his hand onto Delilah's arm. 'Come along, they're about to start, Delilah. What were you doing out here, anyway?'

Delilah steered him back towards the courtyard, and pulled his arm close into hers. 'I was avoiding Ariadnh. She was very rude about my dress.'

'Never mind. This is Hemin's day, and she'll be nervous about it.'

'You really do sound like Lord Phicol, Ekron. You have to do something about that, or you'll turn into a stuffy elder of the community before you've reached twenty.'

As they walked together, her mind returned to Joshua. Her mother definitely wouldn't approve, but Delilah was already wondering how she might find a few moments alone with the servant. Ekron could be terribly tiresome, and Hemin's friends managed to look right through her whenever they met.

She came around the corner and stopped dead, stifling a gasp. In the courtyard, the guests were quiet, and all focused on the man who stood in the centre. He was quite simply the biggest man Delilah had ever seen. Surely the biggest in the known world. Her first thought was of the giants whom the gods had fought before people existed at all. Even his shadow, which stretched along the ground and almost touched Delilah's feet, seemed solid. He might not have been twice the size of his followers, but Delilah found herself mentally measuring her body against his, handspan for handspan. And down his back, as beautifully dressed as her own tresses, were seven braids of hair, held together by bands. The tresses seemed almost golden as the sun fell on them, then a rich polished ochre as he passed through the shade. It ought to be funny, she felt, this man with a woman's hair, but the urge to laugh was tempered by a grudging respect. He must have been growing it since boyhood. Even though the braids were oiled and smooth, they looked like seven ropes that had been tied to his head in case he ever needed to be controlled.

He surveyed the gathered guests, and for a moment his gaze settled heavily on hers. Those eyes — they were the deepest blue, like the cornflowers that grew in the rough edges of the vineyard. He must have been in his late twenties at the most, and yet her mother spoke of him as some kind of venerated leader. Delilah forgot her manners and stared back for as long as she was able. Then she glanced downwards, sure he'd somehow read her mind. Ekron tugged on her arm and with her attention still firmly fixed on the floor she followed him into the courtyard to take a seat so the betrothal could begin. Well, he certainly lived up to his reputation, at least in terms of description. He wasn't handsome in the same way as Joshua, but with his broad forehead and strong straight nose, there was something regal about him. His beard, though full and long, didn't dominate his face any more than those extraordinary braids. And as for his clothes — well, he was perhaps the least elaborately dressed man in the room. He wore only a long plain tunic of black linen, devoid of embroidery or any decoration, and a narrow black belt with a silver clasp. Had no one told him what a special day this was? There were two worn slots in the belt and Delilah realised that these would normally have held knives or some other small blade. Well, she supposed it wouldn't have been good manners to turn up to one's betrothal armed to defend oneself, though a person would have to be mad to take him on.

Achish led Samson towards his daughter, like a farmer leading an ox to market. Seeing him in Hemin's company for the first time, Delilah decided that not even the sum total of Ariadnh's wisdom could ever prepare Hemin for marriage to this man. There was a wildness about him that would surely terrify even the most experienced of women.

For the first time in nearly fifteen years, Delilah felt a sliver of sympathy for her stepsister.

4

Due to their late arrival, Delilah had found herself too far back to clearly hear what was being said in the betrothal ceremony. As the vows approached their conclusion, David, her stepfather's chief clerk, beckoned to her from the end of the row. She slipped out of the rear of the courtyard and went to meet him.

'Ariadnh has decided that you are to join the group who are offering the dowry items to Samson,' he whispered.

Delilah pouted. 'Achish would never have asked me to do that, it's a servant's job — '

'I know, and I'm sorry, but he isn't here to overrule her.'

She shouldn't take it out on David, she knew that. He'd been a close friend of her dead father and had always shown kindness to her and her mother.

'So what do I have to do?' she sighed.

'There are jars of the best wine lined up in the kitchen, and there is one small jug of the very special vintage from last year's heavy rains. The jars are about as tall as you, so you are to carry the jug. Come in last, at the end of the line.'

'Is that all he's getting?'

'There are bolts of linen too, but all together it's only a quarter of the dowry. The Philistine way is to give a part at betrothal and the rest at marriage.'

'That sounds exactly like the sort of business Achish would normally do.'

David gave her a dry smile and turned away without responding. Delilah set off for the kitchen, where she found Joshua with the rest of the staff. Every single servant on the estate had been commandeered to help with the ceremony, and here were all the other stable boys smartly dressed up just like Joshua, though not to the same knee-weakening effect. At the far end of the table the special round-bottomed jug stood in its stand, and as she reached it Joshua sidled up to her.

'What are you doing out here with us?'

'I think it's my punishment for not changing my dress.'

He wasn't standing quite as close this time but she could smell the oil on his skin, and a sweetness too.

'Have you been sampling the dowry, Joshua?'

He grinned. 'Of course not. The master is much too good a man to trick anyone like that. But we have been testing each of the jugs we are using to serve the guests. It's Lord Phicol's orders. Just because he's an important Philistine, he thinks all these Israelites are trying to poison him.'

'That's ridiculous.'

'It's how it is, though, isn't it?'

'So they send Hemin to put a bandage on the sore.'

Joshua grinned again. 'They should have sent you. You could have healed any wound just by kissing it — '

Before Delilah could decide how to answer, one of the senior house servants came in and clapped his hands. Joshua quickly took his place in the line again. The servants moved out into the hallway carrying their heavy loads.

Delilah followed, lifting her head self-consciously as she entered the hallway, ready to assume her role as the jewel at the end of the staff. Here she was no longer simply Hemin's sister in a pretty new dress; she was an unmarried daughter of a rich Philistine. Her mother was right. *I'll be next.*

As they entered the sunlight again, Achish was standing with Hemin before the crowd and Samson had planted his feet like a statue beside them. He watched impassively as the men carried the jars and leaned them with care against the wall. The bolts of linen, protected by hemp lining, were stacked on a table. Delilah came last with the jug, and gave a small bow before standing it beside them. She took her place next to the servants and looked up to see her mother, seated in the front row with the other important guests, give her a proud smile. With the oath-taking over, the guests were muttering among themselves.

Samson said something to the man who stood beside him — the young Israelite whom Delilah had smiled at when serving wine. He spoke to Achish in abrupt though surprisingly fluent Philistine.

'Is this all you have for our leader? You dignify him with just five jars and six bolts of cloth?'

The guests towards the front went quiet, and

the silence spread over the others.

Delilah had never seen her stepfather challenged before. Achish was pale-faced, taken aback. David scurried forward, unrolling a scroll in his hand.

'It's merely a deposit, a small portion of the full dowry as a token of good will. I'm sure my master explained that this is the Philistine way — '

At this, two of the visiting Israelites stepped up beside Samson, shorter and leaner, but still intimidating bodyguards. The atmosphere had turned in an instant. 'We don't want to hear about the Philistine way,' continued the spokesman. 'What about our customs?'

Delilah was worried for David and edged closer. Hemin looked like she was about to faint, and her face searched her father's. Delilah remembered Ariadnh's chuckled words about luxuriating for the first time against the body of a new husband. Any hope of that seemed to have evaporated in sheer terror.

'I thought I had made myself clear this morning,' Achish said in his quiet way. 'I respect the customs of both our cultures and I had hoped that this would be a compromise that you would accept. I've already agreed to bring the wedding further forward than we would normally — '

'You persuaded me to take your daughter's hand,' said Samson, equally quietly, but infinitely more menacing, 'at least offer what is due with no haggling.' He batted the scroll from David's hand. A murmur of disapproval rippled through the spectators, and even from the edge of the courtyard, Delilah felt herself lean back a little. 'For a man of such wealth, you offer me a pittance — '

'She is my only daughter, and she'll one day inherit a full third share of my estate — '

'How dare you insult my sister!' Ekron appeared from nowhere and grabbed hold of Samson's wrist. The giant's eyes dropped to her stepbrother's hand, but he looked surprised more than angry. His two bodyguards weren't as relaxed and one of them, wiry and agile, immediately jumped forward and planted a fist into Ekron's waist. He grunted and seemed to fold with the impact. Delilah felt her breath jolt.

Almost immediately one of the cousins, a man in his twenties called Ariston, came from the second row of the spectators and threw a punch at Ekron's assailant. Chaos ensued. In just a few moments, more of the men had joined the fight, swapping blows with the Israelites, who had swelled up around Samson without warning.

Delilah had witnessed boys fighting in the fields before, scraps over games of dice or some verbal slight, but this was different. There were no rules, no grown-ups to separate the opposing parties. Chairs were tipped over as the women and older men shrank to the back of the courtyard near the gate, while the peace of her family home disintegrated. Hemin, her face streaming with tears, stood near Ariadnh. Lord Phicol disappeared through a side door, pursued by his three escorts. *Shouldn't he be trying to stop the brawl?* Delilah thought. Then she saw her stepfather through a gap in the writhing bodies. Samson had snatched the neck of Achish's gown, and was dragging him like a cat with its paws on a mouse.

Delilah ran forward, seizing the precious wine-jug that moments before had been a symbol of the union. She slipped through the cordon of screaming women who were now clustered together and ran to Achish's side, her face throbbing with anger.

'Let him go!'

'Delilah, no — ' Achish gasped.

'Let him go, you monster! What has he done to you that you would use your weight and height against him — '

Samson didn't seem to hear her at all, so intent was he on his fury, but Delilah knew only Achish's fear and without thinking she jumped on the bench and brought the jug down squarely on Samson's head. It shattered, leaving only a curved handle in her fingers. The Israelite bully was slow to notice the wine that was now pouring down his face, and Delilah thought he could hardly have felt it through those thick braids on his head.

But when the realisation came to him, it came quickly and in a furious guttural roar of Philistine. 'This is a man's business, little girl — '

'Don't call me a little girl, I'm fifteen' — in her anger she lied — 'and I know the business of this house as well as anyone!'

'Then let your father do your fighting for you.'

37

'Only a coward would fight a man so much weaker than himself.'

A grunt of irritation exploded from Samson's mouth, and he let go of Achish and turned on her. Delilah's stomach rolled over and she cast around quickly for something to defend herself with. But there was nothing within reach, apart from —

With a speed that surprised them both, she yanked at one of his braids. But he was snatched from her grasp and bundled away across the room by three of the Israelite men. Ekron clung to the arm of one of them, but he was flung off like an insect, and went crashing into a low table. Delilah ran to his side.

Samson and his men barrelled through the remaining guests and out of the courtyard, set about by Achish's male relatives as they went.

Ekron's forehead was grazed and bloodied. Delilah looked around the broken furniture to find a clean napkin to dab at his face.

'Are you all right?'

'We should have known better than to make an agreement with *them*!' cried Ekron from the safety of the floor.

Delilah sat back on her heels and surveyed the wreckage of the courtyard. Seats and stools had been toppled over and lay broken. Wine stained the dowry bolts of cloth and all the new napkins. Groans and whimpers came from all around. Achish sat on a bench, his head in his hands.

'What a mess!' she said.

'Israelites are all the same,' snapped Ekron. 'Barbarians!'

Delilah dabbed harder than she needed to at Ekron's head, making him yelp. Delilah ignored his pain and dabbed again. 'Remind me of that the next time I jump in to save our family's honour.'

5

'How could you have let it come to that, Father?' Hemin sobbed. She was sitting on a couch in Achish's study. Even though the brawl had not extended this far, the inhabitants of the room — the immediate family, plus several of the cousins — had turned its usual order into disarray, stained as they were with blood or wine, their clothes crumpled and torn. Achish's tunic sat lopsidedly across his shoulders from when Samson had dropped him. His face was still pale. Unlike the rest of his family, though, he showed no anger, only disbelief and confusion. She knew he was replaying the conflict over and over in his mind, waiting for the story to end differently.

'I was humiliated!' Hemin continued. 'And in front of all those people! How could you have let that happen to me?'

'Hemin is right,' said Ekron, wiping his own dried blood from his knuckles. He'd recovered quickly, and seemed proud of his injuries. 'With Samson's reputation, we should have known that something like this was possible. He probably only agreed to the ceremony to see what chance there was of stealing the dowry. He had no intention of marrying Hemin at all.'

'I can't see why not,' squeaked Hemin. 'I'm a desirable woman and would make a very good wife.'

'So if he returns, you will marry him then?' asked Achish. Above his left eye, the skin was swollen.

'Absolutely not!'

Make your mind up, thought Delilah. ' — so you must break the contract, Father,' Hemin was saying.

'If it still even exists,' said Ekron. 'I imagine Lord Phicol would be able to give a legal interpretation, but I'd think — '

'Who cares about the law?' said Ariadnh. 'His brutish *Israelite* manners are reason enough to refuse to marry him.'

You were all for his Israelite manners yesterday, thought Delilah, remembering the conversation she'd overheard between mother and daughter.

'But that's the point, Ariadnh,' said Achish. 'That's what I just don't understand. Betrothal is very important to the Israelites and I cannot quite believe that Samson would back out of what was an important contract to his people and to ours over such a trivial matter as the dowry. But how else can I interpret it? He knew the conditions, and yet he took issue and left. That at least can only be taken as a rejection of the marriage.'

'And of me!' wailed Hemin, dissolving into tears and falling onto her father's shoulder.

Even Ariadnh rolled her eyes at this display of hysteria, Delilah noted. She leaned back against the wall and ran the beads of her belt through her fingers. Hemin's studied misery was rapidly erasing what little sympathy she had for her

41

stepsister. Despite the obvious personal rejection, the slight was shared by the whole household.

'Perhaps he thought me ugly,' Hemin whimpered, looking up at her mother.

'Of course not!' reassured Ariadnh.

Delilah managed not to smile. It was tradition that the bride and groom didn't see each other before marriage, and it was in the hands of Se't, the God of Chaos, whether he'd smile favourably on the match and allow the partners to find each other attractive. Samson was celebrated well enough for his reputation to have reached Hemin's ears, but Hemin wasn't known outside Ashkelon. Perhaps, thought Delilah indulgently, the groom had been shocked by her plainness.

But this small satisfaction was disturbed by a niggling humiliation. Samson had behaved abominably. And like it or not, they shared a common blood that now shamed her. It was perhaps to be expected that a huge, unruly man who wore knives on his belt would bully those who displeased him. But his rudeness, his contempt for Achish and for the honour of the arrangement had vindicated all those who harboured suspicions about the children of Israel. While Samson could leave for another town, Delilah and her mother would have to bear the consequences of his behaviour within the community, and particularly within the household.

Already, in the immediate aftermath, Beulah had suffered the brunt of Ariadnh's anger — 'the disgraceful behaviour of *your* people' — as though she was head of all the Twelve Tribes.

But it was Achish that Delilah really felt sorry for. He'd lost face today among his own people. That was bad enough, but he was clearly troubled by Samson's unexpected rejection of the betrothal. With the vineyard, it was possible to find a reason for a bad harvest, a poor vintage, or even the unruliness of the weather, for there was always himself or a servant or the god Dagon to blame. But he looked out of his depth between Samson and Hemin, unable to use reason to help him.

Delilah slipped over to his chair and rested her hand on his. She knew there was nothing to say that would help, but she could see that no one else had thought to comfort him.

Hemin suddenly whipped her head up off her father's shoulder and squared up to Delilah. 'Your people have brought shame on this family today.'

'It's my family too, Hemin — '

'We are not your family, Delilah. Your true family, your people are liars and brutes, cheats and thieves — '

'Hemin,' said Ekron, 'that's going too far.'

But Delilah couldn't stop herself.

'I don't blame Samson,' she said. 'In his place, I too would've run for my life!'

Before anyone could reply, least of all Achish, she darted across the room, flinging back the curtain that hung across the doorway and scattering the servants who were clustered outside listening in. Joshua called after her as she ran towards the courtyard, but her fury at

Hemin, at Samson, even at Achish for his bewilderment, made her deaf to his plea. She threw herself round the corner, and found herself suddenly kicking at air, suspended as she was between the strong arms of two bare-chested men.

'What? Put me down!'

'Young lady!'

Delilah wriggled furiously and in a moment she'd been set back on the floor, the grip on her was released, but before she could dart off again, the two fat and greasy paws of Lord Phicol slid themselves over her bare shoulders.

'Young lady.'

His touch made her skin crawl, and she shrugged in the hope that he'd release her. But he merely lifted his chin so as to look down his nose at her.

'I need to speak to Ekron's father, child.'

'What about?'

'I hardly think that's any of your business.'

'As his *daughter*, I consider it my business.'

Lord Phicol ran his fingers slowly down her arms. 'Yes. You are truly his daughter now, though typically your spirit reflects that of our most recent house guest.'

'Then what do you want to see Achish about?'

'I've returned to this house because I have a solution to our tricky problem.'

Delilah turned to free herself from his grasp, but he kept his hand firmly on her shoulder and she was forced to lead him back to the study. The servants parted as the little procession strode through the house and at the doorway Lord

Phicol's escorts drew the curtain back. They bowed as their master passed through.

Achish rose from his chair to welcome the new arrival. As soon as Lord Phicol raised his hands in the customary gesture of greeting, Delilah hopped out of his reach and retreated to the edge of the room, behind Ekron. The escorts now stood either side of the doorway, arms folded, feet spread. All the household servants had slunk out of sight. She wondered if she'd be prevented from leaving again, but the atmosphere in the room had shifted to mild curiosity at Lord Phicol's arrival. Just what did the old fool have in mind? His explanation didn't start well though.

'It's my opinion that we have all been injured by the events of this morning, and were we to list the nature of those injuries in both material and less tangible terms, we would find — '

Delilah yawned, leaned back against the wall and looked around the room again. Phicol's presence had certainly given everyone an excuse to spruce themselves up a bit — clothes were now being quietly straightened, the women were more neatly arranged on their benches or chairs, and all the men stood attentively. Not least Ekron, whose chin had lifted to mirror his employer's. Even Hemin seemed to be paying attention, though when Delilah shifted her position, she realised that her stepsister wasn't looking at Lord Phicol, but straight past him at the well-oiled chest of one of his escorts. 'Your Lordship makes an offer of exceptional generosity,' Achish was saying.

'It would be more generous were you to accept it,' said Phicol, now bowing towards Hemin. 'Your daughter is a beautiful young woman, who would be an asset to my household.'

Delilah jerked with surprise. Surely the old fool wasn't offering to marry Hemin himself? She glanced across the room to her mother who, despite her usual grace, had allowed her astonishment to show in the upward tilt of her eyebrows. Beside her, Ariadnh was preening and cooing, her fingers fluttering against her chest, but the truth of the situation was shown in Hemin's new composure, head slightly lowered, eyes gazing up at Lord Phicol, a modest smile playing at her lips.

'Your Lordship is indeed kind and we are grateful for your compliment. But I wouldn't want this offer of marriage to be a gesture of pity,' said Achish.

'Pity doesn't enter into it,' said Ekron enthusiastically. 'This is obviously a far superior match to Samson — with respect, My Lord.' He bowed at his employer.

'My point is, Ekron, that we must consider Hemin's feelings,' continued Achish. 'The events at the betrothal were embarrassing to her, and I wouldn't want His Lordship to feel that he'd taken on the burden of that embarrassment, both within our community and beyond.'

Delilah thought it would have been more polite had Phicol left the family to discuss his offer in private, but he showed no signs of being ready to leave. Delilah looked at Hemin, and saw that her embarrassment had been long forgotten

46

in the wake of this new opportunity. Her stepsister was surveying the room, taking in the congratulations of her family with a smile of radiant delight.

'I can assure you, Achish, old *friend*, that I don't feel it to be a burden at all. I'd consider it a compliment were you to accept my offer, and I'd also add that from a strategic point of view, this alliance will not only restore your family's reputation but also enhance it.'

'Your Lordship is too kind,' said Ekron.

'Indeed,' said Achish, perhaps a little drily.

'Then it's settled,' said Lord Phicol. He bowed deep and low to Hemin, then, with a swish of skirts, he and his escorts swept out of the room.

The room was silent for a moment after he left, then a burst of chatter spilled forth, punctuated by Hemin's girlish laughter.

'I suppose this calls for a celebration,' said Achish above the noise. 'Have some wine brought in from the courtyard,' he added to Ekron, 'if there are any jars still unbroken.'

Ekron grinned at Delilah. 'This is a very special day,' he said. 'Lord Phicol has rescued us from disgrace and ignominy.'

'Lord Phicol doesn't know what he's let himself in for,' she replied.

'Be fair to Hemin. She has had a difficult day.' He stuck his head out into the hallway and called for a servant, and Delilah found herself smiling as Joshua appeared instantly from a nearby doorway.

'You'll do. Get two of the jars from the dowry

brought in here immediately, and a dozen drinking bowls.'

'As you wish.'

'And — And — ' Ekron said.

'Yes?'

Ekron glanced at Delilah, then moved out into the hallway. But if he was hoping not to be overheard, then it was in vain.

'And one other thing. I've seen you looking at Delilah in that way you do. But you're just a servant in this house, and she's not here for you to look at like that. Do you understand? Remember your place.'

Delilah glanced quickly through the doorway. Joshua was turning away, but he caught her gaze and smiled as Delilah rolled her eyes.

Ekron moved back into the room, and squeezed Delilah's arm.

'Be kind to Hemin, please?'

Almost as though she knew her siblings were discussing her, her stepsister fixed Delilah with a look of unmistakeable triumph. Hemin didn't need her kindness, but she smiled nonetheless, for it was difficult to ignore the unspoken significance in Phicol's offer. A marriage between them would rescue the family from the disaster of Samson's rejection, it would cement ties within the Philistine community. Though it galled Delilah to think of Hemin gaining undeserved distinction, the thought of him pulling the secret tie of her dress could hardly fill Hemin with joyful anticipation.

That was the nub of the matter, wasn't it? Hemin might have all the fine dresses and status she wanted, but she still had to marry the pompous, unpleasant and boring old fool, live with him, and share a bed with him. Delilah glanced back at Ariadnh, and realised that her gnawing jealousy had vanished. What on earth would the wedding night advice be this time?

6

Delilah would have been happy never to see Samson again. As it was, their paths crossed again sooner than she could have expected.

It was a busy two weeks for everyone in the household, putting matters in order for the wedding. The preparations were made mostly by Phicol's household as the ceremony was to take place there. Almost every trace of the betrothal to Samson had been erased in these new arrangements: the food, the drink, the dowry gifts, the flowers, the setting, even Hemin's dress — the simple linen shift had been discarded in favour of a fussy red arrangement of pleats and folds, a gift from the groom — were all different from the first wedding. Delilah had the only remnant of that earlier day, insisting on wearing the orange dress, which Ariadnh naturally disliked now that it could be worn comfortably. Delilah had washed it herself four times, so that it would be soft against her skin.

With the focus almost entirely on the wedding, Delilah had managed to spend more time with Joshua, or 'distracting him from his duties' as her mother had put it with a raised eyebrow. He would come and go from the house with various deliveries, but Delilah made it her business to find out his movements, and would often be waiting for him as he returned. She found that from the verandah she could spy him as he stripped to the waist beside the well, and then 'chance' upon him before he was clothed again. She could tell he knew what game she was playing, and that shared knowledge only made the game more thrilling.

Inevitably, Ekron had been torn throughout the wedding between fawning over his employer and gazing wide-eyed at Delilah. The ceremony itself was a long and boring affair, with Phicol taking every opportunity to pronounce judgement on this or that, between introducing his new fourth wife to every one of the three hundred guests. People had come from as far away as Ashdod and other towns up the coast, and Achish had been required to meet many of them as well. His enthusiasm had never waned but the day had clearly taken its toll on him. The bruise beneath his eye had almost healed, barely noticeable in the dark smudges of tiredness. He was all but mute on the way back to the vineyard, and the stillness of the late afternoon air reflected everyone's tired mood.

The cart was just through the stable gates when David, the chief clerk to the estate, came running out of the rear of the house.

'What is it?' asked Achish.

'It's Samson. He's outside the front. He won't come in but he won't leave until he's seen you.'

A wave of fear started in Delilah's knees and spread through her limbs. She lifted herself up in the cart to peer at the house.

'We'll see him soon enough,' said Ekron. 'Anyway, you should keep your head down after

51

the bashing you gave him with that jug.'

'Wait here, please, everyone,' said Achish, climbing out of the cart. 'I'll speak to him.'

But as soon as Achish had disappeared into the house, Delilah clambered out after him.

'You should wait here with us,' said Ariadnh. 'That man is dangerous.'

'Ariadnh is right,' said Beulah.

'But I was the only one who stepped in to rescue Father last time,' said Delilah, disappointed at this show of unity between mother and stepmother. 'I think Samson knows what threat I pose.'

'Then I'm coming with you,' said Ekron, jumping down beside her. 'You shouldn't be alone.'

It was easy enough to find them, for Samson's voice was already booming through the house. Delilah and Ekron crawled into the hallway and crouched behind a pair of large terracotta urns that flanked the front door, taking in the unequal argument. Only half a moon had passed since the disastrous ceremony, but Delilah was quite sure that Samson was far bigger than she remembered. But perhaps it was simply his anger that had grown.

'So you marry your daughter off to Phicol the Philistine?' he said to Achish.

'Please come into the house, and we can talk about this more comfortably.'

'Comfort is irrelevant. You have broken the contract.'

'Please, Samson. Let us not discuss it out here.'

52

'The setting does not change what has happened.'

Achish sighed and shook his head. 'I don't wish to argue with you about this, but you must admit that it was you who took issue with the arrangements after they had been agreed. You rejected the dowry we had given our mutual consent to, you insulted my family, you threatened them, and finally you left the ceremony before its completion. I've known marriages to go ahead after a dowry has been resettled, but never after a groom has left the bride before the betrothal has been completed. What else were we to think but that you no longer wanted to marry Hemin?'

'I thought we had an understanding,' said Samson. 'For all those months you courted me. You spoke such high words about making an example to end the petty squabbles between our peoples. Was that empty talk?'

For a moment, Samson's anger seemed subdued.

Achish lifted both arms in frustration. 'Of course not.'

'Then she is still to be married to me.'

Delilah rolled her eyes. He was going round in circles!

Achish's tone changed to that of a father speaking to an unruly child. 'Not now that she has married Lord Phicol.'

'Then you agree you have broken the contract.' Samson pounded his fist into his palm.

Delilah winced at Ekron across the hallway. It seemed that the giant was exhibiting some self-restraint, but how long would it last? If anything, he was more terrifying than he'd been at the ceremony, for his rage was just below the surface now, dark and threatening like a late summer storm.

'But surely you see that the marriage to Hemin could never have taken place after the way you behaved,' said Achish. 'You terrified her, you *assaulted* me, and the spectacle you caused disgraced my family in front of our community.'

'Your miserable dowry disgraced me in front of my people too — '

'It's our custom!' said Achish.

'You must compensate me then for the broken contract. That's your responsibility.'

'I will not compensate you while we disagree about who broke the contract.'

Delilah's fear gave way to pride. *That's the way to deal with a bully. Tell him straight.*

It seemed to work. Samson softened his wide stance and took a deep breath. 'When we first met, Achish, when we negotiated, you assured me that this match had your blessing, that it would bind our peoples together. Did your words mean nothing? You said the seeds of distrust were sown in the land our peoples share; would you now water them?'

Samson's words were spoken in, if not a gentle tone, at least a reasoned one. And they took Delilah by surprise. Achish sighed, and let his hands drop to his side. He uttered a word, and Delilah could have sworn it was her name. Ekron looked suddenly pale. She strained her ears.

'I will offer you my other daughter,' said Achish. 'Delilah.'

She was on her feet before her stepbrother could stop her, running out onto the verandah.

'How could you do that, Father? How could you possibly offer me to this brute without consulting me first?'

Achish opened his mouth to speak, but no words came.

Samson glowered down at Delilah, then flicked at the air with his huge fingers. 'You offer me this shred of a girl who tried to break my skull?'

'You broke the jug with your big fat head!' Delilah shouted back.

Samson's face flushed dark with blood, and he ran a hand roughly through his braided locks.

'Daughter, please — ' said Achish.

'How can you possibly plead with me, Father, when you offer me up like a sacrificial lamb? I'd rather walk into the arms of Molech, God of Fire, than lie with him!'

'Delilah, this is a business transaction — '

'Is that what you think of me? Like a jar of wine or a bolt of cloth? I saved your life from this animal, and now, when he turns up his nose at your first daughter, you offer him your second!'

'Lilah!' Ekron pulled at her arm, but she shoved him back.

'And you,' at this she turned on Samson, 'you're probably used to people bowing down in fear and getting what you want. Well, I'm no girl: I'm woman enough to stand up to you and your ways.'

Samson shook with a deep, guttural laugh and poked his finger into Achish's shoulder. 'Your first daughter was a disappointment, but this one is an insult.'

'Don't talk about her like that,' said Ekron, stepping in front of her.

Samson peered down and faced him full square. 'Will you take me on again? Must I swat you like a locust?'

'No!' said Achish, moving Ekron out of the way. 'I won't have more bloodshed on my property.'

Ekron unclenched his fists but didn't step back. 'If you're going to marry my sister,' he shouted at Samson, 'you should treat her with the respect she deserves.'

'Ekron!' Delilah turned to face him. 'How could you take your father's side?'

'The girl is right,' snapped Samson, 'you know nothing of the ways of my people or our troubles in this land. You meddle with all the confident stupidity of youth.'

'You're nothing but an Israelite brute!' she shouted.

Samson's blue eyes were as cold as mountain snow. 'You would rather lie with Molech than me, would you? Then you shall have your wish.'

Delilah held his gaze for as long as she dared, and every moment seemed to shrink her further, but just as she feared her nerve would fail her, he turned away and strode rapidly down the track towards the road.

'Thank Ba'al he has gone,' said Ekron. 'Father, are you all right?'

'I'm as well as can be expected — Delilah, wait. Wait, please!'

But Delilah was running off down the hill into the vineyard as fast as she could. The plaintive calls of Ekron and Achish fluttered at her shoulders but soon she was out of sight of the house and she doubled back across the rows, seeking out her childhood hiding place among the vines. Ekron would look for her at her father's grave; he still didn't know about this little burrow.

She paused in the cool, quiet leafy haven. Her nerves felt raw, her anger all-consuming. How could Achish have said those things? A business transaction! She knew that wives were listed by many men in the family accounts, and that when the time came she'd have to accept her place. But to be given up like that, without any apparent thought or consideration as to her feelings. It was too much to bear.

Thank goodness Hemin had not been there to witness the scene. She'd hear about it in time, surely. If not from Ekron, then via Ariadnh. And then she would gloat over how Delilah had been offered as second-rate compensation to the mountain thug.

Even after her fury had abated and she began to calm down, she couldn't decide which was worse — to be offered to Samson or be rejected by him. Had Achish consulted her first, perhaps she might have agreed to be offered in Hemin's place as a way of keeping face for the family she'd grown up in. Achish had been so good to her, and for some time now he'd let her help cut the vines and learn to blend the vintages. If he had only asked her first. Well, it would have been a way to show him she was grateful for all he'd done for her and her mother.

Her thoughts were disturbed by the rustling of branches in the next row, and Delilah peered out expecting to see Ekron. But instead she saw a number of small paws running swiftly between the vines, pale bushy tails with their black tips dragging in the dust.

Foxes!

It was unusual to see them so early in the evening, for sunset must be at least an hour away still. Delilah crawled out and stood up. Now she could see a haze hanging over the rows of vines nearer the bottom of the hill, and her nose wrinkled at the faint but distinctively sweet smell of burning vines.

'Achish! David!' she shouted. 'Come quick! Fire!'

Delilah raced up the hill towards the house, desperate to get someone's attention before it was too late. The latest crop of grapes was just weeks from harvest and to lose them now would be devastating.

'Fire! Get water!'

Ekron was the first to hear her shouts and came running down into the courtyard. 'The bell!'

Delilah hopped up on the bench in the corner and began swinging the rope to sound the alarm. The bell had hung there in the courtyard as long as she could remember, the portent of fire or flood, but she'd never once heard it rung. But in moments, Achish had appeared from the house, followed by servants, stable boys, Ariadnh and Beulah.

Ekron was grabbing buckets from a nook and handing them out to all the men and boys. 'I saw the smoke from upstairs,' he said breathlessly. 'I was watching the fields to see if Samson was going to come back and I thought I saw him at the bottom of the hill. Then Delilah appeared over there and started screaming.'

'Did Samson do this?' asked Achish. 'Are you sure?'

'He is capable of it,' said Ekron. 'You heard him threaten us as he left.'

Molech, thought Delilah. *This is all my fault. I mentioned the Fire God and now look what's happened.*

She snatched a bucket from Ekron's hands and ran out to the well.

'Delilah!' called Achish, running after her. 'You must stay here where it's safe.'

'Fire does not care what it burns,' she shouted, hauling the pail up from the dark well. 'But Samson has chosen us to fight it.'

★　★　★

They were lucky. That was all they could say about it. The lower half of four rows were lost to the blaze, but they had reached the flames before they could do serious damage to the roots of the plants. Shouts and screams of panic had given way to a determined, silent routine: a chain of women and men, boys and girls, Delilah among them, had quickly formed lines from the two wells to the burning vines. They had managed to put out the fire by the time the sun's rim touched the horizon. The smoke from the blaze was now a dark stain drifting west on a light breeze, masking the stars.

When it was all over, and Achish was sadly pruning back the blackened wood by lamplight, Delilah slipped away from the crowd and went back to the house. Her hair was thick with the sickly smoke. Her beautiful orange dress was filthy, the hem heavy with wet earth, the bodice smudged with soot and water. It would perhaps wash out. She couldn't wait to clean herself up. There was a small well round the back of the house, near the stable block, and she could rinse her hair there and wash her face before she went into the house.

She pulled up a bucket of fresh cold water, then plunged her head down into it, swirling her hair around in the water with her hands. Then she twisted it against itself into a thick coil and raised her head, blinking the water away and drawing the wet tresses over her shoulder. She wiped her eyes with the back of her hand and opened them to find Joshua right in front of her, leaning against the well.

'I think you're the bravest person I know, Delilah.'

'We had to be,' she said, deflecting the compliment. 'The vineyard means everything to all of us.'

As he nodded silently she looked him over. The lamplight from the stable walls fell across

60

the yard, glinting on Joshua's damp skin, outlining his muscular arms against his grubby tunic.

'I'm a mess,' she said quietly.

'So am I. We should clean up.'

Delilah held his gaze for a moment, then took a step towards him. She could smell the smoke and sweat on his skin, hear his breathing. 'Then do you want to help me get out of these wet things?'

Joshua pulled her against him, and as her breasts pressed against his taut chest, she was sure she could feel his heart thudding. His cheek brushed hers, then his tongue began to lick drops of water from her neck, his breath drying her skin.

She heard her own soft moans, but she couldn't quite relax. Her eyes searched the dark corners near the house, expecting someone — another slave, perhaps, or even Ariadnh, to step out. She eased Joshua's lips away.

'What's the matter?' he asked.

'Not here,' she said. 'If Achish finds you . . .'

'I'll be banished to the salt mines,' he smiled.

Taking her hand, he led her to a patch of ground behind the house, overlooked by no window. 'Is this all right?' he asked.

Her throat felt dry, and she nodded. As Joshua wrapped his arms around her once more, Delilah closed her eyes and tried to give herself to the moment. To her surprise, it was Samson's face she saw, and his hands she imagined moving down her back. Why did he have to appear again now? She let her own hands touch Joshua's

61

shoulders, and saw the gooseflesh rise across them. At his waist, she felt his hardness press against her. Suddenly, the laughter with Beulah, speaking and laughing of Qadeshtu, seemed childish and hollow.

He kissed her softly on the lips, unclipping the shoulder clips of her dress. The material dropped over her skin, revealing the soft swelling of her breasts and stomach. Joshua backed away a little, his eyes travelling down her body. Her hands automatically went to cover her chest, but Joshua took her wrists gently and placed them on his own chest. In the light of the half moon she suddenly felt shy — she realised she'd been thinking about this moment quite often over the last two weeks, but now that it was here she wasn't entirely sure what she was supposed to do.

'There's nothing to be afraid of,' Joshua whispered.

He unbuckled his belt and drew his tunic off over his head, then laid it down on the floor. Shadows and light played over his smooth body, taut with muscle, and the only marking was a streak of fine hairs leading from his belly to the nest of hair from which his manhood stood proud but vulnerable against the patch of almost white flesh.

'I've never seen . . . ' she said, letting her fingers trail across his chest and down. He groaned, and now kissed her deeply, giving way to his lust. She pulled him down beside her, and they lay side by side, his hand stroking softly at her buttocks, then gripping her flesh harder. The heat between their bodies spread across her skin. She arched her back as his lips moved to her throat once more and then to her breasts. She ran her fingers through his hair as his teeth plucked lightly at her nipple. Sensation fizzed across her skin, as if every tiny hair on her body were lifting as one.

Then his hands took the place of his mouth, and he moved lower still. His hot breath tingled on her hip-bone and she let her legs part for him. She gasped in surprise as his tongue found her sex. No one had told her of this. Their bodies seemed intertwined. The day had been one of endless thinking and shouting, and she was grateful to give way to touch and sensation.

'Come to me,' she said.

Joshua's hair stood up where she had ruffled it, and he grinned, looking suddenly very young. He leaned to kiss her again, and instinctively, Delilah let her legs part for him. He moved his hips forward and she reached down to take his hardness in her hand. Their lips didn't part as she guided him inside her. For a moment, there was a dull pain, growing sharper, but the next there was only softness, and their bodies came together and parted like the tide rolling up and down the beach. She pulled his body tightly against her, wrapping her arms around his shoulders and hooking her legs over his pale buttocks. His breath, on her neck, was a series of thin, quivering exhalations, and she abandoned herself to his rhythm. Would it be like this with Samson, she wondered, then felt guilty for letting her mind drift from the moment.

All at once, Joshua's breathing became laboured, and his hips shuddered. She waited for the spasms of his pleasure to finish, stroking his cheek. His damp hair was stuck to his forehead, and suddenly the night seemed too warm.

For a while he lay inside her, and she felt her body sink from the height of their shared passion. The moon had moved over the house by the time they parted. Still dizzy from the new sensations Joshua had left in her, she said a simple goodnight. Joshua went back to the servant quarters first, checking to make sure the path was clear. Adjusting her clothes, Delilah walked lazily towards the darkened house, so engrossed in the novelty of what they had discovered together, that she failed to notice a small light hanging in the courtyard until she was close enough to see someone framed in the doorway. Ekron sat alone beneath the light, staring out. He hadn't yet washed, and behind the streaked dirt, his eyes looked very white.

Delilah drew her dress more tightly to her body and walked slowly into the shadowy house. It was some time before she fell asleep, troubled as she was by the sadness and confusion she'd seen on Ekron's face.

7

Three years later

The man's hollow, watery eyes settled on Delilah for a moment, then fell again to the track. The load of rolled blankets piled precariously on his back looked ready to crush him. Behind him was his wife, her long, bedraggled gown tugged by a sandy squall. Over her shoulder, Delilah saw the face of a sleeping baby boy. He, at least, looked content.

'That's the seventh family we have passed since the bend in the road,' she said when the cart had moved out of earshot.

Her stepfather nodded slowly and glanced back over his shoulder. 'And here comes another one.'

Delilah rearranged the shawl that shaded her head from the midday sun, hoping that anyone who took the time to look up from the dusty road into the cart would see that her features were as Israelite as the driver's. To be travelling in such comfort stirred a vague guilt. Did they wonder what she was doing sitting on a cushioned seat beside a Philistine? For there was no doubt about Achish's provenance; his high forehead and cheekbones were distinctive of his race.

She sighed. It wasn't as simple as that, and she knew it.

They had not long left the vineyard when Delilah first noticed the long trail of travellers, clusters of people all along the main coastal road from Ashkelon to Ashdod. At first she'd barely looked up from the scroll in her lap. Achish was thinking of expanding the vineyard onto land to the east, and she felt honoured that she'd been the first to see the plans. But after a while the warmth of the sun had made her sleepy and the voices drifting up from the road had drawn her attention. She could tell that these people were poor, not only from the state of their clothes but also from how little they carried with them. Their journeys weren't casual — that much was obvious from the way they lugged cooking pots and bundles of fabric, probably bedding or makeshift tents. Even the smallest child dragged some jug or basket along behind its weary feet. Times were desperately hard, she knew, and work even as labourers or servants was scarce in Ashkelon.

'Why are they travelling south? Why don't they turn north towards the Israelite cities, head for home?'

'For a lot of these families, this land is their home,' said Achish. 'Did your mother ever tell you how long your father's family lived on the edge of Ashkelon?'

She shook her head.

'Five generations. Much longer than my people. It was my father's father who started the vineyard when he first came from across the sea. Your father's family had already been living off the land for many, many years before that. But it's different for these people: they don't have time to build a home and a livelihood. They need to eat.'

Delilah smiled wryly. 'That sounded rather political. I shouldn't let old Phicol hear you talking like that else he'll think you're trying to subvert his plans for the Philistine state.'

'You shouldn't call him 'old Phicol' Delilah.'

'I'm sorry. He isn't all that old, I know.'

Achish gave her a small smile, to show his chastisement was only gentle.

'But you do sound almost guilty; it's not your fault what's happening to the Israelites.'

'There will always be battles for supremacy between cultures, one seeking to control another. I've been called a thief more times than I can remember.'

'You're the most honest man I know!'

Achish laughed. 'In my business dealings, perhaps. But my people are like those bees who take over the nests of other bees, stealing their honey and their homes for themselves. The Philistines have always moved into cities built by others and grown them for their own good; for many that is theft.' He squinted a little and raised his hand to shield his eyes from the sun. 'I've simply tried to do what I can to make sure I don't deny those around me a right to a home and a decent living, no matter who they are.'

Delilah reached across the cart and squeezed his arm. 'But you can only do that if your own business is strong. I understand that.'

'I'm glad of it. You have your father's quick grasp of detail.'

'And my stepfather's eye for an opportunity. We can close this deal with Mizraim together.'

'I wouldn't dream of depriving you of that chance.' Achish smiled warmly at her and reached beneath his feet for the jug of water. Delilah held out the little drinking bowl to be filled, then offered it to Achish first.

'Nor would you deprive me of the chance to see his son again,' she said, as innocently as possible.

Achish dabbed at his mouth with the back of his hand, then laughed as he gave the bowl back to Delilah. 'Jered is a nice young man, intelligent, energetic, and interested in wine.'

'Which is no bad thing if you want him and his father to buy rather a lot of it.'

'It would be useful to bring a son into the family who had a taste for such things — '

' — and who could replace the son you have lost to Lord Phicol's side?'

Achish frowned. She'd spoken out of turn. It had taken weeks until she'd spoken to her stepfather after he'd tried to marry her to Samson. Even Beulah had been shocked. Since that time, several suitors had made their attentions clear, but each time Achish had rebuffed them at the merest hint of displeasure from Delilah. Joshua had been a victim of their unspoken conflict. After a scattering of midnight assignations, poor Joshua had been unceremoniously moved one day to work on the port for almost eighteen months. The reason for his exile was never stated explicitly, but it could only have been Ekron's wagging tongue that sent him on his way. And now he had returned, his desire for her seemed to have waned. He kept his distance, except when others were about, and they had developed an understanding that nothing of that sort could ever occur again.

'I tried again last month to get Ekron to try the different vintages,' he said eventually, changing the subject. 'He'd always rather talk about politics than savour the tastes of the wines in his mouth. At least I have you for that.'

'And perhaps Jered one day too.' Delilah smiled bashfully for she knew it would make Achish laugh in that soft way of his. But did he know how her heart thudded at the prospect of seeing the handsome merchant's son again? He and his father, Mizraim, had visited many of the Ashkelon vineyards two months ago in search of wines to sell in Ashdod, and this exclusive invitation to return with samples had the potential to build Achish's business significantly. For not only would Mizraim be present, he'd also invited several other merchants to try the wines. That the invitation had extended to Delilah also, suggested Jered's interest was more than pecuniary.

'You should take a little care, though, Delilah,' said Achish. 'You're apt to be less than modest about your own powers. Your skills in both flattery and argument are as well-balanced as your face, but it would be as well at least to pretend that you are not aware of that.'

'I suppose you are talking about Hemin. You think I was mean to her last night.'

69

Achish arched an eyebrow. 'Do you think you were?'

'She does not care about the vineyard as I do. I was merely reminding her of that. She owes her marriage to old Phi — to Lord Phicol, to the vineyard's prosperity, but she has never bothered to learn anything about our livelihood.'

'The vines were in your father's blood, so they are in yours. Hemin has other interests — '

Delilah scoffed. *Dressing up, mostly.*

*　★　★　★*

Mizraim's home was very different from the vineyard house, set as it was right in the middle of Ashdod. The building was bordered by streets at the front and back, so the eastern half of the house was devoted to the business, and the western half to living. Mizraim was a merchant in foods as well as wines, and even before the cart had pulled up in front of the business part of the property, Delilah could smell the heady fusion of spices and oils and the scents of warm citrus fruits piled up in the late morning sunshine. They had been travelling since first light, and hunger had sharpened her senses. She was so enthralled leaning over baskets of dried fruits, taking in their fragrance, that she didn't notice Jered standing under the awning at the entrance to the house until she was almost in front of him.

'You look like a small child, if I may say so, thrilled by their first trip to the market.'

Delilah lowered her head in the formal way,

then smiled. The merchant's son was even more handsome than she remembered, though he was dressed quite soberly and his hands were slightly oily and his nails stained dark. He saw her studying them and quickly drew them behind his back, but she only laughed and let her eyes linger on his.

'We had a delivery of berries this morning,' he said, 'but they are delicate things and are likely to burst if a person doesn't take enough care.'

Delilah peered teasingly at his face. 'No evidence you have been eating them, though?'

He blushed. 'I put some by especially for you and Achish to try. If you are to trust us with your wines, then you should know what good company they are going to keep.'

'Good company, you say?'

'Food and wine should always make a careful marriage.'

Delilah was about to respond when she noticed Achish and Mizraim standing companionably together, and remembered her promise to behave with more propriety.

'Is there something you would like me to do, Father?'

Achish gestured to the cart. 'Can you supervise the moving of the wines into our host's house, please? Then we can begin the tasting.'

Mizraim — whose ample build and features showed that he ran his business and his life in equally generous portions — had turned a simple tasting into an opportunity to impress his acquaintances, and a splendid array of dried and fresh fruits, olives, breads, oils and cured meats

71

had been arranged on tables for the twenty or more guests to enjoy. This house had a more informal feel than the vineyard house, large open rooms with wooden shutters to divide the indoor space from the outdoor, and to divide off smaller rooms if required. Being bordered by streets on two sides, the house was flanked by a walled garden at one end, and a large courtyard at the other, across which hung a large awning of woven reeds to keep off the heat of the day.

With the wines carefully arranged in a row along one of the courtyard walls, Delilah took her place by Achish's side as he presented the different vintages to the guests. She handed out the little stoneware drinking bowls, adding water as the guests wished, and supplying her own comments about the particular taste of each wine as she did so. Beneath the careful smile she mentally noted the names of the possible clients and their preferences. And all the while she was conscious of Jered watching her from the edge of the crowd, his own cheeks growing a little flushed. She flattered herself that it wasn't just the wine.

Soon enough the tasting was over and she retreated to the food tables to allow Achish to begin with the business. She'd have liked to follow the conversations, but being a young woman among men made this impossible. Besides, with her work done, her appetite was keener than ever. She helped herself to some cucumber relish and bread smeared with a paste made from crushed olives. Jered was talking with one of the other merchants, but when he saw

Delilah he broke off with a hurried excuse and made his way across the courtyard. His straight-backed enthusiasm was almost comic, and with an inky finger he pushed aside the smooth black forelock that fell over one eye.

'You hide your boredom well, Delilah. But I fear discussions have only just begun. Your father drives a hard bargain, but my father has stubbornness on his side.'

'I'm not bored at all, but there's not very much for a girl to do here. Perhaps you'd like to show me a little of Ashdod. To see if it compares with home.'

The implication wasn't lost on Jered, who agreed it was a good idea.

Having obtained permission from Achish, who'd nodded graciously at her request, she left the front of the house with Jered at her side. Out on the street, she arranged her shawl over her head to shade herself from the sun. The mid-afternoon heat had smothered the streets with its soporific spell and after only a few steps even the babble of contentment from the merchant's garden was inaudible. Delilah paused at the corner and looked around her.

'Where is everyone?'

'This is mostly a residential area, so they are probably using their common sense and lying down quietly in the cool of their houses. You're sure you wouldn't rather be indoors?'

'No, I'd rather be out here with you.'

Delilah could feel Jered's pleasure at the compliment without having to look at him, but she decided to heed Achish's advice, for a change, and kept her eyes on the street ahead of her. 'What is it like to live in Ashdod?'

'I've never lived anywhere else, but I like it. The sea is not as close as in Ashkelon, so things are quieter. It's half a morning's walk to the harbour, less by cart. Most of our goods arrive there. I spend a good part of my days travelling back and forth between the docks and the warehouses, meeting the ships, taking an inventory of the goods, and then accompanying them back again to be stored.'

'And where are those?'

'We have two on the western side of the city — they are visible from the roof of the house if you wish to see them for yourself. But I wouldn't take you there on my own. It's not the safest part of town for a young lady.'

Jered's cheeks had reddened, but Delilah pretended not to notice. He was really rather sweet, a beguiling mixture of confident merchant and attentive suitor, yet with a slight awkwardness she hadn't noticed the first time she'd met him. He had none of Joshua's easy charm, but those berry-stained hands and his earnest expression as he tried to decipher whether she was serious or joking, lent him an inner softness that balanced his good looks.

'I won't pretend otherwise, but robbery in the streets and theft from businesses are a problem in Ashdod. This is the wealthiest of the Philistine cities, and we get a lot of customers from the region, and even from as far away as Lachish and Jerusalem. I suppose that those with lots of money will always draw

74

envy from those who haven't any.'

Delilah thought of the Israelite families on the road this morning, but she knew she couldn't talk about them to Jered. Achish had been right. It was possible to be pretty or clever, but not both. As they turned onto the market street she pulled her shawl a little further back on her head to show off a little more of her neck and the clusters of tiny pearls that dropped from her ears.

In the mornings or late afternoons these streets were probably very busy, but now the place was mostly empty and Delilah could see servants dozing on benches in the shade. But the array of wares was amazing and she shook her head at the sheer variety of it all — furniture and carpets, bolts of cloth, and spreads of food that rivalled even Mizraim's stock.

One particular stall immediately caught her eye. It was piled high with plates, bowls, jugs and jars. The edges of each piece had been delicately fluted by some tiny tool, which had presumably been used to pinch the clay back and forth. The base of each piece had been fired white and painted with a geometric design in black.

'This is so beautiful,' she said, 'but I've never seen anything like it before.'

'I believe it comes from a land beyond Egypt,' said Jered.

Delilah picked up one of the very smallest bowls and cupped it in the palm of her hand. The fluting would make it messy to drink from, but it would look beautiful on her dresser, full of hairpins or jewellery, or better still just empty in the centre, white and black against the pale wood. The jugs were wonderful too, and perhaps if there was time she could bring Achish here on the way home so that he might buy some for his finest vintages. That would be a nice touch, presenting the best of the vineyard's riches in something more exotic, more memorable than the usual —

Her attention was caught by movement at the next stall, a saddler, but no sooner had she looked up than she quickly snapped her gaze back to the bowl again, her legs suddenly weak, all imaginings of the future swept away by the cold shadow of the past. It might have been three years since she'd last seen Samson, but nothing about him had changed. He still stood two feet taller than her, with thick woven braids tethered to his head. But it wasn't his size that made Delilah's heart thump under her breast. It was his eyes, those bright blue eyes that seemed to chill and burn her at the same time.

8

Delilah regretted having pushed her shawl back so far from her face. It would be too conspicuous to start playing with it now, and had it been as far forward as it should have been, she could have been reasonably confident of anonymity on this hot afternoon. But it was too late now and the knowledge of Samson's presence only a few paces away was impossible to ignore, as was the unmistakeable feeling of his attention on her. It was all she could do to lay the bowl calmly back on the top of the pile without breaking it.

Her fingers had barely left its edge when she felt a hand on her shoulder and she almost squealed with shock. But it was Jered — yes, Jered — how had she forgotten about him so quickly? She raised her eyes to meet his and forced composure into her expression through a sweet smile, seeking reassurance in his face.

'I was quite carried away,' she murmured. 'It's all so lovely to look at.'

'Well, I'd like to give it to you if you will have it, a small gift to thank you for coming to Ashdod, a memento of a good day's work and, as we would have it, an omen of the plentiful relationship to come.'

'I — I should like that. But I'm sure it's very expensive if it has come from so far away.'

'I thought we were leaving business behind at the house.'

Delilah lowered her head a little, sure that Samson must now be standing right behind her, watching her every move. 'Then I'll accept gracefully. Thank you.'

'The giving of bowls is my favourite Philistine tradition and this particular bowl is almost as beautiful as you are — '

At any other time, a glowing, if unimaginative, compliment such as this from a man like Jered would have lifted Delilah's heart, but seeing Samson again had made her so flustered that all she wanted to do was run back to the courtyard to the soothing comfort of being beside Achish again.

Jered wasn't in such a hurry to leave, and with agonising slowness he picked up the bowl she'd been holding, and offered it to her in the conventional manner, his hands cupped beneath it. She made herself look at him and smile into his eyes as she cupped her own hands to accept the gift, first her hands beneath his, then slowly his hands withdrawing against hers, releasing the bowl into her palms, and then his hands recupping beneath hers.

'Delilah.'

'Jered.' Delilah completed the customary gesture. Her stomach churned, not with the intensity of Jered's wide-eyed gaze in which she might drown, but with the thought that she was now completely trapped. If Jered had not said her name aloud, there might have been a glimmer of hope that Samson wouldn't have known who she was, but now that was all gone.

Jered however seemed suddenly to wake up to

78

the tension in her face, and she saw him glance over her shoulder.

'It's late. We should be getting back.' He held out his arm to guide her, then tucked himself in behind her, almost driving her back along the street.

'Is everything all right?' Delilah forced herself to say as calmly as she could when they were surely out of earshot. Was Samson still standing at the stall, watching them?

'It's as well I didn't notice him sooner, because he might have spoiled a rather special moment. I had hoped to buy you something today as a gift, give it to you in some sort of privacy instead of among our families — '

'Notice whom?' she asked innocently.

'There was a man at the stall with us, a hulking beast. I'm surprised you didn't spot him, though perhaps you might know his name, as I think he spends more of his time in the lands around Ashkelon than here.'

'His name?'

'Samson.'

'Oh. I think I may have heard of him. Isn't he what the Israelites call a Judge of the People?'

'That's an ironic term. He's nothing but a ringleader. He leads a band of Israelite rustlers and thieves, and I imagine he was on the lookout for easy targets in the commercial district. I should probably get a message out to the other stall-holders when we get back to the house. He's known well enough, I'm sure of that, but it doesn't hurt to be vigilant. He's not usually seen in the better parts of town. He is known for consorting with the women who live on the coastal side of the town, women who don't observe the customs of family and community.'

Delilah thought for the first time that Jered might have a rather stuffy streak in him, old-fashioned even, for everyone knew that in every city there were women who offered their bodies to men for money. Yet, his words about Samson's 'band' gave her an angry satisfaction. The men who'd resorted to violence so quickly in Achish's house were like animals, and their leader had done nothing to prevent it. Achish's judgement had been proved misplaced. If Samson could now do no better than seek out the company of whores, obviously no sane woman had consented to marry him in the meantime. As she thought of this, she allowed Jered to slip his hand through hers and gently lead her up the street back towards his home.

★   ★   ★

It annoyed Delilah that she should still be thinking of Samson in the cart on the way home, her anger now mixed up with frustration. *Should I have said something to him?* she wondered. *Something to prick his arrogance, prowling the marketplace as though he owned it.*

She wanted to talk to Achish about it. But no. Reminding him of the slighting of Hemin and the fire at the vineyard would only bring him sorrow and, besides, he was clearly bursting to ask her about Jered, though his usual reserve was holding him back. Delilah had not let go of the

80

bowl since Jered had given it to her. She'd wrapped it carefully in a piece of dark red muslin to protect it on the way home and it sat in her lap, the most precious cargo in the cart now that most of the wine had been drunk and the jars were nearly empty.

The departure from Mizraim's house had been rather hasty in the end, what with packing the cart and harnessing the donkeys for the return journey. The deal had clearly been sealed to Mizraim and Achish's satisfaction going by the ruddy cheeks and wide smiles that had greeted Jered and Delilah on their return. The farewell from Jered had been perfunctory, but neither had expected anything different beneath the attentions of their respective relatives.

Though it had not been dark when they left, the sun fell quickly and now, perhaps halfway home, the stars were beginning to pierce the washed-out indigo of the evening sky.

'If Mizraim honours his word,' said Achish, 'we must implement the expansion this winter. We'll need more men to dig and plant, for a month. I hope there are still Israelites willing to work in Ashkelon.'

'Perhaps Lord Phicol can help.'

'I'd prefer to keep my business and family separate,' said Achish, cryptically.

Delilah understood what he meant. There was something cold and calculating about the Philistine governor. She disliked being in his presence, his eyes often lingering on her longer than decorum warranted.

Much like Samson's.

The cart was moving more quickly than it had on the way to Ashdod as the load was so much lighter, but donkeys are not given to haste and after a while Delilah was roused from reliving the complicated events of the afternoon by Achish moving restlessly in the seat beside her.

'What's wrong, Father?'

'This road is much too quiet. There should be families walking still.'

'It's almost dark, though. Won't everyone have stopped to eat and sleep?'

'Then where are the campfires? There's no sign of anyone. Listen.'

Delilah pulled her shawl right off her head and closed her eyes to concentrate. Achish was right. The road was absolutely silent but for the soft scuffing of the donkeys' feet against the sand and the creak of the cart's wheels. A torch burned in a holster beside the driver, Saul.

Delilah scanned the horizon, a silhouette of tufty dunes, but it was impossible to pick out anything in the dark.

'Master, someone's approaching,' said Saul.

'Then speed up.' Achish turned to Delilah. 'It's probably nothing.' But his hand shook as it patted hers.

Suddenly out of the darkness rose up the thud of hooves and a ring of shouts around them and the cart shuddered and rocked. The donkeys brayed in terror. Pale and ghostly faces on horseback flashed in the dark but it was impossible to see anything clearly beyond the blaze of the torch. Delilah's fingers searched for Achish's arm, as the hollering rose in volume

82

and she twisted back and forth in her seat, trying to follow the sounds.

'Drive on!' shouted Achish, but the donkeys abruptly turned and the frightened snorts became tangled with a guttural yelp as Saul slumped over to the left, knocking the torch onto the road. Sparks fizzed off into the night.

The cart shook beneath them and Delilah tumbled backwards. She thought she'd fallen on Achish but the tang of salty sunburned skin filled her nostrils, and two hands closed around her waist. She screamed and jabbed at her attacker with her elbows, but then the cart shook again and Achish cried out.

'Delilah!'

His voice died in a dreadful groan and Delilah stopped writhing to search for him. She caught his shadowy outline in the base of the cart, pinned down by one of the men against the empty wine jars.

'Father? Father!'

He didn't respond.

'Achish!' she yelled.

Delilah thrust again with her elbows, but the man holding her grunted heavily against her neck and before she knew it he'd twisted her round completely and was ripping at the neck of her dress with his hands.

'Get off! Get off me!'

She struck out with her fists, but he was strong. He reeked of the dark and the dirt. She tore his hands from her neck and as she did so she felt the smooth gold against her fingers and in a moment she'd pulled off her necklaces, thrusting them out in front of the bandit, swinging them in glittering arcs in front of his eyes.

At first, his rough, heavy hands seemed interested only in her jewels. He thrust them inside his tunic. But then he came at her again, and she felt his fingers seek out the base of her throat, his palm pressing down against her shoulder.

'No!' she screamed, slamming her knees together, and curling her feet up instinctively to brace herself against him. He pinned her with both hands and tried to use his body to push her legs apart, his eyes greedy and glinting. 'Father!' she called.

And then suddenly he was gone with a yelp, as though the night had snatched him away. His hands trailed from her skin, and she was alone, the side of the cart jamming against her ribs.

She looked down. Achish held a hand to one side of his head, and looked in confusion at the shards of broken pottery around him.

'In the name of Ba'al!'

Delilah threw her arms around him, and found she was shivering despite the sweat that soaked her skin. 'Are you all right?'

'I think so,' he said, trying to stand. 'What about Saul?'

'I don't know. Are they gone?'

But Achish was staring over her shoulder with alarm. Delilah spun around. Towering beside the cart, his head and shoulders illuminated by the glow of the torch, stood Samson. The wretch who'd attacked her lay crumpled at his feet.

'You!' she shouted.

He surveyed the damage, his arms folded across his wide chest. 'You're lucky you weren't killed. These plains are dangerous after dark.'

Anger flooded Delilah's veins. 'How dare you! *Your* men attacked us.'

'Delilah, no,' said Achish sternly. 'This man saved us.'

'Don't you recognise him?' she said. 'It's Samson. He's a common bandit.'

'I can see well enough who he is,' said Achish. 'It's lucky he was here.'

Delilah's anger swelled up once again, fused with gut-wrenching fear at how horribly the day might have ended. What could she say? She dare not reveal to Achish that this wasn't the first time she'd seen the monster that day. Yet so many thoughts tumbled over each other, and one question rose so quickly above the others that she couldn't help but exclaim:

'Have you been following me?'

9

Samson appeared not to have heard her. 'Your rescue will come at a price.'

So these were his men. All the heroic combat was nothing but a show! Delilah couldn't contain herself, and why should she?

'You rescue us to get our thanks,' she hissed, 'but now you hold us hostage until we pay our own ransom.'

'Delilah,' cautioned Achish. 'We're hardly in a position to argue.'

'That's exactly the problem,' snapped Delilah. 'Samson always makes sure he gets what he wants because no one ever has the courage to challenge him. And if they do, he sets fire to their property.'

'I had nothing to do with the burning of the vines,' said Samson.

'So you say,' said Delilah.

'So I say,' he repeated, his voice as cool and close as the night air. He was lit by a single torch that he held in his hand, his shadow heavier than the dark, his great braids glistening like an army of serpents awaiting his command to strike. 'You are still several miles from Ashkelon and while I may hold influence over some of these more desperate men, I cannot guarantee your safety. You should at least offer these men something to appease them.'

'That's exactly what I mean!'

'Delilah, please,' said Achish quietly.

She slumped back on the cart bench. Her stepfather rarely had cause to use a warning tone with her these days.

'You are a sensible man, Achish,' said Samson, suddenly the peacemaker, 'and a far more accomplished diplomat than your son-in-law Lord Phicol. So I know that you will understand when I claim some small compensation for your people's harsh and unwarranted taxes on my people.' He held out the torch and waved it gently over the cart. 'This will buy off the men who attacked you, and word will go out that you have made a token gesture to repay years of theft.'

Delilah felt Achish sigh quietly in the dark. 'I understand.'

'The men will take one donkey, the remainder of the wine and whatever money you have.' At this, Samson reached out into the dark between them and grabbed Delilah's wrist in his fist.

'Get off me!' She wrestled against him, but she could feel her bones bending beneath his grip and she quickly gave up.

'Seeing as you had already thought to buy yourself out of trouble, you can give up this necklace in your lap, and you,' at this he grasped Achish's hand, spreading the fingers out for inspection, 'you will give up your rings. The sum of those items will buy off these men.'

Delilah looked at Achish, who nodded briskly as he removed the rings from his fingers, including one her own mother had bought for him. Delilah fingered the gold necklace regret-fully then flung it at Samson who snatched it out of the air without a glance at her. He rammed the torch into a holster in the corner of the cart, then reached down and hauled up the still groaning bandit who had been so interested in Delilah.

'Take these things and get out of my sight,' he said, switching to Hebrew. 'You are lucky I didn't leave you bleeding in the dark for the wolves. But if I hear you have crossed my lands again, I'll hunt you down.'

Delilah stifled her surprise. He didn't know she understood Hebrew, so his threat to the bandits must be genuine. These weren't his men after all, though clearly he held some sway over them. She watched as he dropped the jewellery into the man's hand, then swiftly relieved Achish of his purse. He released one of the donkeys from its harness, then reached into the cart and plucked out the remaining jars of wine, two at a time, laying them down on the dirt. The men swarmed over the prizes, snatched them up and were gone as quickly as they had arrived. Almost instantly, the desert was still and quiet again. The remaining donkey brayed wistfully for its lost companion.

'And now what?' demanded Delilah, still enraged despite this confusing development. 'I suppose you're going to leave us here to struggle home with a single donkey.'

'But your cart is now empty,' reasoned Samson, 'so the donkey will have less to pull. Besides, I'll escort you the rest of the way to Ashkelon. Your driver is in no state to look after you.'

'In the name of Ba'al!' muttered Delilah, clambering over the cart to the driver's bench. Saul was slumped to one side, breathing heavily. 'I need light here.'

'Is he badly hurt?' asked Achish.

Delilah peered at the driver beneath the glow of Samson's torch, her fingers working their way across his head and around his face. Saul winced as she found a spongy wound above his temple and her hand became wet with blood. She wiped her hands quickly on her stole. 'I don't think so. Just a nasty cut. Can you sit up, Saul?'

The driver tried to push himself up, but his arms seemed too weak to hold him. 'He should lie down,' said Samson. He lifted Saul easily and laid him with care in the base of the cart where the wine had been stacked. He fiddled around beneath the benches for a moment, then stepped back.

'You can drive the cart,' he said to Delilah.

Delilah glanced at Achish who shrugged. He could drive the cart himself, of course, but Delilah knew he'd suffered quite enough indignity for one night. So she felt in the shadows for the remaining harness, then gave a quick snap of the rope and the donkey hesitantly started forward.

They drove like that for some way in the silent night, Delilah concentrating on the movement of the donkey instead of trying to untangle all that had happened that day. They made an odd party, the quiet, brooding giant trotting along on the road beside them, a young woman of some wealth with reins in her hands, the silent

Philistine with his Israelite escort. She felt the cart sway a little beneath her, and soon felt Achish's quiet presence close at her shoulder.

'We have been lucky,' he murmured.

'I don't know how you can say that.'

'We could be dead.' His eyes passed briefly over her dishevelled clothes. 'Or worse.'

Delilah didn't have the energy to argue, but her stepfather's timidity made her grip the reins tighter. Being in debt to Samson was surely a fate worse than death. She changed the subject.

'Can you look around in the bottom of the cart for me please? Jered gave me a bowl — '

'Did he now?'

Delilah smiled into the dark at Achish's quick understanding of the gift's significance. 'It's a very pretty one, from the south, rather expensive I'm afraid, and I suppose it's broken. Or *stolen*,' she added.

'Your bowl is undamaged,' said Samson from the shadows. 'It's tucked beneath the bench.'

'What do you know — ' Delilah stopped herself. 'I suppose we should be grateful you didn't make us walk home,' she said to him.

'The donkey represents the Philistine tax on Israelite animals and the tax on vehicles,' said Samson. 'The wine represents the tax on farms and vineyards, food and drink. The jewellery represents the tax on imported goods such as gold and jewels, and the money is the tax on banking and lending. These are four of the main taxes made on the Israelite people. You'll be pleased I didn't choose to exploit the tax on families.'

90

Delilah fumed at the implicit threat. She did not wish to confirm his view of her as Philistine but neither did she want to reveal her own Israelite blood. That old sickness rose in her throat at the conflicting demands on her loyalty. Yet if he'd gone through with marrying Hemin in the first place, perhaps a solution to the troubles might have been a little nearer.

'You're not exactly doing your bit for peace,' she murmured.

'You don't know what you are talking about.'

'Then tell me,' cried Delilah in frustration, 'and stop being a pompous fool who treats me like a little girl — '

'Delilah,' warned Achish.

' — And get down off your pedestal. You think you look regal, I suppose, but really you're just as much a fool as Phicol. He's got his fancy clothes and you with your silly hair — '

Samson's torch suddenly blazed in front of Delilah, its flames thrown out as if breathed by the god Molech himself.

'Never speak of that which you don't understand.'

Delilah jerked her attention onto the dark road, her cheeks stinging with his fury. On the horizon, some thousand paces away, the dim lights of Ashkelon's outskirts glowed.

'I leave you here,' said Samson. Without turning to her, he handed his torch to Achish and spurred his horse. She could still hear the thudding of the hooves long after he'd galloped out of sight.

In the darkness, she smiled to herself.

10

Delilah always enjoyed her visits to the centre of Ashkelon. As much as she loved the tranquillity of the vineyard and the muted greens and browns of vines and earth, the smells and noises of the market thrilled her. Although there was an order to the layout of stalls — textiles, metals, pottery, woods, foods and wines, tallows and waxes, all grouped carefully so that a shopper could easily compare goods between vendors — there were innumerable men, women and children who had squeezed a tiny barrow or handcart into the spaces between stalls and disturbed a river of silks with a basket of cucumbers, or put up competing displays of imported spoons with sour-smelling sheep's cheese leaking whey from a rush basket.

For her mother, the market had long since lost its charms. While she would hasten through her shopping early in the morning before the crowds arrived, Delilah sought the throng and bustle that stretched from late morning well into the afternoon. She liked how the Philistine love of order was turned on its head by opportunistic Israelite wives or farmers setting up in the gaps, and how the alleyways between stalls seemed to open and close around the ebb and flow of these temporary merchants and the Philistine soldiers who were supposed to keep them away.

'They're becoming a nuisance,' observed

Ekron, holding a basket of packages. 'That dirty old crone with the bread was here last week.'

Delilah deliberately stepped forward to look at the woman's bread and gave her a quick quiet compliment in Hebrew. The woman smiled, revealing just two teeth, and tore a piece off a corner of a dark loaf, offering it to Ekron who swerved away.

'Don't be so pompous,' said Delilah. 'You were happy enough to eat it for breakfast this morning.'

Ekron pulled a queasy face. 'Don't let Ariadnh hear that your mother gets the bread here.'

'It was Ariadnh's idea. Even she isn't quite the snob you have become. Anyway, if you hate this place so much, why do you insist on coming with me?'

'I don't hate it,' said Ekron. 'It's very — educational.'

Delilah laughed. 'You hate it. Just admit it!'

'Your mother insists I accompany you. It's not safe for you to be here on your own.'

'I lived through the desert dark, so I think I can survive Ashkelon market.'

'I knew I shouldn't have let you and Father travel alone to Ashdod.'

'You wouldn't have enjoyed yourself. There was no talk of politics at all.'

And you wouldn't have liked the way Jered looked at me either, she thought.

Delilah squeezed through the crowd to a small cart from which a Philistine girl of about her own age was selling stone and pottery beads. She smiled when she saw Delilah approach and leaned across the cart, grasping her friend by the hands.

Delilah squeezed her hand, returning the greeting, then leaned back to take a proper look at her friend. 'Are you hot, Sarai? Do you need some water?' she asked, brushing a few curls of hair from Sarai's flushed face.

'My jar's empty but I daren't leave the stall. Father would be very annoyed.'

'Ekron!' Delilah waved at him through the crowd and tried to conceal her smile as he struggled against the tide with the basket held in front of him. 'Can you fill Sarai's jar?'

Ekron glanced sheepishly at Delilah's friend, who smiled shyly back. There was a half-hearted attraction between them, Delilah was sure, but her stepbrother seemed reluctant to pursue it.

Ekron shoved the basket of goods under the front of the cart and took Sarai's jar, striding easily through the crowd. Delilah watched her friend's eyes as they followed him, then patted her on the arm. 'How is business today?'

'Quite good. But we have less to sell, of course . . . Oh, I heard about the robbery. How is your father?'

'More angry than anything else. His face is still healing. Those thugs cut him quite badly on the cheek. He fears people's pity more than anything.'

'It could've happened to anyone.'

'Indeed. Every week I hear stories of Israelites taking from warehouses, shops, homes; robberies on the street. There's supposed to be some sort of scheme to protect the traders but — '

Ekron reappeared with the jar, drops of water glistening at its mouth. Delilah accepted a drink from Sarai's refilled drinking bowl while the other two tried to find something to say to each other.

'You should be more bold with her,' boomed a voice over Delilah's shoulder. 'Women respond to a more direct approach.' She recognised the voice immediately, and managed to turn slowly. Samson was eyeing Ekron with an expression of contempt.

'You have no place here,' Ekron retorted. 'This is a Philistine market.'

Samson glanced under the cart. 'Yet you have bought Israelite honey and Israelite candles. Were they bought to sweeten the wines of beautiful Philistine women and light their baths before they retire to bed?' His eyes moved to Delilah and stayed fixed on her. 'Hello, desert flower.'

Delilah turned back to Sarai and handed her the drinking bowl, trying to ignore the way her friend's eyes darted in astonishment at Samson.

'You seem to have an admirer,' whispered Sarai.

'He is no admirer,' retorted Ekron. 'He's just a bully boy — '

' — who knows that attractive young women like to be complimented,' said Samson. 'Faced with this princess of the beads, you are uncommonly silent. Who steps on your tongue, little Phicol?'

Delilah began fiddling with the baskets of beads. Sarai too lowered her head, but Samson reached out and put his fingers under her chin,

95

lifting her face towards Ekron.

'Why don't you tell her if you think her a beauty?'

'Take your hands off her,' snapped Ekron, knocking Samson's wrist away from Sarai. Delilah's breath caught in her throat, but he seemed hardly to have noticed. Instead he fixed his blue eyes on her.

'If her eyes are like jewels and her cheeks like the firm flesh of a ripe peach,' he said, 'if her lips the colour of crushed raspberries dripping with juice — '

Delilah felt the blood rush to her face. She knew he was making fun of her, but there was something more beneath the words, and his eyes communicated a longing that couldn't be detected in the easy lilt of his words. She felt the basket bang against her ankle as Ekron dragged it out from under the cart.

'Come, Delilah, leave the gaudy compliments in the market where they belong. Father will be expecting us.'

'Then run home to daddy, little Phicol,' said Samson. 'I hear he has had two wives, so he ought to be able to teach you something of how to love a woman.'

Delilah's ear was drawn to Samson's companions who were chatting in Hebrew behind him.

' — and they say the Philistine girls go like mares when you show them a rod of hot steel,' said one.

'I imagine your rod is more of a broken nail,' Delilah replied in Hebrew to Samson's companion, 'and as for hot steel — more of a wet fish.'

Samson reeled, more in surprise, she suspected, than at the insult.

'You speak in my tongue,' he said, also in Hebrew.

'Come along, Delilah,' said Ekron, tugging hard at her elbow.

'It's my tongue too,' replied Delilah, feeling for the first time that she was able to match Samson's gaze with her own. 'I was born an Israelite but raised in a Philistine family after my father died.'

Samson's mouth twisted around a reply but no words came out. Behind him, his garrulous companion was now red in the face. It was a sensible moment to depart. But Delilah had barely flashed a smile at Sarai and begun to follow Ekron, than she felt Samson at her heel.

'Then you are one of us, Delilah.'

'I'm no more one of you than one of them. I'm simply one of me.'

'I told you in the desert that you lacked wisdom.'

'And I told you that you couldn't build your precious state on threats of violence. I assume the robber has not been stupid enough to cross your path again.' Delilah didn't bother to look back, but she heard the falter in Samson's step as he remembered his words, and realised now that Delilah had understood them too.

Ekron had quickly crossed to a group of Philistine soldiers on one side of the square and Delilah saw him whisper urgently in the captain's ear as Samson regained his ground on her.

'You will always be an Israelite, Delilah,' he said.

'But I merely have eyes like jewels and cheeks like peaches and lips like raspberries — '

The phalanx of soldiers slid quickly between Samson and Delilah, and the captain ordered Samson to remove himself and his companions from the market. Samson made no effort to move or to reply for Delilah had his entire attention. Then Ekron tugged at her arm.

'Come along, Lilah, let's get out of here before trouble breaks out.'

'He won't make a scene,' said Delilah. Samson was ignoring the soldiers and staring at her. 'That's not what he wants.'

Samson smiled after her, his expression without any mockery, then he turned away and was soon lost in the crowd, trailing soldiers behind him.

'I suppose you realise that calling on the soldiers only made you look weak,' she said as they left the bustle of the market square.

'The trouble with Samson is that he makes everyone look weak. Anyway, I'm not a street brawler.'

On another day, Delilah would have teased him further about his tactical escape. But it was more interesting to remember how Samson's gaze had turned when he discovered her heritage. The way his eyes had lingered so heavily on her mouth. His composure, in that moment, had vanished, and she'd seen something else lurking beneath his brash, cocky façade.

And he has no right to look at me like that.

Her anger wouldn't settle on the journey home and she took it out on Ekron. 'He was right about you and Sarai. She is interested in you, if only you would wake up and do something about it.'

'A stall-holder?'

'Her father is well respected in the business community, so Lord Phicol would approve.'

'What was Samson saying to you?'

'Nothing you need to worry about.'

'Then why were you speaking in Hebrew? If it wasn't such a secret, we could all have heard.'

'I was being polite to him and speaking his language.'

'He doesn't deserve politeness. Remember the vineyard; he didn't care for manners when he set the fire.'

'Many things have changed since then.'

'Nothing has changed, Delilah, at least not for the better. Lord Phicol says — '

'Sometimes I think you'd rather marry him than Sarai.'

★ ★ ★

'If I catch you smiling at yourself in the mirror once more, Delilah,' said her mother, 'I'll think that you are hiding something.' Beulah was seated on a couch at the end of Delilah's bed. 'What have you been doing?'

Cheeks like the firm flesh of a ripe peach? Lips the colour of crushed raspberries? Perhaps not, but her skin was clear and seemed to glow. She ran her tongue between her even white teeth and pouted. He'd wanted to kiss her, she was sure of it. *And what would I have done if he had?*

'Well?' said her mother.

Delilah turned away from the polished obsidian oval that hung from her wall and sank down beside her mother.

'Ekron and I met Samson at the market today. Some words were exchanged.'

'Angry ones?' said her mother, sitting straighter. 'Were you in any danger?'

'Only of his clumsy charm. He stumbled upon us at Sarai's stall, where Ekron was his usual tongue-tied idiotic self. Sarai has too much patience for him. Anyway, Samson — with all his reputation for a forthright manner with women — blundered in and started showing off to Ekron, who took the instruction badly. Then his friend tried to insult me in Hebrew, so I answered back.'

'Ah.'

Delilah sat in silence for a moment, fingering her copper bracelet. It had not yet begun to turn green but it was already leaving a tiny smudge around her wrist. It was strange how it changed, the opposite of plants that went brown when they died. Achish said the Egyptians understood its power and called it *keme*, the special property of rocks and metals of the earth, but there was something curious and unpredictable about it. You never knew when or how or why it happened.

Delilah glanced up at her mother. 'It wasn't until I saw Samson today that I realised how much I had been dreading seeing him again.'

'Since the desert? But he saved your lives, and for that I am very grateful. I would tell him if I saw him.'

Delilah gave her a wry smile. 'Then I suppose that Achish didn't tell you all that happened.'

Beulah frowned but listened patiently as Delilah recalled the verbal combat that had defined their last meeting.

'I think he may have taken offence when I compared him to Phicol, because we travelled the last three miles in total silence.'

'I imagine so. What in Dagon's name did you say?'

'Nothing bad. I just made fun of his hair.'

Beulah's expression sobered. 'Oh, Delilah.'

'I knew it was something bad because he threatened me.'

'With what?'

'With nothing at all,' said Delilah. 'Isn't that the worst kind?'

Beulah reached for her hand. 'Perhaps some of this is my fault. After your father died, I was so grateful to Achish for taking us in, so eager that you should feel like you belonged here. I didn't tell you as much about our heritage as your father would probably have wished. Samson is a Nazirite. They take several vows of abstinence as part of their commitment to Yahweh.'

'Like what?'

'You might have noticed that Samson didn't drink the wine at Hemin's betrothal.'

'His friends did, and plenty of it too.'

'They are not all Nazirites, and it's true that not all Nazirites take the same vows. Samson's are to do with what he eats and drinks, and also the cutting of his hair. Other Nazirites also take vows of a more intimate nature.'

Delilah chewed her lip to control her smile. 'But if Samson's reputation is to be believed — '

'Indeed,' said Beulah carefully. 'But his hair is sacred to him. You must have offended him very badly.' Beulah kissed her daughter's forehead, and stood up. 'But you'll have to be more careful, Delilah. Your freeness with words will cause you trouble one day if you're not.'

Delilah guiltily watched her mother go. She'd embarrassed Beulah with her ignorance and, though she wasn't quite sure why, she felt awkward at the insult to Samson. She'd savoured the look on his face in the marketplace, when she'd answered his friend's boorish remarks, but the insult in the desert had shown him she wasn't as worldly as she would like. Either that, or he'd think her equally boorish too. Both interpretations gave him the upper hand.

She glanced back at the mirror stone. Peaches and raspberries. Perhaps they *were* just clichéd words, uttered for show, to tease Ekron. If so, how dare he use her in such a bold manner!

Yet somehow in the light of day, he'd also become more human than that sinister figure in the dark. If words dripped like honey from his mouth, then there had still been a flicker of interest in his gaze. She was no longer the shred of a girl he'd dismissed with a wave of his hand, she knew that much.

But Samson was the last man she'd expected to be touched by lust. Especially for her. It had come from nowhere, a sudden change she couldn't have predicted.

11

'So the Chass'ela vines have done better than we expected this year,' said Delilah, 'but I'm still trying to convince Achish to plant more fig trees down there at the bottom of the hill.'

'Why would he do that?' asked Ekron, trying to conceal a yawn among his words. 'He doesn't sell fruit.'

'I wish just once in a while you would say 'We don't' instead of 'He doesn't'. This is your family, your family's business.'

'To which you have become a natural heir.'

'Only because you wouldn't.'

Ekron frowned and rubbed his forehead. The afternoon sun was high and despite the sea wind that blew in across the city and up onto the vineyard slopes, Delilah could see a thin line of sweat forming beneath the band of his Philistine headdress. 'I suppose you mean the figs should be used for making wine,' he said eventually.

'Exactly! You see, if you use your brain — '

'I spend much too much time using my brain already.'

' — you will remember that the Egyptians exported a very fine fig vintage last year.' Delilah turned off the path. 'Let me show you the field I want to dig out for the new trees.'

But Ekron kept walking.

'Don't go back to work yet. You only just arrived.' Delilah dodged up onto the path beside him. 'I'm sorry you missed him at lunch, but Achish will be so pleased to know that you're taking an interest. Can't you stay a while longer and I'll show you what we have planned?'

Ekron's shoulders heaved up and down, but he said nothing.

'Do you regret not taking more of a part in it?' said Delilah quietly. 'Is that what troubles you? It's not too late to come home and get involved.'

'It's not that.' He suddenly lifted his chin, as though bracing himself to say something important.

'What's wrong?'

Ekron cleared his throat then straightened his headdress on his forehead as he strode purposefully through the vineyard's northern gate. 'Lord Phicol wishes to talk to you.'

He kept walking, but Delilah stood her ground.

'What does he want with me? Oh Se't! I'm absolutely not going to nursemaid for Hemin. She has all the grace of a mad dog.'

'It's difficult to be pregnant in this heat.'

'Hemin is always difficult. Pregnancy has made her impossible. She can struggle on her own. She has a whole house full of staff to look after her.'

'This is not about Hemin.'

Ekron faced her and clasped his hands in front of him as though he was about to make a speech.

'Prayers to El, here it comes.'

'The Philistine lords have asked Lord Phicol to meet with you to discuss a matter of considerable importance.'

'Get on with it, Ekron.'

He cleared his throat again. 'They have noticed — well, it has come to their attention that Samson has developed an interest — a romantic interest — in you.'

Delilah felt her cheeks redden. She steeled her expression to irritation. 'What do you mean?'

'Several senior Philistine citizens noticed his attentions towards you in the market the other day, and apparently he has been asking questions about you around Ashkelon.'

'I don't believe that,' said Delilah calmly. This was ridiculous. A romantic interest! She glanced towards the city, trying to imagine Samson enquiring at Sarai's stall after her. Ekron opened his palms. 'My Lord wishes to meet with you to discuss the situation.'

'What does it have to do with him?'

'Please, Delilah. I'm only the messenger.'

'And how you're enjoying that!' Delilah turned away from him and continued towards home.

'Just see him at least,' begged Ekron. 'Hear what he has to say.'

'Politics doesn't interest me, Ekron, you know that.'

'This isn't about politics. It's just a chat. Lord Phicol wants to get your opinion.'

Delilah paused, staring down at her toes, a little dusty in her elegant sandals. No wonder Ekron had suggested she dress nicely for their walk. And how stupid she was to be flattered by the thought that he was proud to be seen with her.

'I can't imagine Lord Phicol is capable of a *chat*,' she said

'He really wants to know what you think,' urged Ekron.

Delilah's heart was thumping in her chest, and she was angry with herself. The fact was, her curiosity was genuinely piqued by Lord Phicol's request. Of course, she would listen carefully to what he had to say before she said anything of her own on the matter.

She turned back towards Ekron. 'Does Achish know we're here?'

Ekron flushed. 'No. Lord Phicol suggested the matter might embarrass my father, given the unsuccessful attempt to marry you off to Samson.'

'Marry me off? It sounds like disposing of rotten grapes.'

Ekron's shoulders sagged. 'I don't mean it like that.'

'And you're sure Hemin isn't going to be there?'

'We'll enter by His Lordship's own private entrance.'

'In the interests of peace — ' Delilah let her voice tail off but her eyes remained firmly on Ekron's.

'Of course.'

'Very well,' she said. She rejoined her stepbrother's side, training her face to a sombre expression. But her mind was buzzing. Old Phicol gave no value to other people's opinions, she knew that. She couldn't imagine it was a matter of public security, so perhaps he simply wanted to preach about avoiding the indecent attentions of the Israelite. Nonetheless, Delilah quickened her step to match Ekron's and they continued on their way in silence.

* * *

Delilah had never seen the private spaces of Lord Phicol's enormous house, and Ekron had been as good as his word, bringing her through the most secure route to the grouped buildings, which was overlooked only by the guards' quarters. Hemin couldn't possibly know she was there. Ekron put his finger to his lips as they entered the house, and she followed him through a narrow maze of shady corridors that seemed to burrow within walls, passing between rooms rather than through them. Ekron knew his way around and clearly came this way often, though Delilah found it hard to imagine that old Phicol could fit his bulky frame in these thin spaces.

After what felt like a considerable time wandering, they emerged from behind a heavy wall tapestry into an empty whitewashed room in which three wooden desks were arranged, each piled neatly with scrolls and tablets.

'This is my office,' said Ekron proudly.

'Are all these desks yours?'

'No, well, I share it with two other scribes.'

'Where are they?'

Ekron didn't answer, but crossed the room to a heavy door made of terebinth wood, on which he knocked firmly, twice, then once more. There was a pause, then the door was opened and a guard beckoned Ekron to enter. Ekron glanced at Delilah and nodded to her to follow. She gave a mock smile of disdain at the performance, but her hands felt damp and she wiped them surreptitiously on the back of her dress.

The inner sanctum was also whitewashed, though there was little space on the walls to see the fine finish, for every cubit seemed smothered in more tapestries, wooden carvings, silk wall hangings, and painted pottery in exotic colours and shapes the like of which Delilah had never seen before. In the furthest corner stood twin statues in gold of the Great God El and his wife Asherah, the Mother Goddess, facing each other in a pairing Delilah had never seen in any temple. El was crouching provocatively before his wife, his head level with her waist, her body curved in a sensual way to reflect her fertility.

In the centre of the room was an enormous wooden bench on which sat the fattest cushion of sumptuous purple cloth, and atop this perched old Phicol, his feet resting on a matching stool. Two enormous Philistine guards, their bare chests moist with glistening oil, fanned him with feathered fronds.

Phicol took his time to look up from the scroll he was studying, but Delilah was quite sure he knew they were there, and eventually he dismissed the guards with a flick of his fingers and the three of them were left alone. He put the scroll on a table beside him, and laid his fat paws on his thighs.

'Delilah, my dear.'

You old goat, thought Delilah, smiling sweetly. 'May I enquire after the health of my sister?'

'You may. She is managing tolerably given her

condition, though clearly the burden of gestation is considerable for such a tiny slip of a woman.'

Delilah could sense Ekron's agonised anticipation at how she might respond to this, but she nodded politely.

'My Lord — ' began Ekron, but Delilah cut across him, determined that now that she'd decided to cross the threshold, it would be on her own terms.

'Your Lordship wished to see me,' she said.

'Ekron has explained the situation?'

'Only briefly, Lord Phicol. You have an interest in Samson.'

Phicol's eyes blazed with amusement. 'More to the point, my dear, Samson has an interest in *you*.' He clasped his hands in his lap. 'Can I ask how do you feel about him?'

Delilah was torn between telling Phicol to mind his own business, and giving voice to her feelings on Samson. The latter won out. 'He's a charmless ogre,' she said quickly.

Phicol grinned. 'Then we are in agreement.' The grin vanished. 'But he is more than that too — '

'He's a petty thief as well,' said Delilah, warming to her theme. 'He bullies, he robs, he takes what he wants. And there's no one to stop him — '

Phicol raised his hands in a little wave and she stopped. 'And besides those matters, he's a dangerous man, who commands many followers.'

'Then why don't you just arrest him?' asked Delilah.

Phicol laughed as if she'd missed the point entirely. Delilah bristled.

'What is it you wanted to see me for, exactly?'

Phicol's face was suddenly serious. 'I should have made myself clear from the outset,' he said. 'I've been authorised by the Philistine elders to pay you a considerable sum of money to make sure Samson remains interested in you. He is a threat to the safety of our people and the stability of our nation, and the dissent he has been fomenting among the Israelites must be brought to an end. The only way to do that is to control Samson, and the only way to control Samson is through you.'

Delilah's poise crumbled. 'But — But he's flirted with me, My Lord, that's all. I hold no power over him.'

'On the contrary; reports I've received indicate that you wield considerable influence. A single look from you seems to have him playing like a puppy dog around your ankles.'

'But what can I possibly achieve with that?'

Phicol gave a snort, a fine spray of spittle filling the air. 'My dear, my dear, have you never heard of bringing a man to his knees? Of that I'm utterly sure you are capable. Your challenge will be to keep him there long enough for us to make sure he never gets up again.'

'But why me?' asked Delilah. 'There are plenty of women down near the harbour — '

Lord Phicol waved his paw dismissively. 'They cannot be trusted. And we need to be more subtle than that. They might detain him for a night or two, but we are looking for a more *strategic* approach.'

'What you're suggesting doesn't sound like it merits that description. Does my stepfather know about this?'

Phicol took a deep breath through his nose. 'He does not, and I'd like to keep things that way, for everyone's sake.'

'I'm sure you would,' said Delilah. 'And you think I can just be bought?'

'I wouldn't choose such a crude term. You and I are entering into a business arrangement. You are providing a service and I'm paying for it, with the consent of my fellow Lordships.'

His offer was a brazen one.

'Surely a big enough amount of money would ensure the 'trust' of anyone. After all, I imagine you'll be offering me — '

'We'll come to that shortly. But your question is valid, I suppose. Why you?' Phicol smoothed the rich weave of his ceremonial skirt against his thighs and picked idly at a small decorative bead on the fringe. 'It's quite simple. Samson will learn to trust you because he is attracted to you and, for the moment at least, he thinks he can't have you. I heard about what happened that night on the desert road, and how he couldn't take his eyes off you in Ashdod.'

Delilah felt rocked. 'How do you know this?'

'It's my job to know,' he replied coolly. 'The man's a brute, but he isn't a fool. He'd sniff a plot a mile off. But I've seen how you operate, young lady. You've got that apprentice of mine wrapped around your little finger. Samson can't

112

keep his eyes off you, and you speak his Hebrew tongue. That's an intoxicating combination to a lonely figure, however powerful he might be.'

Phicol's eyes glittered, as though he'd imagined the depths of this intoxication for himself.

'So how much will you pay me?' she asked.

Ekron swayed slightly beside her, but Phicol seemed amused. 'I like your manner, but you will of course need to be more subtle with the Israelite.' He kicked the footstool aside and slid off his cushion, reaching out for her with his short fingers.

'Seduction is a game best played slowly and carefully. Like the incoming tide, it must lap steadily higher at the ankle, the knee, the thigh — ' Phicol slipped his fingers over Delilah's shoulder, letting them come to rest just beneath the cut of her dress. His eyes flickered across at Ekron.

'I can assure you I'm familiar with the principle,' she said, removing Phicol's hand from her skin. 'How much?'

Phicol clapped his hands together. 'I've a figure in mind, but I'd be interested to hear what price you will put on Samson's head.'

'I haven't much experience of valuing such transactions,' said Delilah. 'If you wanted to talk wine then I might be better — '

'It's still a trade, my dear. I pay you money, you bring him down.' He peered at her. 'Are you hesitating because you are suddenly in search of a conscience on this matter? I'd have thought that with all that he has inflicted on your family, you would be eager for revenge.'

Delilah's mouth felt dry. It was unpleasant to think that Phicol knew her well enough to have found a weakness in her, yet there was a simplicity to the idea of pricing revenge that made a certain chilling sense.

'So? Name your fee,' said Phicol, retreating to his cushion.

Delilah straightened her shoulders. 'Two thousand pieces of silver.'

Ekron gasped, annoying Delilah, but Phicol replied with a sliver of laughter.

'Two thousand! You would bankrupt our state.'

'I'm not so naive about money as to believe that,' she said coyly. 'Your Lordship's taste in fine fabrics and furniture betrays that he knows the value of things. Two thousand would probably furnish a single room in this house.'

'And what would you do with such a sum, were I to agree to it?'

Delilah's eyes glanced over the shimmering opulence of the room, and down at her dress and sandals, so smart and elegant at home, so plain and dowdy here. She thought of Hemin's ludicrously ornate wardrobe, that white maternity shift embroidered with pearls which she kept being sick on, those turquoise silken robes she lounged about in, trimmed with fine shells from the south. Such garments could be hers and her mother's were they both to abandon any semblance of taste and buy them.

But more to the point, the money would give her mother status in her own family. Beulah wouldn't be reliant on Achish for every penny, and when she wanted to buy her husband a gift — such as a new ring to replace the one Samson had taken, for which she'd saved from the housekeeping for a year — it would truly come from her own pocket. Delilah and Beulah would no longer be the poor wife and child, no longer inferior to Ariadnh and Hemin, or to any other Philistine wife and child.

'I believe that's none of your business, any more than the means of my ensnaring of Samson will be.'

Phicol glanced at Ekron. 'Your young lady sets her own terms.'

'You might be paying me, but you will not buy me,' said Delilah. 'I'm not Ekron's young lady, any more than I'll be yours or Samson's. You said it's a trade, and so it is.'

'Five hundred,' said Phicol.

'No.' Delilah turned for the door.

'Six.'

Delilah kept walking.

'Nine. Nine hundred pieces of silver.'

'Fifteen hundred,' said Delilah, putting her hand on the heavy wooden door.

'Delilah.'

Phicol's tone was serious enough to give her pause, and Delilah glanced over her shoulder.

'The lords have authorised me to give only one thousand pieces of silver.'

'And you?'

Phicol nodded slowly. 'And I'll give you one hundred more. To keep your silence from Achish and from everyone else. He'd be upset by this

115

arrangement, and I cannot afford for Hemin to become distressed.'

'Eleven hundred pieces of silver.'

'For Samson.'

Delilah turned to face Phicol, though she remained by the door. Eleven hundred pieces of silver was more than Achish's vineyard turned over each year. After a moment's thought, she crossed her hands, then clasped them together in the traditional gesture of agreement used for business, and nodded while Phicol did the same in return.

'Ekron, fetch the silver.'

Ekron finally turned to face Delilah and she saw how white his face had become. It appalled her to think of it, but she'd found an unexpected ease in her dealings with old Phicol. She'd managed to stand her ground, and now she had a curious equality with her stepbrother, both of them on Phicol's staff. He barely glanced at her as he went out to the scribes' office, and she wondered if he was ashamed of her for agreeing to this arrangement. Perhaps this was the first he'd learned of the details and, being merely a scribe, he could only listen in shock and without comment.

Such notions were quickly disabused as Ekron returned almost immediately with two large bags heavy with silver, each made of common flaxen weave and tied with cords of twisted hemp. He also held a small purse of rich blue silk, tied with a golden cord, which he offered to Lord Phicol. Phicol swiftly counted the coins, then slid them back into the purse and held it out in front of him. 'You might as well have a pretty token to mark our arrangement.'

'If I may suggest, My Lord — ' began Ekron, but Phicol nodded and snatched back the purse.

'You're right. It will probably give her away when she starts showing it off in the market.'

'I need no trinkets of yours,' said Delilah. 'The silver is quite enough.'

Phicol threw the purse at Ekron, who caught it so neatly that Delilah wondered if Phicol often threw things at him. He poured its silver into one of the sacks and drew it shut as Phicol spoke again.

'You will need a reason, an excuse for being away from home in the company of Samson, for when you are successful you will also be away at night-time, I imagine.'

'I'll think of something.'

'No, I have a suggestion. As Hemin is with child, your excuse is already prepared. You will offer to spend time here each day, acting as her companion and assistant, catering to her emotional and physical needs as a good sister would.'

'Your Lordship has thought of everything,' said Delilah, inwardly asking the mischievous god Se't that such an excuse wouldn't require her actual participation.

Phicol picked up his scroll once more, indicating the meeting was over and Delilah was dismissed without any further acknowledgement. She pulled the heavy door closed behind Ekron and they faced each other in the scribes office, so

117

conspicuously plain in comparison to Phicol's chamber.

'What are you going to do with this?' he asked, lifting the heavy bags slightly. 'I'll carry it back for you, if you want.'

Delilah looked at his thin arms, the muscles straining beneath the golden skin. Ekron had remained slender as he grew older, and had never really engaged in physical games and pastimes like other young men of his own age. He had a narrow face and narrow body, and none of the ease in his own skin of other men, even Phicol, let alone Samson. He seemed uncomfortable beneath her gaze, yet his eyes searched out hers with that pleading, puppyish look that he'd never grown out of, and she suddenly had an idea.

'I'll hide it in Joshua's room, above the barn.'

'Yes, I heard about you and the stable boy.'

'He is a good friend to me, and I trust him absolutely.'

'And I don't. Besides, I don't think he'll take kindly to your — your assignment.'

'What assignment?' she replied innocently.

12

It took a lot of eyelash-fluttering to convince Ekron to let her carry the money to the stable on her own. In the end she only got her way by suggesting that his presence in Joshua's room would arouse unwelcome suspicion among everyone in the household. Though she had no intention of explaining to Joshua what was hidden in the pouches between the bundles of roof thatch, she was certain that if she were forced to, he would simply listen without comment.

As it was, everyone was at lunch when she returned to the vineyard and she'd been able to sneak in and out unobserved. As she squeezed the pouches into their hiding place, it struck her that though the money was heavy, it occupied relatively little space. It was more money than she'd ever seen before, but it was still a compact trophy for such a significant act. Nonetheless, there was a burden about it that she felt eager to begin shifting, and she ran quickly out into the rows of vines and back towards the town without calling in at the house.

As she made her way from the house towards the city, the doubts began to cloud around her. What, exactly, was it that she'd agreed to do? To act as a spy for the Philistines, to seduce Samson. That would be easy enough, she thought. Or was her mission something more?

What was Phicol's endgame in all this? She comforted herself that her role was merely to keep an eye on Samson's activities, and to pass on details of any wrongdoing, should she discover it. But anxieties continued to bubble up. She'd accepted the money so readily, without truly dwelling on its consequences.

The buzz of Ashkelon's streets had already begun to subside in the stupefying heat of the early afternoon, as anyone with any sense withdrew to the cool of their houses. Those who lived too far outside the city, or who counted the makeshift settlements beyond the city gates to be home, retreated to the shaded terraces of bars or clustered in lazy chatter beneath the umbrella thorn trees. It was to these people that Delilah was heading, for being poorer, they were mostly Israelite, and would be much more likely to know where their giant hero might be lurking. She was aware, as she bought a handful of date-plums to make up for a missed lunch, that whatever she said about Samson to these people might well be reported back to him by some means. From now on, she must watch everything she said. She couldn't help remembering her mother's recent caution to choose her words more carefully, and she wondered what Beulah would make of the money and the mission.

Chewing on a juicy date-plum, Delilah joined a group of young women gathered near the market. They were swapping goods from their baskets and panniers, trading unsold wares and joking about how they had evaded the attentions of the Philistine soldiers for yet another day. One woman was demonstrating how she'd tucked a bundle of pine cooking utensils under her skirt and waddled gracelessly past an entire cohort without detection. It was easy to join in the women's laughter. Delilah knew she stood out with her expensive dress and delicate jewellery, but her fluency in the coarser Hebrew expressions immediately defused any uncertainty they had about her. She also made sure she bought goods from the women, a square of honey cake now heavy with sweet scent from the heat, and a hair comb carved from a piece of driftwood. She asked for help to arrange her hair around it, and before long she was joking with them about the shortcomings of men.

Delilah had been nervous about how she would steer conversation towards Samson without being obvious, but it turned out that she'd only had to mention the value of a husband who could carry three panniers on each arm, and suddenly everyone had something to say about the strongest man in all the land. He'd apparently been seen by several of the women as they made their way from the coastal encampments into Ashkelon during the morning, exercising with his followers on a patch of waste ground outside the city. There was much discussion of the girth of various parts of his anatomy, which made Delilah feel quite hot beneath the thorn tree shade. There was also talk of a recent fight between him and a group of Philistines in the harbour.

Samson's status as a hero to these people was obvious, but she forced herself to keep her

121

mouth shut about the impact of his violence. She'd seen it for herself all too clearly — the man didn't discriminate between the weak, the strong, the old or the able. He saw only *his* right and *his* wrong.

She left them with only half a hope that Samson would still be found in the same place, but as she passed through the city gates, she immediately picked him out. Even from some way off he was hard to miss, head and shoulders above his companions. From here, he looked to be the size of a tree, as still and stable too. Delilah's hair whipped at her face, as a strong breeze blew from the east and she was glad of the comb to keep it in place. She couldn't possibly be seductive if it looked as though she'd blown in from the desert on the tail of the khamsin winds.

She stood for a few moments watching him, then traced a route for herself that would bring her past his group on her way back to the city. She didn't want to take too long over it in case he left before she returned, but she must make her passing seem casual and unintended.

It was harder to walk on ground that had not been firmed by the flow of traffic between the city and the port, and it took longer than she thought to trace the circle back towards the group of men. As she came within clear sight, she could see Samson. He was surrounded by his men, in some sort of combat training exercise, fending off each of them in turn as they came at him from all sides. Sometimes he'd fell one easily, then grab him by the scruff of his neck, put him back on his feet, and then show him how to defend himself better. But mostly, he simply knocked them over with a single graceful strike. He reminded her of the dancers at the end-of-summer festival, strong yet light on their feet, and there was something painfully beautiful about how his men rose and fell around him.

As Delilah approached, he whirled on his toes to take on the next assailant and his eyes met hers. In a moment three of his men lay in a heap on the ground, moaning and winded, and Samson was dusting off his hands. If he did that to his own men, what must it be like to receive his blows as a Philistine?

Delilah clasped her hands at her waist and took a deep breath to still her nerves. 'You're working up quite a sweat,' she said in Hebrew.

His eyes lingered on her before he answered. 'This is just practice.'

'For what?'

'You will know when the time comes.'

'I hear that there isn't a man in the whole land who compares to you, Samson.'

He hesitated before answering, and she wondered if she'd gone too far. But as he studied her, Delilah could see the sweat shimmer and grow at the base of his throat. His gaze seemed to melt against hers, and she grew warmer beneath the cool folds of her dress.

'It looks like sport, as if grown men play like boys,' said Samson. 'But the threat is real and — ' He crouched and caught the leg of a silent attacker, sending him flying into his companion.

'I'm not as easily distracted as you think, Jubal,' he laughed. 'If you and Abidan are to pair off in combat, you must each take a different tack or your little army will be wiped out in a single strike.'

The one who seemed to be called Jubal spluttered an ironic 'Ha!' from his heap on the floor and Abidan hauled him clumsily upright again. But Delilah had seen enough. She began to walk on, a part of her still shocked by the simple power of his strength, the ruthless focus of his violence, another part of her still hot beneath her dress. Yet she couldn't leave without the last word.

'I wonder if you have any weaknesses at all?' she called, without looking back over her shoulder. Samson didn't reply, but Delilah was quite sure she felt his eyes on her all the way back to the city gates.

★ ★ ★

She made her way up the sloping rows of vines to the house, letting her hands brush through the soft green leaves. Achish was standing on the verandah of his study. He was surveying his lands, his arms folded across his chest, a broad hat of woven reeds shading his head. She was reminded briefly of her own father, and a memory she had not considered in many, many years came to her, of him standing at Achish's side, each of them looking out over the vines.

What would he have made of her assignment from old Phicol? Even though she'd been just a little girl, she couldn't remember any difference between Achish and her father as a consequence of their race. They had been united by their love of the land. Simple men, with simple pleasures. Achish would be no more happy than her own father to know that she'd become embroiled in the matter of their difference, not their similarities. Almost guiltily she cut through the rows towards her stepfather.

Achish spotted her, and held out his hand to greet her.

'I've been looking for you, Delilah. I wanted to talk to you.'

'I'm sorry to have delayed you.'

Achish studied her face. 'I thought that perhaps you had been for a long walk to assuage your sorrows.'

'Sorrows?'

'Well, perhaps an aching in your soul. A mourning for the absence of a certain handsome young man of Ashdod?'

Delilah smiled uncomfortably. If she was going to go after Samson, clearly the merchant's son would have to wait. 'Jered! You thought I was moping about him?'

'Beulah tells me his bowl remains beside your bed.'

Delilah smiled. 'It does.'

'Then all I want to know is whether you would like me to arrange a match for you with him. I believe Mizraim would be willing, and I'm in no doubt that Jered is more than agreeable.'

Delilah squinted into the sun for a moment, then turned back to Achish. 'I think I'd prefer to wait. If that's going to be acceptable to you.'

'Of course. I don't wish to pressure you. I'm quite beyond understanding the wishes of young women when it comes to young men. I'm fully aware of what is supposed to happen, but I've known you long enough to know that, unlike Hemin, you will not be directed in matters of marriage.'

Delilah slipped her hand through Achish's elbow and squeezed his arm gently. 'I just don't feel ready to settle down yet. I was just thinking as I walked up here how much I love the vineyard, how much it has grown since I was a child, and how much there still is to do. Mizraim, being the sensible trader he is, would rather gain a daughter than lose a son — so for Jered to come here wouldn't be a good deal as far as he is concerned. And I'm not yet ready to leave.'

'I'm not entirely surprised,' said Achish, smiling. 'But your mother felt that you should be offered the choice, and we both want only what is best for you.'

Delilah rolled forward onto her tiptoes, tucked her head beneath the brim of his hat and kissed Achish on the cheek. 'You are kind to think of me.'

'I shall not mention it again, until you do.'

Delilah smiled and turned away towards the house. It was indeed thoughtful of Achish to suggest it, and it was typical of his tidiness in matters of business. She realised now that he and Mizraim had probably discussed it as part of their business transaction in Ashdod, and Achish

126

had tactfully waited for the right moment to discuss it with Delilah. A delivery of wine was due to travel to Ashdod in a few days, and perhaps a bride-to-be might have accompanied it.

But not now. It was a curious coincidence that Achish should ask her about Jered on the same day that fat Lord Phicol had offered her a different deal. Perhaps if Achish had got to her first —

Well, she'd never know.

13

'So Achish has you investigating your competitor's wines.'

Delilah smiled to herself at how quickly Samson had found her in the market, then dramatically dropped her basket of purchases and gave a little whoop of surprise.

'Oh! It's you. You shouldn't creep up on a person like that.' She glanced up at Samson, gave him a bemused smile, then looked down at the ground where her basket lay upturned, its contents scattered around her feet. The figs would be bruised from their fall, but they were a reasonable sacrifice for putting herself exactly where Samson could find her.

'It's well known that Rabet has more honeybees on his land than Achish does on his,' continued Samson. 'Though if Achish is going to go through with that insane idea of planting fruit trees for wine, then I suppose he'll need more bees too.'

'It was my idea, actually, and it makes perfect sense. Or it would if you had ever been to Egypt.'

'Have you ever been to Egypt?' asked Samson, crouching down to pick up Delilah's purchases, his eyes still locked onto hers.

'Of course not. Anyway, what is a Nazirite doing at a wine-seller's stall?'

Samson raised his eyebrows slightly; they appeared as dark lines that cut through his wide forehead. 'I see you have been studying me.'

'Why would I waste my time doing that?'

'For the same reason that you are wasting Rabet's time, dithering in front of his stall.' Samson gave a polite nod to the rival winemaker then turned into the crowd, bearing Delilah's small basket in his enormous hand. She had to move quite quickly to keep up with his long strides. The crowd parted easily in front of him. What must everyone think of them, her trailing in his wake like this?

'If you are walking with me, then please walk with me,' she said, 'not in front of me. I'm not an obedient donkey.'

Samson laughed, a deep musical sound that drew stares from several people. But it was genuine, not mocking.

'You are definitely not obedient,' he said. 'Of that I'm absolutely sure.'

Delilah thought momentarily of Phicol and the silver. But that wasn't obedience, was it?

'And though you are a strong little thing,' he continued, 'I wouldn't have you tow any cart of mine. I imagine you are quite content to sit yourself down in the middle of the road if the fancy for hard work leaves you.'

'What a charming vision you have of me,' said Delilah.

Samson looked down at her, and Delilah realised they had already reached the northwestern edge of the market. She didn't know this area of the town very well. But whether he'd seen through her loitering in the market or not — and it looked as though he had — he seemed content to be seen with her and this was too good an opportunity to turn down. She'd simply have to step out into the unknown. Besides, it was hardly likely that anyone was going to try to rob her with Samson at her side.

'What I'm trying to say,' continued Samson, 'is that I had not realised how pretty you have become. I ignored you as a choice instead of your plain sister — '

'Stepsister.'

'She is still plain, whether you are related or not. You are certainly the more attractive one, and I should have paid more attention. We could have been married by now if I had thought more carefully.' Delilah was studiously not looking at him, but she could hear the smile on his lips as he spoke.

'As I remember,' she said indignantly, 'I refused to be offered.'

Samson seemed to ignore that and turned to the left along a street Delilah had never seen before.

'But your stepfather is a clumsy broker,' he continued. 'He might be a good winemaker but he is a poor businessman and a poor diplomat.'

'A poor businessman he must be,' said Delilah, 'to have increased the size of his vineyard twofold in three years.'

'Largely due to your involvement, I hear.'

'Achish has the vision, the commitment, and — '

'The finest land, stolen from the Israelites; from *your* ancestors, from *my* ancestors. There was no business about it. Achish has just reaped the rewards of someone else's good judgement.'

How quickly he could spark her anger!

'And now I'm exercising my judgement. Goodbye.' Delilah reached for her basket, not an easy feat given Samson's height and breadth, determined to return the way she'd come. She could ask for directions around the next corner.

But she had to stretch across him for the basket and her arm brushed against his. The honey-coloured hairs were surprisingly soft, and though she tugged on the handle he didn't release the basket.

'You are too intelligent to run away from the truth, Delilah.'

'I've no wish to hear myself, or my family, insulted.'

Samson sighed irritably. 'For a man of my size, I'm occasionally clumsy with words, I admit it.'

'You admit you have made mistakes?'

'I'm quite sure I'm about to make another one,' he muttered, sliding his free hand down Delilah's back and steering her towards a narrow alleyway between two houses. He lifted the basket out of her reach, holding it out like bait to a fish, and led the way.

'I'm trying to apologise,' he said, his voice clear and strong. 'I may have been rude to you in rejecting the prospect of marriage to you.'

'You are rude,' said Delilah firmly, trying to work out where they were. 'I was right to reject you. Marriage to you would have been a disaster.'

'It would have been a war.'

'A constant battle.'

Samson stopped in front of a doorway, half-shielded by a heavy calico cloth. 'Then we agree on something. That's a new beginning for us.'

Delilah gave him a firm stare that dissolved into a smile.

'So what is this place?' she asked, looking into the darkened space. Chatter in Hebrew spilled out onto the street, and she could make out a few figures at tables inside.

'The sort of place you will never have been to before. Come.' He swung the basket over her head, ducked beneath the doorway and went in.

Delilah looked up and down the street, but there was no one to see her follow him. Thank goodness he hadn't tried to get her alone already. If she was to seduce Samson on her own terms, instead of falling for what were his obvious physical charms, she must be able to make the opportunity last long enough to get word to old Phicol. She wouldn't let Samson have his way with her, then dump her like all the other girls.

The sweet smell of wine that hung in the air suggested it was some sort of drinking establishment but, unlike the Philistine taverns, there was no carving of a jug on a tile by the door.

She stepped cautiously across the threshold, blinking to adjust to the shadowy interior. Wooden stools were clustered around tables, and against one wall stood a tall rack stacked with jars of wine. On a low table near the shelves rested piles of drinking bowls, spoons and smaller drinking jars, large bowls of sticky honeycomb, and of lemons piled high, as well as a huge jug of water. Beyond the shelves, Delilah saw a small stove on which something was simmering.

Samson gestured to her to follow, and she climbed up a small flight of stone steps to a raised terrace behind the main building. It wasn't overlooked because it was surrounded by high walls, and the space was kept cool by an enormous awning of woven palm, as big as a ship's sail. Several men and a few women were already gathered on the terrace; the men perched on benches or stools, the women draped across some of them like wilting flowers. There was a slight stirring of interest as Samson arrived, but Delilah found the women's expressions turned swiftly from adoration to sullen disappointment when they noticed that she had come too.

The men reached out for Samson, grasping his forearm with their spread palms, joking with each other about how difficult it was to get a decent grip. Samson laid Delilah's basket carefully out of reach in a high nook in the wall, then put a bench against a wall in a shady spot at the rear of the terrace, and gestured for her to sit down. She picked her way through the crowd and lowered herself onto the bench, arranging her dress carefully across her shoulders. She was slightly apart from the crowd here: perhaps Samson was still uncertain about allowing her to mix with his friends. Yet it was the perfect place to watch and listen. Through Ekron, Phicol had passed on more detailed instructions. He wanted information on Samson's followers too, details of how he was protected, what personal bodyguard he could rely on, and here she'd surely see it all. Two of his men seemed as interested in her as she was in them. They seemed familiar, but she couldn't remember if she'd seen them at the training ground, or perhaps just around the market. One, a wiry, serious looking fellow, was pretending not to notice her at all, but the eyes of his companion, a handsome young man with curly hair, kept darting over her. She met his gaze once, smiled politely, then turned her attention to her new surroundings.

She couldn't quite believe that she'd won Samson's confidence so quickly that he'd bring her to such a place, but here she was nonetheless. The tavern might seem insalubrious but there was no doubt that she was deep in the heart of the Israelite quarter of the city, a place no Philistine would ever go to unarmed and certainly where no Philistine woman would be invited. That part of her duplicity made her nervous, yet she convinced herself that as an Israelite she had every reason to be here among her own people, and she lightly rested her hands on her stomach in the hope that they would still the nerves jumping inside her. It was just a tavern, after all, a social meeting place. She'd made it through the first challenge and she could relax now.

But she had barely settled herself to study Samson, who was engaged in conversation across the terrace, when two young men she recognised moved in on her, and sat themselves on either side of her. One — she thought it was Jubal?

— offered her a small drinking bowl and she sniffed carefully at it.

'It's wine. It won't hurt you,' he said.

'Thank you.' Delilah smiled at him and took a small sip. He clearly didn't know that she spent an hour of every week tasting wines with Achish, and was now supervising some of the blendings. She could tell this wasn't one of their vintages. It had a bitter edge, and she thought of Rabet in the market. His land wasn't perfectly aligned with the passage of the sun, and his wines weren't quite as sweet as theirs. Nor as expensive.

'Have your bruises healed yet, Jubal?' asked Delilah.

He smiled, pleased that she knew his name. 'I reckon even if we all tried together, we still couldn't knock him down,' he said. Delilah smiled and looked through the crowd that was now gathered around Samson. An older man had joined the group. His clothes were rather dusty and worn, and he wore no sandals on his feet. His hands were clasped around a drinking bowl that he offered to Samson, bowing his head over and over.

'Who's that?' asked Delilah.

'I don't know his name, but he lives in one of the settlements beyond the city gates,' said Jubal. 'His son got into trouble with a Philistine patrol near the harbour, and was all for going after one of them with a knife. Samson had a talk with the lad, showed him how to defend himself better.'

'And got him to calm down a bit,' added Abidan. 'He did that for a lot of us. But we don't

135

all have fathers to thank him.'

'We show our gratitude by joining him,' said Jubal.

Delilah looked from one to the other, only now seeing just how young they were — perhaps not even as old as her — yet they wore their responsibility with great seriousness, and the weight of this seemed to age them. They were strong too, as muscular as Phicol's guards, but their hands and arms and legs bore scars and bruises that must have come from Samson's training, or perhaps less sympathetic Philistine soldiers.

Samson was now bidding farewell to the man, and he crossed to join Delilah, holding out a drinking bowl to her. 'Try this.'

'What is it?'

'You're so full of questions. Just drink it.'

Delilah gave a half smile. The sharing of a drinking bowl was the second step in the Philistine marriage custom that Jered had begun with her in the market in Ashdod. First you gave bowls, which was an indication of interest but didn't signal commitment by either party. But the sharing of a drink from the same bowl was a gesture of intimacy, and Delilah was absolutely sure that Samson knew enough about Philistine customs to know the significance of his offer.

Delilah took the bowl from him and smelled it carefully. 'Honey, water, lemon peel — and cloves? And something else.'

'Cinnamon.'

'How exotic.'

'Exotic enough for you to share it with me?'

She certainly had his attention now. But it was a little soon to act on it; she wouldn't be rushed.

'I should be getting home,' she said, returning the drink untouched. 'I promised Achish I'd be back in time to help him this afternoon.'

Samson took the bowl from her without comment, then lifted down her basket and made his way to the stairs. Delilah smiled politely at Abidan and Jubal, and at the two young men who had been silently observing her, then she followed Samson down into the darkened room. As he stopped to chat with someone at a table, she passed him and went out onto the street, looking around for some way to identify the house. Phicol would be surprised by how civilised and normal everyone was; they were certainly not the pack of rabid and undisciplined thugs he believed them to be.

As Samson came out of the tavern, Delilah spotted a crack in one of the tiles below the window shutters. It ran almost straight from the tile to the end of the wall. It wasn't much to go on, but she knew she'd recognise it again.

'Thank you for your hospitality,' she said.

'You didn't give me the chance to show you any.'

'I'm sure you will try again.'

Samson looked as though he was about to answer, but he suddenly leaned forward and kissed her. His mouth was firm yet yielding against hers and Delilah felt a little dizzy at how swiftly he breathed his passion into her. She stumbled against him, weakened by the intensity of his kiss. And then, just as unexpectedly as it

137

had begun he drew away and began walking along the alley. Delilah was left standing there, still feeling his lips on hers, still tasting the honey and cinnamon on his breath.

She watched him disappear down the street. This would be easier than she'd thought.

14

'I don't remember you wearing out your sandals so quickly last year,' observed Beulah as she threaded a pair of leather straps through the loops on the sole. 'You must be walking to Ashdod once a week.'

'Why would I do that?' asked Delilah absently, as she rearranged her hair around the driftwood comb for the fourth time since lunch. She'd painted some subtle lines of kohl around the rims of her eyes, but that was all.

'I hear there are some very nice young men in Ashdod. A girl might walk a long way to see such a fellow.'

'Hmm.'

'Delilah? Are you paying any attention to me at all?'

Delilah turned away from the mirror stone that hung from one of the courtyard arches and sat down on a stool beside her mother's chair. Beulah's greying hair hung in neat ringlets framing her round face. The tiny laughter lines around her eyes and the creases of worry in her forehead gave Delilah guilty pause. 'I'm sorry, Mother. My hair seems to have a mind of its own today.'

'It's not the only thing that keeps wandering off. Where are you going in these sandals every day? This is the third pair of straps I've had to thread since the end-of-winter festival.'

'It must be that Egyptian leather. Perhaps their cows are so sacred that the Gods forbid their leather to be used for anything as mundane as my shoes. I shall buy from another stall next time.'

'Delilah.'

'Mother?'

'If you refuse to discuss Jered with me, then I respect that. But I simply don't believe that you are wearing out these shoes going to see Hemin every day. You can't abide being in her presence, particularly not now that she is with child and Se't has control of her emotions.'

'Se't had control of Hemin's emotions from the moment she arrived on this earth.'

'Which only proves my point, Delilah.'

Delilah squeezed her mother's hand then leaned across and kissed her gently on the forehead. 'Don't fret over Hemin and me.'

'Then who should I be fretting over? I never see you any more, and what is worse, I don't even know where you go when you are not here.'

'You have nothing to worry about,' said Delilah, slipping her shawl over her arm. 'I'll be home in time to join Achish on his afternoon round of the vines.' She picked up her purse containing a fan and a few coins, and ran out of the courtyard before her mother could say another word. Delilah hated lying to her, but there was no alternative. Soon she'd be able to give her mother the money that would ensure her security, but first there was work to be done.

★ ★ ★

Delilah conscientiously bought a pair of Philistine leather straps for her sandals on her way through the market, then took the long way round to her destination. It always felt so illicit to pass into the predominantly Israelite quarter, and she instinctively looked over her shoulder before stepping into the alley. She'd come here four times since Samson had first brought her, and though she usually came around the same time of day — between late morning and mid-afternoon — Samson didn't seem to have any sort of routine. Sometimes he'd be there when she arrived, and on one occasion he hadn't come at all. Still, it would help him to think her reliable.

The tavern was busier than usual, and she could hear some discontented moaning as she entered the inner room. Philistine soldiers had been breaking up gatherings of Israelites in public places in the last few days, and many of them seemed to have gathered here to complain about it. Women, it seemed, were likely to be no threat, and were responding to the restrictions by gathering in ever greater numbers in awkward places, like just inside the city gates where they could obstruct the flow of Philistine carts from the harbour. But the men were obviously expected to be trouble, and Delilah couldn't help wondering whether Phicol realised that he was simply driving them underground, rather than keeping them apart. Although there were several Philistine landlords in this part of the city, very few dared to wander through the quarter without specific business to attend to.

Delilah paused to buy a bowl of Samson's favourite honey drink, then wandered casually through to the terrace, but once again he was nowhere to be seen. Perhaps he was out exercising with his followers still; she should consider delaying her visits, though that would mean joining Achish to tour the vineyard at a different time of day. She settled herself into her usual corner, sipping her drink patiently. But she couldn't stop herself peering into the shadowy room every time someone arrived. It was irritating to have her plans held up like this. She'd thought carefully about which days to come here, what to wear, what to say, how to behave, but none of that trouble was worth anything if Samson wasn't here to see her.

'Waiting for someone?'

Delilah focused on the voice, which belonged to a woman perhaps ten years older than she was. She wore a green scoop-necked shift in the Egyptian style, which was perhaps a span too small for her, for it was tight across her ample chest, and reminded Delilah unkindly of vine rolls stuffed with minced lamb. Her hair was very long and raven black and was drawn together over one shoulder. Her eyes were carefully rimmed with dark kohl. She was studying Delilah as closely as Delilah was studying her, and after a moment her lip curled in a smile.

'You aren't the first girl to hang around here waiting for Samson. Some nights there's a queue right down the street of girls wanting to get a sip of his honey.'

'And I suppose you know how sweet it is.'

The woman tilted her head in wry acknowledgement. 'He's not the committing kind, sweetheart.'

'I know his reputation well enough,' said Delilah smiling. 'Happily, I didn't help him earn it.'

'A remark as sharp as that could cut your throat,' said the woman, turning away.

Delilah watched her slope back down the stairs. Had all the other women who called at the tavern also been Samson's lovers at one time or another? He probably knew every woman in the quarter intimately.

Well, every woman but this one. For this particular woman, he'll have to be a little more patient.

Delilah smoothed her skirt over her lap and wondered whether she should have a new dress made, something that fitted her more closely and was less Philistine in design. It wasn't that the Israelite women bared more of their skin, although the ones who visited the tavern certainly seemed to. But their clothing was less formally arranged, with fewer pleats and fussiness. She'd call in at the dressmaker on her way back through the city later. That would be a surprise for Samson, to see her in a new dress. She was beginning to run out of things to wear that he hadn't seen her in before, and at least now she had money to buy whatever she wanted.

She was trying to decide on the colour when a great roar of laughter swelled up in the tavern room, and her heart beat a little faster. A moment later Abidan and Jubal came bounding up the steps, and flopped down on benches to either side of her. She stifled her disappointment, and took a sip of her drink.

'I can't believe you ever catch a Philistine unawares if you make such an entrance everywhere you go,' she said.

'We heard a great joke in the market,' said Abidan. 'I was just telling the others.'

'Tell me.'

Jubal grinned. 'It's much too rude for a lady like you.'

Delilah pulled a face. 'It's nice of you to think so highly of me.'

'We dare not do otherwise.'

Delilah smiled inwardly.

'At least tell me what the joke was about.'

'Well, let's just say it has something to do with Lord Phicol and that ridiculous bullrush he wears in his headdress.' Abidan raised his eyebrows suggestively and Delilah began to laugh.

★ ★ ★

'What's the difference between Lord Phicol and the Holy Ass of Lachish?' recited Jubal.

'No, no, what about this one,' interrupted Abidan. 'Have you heard the one about the Philistine tax collector? He thought the Israelites were following him because they finally chose to honour his ways. But then he found he had a hole in his purse and had been dropping money all the way from Ashdod!'

'They say Lord Phicol doesn't need a rug in

his bedroom. He just walks all over his wife!'

Delilah's eyes widened. Hemin would be horrified. And yet she married the man, and willingly at that. As Abidan and Jubal continued to swap jokes, laughing ever more outrageously, Delilah realised she'd never heard a Philistine mock Samson. They spoke of him only in fear or anger. But there was no fear of Phicol among the Israelites, just contempt. No wonder he needed her help to bring Samson down. How could you frighten a people who will only laugh at you?

She was so lost in her thoughts that she didn't notice Samson climb onto the terrace and she felt almost guilty to have been caught laughing by such a serious man. He was studying her in his usual intense manner.

'We've made her laugh so much,' said Jubal, getting up from the bench, 'she has no breath to speak now. You can talk for an hour without interruption.'

'Do you hear that?' said Samson to Delilah. 'Silence is expected from you.'

'As you wish.' She looked piously at him for several long moments, then he shook his head.

'It's too unnatural. The tide will turn too soon and the sun will change its course if you stay so quiet.'

Delilah let her serious expression crack into a smile and offered him her drinking bowl. 'You look hot.'

'Do I?'

'Yes. What have you been doing?'

But Samson only took the bowl from her and drank, watching her over the rim of the bowl as he drained it. Delilah saw grains of sand and tiny crystals of salt clustered among his eyebrows and in a line along his forehead.

'Then let me guess. I think you've been riding along the shore.' She lifted her finger to his brow line but didn't touch his hair. 'And here you had a cloth tied to keep the wind out of your braids but its cargo has stuck to your face instead.'

Samson wiped his forehead with the palm of his hand and grinned. 'I've been in the north near Ashdod, settling a dispute between farmers from different tribes. I thought I might miss seeing you.'

Delilah glanced at the sky. 'Well, you almost did. It's time I returned home,' she said, getting up from the bench. 'You have done your work but I must begin mine.'

Samson led the way through the tavern and Delilah followed him, deliberately ignoring the envious gaze of the woman in the green dress, who was now draped over the curly-haired man who'd studied her on her first visit. She'd learned that his name was Caleb but she didn't know the name of the woman he was with. She felt their eyes on her and Samson as they left the tavern, but she didn't care what the woman thought now that she was at Samson's side. For though they walked the length of the street in careful and silent separation, she knew that as soon as they turned the corner, Samson would reach for her, drawing her to him, his mouth searching out hers.

This afternoon was no exception, and she was sure she wasn't imagining that Samson's physical heat was pouring into the way he kissed her. For such a huge man, he was tender, yet his passion for her was powerful and today more than ever she felt that he was on the verge of unleashing a desire that wasn't quite fully formed. For herself, she always tried to hold some part of herself back, enjoying it but not giving in to it, but the intoxication was growing with each of these moments. They had reached the cusp of a far greater intimacy, one that couldn't be explored in the street. She spread her fingers over his muscular arms, pulled her mouth a little away from his and looked into eyes that never closed, even when she knew her kisses were carrying him out of himself.

'Let's find somewhere more private,' she breathed.

But Samson seemed to swallow the words from her, his tongue gently licking tiny beads of sweat from around her mouth, his lips finding hers again, and Delilah felt the burn of restraint pull painfully tight against a desire that was beginning to take her over.

We can't go on like this, she pleaded with him in her head. *When will you give yourself to me completely?*

As abruptly as ever, he moved away from her. She cursed him silently for his patience, yet shook her head in disbelief at his self-control. Was he really master of the same feelings she was struggling more and more to manage?

And then — yes, there it was, that odd little darkness in those bright blue eyes, that bottomless pit of yearning for her, masked by such ordinary words. 'I'll see you again, Delilah.'

She wanted to ask when, but he was already walking away. Her lips were still sensitive to the absence of his.

'Yes,' she whispered, 'you will.'

15

Delilah had not noticed it the first time she entered Phicol's private office, but as she waited for him to enter from an adjoining chamber, she realised how cold the room felt. It wasn't that it lacked sunlight, but rather that despite its opulent furnishings, there was no comfort in the place. The terrace at the tavern, with its worn benches and misshapen candles, was more welcoming than this place.

When Phicol finally entered, she willed herself not to look irritated at the deliberate delay, for that would only puff up his arrogance even further. In the corner, the statues of El and Asherah sparkled, and she cheerfully sucked in her cheeks to stop herself from laughing at the memory of Abidan and Jubal's jokes.

'What can you report?' asked Phicol. 'Ekron has been able to tell me very little of your movements, except that you are never at home any more.'

'I've been busy.'

'What do you have to show for it?'

'What is it you want?'

'I want a detailed report of what Samson has been doing lately to incite violence in his men. They are causing trouble all over town. This is exactly what I wanted to prevent from happening.'

'I've seen no evidence of that.'

149

'The evidence is in blood, my dear. Eight of my soldiers have been wounded in the last week, breaking up fights between drunken Israelites and innocent Philistine citizens — '

'I don't know anything about that.'

'Well you should. I'm not paying you for ignorance.'

'Samson spends his time training and exercising with his followers outside the city. The guards on the gates could tell you that, though.'

'He's commandeered a patch of waste land there. We let him use it so we can keep an eye on him.'

'Then you know he spends several hours there every day.'

'And the rest of the time?'

Delilah stifled a sigh. 'He spends a good part of every day visiting the Israelite areas in and outside the city, mediating disputes between neighbours, tying up deals between traders, and generally keeping the peace much more effectively than your men seem to do. He also spends a lot of time praying.'

'Where?'

'I don't know. But I do know his God is very important to him. Just as important as yours.' She cast a deliberate glance towards the statues in the corner.

'Clearly there are other women in the picture still, for I imagine what you think of as praying, he thinks of as devotion to more earthly goddesses.'

Delilah felt herself redden, not least at the memory of Samson's last kiss. 'I couldn't say.

150

But given how much time he devotes to looking after the interests of his people — '

'Pah! He is sowing the seeds of dissent,' barked Phicol, 'not helping them to build a happy and contented future among their enemies. The man is an emissary of trouble from Ba'al — '

'Of course he isn't, he's an Israelite, not a Philistine. He doesn't worship Ba'al — '

'I don't care who he worships. He is powerful enough to bring together the Israelites in his name, and instead of dozens of small groups who fight amongst themselves, you have just confirmed that he is bringing them together to oppose us.'

Delilah listened in silence, her eye caught by the way Phicol's feet swung in front of his bench, caught in the rhythm of his speech. He looked ridiculous, yet his fury was evident. He'd be no match for Samson in direct combat, of course, but in this room his words seemed to echo with an almost divine authority.

'Every day there is more trouble,' he boomed. 'Street brawls near the market, fights outside brothels and down at the harbour, decent Philistine traders attacked in their shops and out on the road. Samson is orchestrating a campaign of terror against us, he is frightening our people, and he must be stopped. The man you describe is a devout little boy next to the warrior we are facing on the streets. You clearly know nothing of value about him at all. I should ask for the return of my silver.'

'I still know more than you do,' said Delilah

quickly. 'All you see is the fighting, but you have no actual evidence that Samson has begun a much larger campaign.'

'And you do?'

'I can tell you that the loyalty he inspires will not be easily broken, so I'm your only hope for winning his confidence.'

'I don't believe he's shared any confidences with you at all yet.' Phicol cast his eye over her from head to toe. 'The women who live near the docks probably know more about his political ambitions than you do.'

Delilah thought of the woman in the olive dress at the tavern, and hardened her stare at Phicol. 'I already know Samson well enough to tell you two things about him. Firstly, he doesn't have political ambitions, as you call them. He doesn't want to sit on a throne and tell people what to do, but people do listen to him and his judgement is widely sought by those who are tired of fighting among themselves. And secondly, the few who are in his confidence have had to earn his trust, for he is a patient man, far more patient than you.'

Involuntarily, Delilah ran her tongue over her lips, searching out the long-lost taste of Samson's mouth. Phicol watched her with cruel amusement.

'Clearly he's got under your skin, but you need to work harder to get under his. I'll make it easy for you. Don't bother your pretty head with battle plans and an inventory of his armoury. Just find out where he spends his nights. It shouldn't be difficult for you to charm your way to such a place. Just tell me that and I'll do the rest. But I want answers by the next full moon.'

'That's only three days away.'

'Then you'd better get on with it. And, Delilah, remember this. He might be a patient man, but he is also a violent man. Your little friend at the market, Sarai — her father's business has been targeted by Samson's men again, and two of Sarai's brothers were badly hurt this time. Samson has started a war against all of us and you would do well to remember how much is at stake.'

★ ★ ★

Delilah left Phicol's study with her chin held high, but inside she was burning with indignation. The Philistine lord had been effective in both his instructions and his insults, and she realised for the first time that behind that arrogant exterior was a skilful manipulator; he'd clearly risen to power through knowing how to control his friends as well as his enemies. As she passed the armed guard by the front door, Delilah straightened her shoulders in imitation of their proud posture, for she felt like a soldier in possession of orders.

She set off on the road towards the vineyard, recalling Phicol's final words. Samson's anger against the Philistine people was spreading quickly, and she was worried for Sarai's brothers, two charming young men just entering adulthood. Had Samson really ordered them harmed? Perhaps he was nothing but a brute, after all. She felt uneasy about it, though, and wondered if there was a way to ask him about it without arousing his suspicions. He'd remember Sarai from the market, she was sure.

Her thoughts were interrupted by a shout, and Delilah turned to see Ekron running out of the house towards her. He was moving awkwardly, and as he approached, Delilah saw that he was limping slightly and that his jaw was badly bruised.

'What happened to you?' she asked.

'Have you just seen His Lordship?'

'I've had the honour,' replied Delilah.

Ekron gave her an odd look. 'Don't ever let him hear you speak like that.'

Delilah bowed again. 'I'm nothing but respectful in His Lordship's presence. Anyway, what happened to you? Did you try to climb up onto his pedestal and fall off?'

Ekron waved away her flippancy.

'It doesn't matter.'

'Ekron — '

'Did His Lordship update you on the latest acts of war by Samson against our people?'

'I'm an Israelite now,' said Delilah. 'That's what I'm being paid to be.'

'You shouldn't defend them. You haven't seen what he did to Sarai's brothers.'

'Were you there? Is that how you got hurt?'

Ekron absently rubbed his hand over his jaw. 'Niq has a broken arm, and Ammit was knocked unconscious by a blow to the head. He didn't wake up for two days. Their father Sihon didn't leave his bedside in all that time, even though

154

half his stock of ceramics was destroyed.'

'I haven't been to the market recently, so I haven't seen Sarai.'

'She's very upset.'

'How do you know so much about it?'

Ekron waved his hands vaguely. 'His Lordship requires me to get information for him. But I know — from what I've heard, of course, that Samson was directly involved in this attack. The Israelites were drunken animals, turning over crates and boxes in Sihon's warehouse, and breaking as much as they could.'

'Drunk? Are you sure?'

'Absolutely.'

'But Samson doesn't drink. His Nazirite vows forbid — '

'Again, you defend him! Whose side are you on, Delilah?'

'I know the difference between gossip and truth.'

'You leap to his defence without a second thought and yet you weren't there and you have no idea what really happened.'

'And you do?'

'You're spending far too much time with that brute.'

'His Lordship doesn't think I'm spending enough time with him.'

Ekron fell silent for a moment. When he replied, his voice was steadier and more controlled. 'You need to know how dangerous Samson's people are. Ammit was so badly hurt, they thought he wouldn't survive. As it is, he may never speak or stand up again.'

155

'But you have to see that I can't help the Philistine people if I don't know how Samson operates. You wouldn't catch a fish by standing on the beach waiting for it to flop up onto the sand. Samson won't be caught by Phicol's soldiers if they are looking in the wrong places. They clearly haven't been very successful so far, have they?' Delilah lifted her hand to touch Ekron's bruised jaw, but he grabbed it before it could reach his face.

'I'm just worried about you,' he said. 'He is not to be trusted.'

'I don't trust him. But I do have to get to know him.'

Ekron rubbed the back of Delilah's hand with his thumb. 'I'd be very upset if something happened to you.'

'I know you would. But I do know how to behave around men.'

'I'm sure you do,' he said resentfully.

'You just have to trust *me*,' said Delilah. Then, thinking that the idea of it might lead his mind to uncomfortable places, she leaned across and kissed him lightly on the cheek, just above his bruises.

Ekron blinked and smiled, distracted by her gesture. 'Very well.'

But can I trust myself? wondered Delilah.

16

The vineyard shimmered in the afternoon sun.
The green leaves and new fruit blurred into a
rich tapestry between the lapis sweep of the
cloudless sky and the searing golden heat of the
earth. Delilah lingered in the cool of the hallway
and wondered for a moment if she could bear
the hot walk to the city to seek out Samson. His
desire for her could surely stand another day, but
Phicol's deadline wouldn't wait and she'd have
to go.

In the courtyard, Joshua was trying to distract
Beulah with a pointless enquiry about household
management so that Delilah could escape
unnoticed, but Delilah picked the wrong
moment to dart out of the hallway, and Beulah
sat up quickly at the sound of footsteps.

'Are you going out again, Delilah?'

Delilah turned towards her mother, smiling
broadly. 'Oh, there you are. I was looking for you
indoors.'

Beulah gave Joshua a wry shake of the head
and he slid away, avoiding Delilah's rueful gaze.

Delilah dropped down on the edge of her
mother's couch and gave her mother a quick
hug. 'It's such a beautiful afternoon I thought I'd
go down to the sea.'

'Is it safe? Ekron told me this morning there
has been a lot of trouble along the coast.'

'Ekron is very cautious about everything. I

wouldn't expect anything different from Little Phicol.'

Beulah stifled a smile and took Delilah's hand in hers. 'Anyway, I'm glad I found you before Achish did. I have some news. We have received word from Mizraim that he and Jered will be attending the end-of-summer festival of Dagon. I think Achish and Mizraim would like to confirm your betrothal then. It would be very auspicious to have the ceremony — '

'I'm not ready to marry,' Delilah replied quickly. 'Jered is sweet. Very sweet. But he is also very traditional and prefers a woman to enjoy the comforts of home and not run a business. I'm not ready to leave that behind.'

'And yet you were just leaving it to go down to the sea.'

Delilah sighed. 'I know you worry about me. But I know so little about the world beyond the vineyard and if I'm to do business out there, I should learn about it first.'

'Mizraim is a successful trader, you could learn from him if you married Jered.'

Delilah had been employing reason, but she saw suddenly that her mother might understand better if she simply said what she felt. 'I'm not ready to marry, Mother. I haven't yet learned your patience and devotion. There's too much out there to interest me.'

'Out there is a complicated world, Delilah, and you are uniquely placed to be hurt by both sides, especially at the moment with tensions running so high. You would be safer in Ashdod, I'm quite sure of that.'

I wonder what Ekron has been saying, thought Delilah, kissing her mother on the cheek.

'If I promise to be careful, will you promise to explain to Achish that I'm not ready to marry Jered?'

Beulah smiled sadly. 'It seems to me that you are asking for your freedom on both counts.'

Delilah felt guilty that her mother had judged her so well, but there was nothing to be done about it. Even without Phicol's mission, she was sure she wasn't ready to settle down, and there was no point in lying about that as well. One thing was certain, she planned to be hurt by neither side, Israelite or Philistine.

In many ways, Ekron had a very narrow view of the world. He'd never been able to see that wine could be made with more than grapes, that an enemy is not fought with knives and spears alone. He'd always been a faithful disciple to Lord Phicol and there seemed no doubt in his mind that Phicol's policies were right and Samson's were wrong.

Delilah was so preoccupied with these thoughts that she took a wrong turning out of the market on her way to the tavern, and it was a moment before she realised she was still in the Philistine quarter. She was about to retrace her steps when she heard a booming voice she recognised as Samson's, and she followed it to the next corner. At the far end of the street she spotted him with a woman, around whom four small toddlers clustered, their hands tightly grasped to her skirt, and for a moment Delilah's heart was in her mouth.

Did Samson have a wife?

Children?

You fool! she thought. *All this time I thought he was only interested in me. But I don't know him at all —*

As she drew closer, Delilah spotted a second man standing in a doorway swinging a sack in his hand, and she began to hear raised voices.

'If she doesn't pay, she can't stay here,' said the man in Philistine.

'Her husband was killed two weeks ago in a fishing accident,' replied Samson. 'She is still in mourning and she has barely enough money to buy food for her children, let alone to pay the rent.'

'I have to feed my children too. Anyway, don't the Israelite men look after their widows, share them out between them — Hey!'

The man shrieked as Samson snatched his throat and hoisted him high, and Delilah ran down the street to intervene.

'Put him down,' she said firmly. The man's eyes were already goggling with fear and asphyxiation.

Samson glanced over his shoulder at her. 'Stay out of this. And take Petra and the little ones with you.'

'We aren't going anywhere and you're not going to do anything to this man.'

'He insulted my people.'

'And mine. But there will only be revenge if you kill him and Petra will be left to fend for herself.'

The landlord was now puce in the face from

160

struggling against Samson's hold. Delilah dug quickly into her purse. She pulled out three silver coins and held them between her fingers in front of the man's face. 'Will this cover what she owes?'

Samson abruptly let go of the landlord, who fell to the ground in a heap. His eyes were still wide, but they gleamed at the silver and he reached for it.

'What does she get for this?' asked Delilah holding the coins just out of reach.

'That will pay what she owes,' coughed the landlord, 'and cover the next two months.'

'Then that will give her time to get back on her feet again.' Delilah glanced at the woman, who was now crying. The children gazed up at her, mostly too young to understand what was happening, but enthralled by the glitter of the coins.

The exchange was completed quickly, but Delilah suddenly felt embarrassed and she turned away before the woman had finished thanking Samson. Even so, he had caught her up by the time she reached the corner and passed into a shady alley.

'He would have given up,' he said gruffly, falling into stride beside her.

'He'd have fainted first. And she would still have owed the money. You weren't going to pay it, were you?'

'I never put money in the pockets of Philistines.'

'Then it's lucky you have me to do it for you.'

'Why did you pay him?'

161

'I find no joy in other people's suffering. And besides, he'd only have come back for the rent tomorrow or someone else would have come in his place. She needs time to get her family back on its feet and she can't do that if she's worrying about the rent. Or about you causing trouble on her doorstep.'

'I simply right things that are wrong.'

Delilah looked up at him finally. 'You have no conscience about — '

The rest of her words were lost in Samson's kiss, and her firmness seemed to dissolve beneath his touch. His mouth sought out her throat for the first time. As she let her head fall back into the palm of his hand, her heart pounded so hard, she was sure his lips would feel it beneath her skin. She could hardly breathe. Unwillingly the image of the strangled landlord flooded into her mind; there seemed to be such a fine line between passion and violence in Samson's world.

It was almost with relief that she felt his mouth lift from her neck.

'There is an old granary two streets from the tavern,' he said, close to her cheek. 'Come upstairs, after dark.'

'Tonight?'

'Tell no one. Absolutely no one. Not even those closest to you.'

'I understand.'

'Betrayal comes all too easily.'

Delilah met his gaze, so heavy with promise yet cold and clear. In that moment she wondered if he could see right into her mind, see the silver bagged up beneath the stable roof, hidden from everyone except those who knew what it had bought.

Her heart shuddered within her, but Samson lowered his mouth all too briefly against hers once more.

'Tonight,' he murmured.

Then he was gone, striding quickly away towards the market.

Delilah leaned back against the wall of a house to steady herself, and closed her eyes. She still had two nights before the full moon. Phicol would be happy enough.

And so would she. Samson's desire for her had reached down inside her this time, and she knew that had he suggested they go to the granary right now, she'd probably have accepted without giving Phicol a thought.

17

Phicol might have spies everywhere, but she doubted Samson's reach was as long. Despite this, she took the back path to Phicol's house rather than the main approach. If news ever did reach Samson of her visits, she could easily claim to be visiting her sister. She was still high from what she had achieved. Not only did she know where he was spending the night, she'd actually be there *with* him. At this rate, she could earn her silver and forget all about Samson and Phicol by the next day.

Ekron was nowhere to be seen when Delilah reached Phicol's house, but the senior scribe apparently knew all about her mission. As soon as she entered the outer office he said, 'His Lordship said you would return.'

'The granary where we are to meet tonight is on the edge of the Israelite district near the western gates. There are torch stands on the gateposts.'

'Is it close to the tavern Samson frequents?' asked the scribe.

'How do you know about that?'

The scribe looked at her down his long straight nose. Delilah wondered if he was Amqu, from the far, far north, for though his accent was clean and he dressed in the formal Philistine style, his forehead was high and he wore his black hair long and smoothed back from his face with a spice-scented oil.

'His Lordship knows a great deal about Samson already,' he said, returning to his scroll. 'When is your assignation?'

'After dark tonight. I intend to keep him busy all night, but it you want to find him incapacitated, I'll need time to make that possible.'

'I'm sure you can find a way to tire him out.'

Delilah wondered if the scribe had ever been seduced himself, for he spoke without any wit or innuendo of what was to take place. In that he was an ideal foil for Phicol.

'We'll come before dawn. Go now.'

His dismissive attitude made her realise that as far as he was concerned she was little more than a servant. Was this how those women down at the harbour felt?

He hardly noticed her departure. Delilah had expected to spend a good part of the afternoon being briefed by Lord Phicol on what to expect, but instead found herself out in the atrium with nothing to do. She didn't want to go back to the vineyard yet, in case Beulah saw her and stopped her from going out. Joshua had agreed to run into the city to collect her new dresses from the dressmaker while he visited a cousin, and there was still plenty of time before she had to sneak back to the vineyard stables to change.

She didn't want to admit it, but her confidence was waning and she began to wonder if she'd be able to keep her nerve. In Samson's company, she never doubted his interest in her, but here, in the cold, passionless halls of politics, its walls decorated with maps of territories near and far, she wondered if she was little more than a soldier in one of Phicol's armies.

She was roused from contemplation by the slap of bare feet on the stone and she looked up to see one of Phicol's beautiful bare-chested guards approaching her. Buoyed by thoughts of Samson, she gave him a lazy smile, but he merely opened the door for her to leave.

'I'm to be kicked out, am I?'

The guard said nothing but a hellish yell rose up and they both glanced out into the courtyard.

Hemin was waddling across the stones, supported by two maidservants, like a hen unused to gliding on water. She was draped in a brown shift with black stitching around the hem and sleeves and had put on a lot of weight since Delilah had last seen her, her belly a sizeable mound beneath the dress. Delilah hoped to slip away unnoticed, but for all her indignity, Hemin's eyes were still sharp. 'What are you doing here?' she snapped at Delilah through the doorway.

'I've come to visit you.'

'Why?'

'Sisterly compassion.'

Hemin uttered an expletive designed to embarrass Kathirat, the goddess of pregnancy and marriage, and slumped down onto a padded couch in the courtyard.

'Get me cushions.'

The maids hung back, as though they knew Delilah surpassed them in servitude, so she shrugged and grabbed four huge cushions from a she knew before she got to the granary. Aside from Phicol's scribe she'd told no one of the assignation and she didn't want to meet any of Samson's men on the way, but she didn't know how to get there without passing the tavern. She slowed her steps as she turned off the square into the Israelite quarter, and fussed a little with her hair and the links of her silver belt. Fortunately the street with the tavern was dark with thick shadows that fell from the buildings, and she paused long enough outside the tavern to see that there were fewer people inside than usual. Abidan was there, without Jubal, and was perched on a bench with another of Samson's followers, Ariel, the wiry fellow who had observed her so surreptitiously on her first visit to the tavern. In the corner, Delilah noticed the black-haired woman who had mocked her just a few days ago. She was leaning against Caleb's shoulder again, running her fingers through his dark curly hair. He didn't seem to be soothed by her touch, though. As Delilah watched, he pushed her away and got up to join Ariel.

But no Samson. He must be waiting for her at the granary. She moved swiftly along the street, turning the sequence of corners and wondered whether he'd welcome her with a drink, or if he'd simply embrace her as soon as he caught sight of her and lead her straight to his bed. Of course it was possible that he had no intention of extending their intimacy any further than the intense kissing she'd come to enjoy, but she'd have to change his mind. He'd need to be subdued by passion if the soldiers were to stand

nearby bench. She pushed them around Hemin's bulk, then stood back to look at the effect.

Hemin scowled at her, and Delilah smiled. 'Please don't thank me.'

'I could have managed.'

'No you couldn't. Besides, I was thinking of the baby. It's going to need all the help it can get.'

Hemin shot her an angry look. 'You've just come to revel in my misery.'

'Aren't you happy? You're giving His Lordship a son and heir.'

Hemin's lips thinned so rapidly that Delilah felt an odd stab of compassion.

'Oh Se't. You're having a girl, aren't you?' she murmured.

'So the midwife says,' hissed Hemin. 'But if you tell anyone — '

'I'm not that mean. You have trouble enough on your hands if it turns out that way.'

Hemin's expression turned suspicious. 'What are you really doing here?'

'I came with a message for His Lordship from your father. Just a business matter. Beulah also wanted me to pay our respects to you.'

'Your mother's respects — '

'I can see you aren't feeling yourself today,' said Delilah brightly. 'Still, only three months to go.'

'May you know Kathirat's hell for yourself one day. Though if you keep sleeping with the servants, it won't be too long coming.'

Thank you, Ekron, thought Delilah. 'You're just jealous,' she said, 'because my lovers are nearby bench. She pushed them around Hemin's bulk, then stood back to look at the effect.

Hemin scowled at her, and Delilah smiled. 'Please don't thank me.'

'I could have managed.'

'No you couldn't. Besides, I was thinking of the baby. It's going to need all the help it can get.'

Hemin shot her an angry look. 'You've just come to revel in my misery.'

'Aren't you happy? You're giving His Lordship a son and heir.'

Hemin's lips thinned so rapidly that Delilah felt an odd stab of compassion.

'Oh Se't. You're having a girl, aren't you?' she murmured.

'So the midwife says,' hissed Hemin. 'But if you tell anyone — '

'I'm not that mean. You have trouble enough on your hands if it turns out that way.'

Hemin's expression turned suspicious. 'What are you really doing here?'

'I came with a message for His Lordship from your father. Just a business matter. Beulah also wanted me to pay our respects to you.'

'Your mother's respects — '

'I can see you aren't feeling yourself today,' said Delilah brightly. 'Still, only three months to go.'

'May you know Kathirat's hell for yourself one day. Though if you keep sleeping with the servants, it won't be too long coming.'

Thank you, Ekron, thought Delilah. 'You're just jealous,' she said, 'because my lovers are handsome, not to mention tall, and I choose them because they have the stamina of racing horses. I'll be spending tonight with a man so virile he'd make your eyes water and your — '

A cushion flew past Delilah's ears and thudded into the wall beside the doorway.

'Get out!' yelled Hemin. 'Get out of here!'

In the atrium the soldier was still waiting and he gave Delilah a sly look that revealed he'd eavesdropped on the last part of their conversation. For a fleeting moment she allowed her eyes to fall across his chest, admiring the way his smooth, hairless skin curved in perfect symmetry about his breastbone. But her imagination had been filled with the prospect of Samson for too long and she felt no stirring of interest in this sculpted imitation of Philistine perfection.

Besides, her stomach was beginning to twist around itself in anticipation of the evening and Delilah felt a wash of nerves. Their kisses had given her an idea of what the act itself might be like with Samson, but Joshua was hardly adequate preparation for someone of the Israelite's reputation. Fanning herself with the end of her stole, Delilah stepped out into the sunshine, glad to be alone.

18

By the time Delilah arrived at the market just after sunset, the city's bustle had died with the failing daylight and the streets were largely empty. The traders were weaving out through the gates, their donkeys braying at each other. She walked quickly towards the market square, her footsteps deadened by the fine dusting of sand blown in on the day's winds. There were a few soldiers around, some Philistines steadily making their way to the northern quarter, but no Israelites to be seen.

Delilah felt conspicuous by her mere presence in such empty streets, but she was less likely to be noticed if she walked confidently instead of scurrying through the shadows. That was the curious part of being both Philistine and Israelite. Joshua had told her that the latest curfew of Israelites had virtually shut down the city after nightfall, but Delilah wondered whether the Philistines didn't know they were exempt from the curfew. Perhaps having the city darkness to themselves was just too unnerving.

Maybe her own nerves were still not under control, but the city felt odd to Delilah. The emptiness might make Samson suspicious and more alert than usual. She'd simply have to make sure his mind was suitably occupied to ignore such worries.

Her own anxiety was that she'd see someone

she knew before she got to the granary. Aside from Phicol's scribe she'd told no one of the assignation and she didn't want to meet any of Samson's men on the way, but she didn't know how to get there without passing the tavern. She slowed her steps as she turned off the square into the Israelite quarter, and fussed a little with her hair and the links of her silver belt. Fortunately the street with the tavern was dark with thick shadows that fell from the buildings, and she paused long enough outside the tavern to see that there were fewer people inside than usual. Abidan was there, without Jubal, and was perched on a bench with another of Samson's followers, Ariel, the wiry fellow who had observed her so surreptitiously on her first visit to the tavern. In the corner, Delilah noticed the black-haired woman who had mocked her just a few days ago. She was leaning against Caleb's shoulder again, running her fingers through his dark curly hair. He didn't seem to be soothed by her touch, though. As Delilah watched, he pushed her away and got up to join Ariel.

But no Samson. He must be waiting for her at the granary. She moved swiftly along the street, turning the sequence of corners and wondered whether he'd welcome her with a drink, or if he'd simply embrace her as soon as he caught sight of her and lead her straight to his bed. Of course it was possible that he had no intention of extending their intimacy any further than the intense kissing she'd come to enjoy, but she'd have to change his mind. He'd need to be subdued by passion if the soldiers were to stand any chance of capturing him, and Delilah had already amused herself at length by imagining how this might be accomplished in a manner that wasn't disagreeable to either of them.

The street on which the granary stood was wider than its neighbours, and the pale stone of the buildings glowed in the milky moonlight. There was no sign of the Philistine soldiers Phicol would send for Samson, or they were at least very well hidden. Delilah was reasonably certain she hadn't been seen as she slipped inside the heavy wooden gates. The granary was fronted by a small yard that was completely empty, and she couldn't see any lights anywhere in the building. The place looked abandoned.

Had he not come, after all? Had he somehow got wind of the trap? Worse, perhaps this was a trap for her! Samson might have realised that she wasn't who she seemed to be, and drawn her in with his seductive behaviour, only to capture her and subject her to interrogation over the intentions of Lord Phicol. She hesitated by the side door he'd told her to use, wondering if it was really possible that he'd seen through her allure. There was no way to know. She'd simply have to use her wits.

She pulled open the door and went inside. For a moment she thought she was still seeing the stars in the sky, for all around her were tiny pools of light hanging in the air. She edged forward, a little uncertain, but in a moment was smiling at the beauty of it. In the centre of the otherwise completely empty granary stood a spiral wooden staircase, which was lit with small candles at even intervals, up into the darkened roof space. Other candles hung in tiny black bowls strung with jute from the rafters, their little flames glimmering in the air, and in the utter stillness of it all, Delilah felt she was walking through the night sky.

It seemed that she was meant to go up the staircase, for the candles led upwards. She slipped off her sandals, lifted her skirt between her fingers and began to climb as quietly as she could. As she turned back for the first time she noticed the candles were going out behind her, and she felt tiny tufts of air caress her ankles. She paused for a moment, enchanted by the silent magic of it, then continued to climb, nervous at the sensation that she was surely being watched. The stairs levelled off and more candles illuminated a large wide platform that filled perhaps half of the upper floor. To one side of the room lay a wide dark pile of furs and blankets, but around her the walls sparkled with silver.

Having assured herself that the floorboards were steady, she moved to take a closer look. But what shone in the candlelight here were the edges of knives, short swords, and ploughshare blades. It was a glittering armoury hanging from the wall, and beneath it she could see the dark outlines of clubs, staffs and sharpened animal bones. Next to that lay a pile of feathers, slender poles of different lengths, and some long jute strings, the components for making bows and arrows. Her whimsical delight fell away. Phicol had been right. Samson was planning some sort

172

of rebellion, and these sharpened tools would fill the hands of at least a hundred angry Israelite men. It would be carnage, of that there was no doubt. She shivered a little in the darkness at the thought of it. It must not be allowed to happen.

She turned her back on the wall and gasped at the sight of Samson standing behind her, watching her steadily. She expected he was nearby, but to see him waiting for her brought home the reality of her task. He wore a tunic of black linen, similar to the one he'd worn for his betrothal to Hemin. It was open to the waist and unbelted. For a brief moment, she thought she'd dressed too elaborately for this meeting in an abandoned storage building. But she could feel his eyes moving over her and she smiled. Perhaps she should say something, greet him, thank him for the candles, anything to stop herself blurting out a question about the weapons that seemed to have forged a cold hard wall behind her. But his stillness was so absolute in this vast space that she steadied her eyes on his and without saying a word, she slid her fingers beneath the panels of his tunic and over his chest, then tilted her head up to kiss him.

He pulled her to him wordlessly, the partial restraint of his public affection so easily discarded in this private darkness. His mouth sought hers, but she'd barely begun to return his kisses when his lips began to wander over her neck, and she arched against him, caught by the heat of his breath on her skin and the response it awoke in her. Her fingers spread against the muscles of his chest, and his skin yielded at her touch like molten candle wax, as though he was allowing her to leave her mark upon him. The linen of his tunic strained under her hands as she sought out more and more of him and she smelled the sweetness of the sun rise up from his skin. His fingers reached round her waist, untying her belt and in a moment the dress slid smoothly from her shoulders in a cascade of sea blue to the floor. She opened the remaining ties on his shift, fumbling a little. He pushed her hands aside and tore the fabric quickly, casting it off like a shadow at his feet.

He reached out to pull her nakedness against his own, and his manhood pressed hot and heavy against her ribs. But Delilah denied him for a moment more, backing away towards the pile of furs against the far wall. He followed, and stood over her at the edge of the makeshift bed. With one hand cupped under her breast and the other supporting her behind, he lifted her easily from where she stood, and laid her gently down. She sank back within the furs as he knelt in front of her, his fingers caressing her abdomen in gentle circles then traced out by his tongue, spiralling towards her breasts. His plaits fell against her with every turn of his head, brushing her thighs, and her sex. She was near powerless now, and a dizzy anticipation rose inside her, but she raised herself out of the warm embrace of the furs and knelt up in front of him, drawing his head level with hers.

In the candlelight she could see the surprise in his eyes. It wasn't the look she had seen in Joshua's; they had met as equals. She could see that Samson's desire was a surprise even to himself. He had succumbed. She pressed his lids down over his eyes, feeling how they yielded beneath. Even mighty Samson had softness among the hard. From there she trailed her fingers over his body, burying them in the rich silky hair below. She tried to push him over, to assert control again, but his breath quickened in her ear, and he began to kiss her again, more deeply than before. She kept her body hard against him, and in time he gave way and lay on his back, his eyes wide as she lowered her body onto his, gentle moans escaping from him into the curls of her hair. Bewildered at how easily she'd mastered his desire, he rocked beneath her. She held his gaze, her breasts brushing softly against his chest.

'You always want your own way,' he murmured, the words trapped between his quick breaths of pleasure.

Delilah laughed gently, resisting him a little with her weight. 'That's what you like about me.'

He began to move into her with a more steady rhythm, his hands sliding to her waist, but she reached for his wrists and drew them apart, pinning them gently to the bed beside him. The muscles of his arms offered tensed, but token resistance, to her manipulation. Delilah felt her heart thud to her throat, as her passion clashed with another, more rational train of thought. She saw what she must do. She lowered her mouth close to his.

'I don't want this to be over so quickly,' she murmured, trying to hide the nerves in her voice. 'You might never want to see me again.'

'Not you,' whispered Samson, his voice catching in his throat. 'Not you.'

The deep dark in his eyes was almost believable but Delilah was suddenly shy of her own powers. She was relieved she'd spotted the bowstrings by the wall.

'Then just for tonight,' she whispered, 'let me bind you, so you can't leave as soon as you've had your fill of me.'

Samson tried to wriggle his wrists free to draw her down onto him, but Delilah kept her grasp firm and her eyes fixed on Samson's face, her hot breath mingling with his.

'Just tonight,' she whispered. 'Let me. Let me.'

'But — ' Uncertainty crossed his face, but she kept her gaze steady and true, and his wrists gradually grew limp beneath her grip, his will to dominate her dissolved in the dark.

To test him she released one hand to loosen her hair from its comb, but he just lay there, enthralled by her, so she lowered her head to his chest and slowly moved down him, letting her hair slip over his body, its passage drawing a deep moan from him. Her heart was beating so fast in her chest she could hardly breathe, and she couldn't quite believe that he just lay there, waiting for her. She reached into the shadows and snatched up a handful of bowstrings.

'Now, my darling,' she said, 'you will not leave this bed until the dawn comes.'

He lifted his head to search for her, but Delilah quickly tied four of the strings in pairs and looped them delicately around his ankles so

176

as not to alarm him. Her breasts nuzzled the soles of his feet so that he might feel more than her tying him, and in a moment his ankles were securely bound. He twisted a little against the unfamiliar sensation, but she writhed herself back along him, darting her tongue along his thighs and the smooth, shifting muscles of his stomach. His head fell back in mute acceptance, and his body began to move rhythmically in anticipation of their physical union. Once again, she let him enter her, and now he moved faster. His hands reached for her breasts and she knew she had just a few moments to complete his captivity before she gave in to the surge of desire that was overtaking them both. She crossed his wrists against each other, and snagged them quickly into another loop of strings, drawing them tight.

He twisted with surprise, wriggling to free himself, but Delilah quickly, gratefully, pushed her hands into the well of his chest as her desire swelled, building to a hot ball deep inside. The binding was complete and he was hers. Her heart was pounding in her ears and her skin burned. She was ready to give in to oblivion, and from the rasping breaths that left his mouth, she knew that he was approaching the same precipice. She felt the shuddering of her own intoxication take over, but Samson suddenly went still. But it wasn't a look of ecstasy that crossed his face. He turned his head towards the stairs, and his breathing slowed.

'What is it?' she whispered. She'd heard nothing.

'Get your clothes,' Samson hissed, his rough tone shaking her out of glorious numbness. She lifted her head limply from his shoulder to see him nodding sharply to a low cupboard in the corner of the eaves. 'In there!'

'What's happening?'

'Go!'

19

She lifted herself from him, genuinely alarmed. Were Phicol's men really here, already? Could they not have waited a little longer? She was up and off the bed quickly, but she could still feel Samson's skin against her own. Or perhaps that was the heavy, damp cloak of guilt.

She snatched up her dress and belt and ran quickly towards the cupboard, shivering from the sudden dissipation of her desire. Yes, there were sounds below now. She fumbled for the latch and crawled into the hiding place, casting a glance back at Samson. He'd managed to get off the bed, but his hands and feet were still tied and he wobbled uneasily. The aroused lover had been replaced by a naked giant, huge and angry at an intruder. As she drew the door almost closed in front of her, she saw him kick out at her sandals, sending them flying into a darkened corner. Simultaneously he broke the strings that bound his feet.

Delilah was aghast at how easily he'd freed himself but, before he could release his hands, three men, dressed only in rough brown shorts, charged up the stairs into the attic. One carried a flaming torch and a short blade, the other two, long knives.

'What's the meaning of this?' said Samson. They didn't respond, but regrouped at the top of the stairs. The pair rushed at Samson from either side, instinctively sure of their advantage, their blades slicing blinding arcs in the shadows. Samson dodged the first attack, a hard kick knocking one of the assassins back.

Delilah winced. *I should have used more strings . . .*

Samson seemed to have heard the thought for he suddenly clenched his fists, twisted his wrists across each other and jerked his elbows in opposite directions, snapping his remaining restraint. Now he was free and the armed men sprang back into their attacking formation. Delilah could barely see Samson's fists and feet moving in the dark. Suddenly one of the Philistine knifemen crashed into a wall in a shower of sparks, falling heavily and dislodging a strap of knives and a ploughshare. Samson followed him and brought down his heel with a sickening thud on the soldier's cheekbone. The man twitched as Samson snatched up his knife.

The other two looked more unsure now, and circled slowly around their target. Samson's feet moved precisely over the creaking floorboards, anticipating the movements of his enemies as if taking part in some deadly ceremonial dance. The second long knife suddenly thrust out of the dark towards Samson, but he spun quickly and drove his foot into the ribs of the torch-holder behind him. Both long and short knives spun in the air, sparks from the torch exploded into the dark and Samson suddenly dropped low.

They'd got him!

But then the floor shook, the flames seared an arc in the darkness and Delilah stared as the

180

together, and they knew his weaknesses — such as they might be. Phicol should have known better. Blast his arrogance!

The cupboard door opened. Samson was standing there, dressed once again but barefoot. There was blood on his legs, arms and face and sweat across his brow. His eyes were steady on hers as though he was studying her for some sign that she wasn't as afraid as she should be.

'We have to leave here,' he said, holding out his hand to her.

'What happened?' she said. The weakness in her voice was genuine.

'Philistine assassins.'

'Did you — '

'One of them lived.'

Delilah dragged her dress out of the cupboard, awkward at her nakedness. The magical trysting-place now smelled of blood and death and she couldn't look at the bed where so recently they had known such intense passion.

'Put that on,' said Samson. 'We need to leave this place before more soldiers arrive.'

Delilah stepped into her dress, quickly straightening the fabric over her shoulders and hooking the length of silver links around her waist. *I should have tied him up with this*, she thought. *A chain might have been enough.*

She felt Samson's arm around her shoulders and he guided her across the room, between the bodies of the soldiers. But Delilah couldn't keep herself from looking at their faces, and she stifled a retch of misery as she recognised the assassin with the slashed throat as the soldier who had eyed her that afternoon at Phicol's house. He must have been a part of Phicol's elite personal guard, the first choice for a mission of assassination from His Lordship. Now his head was twisted awkwardly, and his eyes stared at her vacantly.

Delilah gulped down the memory, faint at the mingling of past and present, and it took a moment to realise she'd not collapsed but that Samson had swept her up into his arms. He dropped her sandals into her lap, then strode quickly down the staircase to the darkened floor below. The soldier who had fallen down the stairs had disappeared, and Samson crossed quickly to the wall where he slid back a panel.

'We need to move on from here as quickly as we can,' he said. 'They will send someone else, now that the injured one has gone to raise the alarm. I don't want you to be in any further danger.'

Delilah nodded, wondering if he really hadn't seen the clumsy coincidence of her seduction with the assassins' attack. But she didn't trust her judgement at that moment. The dizziness of passion had been replaced by an awful weakness in the presence of sudden death, and she was glad Samson was carrying her. The subterfuge had to go on now, and hopefully he'd interpret her distress as girlish shock rather than wretched disappointment. She closed her eyes, trying to shut out everything but the steady beat of his heart and the gentle rocking as he carried her out into the night. She had no idea where they were going, but it was her turn to trust him.

Perhaps she dozed off, for she was surprised when he set her down on her feet. Glancing around, she thought at first that they must still be in the city, for the curfew would surely restrict passage through the city gates. But there was too much space between the buildings, and she realised she could hear the waves against the sand. He'd somehow brought her outside the city limits and down to the beach, and she inhaled deeply, inviting the fresh sea air to cleanse her memories. Samson took her hand and led her between two buildings, ducking through a low door to the right.

'Where are we?' asked Delilah as she straightened up. The building was old and derelict, for she could see the stars through gaps in the roofing rushes and the wind blew gently through the wooden wall slats.

'Far enough away,' said Samson. He went to the corner of the room, wetted a cloth in a bowl, and began washing the blood from his arms, legs and face.

Delilah looked around. Moonlight fell in thick opalescent shafts through the roof illuminating an assortment of crates and baskets, tall wine jars, huge coils of rope and tangles of jute, and bundles of empty sacks. There was also a row of simple bunks along the far wall, and she let him lead her to the bunk on the end, covered with a pair of woven blankets and a fine coating of sand. Through a gap in the wall she could see the posts of a mooring point and faint tracks in the sand where a pair of boats had been pushed out to sea. This must be a fishermen's bunkhouse, its

185

inhabitants out for a night's work.

Samson crossed to the bed, picked up the blankets and shook them briskly, then laid them back down.

'The tide has only just turned. No one will return until dawn,' he said, sitting down on the bunk.

He placed his hand around her waist and held her, watching silently. She couldn't stop herself from seeing the soldiers' faces, couldn't shut out the awful sound of their dying whimpers, and after a long moment, she moved towards the only solace she had and let his face rest against the folds of silk that hung across her breasts. Desire rose up within her with frightening speed once more, and she knew she wouldn't delay its embrace this time. His mouth was at her throat again, and she felt her heart pound beneath his lips, felt him unclasp her belt and heard it fall like a peal of tiny bells on a dozen ships far out at sea. He loosened his tunic with one hand and spread it on the blankets behind him, then he cradled her gently onto the bunk, kneeling astride her, his hair falling in dark ropes over his shoulders.

He was ready to enter her, but that extraordinary tenderness seemed to take hold of him again and he kissed her forehead, her ears, her nose, her mouth and neck, steadily anointing the whole length of her body. He pressed his lips over each of her ribs in turn, pausing over her navel before moving lower still. She could hear her desperation for him forming in a mewling breath. In that moment she hated herself for giving in to him, and yet she wanted him even more than she had in the granary for now he was the only safety she had. And then he was inside her and she let him move her, over and over until she couldn't tell their breathing from the swell of the sea and she let out her cry into his mouth and he into hers.

They made love again and again through the night, until the moonlight began to turn golden and the waves lapped close to the shack. Delilah said nothing, allowing her body to speak for her. Between embraces they slept, letting passion wake them of its own accord.

But as the darkness thinned, so the reality of her situation became clearer. Her doubts multiplied. She had failed. She couldn't hide in this shack forever. Phicol would demand a debriefing, to dissect this catastrophic turn of events. He would want details of another location where Samson might be ambushed for a second time.

Dawn was just picking pale shapes out of the shadows, when Samson eventually sat up and moved to the end of the bunk. He picked up her dress from the floor and draped the silk across her.

'You should leave soon.'

'Alone?'

Samson nodded. 'Besides, I know these fishermen and I want to talk to them. There have been disputes along the coast which need resolving.'

'I don't want to leave,' said Delilah.

Even now the Philistine lord would be pacing

in his study, bellowing at Ekron and the scribe over the disastrous attack, demanding an explanation from the absent Delilah. She'd rather be in this bed with Samson than anywhere near Phicol, that was certain, but she would have to take him some very special information next time if he was to be convinced of her loyalty. The ease with which Samson had broken his bonds would have made it look as though she hadn't really tried to tie him at all, and the torch-holding assassin would surely be making that very point to Phicol from the surgeon's couch.

She realised Samson was watching her as she considered this, so she smiled languidly.

'When will I see you again?' she asked quietly.

'Tonight.'

'Here?'

Samson grinned. 'I'm not that lucky. Come to the tavern at dusk. I will find you there.'

She slid her legs over the side of the bunk, pulled on her dress and clasped the belt around her waist. She tied her hair into a knot and let it hang at the nape of her neck, then picked up her sandals and looked down at herself. The dress that had felt so beautiful last night looked wrong this morning and she wondered if she'd ever wear it again.

Samson was still watching her and, perhaps sensing her discomfort, he drew her to him. He was still naked and she began to twist the hairs that grew down from his navel, wondering if he could be convinced to undress her again. But he removed her inquisitive fingers and kissed her so formally on the mouth that she wondered for a moment if he was saying goodbye for good.

'I *will* see you tonight?' she asked. She hadn't intended to sound so desperate.

He nodded, then looked past her to the doorway, and she reluctantly turned away and walked out into the dawn. She glanced back at him from outside but he was tying his tunic around himself and already seemed to have forgotten she'd ever been there. Delilah headed up the beach towards the city. People were bound to give her strange looks dressed like this, and perhaps she ought to walk around the city gates, rather than right through the centre. Word would surely have got round Phicol's closest allies by now that the assassination attempt had failed, and she wondered if she would be blamed for the lives that were lost. Certainly their memory would be long leaving her.

And then there was that other memory, the lingering sensation of Samson's skin against hers that simply wouldn't be brushed off by the sun or the morning breeze.

20

Joshua was terrified. 'You shouldn't have told your mother that,' he said. 'I'll be sent back to the harbour warehouses.'

'I'm sorry,' Delilah replied with genuine regret. 'She promised not to tell Achish.'

She paused to snap off a vine tendril that was dangling in their path. The vines down here weren't as tidy as they should be. Her own absence, of course, was partly to blame. Achish relied on her to train and trim a good part of the stock because she did it so well. But if she wasn't here, she wasn't helping.

Joshua tucked his hand into Delilah's elbow. 'I miss you — how things were — you know — but we agreed we'd had fun while it lasted, and I'm pleased you thought of me, even if I was just your convenient excuse.'

'You should have seen her face,' said Delilah, suppressing the pang of guilt. 'She asked me directly where I'd been, and I replied equally directly that I'd been sleeping with you in your bed. Of course, the first thing she said was that I shouldn't be having 'such relations' with the house servants, that she thought we'd both learned. I reminded her that I was a house servant, because she and my father both were. Besides, I said, what was so different about it than Achish choosing to marry her?'

Joshua was silent for a moment, then he

squeezed her elbow. 'It's none of my business — '

'No.'

' — but I hope this man is worth it.'

'So do I.'

'He must love you a lot to give you all that
money.'

'Men do pay women to have sex, you know,'
said Delilah elliptically.

'You wouldn't stay out overnight for such a
man,' said Joshua with certainty. At the bottom
of the hill, he kissed her swiftly on the cheek.

'Mother made me promise not to do it again.
She wants me to marry Jered and go to Ashdod
as a well-trained wife.'

'You aren't going to marry him, are you?' said
Joshua, puffing out his chest a little.

'Why?' smiled Delilah. 'Does it bother you?'

'I'm pinning my hopes on your current man.
Even without having met him, I prefer him.'

Delilah pinched Joshua's arm, making him
yelp, then ran off.

'Don't wait up!' she called, not looking back.

★ ★ ★

The tavern was half-empty again when Delilah
arrived. Samson was nowhere to be seen, and
there were only a few old Israelite men chatting
in the corner. One of them stared at Delilah with
considerable interest as she entered, and she was
pleased she had chosen one of her plain
flax-coloured work dresses instead of something
more formal. She had got Samson's attention

now, well and truly, so she could worry less about looking her best all the time, and begin to blend in with the Israelites.

The day following the failed assassination had blunted her fears, and her confidence had blossomed once more. To her surprise, Phicol had not summoned her, nor had she seen Ekron. At first she had supposed that the lives of His Lordship's men came cheaply, whereas she, evidently, did not. Then that he perhaps too was embarrassed at his failure. But as she dwelled further, she realised the truth that Samson must have realised all along. The deadly game they were playing was a secret — if Phicol admitted the attempts on Samson's life were officially sanctioned, there would be anger, even rebellion. No, his machinations had to take place under cover of darkness.

Delilah hesitated by the bartender's table, wondering if she should buy herself a drink. Samson had said to come at dusk, and she was already a little late, so there might not be any point. On the other hand, she had to try to look as normal as possible, so she laid a coin on the table and asked for a bowl of the warmed honey drink. She could feel the eyes of the old men on her back, and she carried the bowl through to the empty covered terrace to be away from them. The candles hadn't been lit yet back here, perhaps there was no point with so few customers —

'Delilah.'

'Oh!' Delilah started, spilling a little of the drink over her hands. 'Who's that?'

She peered into the gloom and realised someone was perched on the back wall, almost invisible in the shadows. It was much too slender to be Samson, but as she squinted at it, the shape slid down into view.

'Caleb?'

'That's right.'

'You made me jump.'

'Then I'm sorry.'

Delilah wanted to know if Samson was nearby, but something in the way he studied her made her wary. She thought of the woman who had been playing with his hair the previous evening, and was surprised to see him run his fingers through his hair at that very moment, as though he could see the thought in her head. She could see why the woman was interested in him. He was very good-looking, with a wide well-proportioned face and smooth unblemished skin, though his left cheek bore a new scar that curved at least a finger's length towards his nose.

Delilah sat on a well-lit bench near the tavern's back door so she could see Samson if he came in, but Caleb stayed in the shadows, perching on the top step. She hadn't spoken to him before, at least that she could remember, and he didn't have Jubal's easy manner or Abidan's sense of humour.

'Have you been training today?' she asked politely.

'All afternoon. I lead the exercises when Samson isn't there.'

Delilah blushed. Perhaps Samson had been sleeping off his exertions of last night. She lifted the bowl to her mouth, and drank. The taste reminded her of Samson's mouth, and the syrupy warmth lingered in her throat as she thought about the hut on the beach.

'Have you finished?' asked Caleb, his words dragging her out of her reverie.

'What? Oh, yes — '

'Then we should leave. Samson has asked me to fetch you.'

Why didn't you just say something? she wondered. *We could have been on our way by now.*

Outside the tavern Caleb moved off quickly into the shadows and Delilah had to run a little to keep up with him. They turned back towards the market, but Delilah soon lost her bearings in the quick turns. Caleb took them through yards and down alleyways. He said nothing as they walked, and she felt furtive and awkward in his company. Several times he glanced back at her, yet he looked right through her.

Abruptly Caleb turned into a doorway Delilah was sure she wouldn't have noticed, and began climbing a flight of stairs. It was very dark inside and she had to put her hands out to find the walls, trusting her feet to follow Caleb's. At the top he grasped her elbow, steered her sharply to the left, then let go. She heard a couple of raps on wood, then footsteps, and a door swung open.

It was a half-covered roof terrace cast only in moonlight. There were at least twenty men gathered here, some that Delilah had never seen before, and in the far corner stood Samson, leaning against the wall. His gaze burned with pleasure at her presence, but he said nothing, made no indication to the others that their intimacy had advanced, nor did he invite her to stand beside him. Delilah was glad of the darkness to hide her blushes.

'We were stupid to keep everything in one place,' said a voice.

'Not everything,' said Samson. 'There is still a significant cache of bows and short knives beneath the cellar floor at the tavern — '

'Which we can't get without alerting everyone in Ashkelon,' snapped the first voice.

'Which also begs the question of exactly how the Philistines found the granary at all,' added a third man. 'It has been completely safe, until now.'

Delilah recognised the voice and saw Ariel perched on the low wall to her right. He was angry, and from the nodding she saw he'd spoken for many of them. Even Abidan and Jubal had lost their usual cheer and were watching Samson silently to see what he would say.

'Well?' Samson said slowly. 'If someone has a point they would like to make, they should do so now.'

'We're all thinking it,' said the first speaker.

'You've brought her here, to another of our hideouts,' said Ariel. 'So we might as well ask her directly.'

Delilah's heart shuddered in her chest. *They know I betrayed him. How will I answer them?*

'You will ask Delilah nothing,' said Samson. 'You will ask me, Ariel, if there is something you wish to know.'

195

Ariel jumped down off the wall and stepped into the middle of the group, his back to Delilah. 'All right then. How can you possibly trust her? She has a Philistine family — '

Delilah's throat tightened and she barely heard Samson say, 'But she is an Israelite. She is one of us.'

'She is not one of us,' offered Jubal, 'but she could be.'

'Don't be naive,' said Ariel. 'We all defend our families first.'

That's where I've seen you before, thought Delilah suddenly. *At Hemin's betrothal. Ariel was one of the bodyguards, and Caleb — Caleb was —*

'Enough,' said Samson, raising his voice a little. 'I know Delilah wouldn't betray us. Phicol is well organised as it is.'

'I agree,' said Caleb from beside Delilah. 'I'm sure I'm being followed. I felt someone behind me on the way to the tavern — '

'They don't know about the tavern, do they?' asked another man, turning to Caleb, his eyes lingering on Delilah.

'It's probable they know of it,' said Samson. 'It's a public place. As Ariel says, we shouldn't be naive.'

'More worryingly,' continued Caleb, 'I was sure I was still followed when we came here, but though I kept looking, I couldn't see anyone. I took a very roundabout route, but still — '

Caleb tailed off and for a moment there was silence. Delilah dared not look around but she was sure everyone's eyes were on her. She kept her gaze on Samson. She'd thought that somehow her seduction of him would have remained separate from his men, that she'd slip in and out of his life unnoticed. But now it felt as though she'd married his whole band of followers, and they wanted to know what he'd brought into the family. They were like brothers, with Samson at their head. And for some unknown reason, not merely fear, she was keen not to disappoint them.

'I will repeat what I say each day,' said Samson, a cool steel in his voice, 'and hope that you are listening properly this time. We must be patient. Overthrowing a nation does not happen in a night, a moon, or even a year. We are building the foundations for a lifetime of change, and while we gather new weapons, we must continue to unsettle the Philistine people with our voices and our actions, not just our violence.'

'Indeed,' said Ariel quietly.

Samson moved to the centre of the group. 'Besides, they sent three men to try to kill me and they failed. So no one acting alone could bring me down.'

His gaze fell briefly on Delilah as it swept around the group and it was all she could do to stop herself nodding in agreement. His logic was flawed, but his self-belief seemed to carry the argument through. Delilah felt a shiver of sympathy for him, and surreptitiously pulled her stole tightly around her. The seduction really had blinded Samson to the truth, and her innocence was a given through his force of will alone.

21

Delilah was studiously tying up the laden vine branches one morning when a rustle in the neighbouring row disturbed her. She looked up to find Ekron watching her. Seven days had passed since the failed assassination, but she had neither been ordered to visit Phicol nor seen Ekron at all in that time. She was annoyed at being ignored and also nervous of a summons, so she hid her confusion at seeing Ekron by giving him a brisk nod and moving along the row.

'I presume it's Samson who makes you smile like that when you think no one can see you,' he said dryly. 'You look quite drunk on your success.'

The comment stung her, but Delilah forced herself not to look up. 'My efforts were wasted by Phicol's incompetence. Why did he send just three soldiers to assassinate Samson? Or was that your idea?'

She knew Ekron's silences well enough to know that her barb had struck home, but she moved on to the next vine without looking at him.

'You are still in His Lordship's employment,' said Ekron eventually, 'so you should tell me everything you have learned in the last few days.'

'It can't be of any importance if you have waited so long to find out.' Delilah looked up at last. She was surprised Ekron had not criticised her for Samson's easy escape from the binding, so perhaps he didn't know all the details.

Ekron got a tablet out of his satchel. 'How does Samson spend each day?'

'Aren't you having him followed?' asked Delilah, remembering what Caleb had said on the terrace.

'You are so much closer to him than we could ever get,' said Ekron.

'I've told Phicol all this before. Samson exercises, trains his followers in physical games and activities, and he also visits Israelite traders and families, sorting out problems and arbitrating disputes.'

'There is rumour he's been meeting with an elder of the tribe of — '

Delilah held up her hand. 'I'm not required to understand the politics, Ekron. That's your job.'

'And yours is to keep right on top of him. So to speak.'

Delilah's anger flared. 'I'm doing you a favour, remember.'

'And it's clearly no hardship to you. But you know little of use, Delilah. You will need to pay more attention. You are a spy now, not just one of his lovers.'

I'm his only lover, thought Delilah. *I'm quite sure of that.*

'We need to know what attacks he is planning,' continued Ekron, 'and whether he's met with the elder from Beersheba. It would be a significant development were Israelites from the southeast to move west. We know you spend more than the

199

nights with him so if you see — '

Delilah waved her hands in mock surrender. 'I'll do what I can. Now just let me get on.'

Ekron tapped his tablet by way of reminder then strode off down the row towards the city. Delilah watched him go, sighing deeply. Samson's natural reticence had been released by his desire for her, but Phicol had been right about how much Samson would still keep from her. Though she resented Ekron's proprietary interrogation, Delilah knew she'd got off quite lightly compared to the grilling that Phicol would have given her. Not for the first time in those last few days, she wondered if she should simply give the money back to Phicol, and accept defeat.

If Ekron could see the pleasure in her face, she hoped he hadn't realised she left all thoughts of Israelites and Philistines with her clothes on the floor beside Samson's bed. Since the failed assassination she and Samson had undressed each other in a different room each night, and there was a restlessness to their liaisons that couldn't be helped. But she sensed that the Nazirite had found a peaceful oblivion in their passion for each other, a tranquil pause in his campaign against the Philistines.

★ ★ ★

Later that day, Delilah followed the directions Samson had given her, and turned into a narrow alley near the south of the city and pushed open a gate near the end. It opened into an orchard belonging to Onan, a wealthy Israelite who was happy to accommodate Samson and his followers in exchange for the promise of future freedom from Philistine trading restrictions. Just the sort of information Phicol would want, and Delilah was beginning to realise that by agreeing to bring down Samson, she was endangering a host of others. Was this Onan really such a bad man as to deserve Phicol's wrath, or just another hard-working Israelite striving for a fairer life? Delilah felt the weight of the coming reckoning, and tried to shrug away her discomfort.

Caleb was training the men this afternoon and he gave Delilah a quick glance as she settled herself beneath a tree. Samson had apparently not noticed her at all.

She was intrigued by the group almost as much as she was by Samson. Caleb was quick and fast, good at assessing the strengths and weaknesses of the others; he preferred action over talking. Conversation was always limited and he spoke only when he had to, but she knew he was attentive; he often sat near to Samson, listening carefully to what his leader said. Ariel, on the other hand, was the diplomat of the group. Even though he'd openly questioned Delilah's trustworthiness that night, she soon understood that he'd done so precisely because the others wouldn't. She wasn't certain that his doubts about her had really gone away, but his way was to talk aloud, not to whisper secretly, and he often accompanied Samson when he went among the Israelites, advocating a case or introducing to Samson the newcomers who wanted to join the fast-growing group of Israelite rebels.

Abidan and Jubal were Delilah's favourites, though. Abidan was as perfect as Jubal was imperfect, one by far the most handsome of the group, the other a mismatch of outsized limbs and the twist of a broken nose. Their constant companionship meant that there was always noise in the group, and they had unofficial roles in sustaining morale, joking with everyone and always leaping up to help out with tasks. They had boundless energy, and with it a boyish immaturity in place of Samson's charisma. They took the cause very seriously, indeed Delilah had been touched by Jubal's defence of her in front of the others, but they did so without Ariel's rhetoric. They seemed like lion cubs in Samson's pride, and she wondered how they would cope after he was gone. And what did that make her — the turncoat lioness?

Her eye was caught by a staff spinning high into the air. Samson, his back to her, caught the staff easily, brandishing it this way and that, switching hands, spinning it, jumping over it, twisting it to and fro over his shoulders as he turned at the waist, his feet firmly planted in the grass. He was wearing just a simple calico skirt, belted with a leather strap, and his seven braids were tied loosely at the neck with a scrap of cloth. They hung heavy and still against his back, and Delilah was enthralled by the rippling of his muscles, like sand beneath a shallow wave. He seemed so peaceful here among the trees, not fighting an imaginary foe but simply testing himself to his limits.

Though she didn't doubt that some of Samson's men engaged in illegal activities, she'd seen little first-hand. Still, there was plenty that warranted the paranoia which so plagued Phicol and the other lords. They talked of little else but the history of their people, and their right to independence. Everything, it seemed, was in preparation for a time in the future when the Philistine yoke would be lifted.

She'd come home in the early hours of each morning when Samson left to join Caleb and the others for training, and she'd bathe in the sunrise and appease her conscience with three or four hours of work on the vines. She might meet Achish to taste a vintage or discuss some aspect of the business, but after lunch she'd return again to Samson and follow him as he wove intricate paths through Ashkelon's streets. The Israelites worshipped him and, if he was drawing the threads of rebellion ever tighter in his wake, he did so through the power of his presence as much as his words.

What she'd not told Ekron was that while Samson had made no mention of the elder from Beersheba, he had told her he was going to the east of the city to meet an Israelite shipowner, to negotiate a price for a cart of ploughshares that had recently arrived from Egypt. Ekron would be desperate to learn that some of them would be melted down in a secret Israelite smelting pit, to be recast into knives and swords, and that others would be sharpened to damage crops, property and livestock. Two weeks ago, Samson wouldn't have trusted her with such knowledge, but that was steadily changing. Phicol would be furious as would Ekron, but here among Samson's men she felt curiously reluctant to make life easy for them.

It was difficult to ignore how compellingly Samson spoke about the simple rights of the Israelites to own their own land and control their own lives. She thought of her father, so long now in the ground, but once such a faithful servant of Achish. Though she'd been a child when he died, she knew that he'd yearned for his own small piece of land on which to build a house for his family and grow food for them to eat. He would look wistfully out of the window of their tied cottage on the edge of the vineyard, not up to the big house but out towards the open land to the northeast. He would never speak of it, and always served Achish and the vineyard well, but she'd grown up among the vines with him and would always remember how he held the grapes in his hand and said to her, 'Look what a man can do with a square of land.'

She was so caught up in this memory that it took Samson's gentle caress for her to realise she'd drifted so far into the past. He rarely touched her in front of the others, always sitting a little distance away from her in a way that only enhanced her longing for him. This time she hadn't even noticed his arrival at her side. He sat down next to her, and she realised that the group had finished their training. Abidan and Jubal were joking around as usual, and Ariel was explaining something to Caleb, who quickly looked away when Delilah caught his eye.

'I was calling your name but your mind was elsewhere,' Samson murmured, studying her face intently. 'Onan's daughters have brought out refreshments.'

She smiled, and brushed a lock of hair from her face. 'Perhaps in a moment.'

'What were you thinking about?'

Delilah hesitated for a moment. 'My father.'

'Your true father?'

She nodded. 'I was wondering what he'd make of you.'

'Your father was a very well-liked and well-respected man.'

Delilah shifted on the ground. 'You knew him?'

'I met him once when I was about twenty, not long before he died.'

'What was he like?'

'You don't remember?'

'Not really. I remember like a child would, not proper things about what sort of man he was.'

'I was surprised he chose to work for Achish. His father worked for Achish's family, and his father before him, and before that Achish's ancestors stole the vineyard from your ancestors.'

'Was it really a simple theft?'

Samson nodded. 'Your father's family comes from Nahal Sorek, the valley lands to the northeast where the rivers drain down from the hills.'

'Isn't that on the edge of the Philistine land?'

'It is.'

'I didn't know we came from that far away.'

'Vines grow well in the valley lands but your great-great-great-grandfather's family had taken up this land closer to the sea because although water comes from the ground and not the rivers in this part of the coast it was both fertile and near to a city where the wine could be sold.'

Samson reached behind him for a drinking bowl and held it out to Delilah. 'When the Philistines invaded these lands, they brought the skill of finding water and were able to make more of the gifts of the land than the Israelites had. They saw the advantages your father's ancestors had seen in the fertility of the earth, the nearness of city and sea, but while our people felt at home wherever they stopped, they didn't think as the Philistines do that land is the one true source of power. Achish's family began to grow vines on an adjoining piece of land to your great-grandfather. Within a generation he had stolen so much business from your father's family, they had no choice but to sell up to Achish's ancestors. Your father's family came to work for Achish's family, but I believe your father was never content, and I know that at one time he considered returning to Nahal Sorek to begin again.'

Delilah found herself rapt as Samson drew out a thread of the past, sounding suddenly much older than his years. He spoke of her father as though they had been companions, even though Beulah's husband must have died when Samson was still in his teens. Delilah nodded, curiously sure of something she had no other way of proving. While she'd always ignored her mother's half-serious encouragements to respect her one God — Yahweh — Samson's words struck a deeper chord. Now she felt drawn in to a sense of tradition that was more about people and shared history, than whose God was more powerful.

'That's why our struggle matters so much,' Samson said quietly. 'It's not just so that we can feed our people, but because we must learn that our instinct to move on denies us security and safety. There is no other solution, Delilah. The Philistines must give back what they stole from us.'

There was such softness in his speech that Delilah found it hard to believe she had just heard a war cry from a man feared across the land for his brute strength and ruthless violence. Yet he was as sure of his words as he was of the tree he leaned against, and Delilah understood how he'd managed to convince so many to follow him. Not just young men who wanted to fight, but the elderly, the widows, the children.

But how could she possibly convey to Phicol that this was the true nature of Samson's threat to the Philistines? Phicol understood only violence because that, after all, was how Samson had begun his campaign and she knew that was how it would continue to the bitter end. But there was so much more to it than that.

'Is it true that the Israelites learned ironwork from the Philistines?' asked Delilah, thinking of the ploughshares.

Samson smiled wryly. 'They did indeed teach

us how to make the weapons we will use to fight them.'

Delilah laughed softly. She certainly wouldn't be pointing that out to Phicol.

Her attention was caught by movement over Samson's shoulder and she nodded towards Abidan and Jubal who were hovering a few strides away. Samson beckoned them over and they crouched down beside him, their faces glowing with excitement.

'I don't think you work them hard enough,' said Delilah. 'They shouldn't look so eager for more.'

Samson shook his head. 'Ah, no. This one,' he pointed to Jubal, 'has an idea, and this one,' he pointed to Abidan, 'thinks he can carry it off.'

The two young men glanced at each other sheepishly, but instead of turning to Samson, they looked at Delilah.

'I do have a plan,' said Jubal to her, 'but it involves you.'

Delilah glanced at Samson, but his attention was on the boys.

'Delilah would make an elegant distraction — ' began Abidan.

'That depends on the target,' said Samson.

'The tax man,' said Jubal, grinning broadly.

Samson frowned, considering the idea, but Delilah found the boys' mood infectious, and she leaned forward. 'What do you want me to do?'

'Just look pretty and helpless in a carriage,' said Abidan.

'Is that all?' said Delilah, disappointed.

'And we thought you'd be so good at it!' joked Jubal.

Delilah glanced again at Samson, and this time found his gaze on her. But his expression was completely neutral and she had no idea what he thought of their suggestion. If there were any lingering doubts about her trustworthiness, this would be a chance to convince everyone of her reliability.

'Will you let me?' she asked him.

Samson studied her for a moment longer, then smiled. 'You always get your own way.'

22

Joshua helped Delilah climb into Achish's best carriage, then he hopped up onto the driver's bench and lifted the reins. 'Where to, madam?'

Delilah hid a smile and smoothed her skirt over her lap. She'd forgotten how comfortable the carriage was, with its silk covered cushions and fringed canopy overhead. It was much smaller than the cart Achish used for almost all his other business, and sat two comfortably at the shaded end.

Achish leaned into the carriage. 'Tell Sarai that I've made a gift of a jar of wine to the god Resheph to speed her brothers' recovery from the attack. Give them all my respects and good wishes.' He glanced at Joshua. 'And take care of both your passenger and the horses.'

'Yes, sir.'

Joshua was schooling two new Arabian bay mares and Achish was keen for him to try them out with the carriage rather than the cart, so the excursion to the country estate where Sarai's father had moved his family had everyone's blessing. Even Beulah seemed content, though she'd warned Delilah to keep a respectful distance from Joshua.

'You cannot ride in the carriage and still hold the driver's hand,' she'd murmured to her daughter as they walked to the carriage.

'No, mother,' Delilah had replied politely. 'I'll

be on my best behaviour.'

Joshua nodded courteously to his employer, gave the reins a twitch and the horses moved off. They were out of earshot before he spoke again. 'Are we really taking the road to Gath?'

'Sarai lives out that way.'

Joshua glanced back over his shoulder. 'All right. What I mean is, are we really going to see Sarai?'

'Yes. I haven't seen her for ages.'

Joshua's shoulders sagged. 'I thought we might be going to meet your lover.'

'You are curious,' laughed Delilah. 'Why would you want to meet such a man?'

'I want to see what all the fuss is about.'

'That's for another day.'

'Are you sure? You're very dressed up — I mean, you look beautiful, but isn't it grand just for visiting Sarai?'

Delilah smiled to herself. Joshua wasn't difficult to impress, but she was glad her efforts were obvious. She wore her second best set of jewellery, a twisted rope of gold as thick as her little finger, made into a torque and bracelet, with a pair of polished garnets hanging from fine hooks in her ears. She'd chosen her other new dress, a formal red ochre shift with copious pleats and a slashed neckline, and she'd arranged her hair in curls around her face and neck.

'Sarai's father may be receiving visitors from the Philistine High Council,' she said, 'so I can't just turn up looking like a vine-worker.'

Joshua turned his attention back to his horses and Delilah sighed inwardly. His curiosity was awkward at times, and it was crucial that today of all days, he didn't suspect that what was about to befall them would be anything other than an appalling coincidence.

In truth, Delilah had little idea herself of what exactly was going to happen during their drive. She knew only that somewhere on the long straight road to Gath before Sarai's house, the tax collector's carriage would come into view as he returned with his small escort towards Ashkelon to deliver the taxes he'd collected in the river valley settlements around Gath.

Jubal had done the sums for her, but it was clear that the recent steep rise in Philistine taxes on Israelites meant the collector's money chests would be much fuller than usual. But Jubal had demonstrated his intelligence beyond numbers, by organising a visit to a small Israelite settlement outside the city gates a few evenings ago. Samson had not joined them, kissing Delilah briefly in farewell as he left for his daily period of prayer, the one part of his life from which she was always kept apart. She accepted it without question, but this time she'd been affected as much by the simplicity of their parting as by Jubal's rather sombre mood. Without Abidan he was as bereft as a man without a shadow, but Delilah quickly discovered that where he was taking her was no place for levity.

Within sight of the city gates, a dark smudge on the golden landscape had turned out to be a makeshift village for a large group of Israelites, camping under scraps of canvas or under the stars, their few possessions stacked neatly in sacks around them.

'How long have these people been here?' asked Delilah as Jubal led her to the edges of the encampment. 'A few weeks?'

'Two years.'

'Two years? Don't they have homes?'

'These are their homes, Delilah. This is my home.'

Delilah had reached for Jubal's hand and squeezed it gently, because she couldn't think what else to do. Columns of thin smoke rose up from a couple of fires, salt-rich from the burning of seaweed instead of wood, and barely a cover for the sour smell of makeshift cesspits on the edge of the camp. Children moaned quietly in their mothers' arms, or scratched in the dirt for play, and Delilah realised there were no men to be seen.

'You see, the tax collectors want paying anyway,' continued Jubal, 'whether you have money or not. The Philistines tax the dead as well as the living, so there is no escape that way either. There is no food on these fires, and the women rely on what little their men bring home.'

Delilah had reached for her purse but Jubal had stopped her. 'Tomorrow they will have food — not money, but food. The taxes we rescue will be used to buy what these people need. And you will help that way.'

So Delilah had spent a restless night in her own bed, her nose still full of the smell of the camp, her sleep fractured by the staring faces of Jubal's desperately poor friends and family. It had felt odd to be alone in bed too, and she wondered fleetingly if Samson had found someone else to keep him warm. But as soon as she thought it, she knew it to be untrue. She comforted herself with the proud smile he'd given her as Jubal led her out of the orchard.

She had her own reasons for helping with this ambush that weren't merely a matter of compassion. Phicol didn't need another obscene statue of Asherah over which to fawn, he didn't need Israelite money to feed his war against people who couldn't feed themselves.

As Joshua turned the carriage onto the Gath road, Delilah ran over the few instructions she'd received from Jubal again. *Once you get onto the Gath road, look for the tax collector's carriage. As soon as you can see his driver's face, find something to hold on to. Remember, nothing bad will happen to you or your driver.*

It was a while since Delilah had been out this way, and she was dismayed to see that it resembled the road to Ashdod, littered with more wretchedly poor Israelite families walking in search of a better life. So many of them had so little, and Delilah wondered whether a robbery really needed to be staged. Couldn't these people simply rise up and take back what had once been theirs? Yet their eyes were fixed on the floor, so focused on survival, they had no will for anything else.

The Gath road was quite narrow for a good distance, barely wide enough for two carriages to pass each other between rows of huts and barns. It would be a good place for an ambush, even

214

this near to the city, and indeed she soon spotted the armed carriage rolling towards them. There were four guards flanking the carriage on foot, plus the driver and the tax collector in the carriage. As they closed, Delilah slid her fingers beneath the cushions, grasping the wooden frame beneath the bench and bracing her feet against the floor.

Suddenly the Arabian mare on the left buckled and swayed, dragging the other one towards it. Joshua yelled, tugging at the reins, but the horse was staggering and neighing, floundering against the bridles as she tried to stay on her feet.

'Is she lame?' shouted Delilah, holding on tightly. The carriage was rocking violently from side to side as the horses struggled against each other, and Joshua was fighting for control.

'Come on, girl! What's wrong with you?' Joshua held the right pair of reins out. 'Jump up, Delilah, and grab these. I can't manage both horses.'

Delilah stumbled forward, banging her arm against the front of the carriage. She had to hitch her dress up over her knees to climb over and she'd barely put one foot on Joshua's bench than he flung the reins into her hands and jumped down beside the agitated mare.

'Try to stop the other one,' he yelled, tugging hard at the mare's bridle and trying to get his hand onto her nose. 'Come on now, what's wrong with you?'

And then suddenly the mare slumped to the ground, her knees folding beneath her, pulling her stablemate down as well and rocking the

215

carriage dangerously forward.

Had she been sitting, rather than standing astride the bench, Delilah might have slid onto the horses. She glanced up, and saw the tax collector's armed guard running towards her, his carriage trotting fast to keep up.

'Are you all right, ma'am?' shouted one of the soldiers. He held out his hand to her to climb down, but she shook her head.

'I feel safer up here.'

'You could easily fall. You ought to come down. What happened to your carriage?'

Delilah pointed to the other side where Joshua was crouched on the ground next to the mare. She was disconcerted to see that the horse had gone very still.

The soldiers worked quickly to release the felled horse from its bridles, and as the Philistine's carriage came to a halt in front of them, the other horse stood up and the carriage rocked back onto its wheels.

'What seems to be the trouble?' asked the tax collector, peering out through a slatted wooden screen. Delilah realised his seat was completely enclosed in a wooden frame, and that his canopy was just cosmetic. He took his security seriously, that was clear.

'One of our horses fell lame and we nearly tipped — '

She was interrupted by a bloodcurdling yell and in a moment, both carriages were completely surrounded by forty or more men who had swarmed out of the barns onto the road, their faces smeared with ashes, their hair

216

hidden beneath rags. They brandished an assortment of crude but sharpened weapons. The soldiers immediately unsheathed their swords, and retreated in formation around their carriage, but they were hopelessly outnumbered. They pointed their swords outwards, but made no move to attack.

'Open up!' barked one of the men at the tax collector. Delilah thought from the voice it might have been Jubal, but he was so well disguised she couldn't be sure. 'Open up your carriage and give us the Israelite money.'

'Under no circumstances,' squeaked the tax collector indignantly. 'This is the rightful property of the Confederation of Philistine Cities, collected under due law of the Philistine High Council and by the orders of Their Lordships — '

Wood screeched as an axe blade scythed through the side of the carriage from top to bottom, causing the tax collector to lurch away from the screen.

He began to squawk, 'In the name of the Great God El, I command you — ' but he was distracted by sudden ribald cheering from the robbers. Delilah looked down to see a fine trickle of coins falling through the floor of the carriage onto the road. The axe blow must have punctured one of the chests.

The robbers needed no further encouragement, and in moments, the side of the tax collector's carriage had been levered off, the tax collector lifted out onto the road and tied up with his soldiers and driver, and the money bagged safely into sacks.

'And you, m'lady,' said a sarcastic voice. 'What do you have for us?'

Delilah turned to find the leader of the brigands had hopped up on the carriage behind her without her noticing. There was real menace in his eyes, and he slid his fingers easily beneath the torque.

'Such a pretty thing you are.' He gave it a quick tug and the clasp gave way, and he twisted it through his fingers.

'And the bracelet, love, and the earrings. Don't want to hurt you!'

'Leave her!' shouted Joshua from where he still knelt by the horse.

Delilah willed him silently to stay where he was and not interfere. Jubal had told her that he and Abidan would be the only ones in the party who knew she was a decoy, so there was still a chance of trouble from the others. But up close, with his dirty face so close to hers, she was even less sure it was Jubal, and she felt suddenly uncertain as she removed her remaining jewellery and handed it over.

'I said, leave her!' Joshua had stood up and was trying to clamber onto the driver's bench, but the robber gave him a light shove and he tumbled back onto the road.

'Don't want to hurt you either, boy. We got what we came for, and more.' He gave a shout, and in moments the robbers had melted away as quickly as they'd come. The tax collector's carriage was being driven down the road towards Ashkelon at a furious pace, and the other men had simply vanished.

Delilah jumped down to the road and pulled Joshua to his feet. 'Are you all right?'

'Just bruised. But what about you? I thought he was going to kill you.'

'It wasn't as bad as it looked. He frightened me, though,' she said truthfully. 'Is the horse dead?'

Joshua smoothed his hand over the mare's neck and pulled a tiny feather dart out of her flesh. 'I spotted this when I was down beside her.' He dabbed his tongue at the end of the dart, making Delilah wince.

'I reckon she jumped from the pain at first, but then the drug took hold and made her legs go. She's breathing all right and I expect she'll come round.'

Delilah looked across at the tax collector, who was shivering against his escort. He'd got off lightly, she thought. Perhaps Samson had told the boys to make sure no one was hurt in Delilah's presence. She knew from that night in the granary it wasn't always like this.

She tottered unsteadily towards the bound men, and began untying their ropes. 'I feel so dreadful about what happened to you. But you surely saved our lives, coming to our rescue to calm the horse.'

'Never mind that,' said the tax collector shakily. 'I need you to come with me to confirm my account of these events to Lord Phicol. He'll be furious.'

'Lord Phicol?' said Delilah sweetly. 'But he's married to my sister.'

23

'If I didn't know better,' said Phicol, 'I'd say you were in on it.'

Thus far he'd kept his anger in check, but Delilah could see he was like a dam, ready to burst.

'I assure you,' she said, trying to keep the fear from her voice. 'The experience wasn't pleasurable for me either.'

Phicol took a deep breath, and sat heavily in his chair. The summons to see her Philistine paymaster had arrived quickly via Ekron, and she'd barely had time to prepare herself mentally before they'd marched over to his house together.

'Have you any idea how much money those scrounging Israelites took from me?' snapped Phicol. 'I've a good mind to subtract it from your fees.'

Delilah decided to stick with her combative responses. 'I was too busy fearing for my life to count your treasure,' she said.

In the corner of the room, Ekron sucked through his teeth, but Phicol actually smiled.

'You're either very clever, my girl, or incredibly foolish.'

'I'm doing my best,' she said, adopting a more conciliatory tone.

★ ★ ★

He dismissed her soon afterwards, and Delilah was grateful to be out in the open air once more. The expected fury had never been unleashed, but in some ways that frightened her more. Could it be that he really was doubting her reliability and was beginning the slow process of cutting her loose?

Outwardly, her situation was transparent. Joshua certainly didn't suspect her, and she was relieved that the mare recovered fully from the dart. The carriage was miraculously undamaged, and they had been received home with considerable relief by Achish. Beulah's nerves stood up less well under narration of the attack, and she banned Delilah from leaving the vineyard at all for two full days. Although she was able to occupy herself usefully by paying extra attention to the vines, Delilah was perturbed to find that her body yearned for Samson to the point that she lay awake for hours wondering where he was. He'd become the rhythm of her days as well as her nights.

It was a relief then when Achish took pity on her three days after the robbery and sent her into town with some bills to present. Delilah finished the business quickly, then went to the tavern, hoping against hope that Samson would be there. She hesitated at the back door when she saw him, perched on the terrace wall talking to Ariel, suddenly unsure of how he'd greet her. But when his gaze finally fell on her, it was so intense it both delighted and unnerved her.

'It was prudent of you to stay away from here for so long,' said Samson after Ariel left. 'We had

221

a lot of Philistine visitors the day after the robbery and it was better you weren't here.'

'It wasn't prudence. My family overreacted to the danger and insisted I remain where they could keep an eye on me.'

'Has the horse recovered?'

'It has, thank God. Jubal made a very convincing thug.'

'That wasn't Jubal. That was Maoch. He knew nothing of who you were and we thought you would be safer if you genuinely didn't recognise your assailant.'

'Was Jubal even there?'

Samson laughed. 'I wouldn't have left you completely unguarded.'

'Oh, thank you,' said Delilah drily.

'He wants to express his gratitude. Will you come back here tonight?'

'I'd like to, but my family have organised a celebration to honour the God El for my safe return from the clutches of the evil Israelite robbers.'

'I should like to attend such a celebration — '

Delilah's eyes were wide open before she realised he was joking. 'Aren't you satisfied with rattling Lord Phicol from afar? He's absolutely ruthless, and since the robbery he's been as angry as Ba'al Hadad with a mouth full of lightning.'

'You have too many gods.'

'Don't you mean the Philistines, not me?'

Samson fell silent for a moment. 'Does that mean that I won't see you later?'

'It will be much later.'

'Come to the beach hut. Do you remember the way?'

Delilah nodded.

'I'll be waiting.'

Delilah lifted her hand to reach for his, but he stood up and with a last lingering look, he left the tavern.

★ ★ ★

The celebration was meant to be a small family affair, although it was difficult to keep it so with Lord Phicol and half his staff in attendance.

The ceremony began with the family gathered in front of the domestic altar to El, where a ritual drinking bowl was filled with fortified pomace spirit from the vineyard's own pressing, and then ignited. Delilah was always enchanted by the colourful flames that ate up the clear liquid, and afterwards Achish gave her the sacred cloth to pick up the bowl as custom dictated. Joshua had been invited to the ceremony, though not the party, and though she knew it would irritate Lord Phicol, Delilah made a point of giving the ceremonial Philistine bowl to the Israelite slave who had protected her during the attack.

'I wouldn't be alive now,' she said, moving through the gathering with the bowl held out before her, 'without Joshua's speed in unbridling the horses.'

She handed the bowl to him and Joshua blushed to be singled out. Though Achish and Beulah nodded gently at her gesture, Delilah could see Ekron out of the corner of her eye, his

223

own face set in white rage.

'I'm sure you would have done the same for me,' Delilah said to Ekron a short while later, after Joshua had been dismissed from the gathering and the family had moved to the courtyard.

'You shouldn't have been out there on the Gath road. It was irresponsible of Father to let you go out that way. Don't either of you listen to a word we tell you about the Israelites?'

'Surely you wouldn't have us all hide in our homes while battles rage on the streets? If we are to survive their oppression, we would be better continuing with our lives as we mean to live them.'

Ekron shot her an angry look, and poured himself another bowl of the special celebration vintage. No one else knew, but Achish had taken two jars from the rack he'd promised Lord Phicol for the birth of Hemin's child, to use for the evening's party. It lingered on the tongue like the fattest berry fruits squashed and bleeding, but Delilah could tell that its perfection was completely lost on Ekron's crude palate.

'You can't have it both ways,' she said, sipping from her bowl.

Ekron sighed irritably and set down his drink, splashing wine over the rim. He strode away to join Phicol, who was holding court on the opposite side. Her stepbrother spoke in Phicol's ear behind a raised fan. The lecture was surely imminent now, and Phicol was bound to deliver it before he took Hemin home for the evening.

Hemin herself was taking the midwife's advice

to eat for two very seriously, but she wriggled uncomfortably on the wide stool from Achish's study that had been brought out especially for her. The presence of the baby in her belly annoyed her and she was shouting at everyone, even her father. Beulah drifted to Delilah's side to pick up a handful of cherries, and they turned discreetly to study the food.

'It's very good of you to spend so much time with her,' said Beulah quietly.

'The sooner the baby is born, the better for us all.'

'There are still three more months to go. I suppose she'll hand it over to a nursemaid soon enough. Philistine women don't dirty their hands with the raising of children.'

'I've always found that a little sad.'

Beulah reached for a cube of sheep's cheese. 'It was nice of you to give the bowl to Joshua.'

'He is a good man, Mother.'

'But not good enough for you.'

Delilah said nothing. Answering would only invite more questions, and there was a seriousness to her mother's expression which Delilah had not often seen before and which worried her. Beulah may have had traditional views on family life, but Delilah knew that her mother had a very keen understanding of people and their ways. She was so steeped in lying now, that the sharp pangs of guilt had become a dull ache, rarely acknowledged. She comforted herself that her mother would soon be able to enjoy the fruits of Phicol's bribe. Once the task was done.

225

With a frustrated yell, Hemin suddenly lurched to her feet and bellowed at Lord Phicol that she wanted to go home. Phicol snapped at her for interrupting him, but he quickly got to his feet. Delilah suspected he was also grateful for an excuse to leave the party. He had kept to a lavish stool in one corner of the courtyard all evening, refusing to talk to anyone unless they approached him. Ekron had hovered about him like a moth, too stupid to see how hot the flame was. As Phicol gathered his skirts about him to leave, sending two of his elite guard to escort Hemin to his carriage, Ekron darted to Delilah's side. She knew what he was going to say before the words left his mouth.

'His Lordship wishes to talk with you,' he murmured. 'Wait outside the rear gate.'

'It's not convenient at the moment.'

Ekron stared at her. 'What do you mean? You can leave at any time, it's just a stupid party.'

'It's my stupid party, in case you've forgotten.'

'If you hadn't been going to see Sarai — '

'To put in a good word for you, Ekron.'

Ekron jerked with surprise and hissed, 'You had no right. And besides, if you hadn't been going to see her, the tax collector wouldn't have been robbed and Lord Phicol wouldn't be in such a filthy temper and taking it out on me.'

'My visit to Sarai had nothing to do with the robbery. Whatever gave you that idea?'

Ekron said nothing but only held her gaze, daring her to challenge him. Delilah was suddenly furious.

'I lost jewellery worth three hundred pieces of silver that day — '

'Which you can easily afford to replace.'

' — I was surrounded by fifty hollering thieves — '

'Some of whom you no doubt knew — '

'Enough!' snapped Delilah.

She'd raised her voice enough to attract Achish's attention, and he was now watching them with concern.

Delilah smiled at Ekron in mock politeness, and turned into the house. She knew there was jealousy beneath Ekron's concerns, but his fondness for her, which had been so pleasing in their youth, now troubled her. It was he who had chosen a life of politics above everything else. Now he must live with the consequences.

Phicol was indeed waiting by the rear gate, his posture suggesting extreme displeasure. His hands were pressed together, the fingers pointing out towards Delilah and she knew she was supposed to give a formal bow.

Instead she said, 'You summoned me?'

'You have not been telling me everything, of that I'm quite certain.'

Delilah watched him carefully. He was right, of course, but it was impossible to know what he suspected her of concealing.

'What is it you wish to know?' she said.

'Many things, Delilah, many things.' He paused, apparently for effect, for he then said, 'But in the meantime, I have a particular request. I want you to make sure Samson attends the festival of Dagon, next week.'

'Because?'

'Despite your reticence on certain key facts, the discovery of the arsenal of weapons at the granary has given me enough evidence to arrest Samson. But — '

'So you are grateful to me.'

' — but, I wish to arrest him in a public place predominantly attended by Philistines, so that anyone who wishes to protect or defend him will be noticeably outnumbered. Samson has many enemies among our people and I'm sure that were there to be difficulties in his arrest, I'd find spontaneous support among a Philistine crowd.'

'You could arrest him anywhere.'

'Not without putting my own men at risk. I'm sure you think me a callous man, my dear, but I've lost enough Philistine blood to this animal that you lie with. I need to capture him and keep him where I can control him. You will be free of me soon, but only when I have him within reach. I have yet to satisfy my curiosity about his plans for the Israelite uprising.'

Delilah's mouth was dry. 'Because without him, the rebellion has no leader and so no purpose.'

'Precisely.' Phicol turned to his carriage. 'The festival of Dagon, my dear. The first evening, in the market square. Don't forget.'

Delilah shivered in the breeze as the carriage drove away. The festival was her favourite time of year, a celebration of fruitfulness and the joy it brought, of lavish feasts and dressing up, of family games and sporting challenges. She had been hoping that she could share some part of the festival with Samson, show him that Philistines weren't all bad, that there were gentle pleasures to be found in their customs that he could enjoy with her. But Phicol had reached into that tiny dream as though he knew she treasured it, and crushed it ruthlessly.

24

The boats were drawn up on the shore, well clear of the lapping tide. Delilah slowed her steps. Had Samson changed his mind about where they were to meet? If the boats were in, then so were the fishermen, and this was where they slept and ate. They would hardly welcome a trysting couple, no matter how well-respected Samson was.

And tonight she didn't want to see anyone else. As she came close to the hut, she felt the stillness of the place and was immediately sure there was no one else around. The waves too hardly stirred, but as she ducked into the hut she noticed Samson was sitting cross-legged on the floor, his back to her. His hands were clasped in front of him, and he was sitting so still that in the moonlight, he looked like one of the lifesize statues of the Philistine gods and goddesses that would be carried through the streets during the evening parade that opened the festival of Dagon. The moonlight cast the outline of his body in even greater relief than usual, so that he looked carved out of marble, and his thick braids of hair lay unbound against his back. They glinted in the silvery light and Delilah longed to touch one, just as she'd reached out to touch the statue of the beautiful protectress god Asherah, the very first time she'd seen the festival parade as a child.

But as her fingers reached out tentatively towards him, Samson rolled his head back and gave a great call to the heavens. Delilah jerked her hands back against her chest, her eyes following his up to the roof and to the starlit sky.

He's praying, she thought, moving backwards as quietly as she could towards the doorway. She'd never seen him at prayer before, though he left her each afternoon to attend to his devotions, and although she remembered her father's nightly prayers from her childhood, since Beulah had married Achish such rituals had been put aside out of respect for the Philistine household.

Delilah carried in her head the memory of the cries Samson made when he was inside her, the sounds she believed she'd put into his mouth with her own. But this came from Samson's heart, not his body, a lighter, purer sound that seemed to float into the sky. She was sure that everyone across the land could hear it, that right now they would be woken from sleep, be lowering their knives to their bowls, looking up from their fishing nets and searching the night for its source. It made her skin tingle, it was so clear and sharp. He stood quickly and seemed startled for a moment to see her waiting.

'I didn't hear you arrive,' he said.

'I didn't want to disturb you. I'm sorry — '

If he was offended, he didn't let it show, and he came to her with a kiss. His passion caught her by surprise, as it had not since that first night in the granary. She'd run here through the darkened city, eager to wipe out the evening's

231

events with the sheer power of his presence, his size simply obliterating everything else around her. But now, as they searched for each other against the sandy floor, the thoughts she'd fought to suppress rose up again.

The festival of Dagon, my dear.

Samson's fingers walked her breastbone and he gently kissed the curve of her ribs. She ran her own fingers over his shoulders, aware of how small her hands were on him. He seemed to sense how much she wanted him, how much she needed him to put out a fire within her, and yet even as he entered her, she could see Ekron's face in the darkness of her head. She remembered the last time they'd spoken in the open courtyard at home.

'How do you feel,' he had asked, 'leading a man to his death?'

'What do you mean?'

'You can't believe that His Lordship really means just to arrest Samson?'

Ekron's laughter, dry, ironic, bitter —

'You are fooling yourself, Delilah, if you take Lord Phicol at his word.'

Delilah allowed the richness of her pleasure to swell more quickly than usual, hungry for it. She pulled him closer still, aware how easily his embrace could crush her, yet half-willing it. And then, from deep within them both, the shuddering gasps of climax rose up.

All too soon it was over, and she lay against him, her head against his chest, the steady thud of his heart in her ears. Samson's fingers ran through her hair, unknowingly soothing her, but

232

the hot agony of guilt lay deep in her chest, beyond his reach. It was just as their first night at the granary had been, when she'd suppressed the true purpose of her visit with her own desire, gladly hiding words that might give her away within Samson's silent embrace. He'd not suspected her then, but did he do so now? Had he learned that her passion for him was at its greatest whenever her betrayal was nearest?

She yawned, willing sleep to come to her as she lay so safe against him. But Phicol's bleating instruction lay heavy on her tongue and she frowned in the dark, trying to think of a way to raise the festival that sounded natural in this magical place, so far from everyone. She was still trying out various remarks in her head, when she felt Samson's voice rumble beneath her.

'How was your celebration?'

Delilah moved a little so that she could see his face. 'You wouldn't have enjoyed it,' she said. 'Hemin made her presence felt.'

Samson laughed quietly, a deep, comforting sound. 'Maybe you are right. But I'm curious about your life at the vineyard.'

She nestled again against his shoulder, amused by his interest. He'd never asked what she did when they were apart before and she'd always assumed that he knew. That was the source of his authority, she felt; he seemed to know so much about everyone and everything, including her. To admit ignorance showed an unusual vulnerability in him.

She slid her fingers through the hair on his

233

chest. 'I've heard that curiosity can be dangerous.'

Samson snorted, his gruffness returned. 'Ruling by deceit and by force is dangerous. Curiosity is natural.'

'Well — ' she hesitated. 'The festival of Dagon is next week. My mother will be there, with Achish of course, and you could watch us from afar.'

'Watching you from afar is definitely dangerous. The further away you are, the more I want you near to me.' Samson's hand drifted over her buttocks and he gently pressed her against him.

She could feel his arousal for her growing again. This was what Phicol intended, of course, that she use her intimacy with Samson to control his movements. But just as at the granary, the proximity of pleasure and death was impossible to ignore, and she couldn't rid herself of Ekron's taunts. She wouldn't see Samson die at the festival, but she would always know she'd led him to his death.

'I had been thinking of attending the festival anyway,' he continued. 'There are competitions of strength, at which prizes of silver and gold are offered. It would please me to rob the Philistines of their money in person, for once.'

'Those competitions are on the first day,' she said quickly.

'I know. After the teams of Philistine boys have carried those ludicrous effigies of their gods through the streets, they line up against each other, do they not? Two teams take opposite ends

234

of a rope and try to pull the other team over a dividing line.'

'The Charioteers' Cup.'

'A silver cup filled with silver coins.'

'You're not going to carry an effigy as well, are you? That would be considered blasphemous.'

'Not if I were to bring that fellow you're always invoking, Se't.'

'The God of Chaos.' Delilah grinned. She could just imagine the scene. Phicol on his raised platform, squealing with indignation as Samson dragged in the huge statue draped chaotically in clothes, crops and vegetables, five small children shrieking away tunelessly on pipes and drums at his sides.

'It would be a very suitable blasphemy then,' said Samson, 'if I were to bring Chaos to the Philistines' own festival.'

Delilah propped herself up on her elbows, peering at Samson's face in the dark. 'You mean to cause trouble?'

'There is always trouble when Israelites and Philistines meet.'

'But at the festival?'

Delilah forced down the panic rising in her chest. This was exactly what Phicol wanted, and she'd barely had to say anything to make it happen. But if Samson were going to attend in such a fashion, he'd be unprepared for an attack by Phicol's men. Worse still, Ekron would be laughing at how easily the giant had allowed himself to be captured and Delilah would be forced to laugh with him, if she were not to give herself away.

The reality of the situation punctured her pleasure. She couldn't let him go ahead. Phicol would surely not make the same mistake he had at the granary; once again, she'd be forced to watch his fate unfold.

'Are you sure that's the most effective way to attack the Philistines?' she asked carefully.

'If they are willing to give up their money so easily, then I want to be the one to take it from them.'

Samson gently drew her head towards his, his words caressing her cheek. 'Don't worry. I'll be perfectly safe, unexpectedly rich, unbearably proud, and you can cheer for me from behind your pretty little hand.'

His enthusiasm for attending the festival would have been charming had Delilah not felt the throb of dread deep within her. She pushed him away again.

'Listen, Samson. I don't want you to go.'

He looked hurt. 'There are no rules forbidding an Israelite to enter these competitions, are there?'

'Not to my knowledge, but . . . '

'Then I will go.'

He tried to kiss her once more, but this time she pushed him harder leaving her palm against his chest, her elbow locked straight. 'No! I forbid you.'

His face showed confusion, but he was still smiling. '*You* forbid *me*?' He hooked a finger in the crook of her arm and easily broke her hold.

She rolled away and stood up in front of him. 'Why can't you take anything I say seriously?' she asked.

'Because you're naked,' he said, reaching for her.

She backed away further. 'Can't you see? If you keep taunting them, they'll lose patience. They'll try to hurt you.'

Samson's smile finally broke. 'They've tried before. They'll fail this time too.'

'You think your God will protect you forever, don't you?' she said. 'They have gods as well.'

Samson sat up, and cast his locks behind his head. He looked at her darkly. 'The difference is that I trust my God. If he chooses to bring about my end, I will accept it.'

Delilah snatched up her clothes and began to put them on in a hurry. 'Then you're a fool!' she said. 'And I won't waste my time with you.'

25

The crowds were already gathering in the centre of Ashkelon.

'You look beautiful,' said Achish to Delilah, offering his hand to her as she climbed down from the carriage, 'even if you are not wearing the new dress I bought for you.'

Delilah brushed at the skirt of her white shift, then stood on tiptoes and kissed her stepfather's cheek. 'Forgive me. I thought I'd save it for the last night. That has always been my favourite part of the festival.'

'I don't pretend to understand the workings of a young woman's mind,' replied Achish, smiling broadly and holding out his hand to Beulah, who had come in the carriage with Delilah.

'It's a lovely dress, though. I'm very lucky,' said Delilah.

'You may just regret not wearing it today,' murmured Achish, turning to his left. Delilah followed his gaze and forced herself to smile. Mizraim stood with his son beside their own carriage, looking on expectantly.

'Jered,' she said quietly.

'I thought it would be a nice surprise for you,' said Achish, and Delilah met her stepfather's searching gaze with as much genuine pleasantness as she could muster. She'd completely forgotten about Jered and Mizraim visiting the festival. The young man looked as handsome as ever, but she could hardly find the energy to socialize. Her mind continued to replay her argument with Samson and her subsequent storming out. How stubborn that man could be!

'He has missed you, I gather,' continued Achish, 'and has come to the festival at my invitation so that he can spend some time with you in your home city. I understand there might be a possibility of Mizraim opening a new warehouse here and Jered would be sent to supervise it. Obviously it would help if you could show him the city, help him to get a sense of what it would be like to live here permanently.'

Delilah gave a courteous bow to Jered, who was apparently so overwhelmed by the sight of her that he was unable to do anything but stare. *Live here permanently? A new warehouse?* It seemed that her unwillingness to go to Ashdod in recent weeks had been interpreted as a desire to stay in her home city. And now an alternative plan had been hatched for the young lovebirds.

Delilah approached Mizraim and Jered. To the older man she gave a respectful bow, then bowed again to Jered.

'How are you, Delilah?' he asked, a broad smile creeping over his face.

'I'm well, Jered. I hope you had a pleasant journey here. Welcome to Ashkelon.'

'It's a good time to visit. The festival of Dagon always shows a city at its best.'

Not if old Phicol gets his way, thought Delilah. She looked about for Abidan and Jubal, Ariel or Caleb among the crowd. She had no idea if Samson was going to go through with his

239

insane plan, and prayed that her anger had moved him to reason. If there was trouble, Jered and Mizraim would probably change their plans to move to Ashkelon as quickly as they had made them.

'I believe we are sitting over there, near the centre,' gestured Jered towards the grandest seats available.

Delilah's heart sank. Not only was she to spend the evening entertaining Jered instead of fretting over Samson, but she'd have to do so within spitting distance of Lord Phicol. While most of the benches on the temporary platforms that now framed three sides of the square were for wealthy Philistine politicians and business-men, there were four rows of elaborate stools and thrones arranged for the royal party and honoured guests. As extended family of His Lordship, Delilah had forgotten that they would be expected to join him, and as Mizraim and Jered were their guests, so they would be seated with him too. It would be a grandstand seat to view the arrest of Samson. Just what Phicol had intended, surely.

Jered offered Delilah his raised hand in the formal gesture of betrothed couples who wish to walk together in public, but Delilah hesitated. His surprise arrival, and Achish's arrangements behind her back, had irritated her. She owed her mother a scowl for her complicity in the plotting too, but everyone's eyes were on her. She took his hand, even though it would signal an intimacy she didn't feel.

Once seated, she began asking Jered polite

questions about the business, about his journey, about where they were staying in Ashkelon and where they were considering renting a warehouse, but his answers washed over her as she scanned the throngs for any sign of Samson. She excused her interest in the crowd that was gathering in their seats and in the statue procession that was massing in the main street, by explaining that the opening of the festival was one of the most exciting parts.

'I'd be remiss,' she said, searching the crowd for Abidan and Jubal, 'if I didn't point out to you every tiny detail of the spectacle.'

'I'm sure that in your company I'll find it even more interesting,' said Jered, without taking his eyes off her.

'You are very kind,' she murmured.

'Not really. Delilah — you see — well — '

'Oh look,' said Delilah, pointing across Jered to the royal party. 'There is Lord Phicol, our honoured host, and my stepsister Hemin, his wife.'

Jered coughed self-consciously and stood up with Delilah and her family, bowing to Lord Phicol. Ekron stared at Jered with particular distaste, and Delilah met his eventual gaze on her with a fury she didn't have to conjure. She knew he felt contempt for Joshua and hatred for Samson: both of those fitted with Ekron's political views of the Israelites as well as his jealousy; but Jered was his equal, in social standing at least.

Jered had apparently caught sight of Ekron's expression, for he cast a wounded look at

Delilah, seemingly aware that he'd stumbled over someone else's passion.

Delilah patted Jered's hand. 'My stepbrother bears great responsibility working for His Lordship, and at times he is inclined to be suspicious of newcomers. But you have my father's blessing — '

'I do?'

Delilah cursed herself for her clumsiness. 'It seems that way,' she said, smiling pleasantly.

★　★　★

Delilah knew she said it every year, but the statues of the gods and goddesses looked even more amazing than ever. His Divine Highness the Lord God El had been painted in gold this year, a glistening figurehead in the late afternoon sun. Molech, the God of Fire, sat in the centre of a ring of flames that were fed by a channel of pomace that flowed around him. Resheph, who was celebrated in alternate years for each of his roles as God of Plague and of Healing, was cast out of pure white this year and floated past in a scented cloud of herb oils, which was quite an improvement on last year's pestilential figure in black surrounded by rotting food.

Lord Phicol was invited, as usual, to come down from his perch to sit in the lap of the figure of the Melqart, King God of the City, and was given a tour round the square lofted on high, his purple robes spilling out over the red robes in which the statue had been dressed. He waved benevolently to his citizens, but Delilah's eyes

242

were on the statue of Se't, who had been brought into the square on the far side too early, disrupting Phicol's personal parade. Delilah peered through the crowd to see if Samson was responsible for this untimely interruption, but she couldn't make anything out clearly at this distance.

'Trust Se't to make trouble,' said Jered rather seriously.

'It doesn't matter. It will remind Lord Phicol that the gods control our fates, not he himself,' said Delilah absently.

Jered laughed nervously. 'Should you be heard saying such a thing?'

'Of course. He is almost family,' said Delilah brightly. 'Besides, politicians cannot lead without the confidence of their people.'

'Lord Phicol has apparently done a very good job,' said Jered, clearly uncertain whether Delilah was joking.

'And he is already quite sure enough of himself, so it won't hurt for him to be reminded of it now and again. Let Se't tease him a little. It will do him good.'

But if Samson was responsible for Se't's arrival, he must have been behind the scenes, for the team of charioteers carrying the deity were clearly Philistine. Perhaps rumour had got out about what Phicol had planned for Samson. More likely, perhaps the Israelites were being more cautious than usual. In theory, the curfew still stood, though with so many people present at the festival, such a ruling would be difficult to enforce.

Se't's unruly entrance was followed by the last of the statues, the festival's host deity, Dagon, the God of Crop Fertility. His platform was carried on the shoulders of several oiled bearers. As usual, Dagon was wreathed with flowers and fruits, and he was carried on a platform decked with bundles of wheat, bales of raw cotton, beehives and an array of fruits, flowers and vegetables. Unlike the other gods who received a new statue each year, the same figure had been used for Dagon for many decades, representing his constancy to the Philistine people and their continuing faith in him. No one was permitted to repaint or mend him, for he was a sacred figure, but miraculously he was never damaged during the festival and looked as good as new every year.

As Dagon was carried to his place in front of the royal party, Phicol wore a smug smile, and was beadily surveying the square as though he too expected trouble. Once or twice, his eyes caught hers and Delilah studiously avoided his gaze. Though she wanted to see Samson stride through the crowd, openly challenging Lord Phicol, Delilah also felt a lingering respect for the festival she'd grown up loving so much. For all that it was Philistine, she understood its purpose as celebrating the joy and the responsibility of a person's ability to grow food from the land, something her father had shown and shared with her from a very early age. As one of the wrestling students unloaded a jar of wine from Dagon's platform and carried it up to Lord Phicol, she reached across Jered and squeezed Achish's hand. In that jar was their own wine, pressed from grapes that had grown on vines she had cared for. That was her wine, and in so many ways this was her festival.

A great cry went up from the far side of the square. Delilah released Achish's hand and looked across to where a cohort of Israelites strode into view. Samson led them. Her heart quickened to see him striding so confidently into the Philistine arena, but her mind screamed at him to turn and leave. In the group that followed him, Delilah saw Caleb and as they neared the platform he glanced up and caught her eye. Delilah dared not respond in case someone noticed and she looked away quickly.

'What is the Israelite troublemaker doing here?' asked Jered angrily, getting up from his seat.

'It's his city too, so I understand,' replied Delilah quietly. 'Perhaps he's come to pay his respects to Dagon.'

'He'd do no such thing.'

Samson marched directly to Phicol's platform, where he stood barely a few strides from her, his arms loose at his sides, the seven great ropes of his hair plaited together down his back. He was bare-chested and wore a simple leather skirt and sandals, and his skin glistened in the fierce torches that drove off the gathering dusk. If he noticed her, he made no sign of it, but he must have known that the eyes of everyone were on him.

'I've come to claim the Charioteers' Cup,' he said in Philistine, his clear voice cutting through the outraged shudder of discontent from the crowd. 'Who will compete against me?'

Ekron jumped up beside Lord Phicol. 'You speak our language, but you are not a Philistine. You are not eligible to take part.'

But Phicol slapped him down with a flailing hand as he leaned forward on his throne. 'There is nothing in the rules to prevent this man from competing. I say, we should let him fight among us.'

'He'll be easily beaten by our men,' said Jered to Delilah. 'He is a fool to try though I suppose it will make a good spectacle.'

But Delilah barely heard him. Pairs of soldiers had formed ranks on either side of the square.

26

Delilah looked at Phicol, searching his face for any sign of what was to follow. Surely he wouldn't risk bloodshed here; not on a festival day.

Phicol was watching Samson patiently. He had the crowd with him too, caught up in his confidence. In her concern, it took Delilah a moment to notice that only Ekron's attention wasn't on Samson. Instead he was watching her across the crowd, studying her intently. She met his stare with a cold one of her own.

The crowd had grown silent around her and she realised that the soldiers were closing in steadily, separating Samson from the other Israelites. Samson turned his back calmly on Phicol to face the god-bearers.

'Are you the first team?' he asked.

'It's us!' shouted one of the young men. 'As bearers of Dagon, it's our right to take the first round in the Cup.'

A cheer went up from his friends, and seven of the wrestling students surged into the space between Samson and the soldiers. They were fit, strong young men, most of them short and stocky as befitted successful wrestlers. They quickly formed into the rope line, the shortest man at the front, the tallest at the rear.

'Bring the rope!' they chanted, 'bring the rope!'

A group of judges at the foot of the royal platform gathered quickly in a flurry of skirts and formal headgear, reminding Delilah of a clutch of chickens. The soldiers had now settled into a stationary arc between Samson and the rest of the Israelites; it seemed the first match was to go ahead without interference from anyone on either side. But after that? Delilah felt beads of sweat along her back. This was *her* fault. *She* had emboldened Samson, convinced him of his invincibility. She couldn't help but feel he was doing this out of some misguided notion of impressing her with his bravery.

The rope was produced and laid out on the ground, and in a moment the wrestlers had picked it up and threaded it among them. Samson swung the rope easily over his head, wrapping it around his back and arm, and it was drawn taut. One of the judges drew two lines in the dirt between the two sides, then he tied a ceremonial belt around the middle of the rope.

'Pull!' he shouted.

The wrestlers dug their heels in and began to haul on the rope, a rhythmic chant rising up as they worked. The excited crowd quickly took up the mantra. At first, Samson seemed just to be holding the rope lightly in his fingers, but slowly Delilah saw his muscles firm across his shoulders, his legs brace against the ground and his grip tighten on the rope. The challengers pulled and pulled, their shouts growing louder and louder, but for all their effort Samson didn't move at all. Then with one sharp tug on the rope during a breath in the chant, he snatched them forward, pulling the front man over his line. The others tumbled into a heap after him.

Delilah wanted to rise from her seat in delight but the crowd had fallen silent with the wrestlers' defeat. Caleb was standing completely still among the Israelites. Were they simply going to wait and see what happened?

The wrestlers picked themselves up, shoving each other with fury at their easy capitulation. The next team rushed forward. They were a group of hauliers from the harbour who had borne the statue of Elat, Mother of the Sea. There was some jostling among the wrestlers and harbourmen, as the wrestlers felt cheated by their loss. It was Samson who snapped the rope to get the competition moving again. The harbourmen took his impatience as a baiting and grabbed at the rope, starting to pull before the judge was ready. There were seven in this team too, by the rules. The harbourmen were much taller than the previous opponents, and broader too. Again Delilah saw Samson's strength build slowly against them, his body tensing as he fought for control of the rope. This time he had to dig his bare heels into the dirt, the sand flying up against his firm calves as he moved slowly backwards. But once more, he dragged all seven over the line.

'A rematch!' bellowed one of the harbourmen.

The crowd bayed in approval as the wrestlers' team joined the line, and Lord Phicol nodded his assent at the judge. If he was angry, it didn't show in his impassive face. Delilah suspected there was more to this than met the eye. Samson merely shrugged and wrapped the rope around him once more, waiting patiently while the wrestlers and harbourmen organised themselves. Delilah couldn't believe how calm he was, how still and strong and deaf to the rising chants against him, like the huge terebinth trees standing tall against the winter winds.

'He'll feel it now,' said Jered, jumping to his feet and waving his fist. 'Go, boys, go!'

Pull, my darling, pull, she urged. *Don't let them beat you.*

Delilah's attention snagged on the end of her thought and she glanced at Jered. His charming boyishness was suddenly naive, his clear view of the world so irritatingly simple. Delilah was no politician, but she knew that Samson's fight for control of the rope meant far more than the right-against-wrong battle with the Philistines that Jered saw.

Delilah slipped out of her seat, and out of Jered's flailing grasp for her. 'I've no taste for such nonsense,' she shouted over her shoulder. 'Can you not find something more sensible to cheer?'

'But Achish told me you loved the Charioteers' Cup — '

'Then consider it spoiled by the Israelite,' snapped Delilah, gratefully slipping out of sight from among the rows of Philistine nobility who were all on their feet, hollering for blood.

There's something wrong about all this, she thought, peering through the crowd for an indication of what was going to happen.

The chants of the crowd were rising higher

and louder and Delilah felt her heartbeat quicken and her palms dampen as she looked around quickly. But the soldiers stood motionless in their cordon with their weapons raised, and Phicol still sat calmly on his bench watching the spectacle.

She climbed up onto the rear of the platform, which gave her the best view of Samson without being visible to Phicol. She could see Ekron looking around for her in the crowd, but she was concealed from sight back here. Samson didn't seem to be feeling the tension, though she could see that every muscle in his body was braced against the rope as he slowly hauled the two teams towards the line. Clearly it was harder work, for his glistening skin rippled with each step. Suddenly with a great holler of disappointment, the first of the challengers skidded over the line.

The crowd broke out in furious shouts, and the Philistine rope-men, buoyed by the support, suddenly lurched at Samson. The other Israelites saw the threat at once and weighed in against the attack. Delilah turned cold with panic.

Is that the plan? Phicol's going to let his people do the killing for him?

She hopped down from her vantage point and crawled between the crowds to avoid the arms that were now punching the air with encouragement for the fighters on the ground. She was quite close to Phicol now, and she could see Ekron's feet just a couple of bodies away from her. But what could she possibly do for Samson?

He and the others were outnumbered four to one.

She pushed her way to the right and emerged next to Ekron.

'I hope you're satisfied,' she said angrily. 'You'll get nothing from him if he's mauled to death.'

'You brought him here,' replied Ekron.

'No,' shouted Delilah, 'you brought him here, with your arrogance and your single-minded obsession with defeating him.'

A bloodcurdling scream rose up from behind Ekron and he glanced over his shoulder. Hemin was hollering from her stool, tucked down among the standing crowd that seethed around her. 'Help me!' she cried.

'Get her out of here,' bellowed Phicol when he noticed Delilah. 'And you,' he shouted at Ekron, 'get down there and make sure that thug is brought under control. He's a danger to my people.'

Ekron scrambled down off the platform, and Delilah moved down to the lowest level. Now nearer, Delilah could see how fluidly Samson was fighting off his attackers, and she felt a surge of confidence at the ease with which he seemed to be coping. His eyes were bright, his face composed despite the sweat that glistened on his forehead. Paradoxically, he was shielded from any fresh attackers by the moaning injured who were piling up around him where they fell. She saw that Caleb and a pocket of Israelites, their backs to each other, were fighting outwards into the Philistine crowd. There was another pocket there, and another. They seemed to have quietly multiplied while the attention was on Samson, and forty or fifty of them were now wreaking their own havoc among the crowd.

Delilah hardly knew where to look and she realised that if the crowd lost control she'd be caught up in the trouble. But where could she go? Ahead of her, Ekron was forcing his way into the tangle of bodies that surrounded Samson, adding his own fists to the barrage, but as Delilah looked around for a way out, she spotted a bright glint in the crowd to her right. One of the wrestlers who had not been in the first team was standing on the edge of the group, a knife clasped in his hand, its blade flat against the inside of his arm. It was concealed from most angles, but here, raised above the ground, she could just see the edge of it, picked out by the blazing torches on the front of the royal platform.

She was about to scream out to Samson when she felt someone squeeze her ankle and she looked down.

'Time for you to go.' Ariel was standing at ground level 'You should get out of here while you can.'

Delilah peered past him to see Jubal, Abidan and several of Samson's closest followers clustered beneath the awning at the front of the platform, right beneath the eyes of the royal party, yet almost completely concealed by the brawling crowd. She looked again and saw that the wrestler had begun to move towards Samson.

'How did you find me?'

'Never mind that,' grinned Ariel. 'Crawl out under the platform. It's going to get pretty bad.'

'That man has a knife,' she cried, pointing into the crowd. But the man had disappeared from view. 'I've lost him, oh Se't, I've lost him!'

'It's all right. Samson knows.'

But before Ariel could explain it, he and the others suddenly swarmed up around Delilah. She crouched beneath the platform for a moment, watching the tangle of feet and legs kicking at each other, trying to track Ariel's thin legs and Jubal's sturdy ankles among the crowd. It felt terribly wrong leaving them here, leaving Samson here, but at least now she knew he wasn't alone. Caleb would coordinate the Israelite unrest on one side of the military cordon, Ariel would extricate Samson, and the others would defend their departure. She felt sick at the roar of the brawl around her but she must let them do what they had trained for.

Somewhere above her head she knew Jered would be trying to explain her sudden departure to Achish, and that there would be considerable embarrassment for all concerned. She couldn't muster any sympathy — they shouldn't have sprung such a surprise on her. Beulah should have known her better than that.

Delilah crawled to the back of the platform then lifted her stole up over her head, twisting the length of ochre silk so it hid most of her now grubby dress. She closed her eyes for a moment, then let her feet take her west, towards the beach.

27

The waves, normally so soothing and peaceful, jarred at Delilah's nerves, their endless swishing against the shore reminding her only of how the night was dragging as she waited for Samson to return. Nowhere within the city would be safe tonight, and the guards would be searching the usual Israelite gathering places immediately beyond the city gates. But even at this little distance, her imagination conjured ways in which Samson could be captured, hurt, tortured or killed.

Fear was beginning to overtake hope. She thought she heard quiet laughter rising among the sand dunes, and listened carefully to the darkness. There it was again, unmistakeably laughter, light, teasing, welcoming in its familiarity. She quickly brushed the sand from her dress and moved quietly towards the beach hut. She began to make out voices speaking in Israelite.

Abidan and Jubal came into view.

'There you are!' said Jubal.

Delilah gasped. His face was covered in blood, and his hair stood up in uneven clumps.

'What happened to you?'

'He's fine,' said Abidan. 'But I'm very badly wounded.' He pushed his arm out towards Delilah and she saw four clear scratches running the length of his arm.

Delilah reached for him, but her tenderness was interrupted by Abidan's quiet laughter.

'A woman did that to me, can you imagine?'

'Was it Hemin?' said Delilah, smiling.

'No,' said Jubal. 'She just screamed constantly throughout from her throne. My head hurts.'

'Where's Samson?'

'He's coming by a different route. We took different ways here, just to be safe.'

'Was anyone badly hurt?'

'Mostly Philistines,' grinned Abidan.

'There you are,' said a voice behind Delilah. She turned to see Ariel, who had a handful of fabric pressed to his upper arm. 'Can you get me some seawater? I need to wash this wound.'

Delilah pulled him out of the shadows into the moonlight, easing back the cloth. The thick blood looked black and sticky. 'It looks pretty serious.'

'That was your knifeman.'

'He wasn't mine — '

Ariel put his hand on Delilah's arm. 'I'm teasing you, I just called him that because you identified him.'

'Does it hurt?'

Ariel snorted derisively. 'He was an amateur.'

'He still managed to nick you,' said Abidan.

'I'll get the seawater.' Delilah picked up a couple of pails from behind the hut door, then ran down to the water's edge where she swilled out the buckets. Then she waded out to the depth of her knees and filled the buckets from the free-flowing water that would be free of grit and weed. They were heavy, but she was used to

256

hauling wine jars around. She balanced herself carefully and headed back up the beach. She was so intent on her task that she didn't notice Samson until she was almost in front of him.

'Oh! Thank the gods.'

'Let me take those.'

Delilah pulled the buckets towards her, peering at Samson. His skin was marked with a few scratches and light cuts, and his shoulders sagged a little. 'You don't look too bad, considering.'

'Give me the buckets.'

Delilah shook her head. 'This is all I can do,' she said firmly. 'So let me do it, please.'

Samson looked her over, as though trying to work out whether he could carry her and the buckets. 'Your dress is wet.'

'It doesn't matter.'

'You looked beautiful up there in the stand.'

'I thought you hadn't seen me.'

'I see everything. Including the way Jered looks at you.'

'You know his name?'

'The market in Ashdod. Do you remember?'

Delilah laughed quietly. It was only a few months ago but so much had happened, so much had changed.

'Was anyone badly hurt?' she asked as she set off up the beach.

'Not really. My men are better fighters. It's easier to be quick when you don't have a weapon to think about.'

'And what about Caleb? I saw him in the crowd.'

'He won't come here tonight. I told him to regroup with the others outside the city.'

Delilah sighed, blowing some of the evening's tension into the breeze. 'I still can't quite believe that you marched into the centre of the square like that. You might as well have challenged Phicol directly.'

'He will have seen it that way.'

'How did you get out of the square, though? The place was full of Philistines.'

'You sound worried.'

Delilah stopped and turned to face Samson, the buckets slopping against her legs. They were behind the beach hut, and inside she could hear the boys joking with each other, comparing wounds and trading tales of combat.

'I thought you'd be killed.'

'It will take more than an angry mob to stop me, Delilah.'

'But how far will you go?'

'As far as is necessary. We must be free.'

Delilah put down the buckets and put her arms around him.

'I know Phicol,' she said. 'I know how far he'll go.'

Samson kissed the top of her head. 'And so do I.'

★   ★   ★

Samson insisted that she shouldn't linger among them, and it was with great reluctance that Delilah left before dawn. He pronounced himself reasonably certain that the soldiers wouldn't search so far from the city, given their arrogant and clearly false assumption that no one could pass through the gates without being observed, but his mood was cautious.

On her way back to the vineyard, Delilah wondered if his confidence had been shaken by the ferocity of the mob's attack on him. Perhaps she was simply seeing how seriously he took his mission. She'd heard his orations, seen his preparations and his prayers, but she'd never seen him after a full-scale confrontation between the two communities, and there was a clear shift in his mood that unsettled her. She couldn't define if there was a brooding anger, uncertainty or perhaps even fear, but something had changed within him. He'd allowed her to bathe Ariel's wound and bind it with clean cloth, then he took her hand and led her away from the hut.

'What about the others?' she'd asked. 'Will they come here?'

'Everyone will lie low now until the festival is over. We'll meet again soon.' He had kissed her deeply, then released her.

'When will I see you again?'

'I'll find you.'

'You dare not come into the city — '

'I will find you.'

Delilah took the long route around the city walls back to the vineyard. Despite the nearness of morning, there were still plenty of people around, and it was easy enough to mingle with the crowds without being noticed. There was blood on her dress from Ariel's wound and the hem was still damp from the sea, but given the state of disarray in which some of the young men staggered home, she was hardly likely to be picked out. There were soldiers everywhere, stopping men and holding their faces in the torchlight. Rumour of the evening's fracas would have spread quickly and she was quite sure that all the Israelites were already in their homes, waiting for the knock on the door instead. Phicol would be furious after last night's failed capture, and no doubt the city would feel the weight of his wrath.

And then there was Jered to worry about. At least he wasn't staying at the vineyard. Achish had arranged for him and Mizraim to stay in the city, so Delilah would have time to prepare to face him and his inevitable disappointment. There would be uncomfortable conversations with Beulah and with Achish, and she shook her head in frustration as she walked, hoping that her confused feelings would settle themselves. She was still formulating excuses for leaving the festival when she turned up the vineyard road, and her heart leapt when she saw a shadow hovering beside a tree just a short distance ahead. The sky was turning from black to indigo but there wasn't quite enough light to see anything clearly.

Delilah stopped for a moment, wondering if she should turn back towards the city. There was no one around at all, and Delilah couldn't remember when she'd last seen a soldier. It would be ironic to have to run for their help, tonight of all nights.

The shadow hovered still half hidden, and

suddenly Delilah felt all the evening's frustrations and fear bubble up to the surface. 'Who's there?' she shouted.

Ekron stepped out.

'What in the name of — ' She shook herself free of his grasp. 'What are you doing here?'

'I could ask you the same question.'

'I asked first.'

Ekron pulled a face. 'Waiting for you.'

'Why?'

'You left your guest at the festival. Father is angry.'

'Achish is no such thing.'

'How do you know — '

'Because I'm the one who spends time with him, Ekron.'

'He's *my* father — '

'*Your* father does not get angry. He gets frightened, anxious, uncertain but never angry. That's his biggest failing, not knowing when to stand up for what he believes in and constantly giving in to everyone else.'

'And what do you believe in, Lilah?'

'Don't call me that.'

'Oh, I do apologise. Anyway, if Father is not angry, then Lord Phicol certainly is.'

'I imagine so,' said Delilah, walking on up the road. 'He was made to look like a fool, and a fool can never stand to see his reflection in the mirror.'

'For an Israelite, you know the Philistine proverbs very well.'

'So I'm an Israelite now, am I?'

'When it suits you.'

'When it suits you and Phicol.'

'You took the silver without much thought. But I imagine your conscience is troubling you now. Samson was lucky tonight — '

'Phicol was careless,' snapped Delilah. 'He was arrogant and careless. Sending one man with a knife to take on a giant, relying on a bunch of badly trained citizens — '

'It's a fine speech,' said Ekron, 'but I don't believe a word of it.'

'You saw what he did,' said Delilah, stopping again. 'He didn't use his soldiers — and there were plenty of them — but he let ordinary people do his fighting. That's a coward's way — '

'It's our leader's way — '

'He's not my leader, Ekron, he's yours.'

'So you *are* an Israelite. I ask you again, whose side are you on, Delilah?'

'I don't have a side, Ekron, not like you. I don't need to hide behind someone else to know myself.'

'Oh no, you're a free agent now, you can be bought for any price. And what have the Israelites paid you to let them in on Lord Phicol's strategy?'

'Don't be ridiculous!'

'Have they won you over with their strong arms and their dark curly hair, their reckless charm and their easy talk beneath the blankets? Why didn't you stay to watch the fight, Delilah? Why didn't you stay to watch Samson triumph over us? Because you were afraid he was going to lose, you were afraid that we were going to capture him and kill him right there in a

Philistine arena. And you couldn't stand to watch your lover fall at our hands.'

Delilah strode away, her face burning, her nails dug hard into her clenched palms.

'Samson is in the city,' shouted Ekron, 'not the vineyard. Run to him, Delilah. Or would that give your newest loyalties away?'

Delilah made herself stop, her breath rising hard and fast in her chest. *He's taunting you because you've hurt him*, she thought. *He's jealous of Samson, that's all it is.* She turned slowly around and walked back towards Ekron. She could feel her anger shimmering around her, but she could no longer control it.

'I'm almost certain that it was *your* idea, Ekron, that I seduce Samson. You have been trying to get your own back ever since I climbed into Joshua's bed instead of yours — '

His fist hit her cheek so fast that Delilah's head jerked back before she realised what was happening. She staggered, her arms flailing around her, the stole catching around her ankles, then the ground rushed up beneath her.

Ekron darted forward, his other hand slapped against his mouth. He gazed down on her, his eyes wide, his head jerking from side to side in disbelief. Delilah stared up at him, too shocked to speak, her cheek already throbbing.

'In the name of El — In the name of El — ' he stuttered, 'I'm so, so sorry — ' Ekron seemed to gather his senses and offered his hand to pull Delilah to her feet, but she smacked his arm away.

'Stay away from me.'

Ekron crouched down in front of her, his eyes glistening wet in the moonlight.

'Please forgive me — '

'Go away!'

Delilah groggily pushed herself onto her knees, then stood up, brushing the dust from her dress and stole.

'Let me see your face,' Ekron reached for her again, but she flinched backwards.

'Don't ever touch me again.'

'Delilah, please — ' His voice choked on the words, and Delilah saw he was crying, the tears slicked around his miserable twisted mouth.

'Why should I, Ekron? You've never forgiven me for what I've done.'

'But I should, I can see that now.'

'And that means I should forgive you too?' she asked bitterly.

She turned towards the vineyard.

'Do you forgive me?' he called after her. 'Lilah?'

'Go back to Lord Phicol,' she said wearily. 'Go home.'

28

Delilah wanted to avoid the breakfast table at all costs, but she knew that if she put off facing her mother and Achish, it would only become more difficult. Leaving the festival was explicable, but the mark on her face would be harder to explain. She carried the mirror stone to the window and made herself inspect the bruise left by Ekron's hand. The obsidian was highly polished but dark, and it exaggerated the colour of the mark so much that she took a bowl of water to the window instead, and peered in its thin reflection to see if she looked as bad as she feared. It would certainly take a few days to heal, but she'd bee~ lucky that Ekron had not damaged her eye. T~ pain had kept her awake for most of the ni~ though she wasn't sure she'd have slept ~ anyway.

Achish leapt up from his stool as soo~ came onto the verandah, and walke~ round the table towards her.

'We were worried about — In the ~ gods, what has happened to you?'

Delilah glanced at her mother, ~ directly so that the bruise would ~ away. It was better to be open ~ seem innocent from the start.

'I fell at Lord Phicol's ~ guilty about abandoning H~ went over there, but there ~

265

I got a bit lost in the dark round the back. I tripped over by the gate, caught my face on the step.'

Achish lifted his hand gently to Delilah's face and patted the bruise with his thumb. 'I'll call the physician.'

'There's no need,' said Delilah, lifting his hand off her face and moving to within reach of her mother.

Beulah got up from her stool and looked carefully at Delilah's face. Delilah cast her eyes away from her mother's gaze, but she could feel the doubt in the way Beulah's fingers rested on her face.

'You see, I'm quite all right. I'll rest this morning with a compress of herbs on my face, and I'm sure the bruise will start to go down.'

Achish was hovering by the table, watching her anxiously.

'Are you sure that you fell?' he said eventually.

Delilah's heart beat jerkily in her chest. 'What do you mean?'

Achish sighed and moved to Beulah's side. 'We know that being with Hemin at the moment [is] not easy, and even Ariadnh has raised [con]cerns about how the pregnancy is affecting [He]min's senses. She's become quite wretched, I [und]erstand, and certainly last night she didn't [___] herself.'

'[W]hat Achish is trying to say,' said Beulah, 'is [if] Hemin has been suffering from her misery [and m]aking you share in it, you should feel able [to tell] us. We want to look after you both.'

[Delila]h felt relief flood through her. 'Oh no,

266

it's nothing like that at all. You don't need to worry about Hemin and me.'

Achish smiled, clearly comforted by her answer. 'I'm so glad. I know that you have not always got along well, but you have been very kind and understanding of her during her confinement. I'd be extremely distressed if I thought Hemin was punishing you for your kindness.'

Delilah sat down at the table. She filled a bowl with fruits and sheep's curd and drizzled some honey over the top.

'You don't seem to have lost your appetite at least,' said Achish. 'If you eat well, then the bruise will heal in no time. But I forbid you from working in the vineyard today.'

'But Achish — '

'No, I absolutely forbid it. Your face is tender and I won't allow you to be out in the sun.'

'Very well.'

Achish kissed his wife and his stepdaughter on their foreheads, then left the verandah. Beulah watched him go, but Delilah concentrated on the bowl of fruit. The easy part was over.

Her mother let her eat in silence, but Delilah could feel her scrutiny, and as she popped the last of the apricots into her mouth, her mother spoke.

'You spin a fine tale,' said Beulah quietly, moving to sit on the bench next to Delilah.

'What do you mean?'

'I'm your mother, and you cannot lie to me. I've seen many things, and I know the mark of a fist when I see it.'

Delilah sighed and lowered the bowl into her lap. 'You are not to worry.'

'I've learned to accept that you spend little time here now, that you have developed a life of your own and friends of your own and, what is more, that there is little future for Jered with you. I've always known your will was strong, and that to try to restrict your choice is both foolish and unkind. But I will counsel you strongly to leave any man who strikes you. If he's hit you once, he'll hit you again, and I know you well enough to be certain that such a relationship would destroy you. No man is worth such a sacrifice.'

Delilah smiled. 'I absolutely promise you that I'm not involved with such a man.'

Beulah narrowed her eyes. 'And for some reason I believe you.'

'I wouldn't lie to you about that.'

'You would merely lie about everything else.'

Delilah shook her head ruefully. 'I don't wish to worry you. I'm learning about what is important to me.'

'And what is that?'

Delilah put her bowl on the table and refilled it. Despite her exhaustion, she had indeed found her appetite and it probably helped to have some sort of activity to divert herself during Beulah's questioning.

'I wonder myself,' she said eventually. 'Isn't that the point of growing up, though? Not just to do what you are told, or what is expected of you, but to know yourself well enough to decide what matters?'

'I left those questions to your father,' said Beulah.

'And I don't criticise you for that. But I'm learning about my background — *our* background — and it is helping me see what is important to me. You know that I've never sat entirely happily in this family, even though Achish has been very kind to us and I've grown very fond of him. I'd never do anything to hurt him.'

'But?'

Delilah licked curd from her spoon. 'Why did my father never move back to Nahal Sorek?'

Beulah lifted her head in surprise. 'I haven't thought of the valley lands in more than twenty years.'

'Really?'

Beulah sighed. 'Well, perhaps once, when your father died. I wondered whether we would be able to bury him there, but there is little time in the burial customs to move a body any great distance, and Achish was so kind to me when your father was taken ill, I didn't think of it further.'

'So why didn't he leave?'

'Because of you.'

'I wasn't born then.'

'No, but we were just married and we were trying to have a baby. I had lost three babies before their time, and when I fell pregnant with you, your father had just decided to move back to Nahal Sorek to grow his own vines. But when I told him I was having a child, he put his plans to one side so that I could have access to

Achish's physicians, in the hope that this time the baby would be born alive. He was right to do it, and I've always been grateful.' She lifted her hand and caressed Delilah's hair, delicately pulling it away from the bruise. 'He gave up his dream to give you a future.'

'You must miss him.'

'I do. And Achish knows that. He misses your father too. Your father had a role much like the one you have grown into here, and Achish has always been very honest about how much he relied on your father and how much he relies on you.'

'Would you have gone to Nahal Sorek?'

'Of course. Your father knew that the worst of the battle between the Israelites and the Philistines was only just starting. He could see that a new leader was coming through the tribes and that people were steadily realising that they had to defend what was rightfully theirs. He took much criticism from other Israelites at times for his close relationship with Achish, and in truth he wanted to live in a place where that wouldn't matter, at least until after he had died. He believed that as a seafaring people, they would always favour the coastal lands and leave the inland valleys alone, but he suspected that eventually their greed for land would draw them in.'

'You sound like a politician. Don't let Phicol hear you talk like that.'

'I try to avoid letting Phicol hear me talk at all.' Beulah glanced at the bruise again.

'It wasn't he who hit me, I promise you.'

'He is the right height, and his temper flares like the desert wind. He was raging last night as I've never seen before.' Beulah was silent for a moment. 'Delilah, your father had a great vision for the Israelite people, and he believed that a time would come when they would free themselves from the Philistines. He had a lot of faith in this new leader I mentioned.'

Delilah watched her mother carefully, sure that she was speaking of Samson. 'That faith wouldn't have been easily given.'

'It would have to be a very special man to convince your father. He would have to be someone who had no fear for himself or for those who followed him. Your father was a good judge of character, and I'd hope that's a quality that he's passed on to you.'

'I hope so too.'

'No one would blame you for choosing to be loyal to your Israelite heritage, Delilah. It would be a difficult decision to make, and it will be unpopular among your extended family. But I believe you understand the risks.'

Delilah began to speak, but Beulah put her hand on her daughter's arm. 'Let me say one more thing. If you have chosen an Israelite lover, then there will be many men who will not only be disappointed, but perhaps very angry too. Revenge is in the air, Delilah, particularly after last night. It poisons those who don't have the strength to keep on a straight road.'

Delilah watched her mother stand up. She wanted to tell her that Samson was on the straightest road of all, that his courage and his conviction were the truest of any man. She wanted to tell her how when she was alone with him, their bodies wrapped around each other, nothing else in the world mattered at all. She wanted to tell her how happy she was, how frightened she was, how angry and confused she was.

But instead she lifted her cheek for Beulah to kiss it, and let her mother walk quietly into the house.

29

It took four long days for the bruise on Delilah's face to begin to heal, but after repeatedly packing the cheekbone with patches of crushed comfrey leaves, the bruise faded to a greenish-yellow. With a fine brushing of Egyptian face powder, it was almost concealed. Despite the aching misery of separation from Samson, Delilah had curiously enjoyed her enforced confinement at the vineyard, away from the fuss of the festival. Jered had come to dinner on the third evening with Mizraim, to celebrate the festival's end, but Delilah had refused her mother's suggestion that she plaster her cheek with powder.

'Let him see me as I am,' she insisted. 'Besides, I imagine his great passion for me has already begun to ebb away.'

In truth, Delilah had been dreading the awkwardness between them and as they were seated together at dinner, she made an extra effort to be kind to him, while restraining her usual flirtatious instinct. He was courteous and pleasant, but he was more wary than she had ever known him, talking only of neutral subjects and staying well away from politics.

'I've frightened you a little,' she said to him quietly as they made their farewells in the courtyard. 'I apologise if that made you uncomfortable.'

Jered smiled ruefully. 'I think I would bore you,' he said, raising his hand to stifle her objections. 'I'm a simple fellow, and I don't know that I can change.'

'I'll always treasure the bowl you gave me,' said Delilah honestly. 'And I wish you luck in finding a suitable girl.'

'Father tells me I'm very eligible.'

'And very handsome,' said Delilah, kissing the tip of her finger and resting it on his cheek. *Just not quite the right man for me.*

The right man was out there somewhere in the city, and every night Delilah sent a silent prayer into the dark that he was still alive and well.

Two days after the festival ended, Delilah decided her face looked almost normal enough to go into the city, and she knew she couldn't go another day without seeing Samson. He'd said he would find her, but while she was sure he wouldn't come to the vineyard, his absence had made her fearful for his safety. So she set off in the morning for the market, seeking talk of him at least.

The mood in the city seemed deflated by the end of the festival, but there was quite a bustle at the city gates. Chalked up on the wall was an official notice, around which a number of Israelites and Philistines were clustered. Delilah squeezed through the crowd, fearful of what news it brought.

It wasn't an announcement of Samson's capture at least, but something almost as bad. Phicol had ordered that anyone caught within the city walls in Samson's company would be executed immediately and without question, and he'd offered eleven hundred pieces of silver for Samson's capture and delivery, alive or dead, to the royal palace.

Delilah shivered despite the warm morning sun. It was clearly a message to her, as much as to the people of Ashkelon. To offer the same prize as he'd already given Delilah was intended to show her that she'd failed in the task for which he'd paid her. What was more, if she was now found with Samson, she would pay with her life. Phicol had her cornered. In order to prove she was eligible to keep the money, she'd surely have to ensnare Samson again, but if she did so, she'd probably be killed for being in his company.

Delilah drew her stole up over her hair and walked on. Normally she'd be happy to flaunt convention and show her undraped hair and face. But Phicol's notice had the desired effect, and she felt conspicuous and vulnerable. The soothing trip to the market would now bring no comfort at all, and had she not promised to run some errands for Beulah, she'd have turned immediately for home.

Sarai wasn't there with her stall, and the lovely Israelite woman who sold the bread was absent too. There were many more gaps between traders than usual, and Delilah suspected that many Israelites were simply staying out of the way until the trouble died down — if it ever did.

She did her chores quickly, diverting glances at her bruise with a charming smile, and was just congratulating herself on her efficiency when her stole got snagged on a trestle table as she passed. She tugged at it lightly but it wouldn't give, and when she turned to unhook it, she saw it was held in someone's hand. A huge man in a dark cape and oversized hat was sitting behind a table of cheeses, with her stole gripped in his fingers.

It was Samson.

Delilah suppressed her gasp of surprise, and approached the table.

'Have you any goat cheese?' she asked quietly.

'Not much call for it.' He paused. 'What happened to your face?'

Delilah sighed. 'Not here.'

'What happened to you? You never wear a stole.'

'And you never wear a hat. It doesn't suit you.'

'I need to see you.'

Delilah felt a welcome nudge of desire twist in her stomach, but it was edged with a different kind of desperation that wasn't welcome.

'It's not safe.'

'For either of us. Come to Onan's orchard.'

'Is he trustworthy?'

'Yes. Go to the lower gate, to the huts. We won't be seen.'

'Very well.' Delilah put a coin down on the table and picked up a cheese, then she nestled it into her basket and turned away.

★ ★ ★

She took the long route to Onan's just in case she was being followed, but somehow she didn't think Phicol would demand discretion any more.

276

His soldiers would attack on sight.

The huts were quite derelict, but Delilah could see new floorboards had been put down recently. Were there weapons hidden beneath? She found Samson in the third hut, farthest from the gate. He'd removed the hat and was running his hand over his hair.

He drew her to him as soon as she entered, and kissed her hungrily.

'I've missed you,' she said. They were perhaps her first truly honest words to him and she hoped it didn't show.

He kissed her again by way of answer, then cupped her face in his palm.

'Who struck you?'

'It isn't important.'

'It is.'

'Samson — '

'There are few people who would have had cause or opportunity to do it. Achish is too weak, Jered too afraid of you, Phicol has his own wife to strike, and then there is the wife herself — '

'Hemin is difficult, it's true — '

'And then there is Ekron.'

Delilah frowned. It was no good hiding it. If Samson knew her life well enough to assess the culprits, then he couldn't be distracted from the truth.

'What gave him the right to strike you?' Samson's voice was heavy with fury.

'It was an accident.'

'He's left the mark of his knuckles on your face, Delilah. This was no accident — '

'You sound like my mother.'

'Then she is truly wise. And he is a fool, a stupid little fool.'

Delilah lifted her own hand to stroke Samson's cheek and calm him, mirroring his hand on her face. 'He knows that.'

'He does not know his own mind, and that's a dangerous way to live. I should teach him a lesson about attacking someone who cannot defend themselves.'

'You will do no such thing,' said Delilah firmly. 'You are to stay out of sight. You wouldn't allow anyone to endanger the campaign against the Philistines with such a rash and petty revenge, and I'm applying the same rules to you.'

Samson ran his fingers tenderly over the bruise. It didn't hurt much any more, but here, in the dangerous heart of the city among his enemies, there was such openness in the way he looked at her; his love for her was so transparent, that Delilah suddenly felt great fear. He must know that she was now in as much danger as he was. The trust he'd always had was vindicated.

The hut was no place for intimacy of any sort, and Delilah had barely arrived when Samson sent her away again. But he made her promise she would meet him at sunrise in two days on the road to Ashdod. He refused to explain why but told her to ask Joshua to drive her out in the cart. She agreed, without thinking at all of the difficulties, and left him. Beyond the city limits, Phicol had no direct authority, so it would be safer to be with Samson out there.

★ ★ ★

278

Delilah's remaining errand for the day was far from pleasant. Achish had asked her to procure a package of dried herbs from the physician, which were meant to be effective for calming nerves. They were intended for Hemin, and Delilah had accepted her stepfather's request to deliver them personally — the gesture, as much as the medicine, was intended to have a soothing effect.

But Ekron would be there too.

Perhaps he'd confessed his deed to his employer. There would be a way for him to put it, no doubt, that cast him in a better light. His duty. Keeping the whore in check.

It was possible that she could get in and out of the house without seeing anyone except Hemin's nursemaid, but as she came through the back gate, she knew it was more than likely that Se't would have shaken up the cup of bones and cast her a bad throw.

And so it was, for Phicol was sitting in his courtyard garden, eating his lunch as he listened to droning advice from another politician. Ekron sat cross-legged on the floor, taking notes on a wax tablet. Delilah hesitated on the far side of the fish pool, but Phicol saw her and beckoned her over, shooing the politician away. Ekron got up to leave. Phicol snapped his fingers and Ekron sat again.

'We're honoured you have deigned to visit,' Phicol said to Delilah. 'We wanted to see how your face looked.'

At least I won't have to pretend, thought Delilah. She approached the couch on which Phicol was reclining, a plate of quartered figs

279

and cheese resting on his stomach. Delilah couldn't help thinking how like Hemin he looked, spread out on his back like that, but Phicol's manner dissipated any humour in the moment.

'The capture at the festival was a disaster,' he snapped, staring at her.

'Your Lordship is disappointed.'

His face said that he was furious, but his voice remained calm. 'I cannot divine how he managed to escape when he was surrounded by seventy of my best soldiers.'

'Perhaps Your Lordship's strategy is too organised. Samson has a talent for improvisation.'

'I don't want to hear how he amuses you in bed.'

Delilah ignored the barb. 'I meant only that Your Lordship has spoken many times of how unpredictable his attacks are — '

'I suggest you stick to your own area of expertise, Delilah. If you want to keep your money, you will arrange a seduction of Samson within the next three days that will not fail. I know that you have spent barely one tenth of your fee yet, so you will feel its loss all the more keenly when I take it back.'

'I've always delivered Samson as you requested,' she said.

'Your past achievements are irrelevant if you fail next time. Besides, I think Ekron has made our feelings clear.'

Her stepbrother shifted uncomfortably.

'He has,' replied Delilah.

Phicol chewed on a quarter fig. 'How will you arrange the seduction?'

'I'll inform Ekron of the details when I'm ready.'

'Not the granary again. Perhaps Onan's orchard.'

Delilah tried to keep any shock out of her face. Phicol seemed to know much more than she thought. 'Very well,' she said. 'In the meantime, I have a package for Hemin.'

'Let Ekron take it. Your face will upset her.'

Delilah thought it would probably delight Hemin to see the bruise her brother had left, but she walked back towards the gate, followed by Ekron. She handed him the package without a word, but he reached for her as she turned away.

'Don't touch me.'

He put up his hands. 'All right, I won't. But you need to understand that His Lordship is absolutely determined to capture Samson this time. If you don't do as he asks, you won't just lose the money. We will lose everything.'

'What do you mean?'

'Just that.'

'What? The vineyard, the land, the house? Is that it? He intends to punish our family for my failure? That's ridiculous and unwarranted. Your father has been a thoroughly loyal subject — '

'Don't underestimate Lord Phicol's determination to have his own way, Delilah.'

Delilah looked at her stepbrother. Something seemed to have broken in him since the night he'd struck her: he looked older than before; yet more vulnerable too. She knew she should feel

281

mercy or at least compassion, but that part of her was dead. He was genuinely frightened. And that frightened her too.

'It won't come to that,' she said.

'You'll do it? You'll give me the details of the place to find Samson?'

Delilah nodded. Lying was easier without uttering the words.

30

The watery sky was just tinged with the first red of the rising sun as Samson lifted Delilah onto the horse. He was shrouded in the same hat he'd worn in the market, but Delilah had been able to identify him from some distance away through the sheer size of his silhouette against the dawn.

'Where's Joshua?' he asked, as he swung himself up behind her. The horse was a huge pale stallion, and Delilah was small enough to sit within Samson's usual riding position, embraced by his legs and held firm between his arms.

'I sent him on his way. He's going to see his brother in Ashdod. He wasn't happy about leaving me in the middle of nowhere, but I didn't want him to see you.'

Samson gave the reins a swift shake and the horse trotted on. 'Who were you protecting, him or me?'

'Both.'

His quiet laughter shook her. The night had been cool and though the day would become hot again in a few hours, she was glad of the heavy woven wrap she'd layered over her plain blue dress. Samson shifted behind her and peered over her shoulder.

'No gold and jewels today?' he said.

'Last time I travelled out of the city, I was robbed by violent Israelites.'

Samson chuckled. 'I'd protect you this time.'

'Anyway, where are we going?'

'To the Sorek Valley.'

'You're taking me home?'

'To my home too.'

Delilah twisted so that she could see his face. 'We come from the same place?'

Samson smiled. 'Several generations ago, our families settled on the same plain. My mother still lives there.'

Delilah reached automatically for her hair, tucking it behind her ears, then fussed a little with the skirt of her dress. She had not eaten yet and her stomach churned.

'I wish you'd told me,' said Delilah. 'I could have brought something for her from the vineyard, a gift — '

'A gift will not change who you are, Delilah. She is an excellent judge of character, not wine, and besides, you don't need to impress her.'

'I'm quite sure you say that to all the young women you take to the Sorek Valley.'

Samson kissed the top of her ear. 'I've never taken a young woman home before.'

They climbed steadily up to a low rise. Delilah smiled into the sun that had begun to glow to the east, but she felt anxious nonetheless. If his mother was so insightful, perhaps she would sense immediately the duplicity in Delilah's past.

She slid her hands over Samson's on the reins. Out here, far from the city, far from their lives and all the claims upon their attention, far from everyone who would love or hate them, fear them or challenge them, life seemed so simple. They rode on in silence, turning towards the hills in the northeast, and she opened her eyes and her mind to him, to the tension in his arms as he held the reins, the feel of his chest against her back, the way his tunic stretched against his thighs, the thick twists of his hair that lay over his shoulder, tucked beneath the hat. She tried to remember every single thing he had ever said to her, and as they drew nearer to the valley, as the greener plains grew fat against the horizon and the sun lifted into the midday sky, he showed her the features of the land her family had once left behind.

It was already well into the afternoon when they crossed a river at a narrow point. The horse struggled over the rocky ridge that separated the plains to the south from the valley itself. On the far side, with the firm ground beneath their feet, Samson dismounted by a small settlement.

Delilah slipped off the horse too, and hung back as Samson strode through a sprinkling of tents that lay beside the river. When he saw that she didn't follow, he took her hand and drew her confidently through the people who had gathered quickly to welcome him. He knew their names, and greeted them warmly, clasping shoulders and hands, ruffling the hair of little children who threw themselves at his legs. But he didn't introduce Delilah to any of them and as they neared the last of the tents, the crowd drew back a little. Delilah could feel their curiosity, but she took a deep breath and focused her attention on a small woman who now came out of the tent, a broad smile on her face.

'I knew you would come,' she said, raising her

hands to her son's face.

Samson gathered his mother to him without a word, and buried his face in her hair. It was extraordinary to think that such a small, slender woman had given birth to this giant of a man, and Delilah was surprised too by how young she looked. She was surely at least fifty years of age, yet her hair wasn't yet entirely grey and her face had fewer lines than Ariadnh's.

'Azubah,' said Samson, drawing back from her. 'I've brought Delilah to meet you.'

The woman turned to Delilah and reached out for her hand. She squeezed it firmly, and drew Delilah closer, smiling warmly. 'You are Abner's daughter. I can see that very clearly.'

Delilah nodded in disbelief. 'I — Yes — But he died — Did you — '

'You must be tired from the journey. Come in and I'll make you something to eat and drink.'

She led Delilah into the tent, a structure of sturdy poles and draped red fabric pulled taut and pegged firmly into the earth. Delilah glanced back at Samson, who was gazing at her with such deep affection that she blushed. She'd been afraid that his mother would take a dislike to her on sight, but Delilah could see that her presence among people who loved him brought him the very purest joy. She felt breathless with his delight as she tore her eyes from his and followed Azubah.

Far from being gloomy, the far side of the tent was open beneath a cleverly constructed canopy that kept out the heat but not the light. It would be hard to rival the interior for comfort.

Cushions and blankets of all sizes and colours were scattered informally around the tent, and though it was empty of other people, it felt cosy and welcoming. Two sections were separated off with awnings and curtains hung from the interior frame, perhaps for sleeping areas. Though the river was some distance away, she could hear its gentle rushing. Delilah felt as though she'd travelled to another land altogether, somewhere even more peaceful than among her beloved vines.

Beneath the canopy stood a pair of cooking benches. Out in the open air, a fire crackled quietly. Opposite the benches was a wooden chest full of small wooden boxes and fabric pouches, and Azubah closed its lid as she passed.

'I hold the medicines for the people of the village. My neighbour's daughter is soon to give birth, and she's been in much discomfort lately.'

'Do you use chicory?' asked Delilah.

'Sometimes,' replied Azubah, pulling a clay pot of honeycomb from beneath the table. 'What do you know of it?'

'My stepsister is also with child and her physician suggested chicory root to ease her wretched temper.'

'You speak of Hemin?'

Delilah stifled her surprise and nodded. If Samson's mother knew of the failed betrothal, did she also know of the aftermath and her own part in it? She said, 'Our father bought some for her a few days ago but I don't know if it's helped at all.'

'Chicory can be used for that purpose, though

287

an infusion of goldflower is better, in small doses.'

'I've not heard of that plant.'

'The Philistines consider it a poison, because it can cause sickness in large doses, and also blindness. But it's very good for easing sadness. I'll give you some to take back for her. You should also take some poppy-blood. It will work well when she is giving birth to the baby, to dull her senses just enough to make the passage of the baby easier. If she is already miserable, the baby shouldn't draw in its mother's fury when it takes its first breath.'

Delilah smiled and wondered just what Samson had told his mother of Hemin. She'd judged the situation almost perfectly without having even met her, though Delilah wasn't sure exactly how she'd offer either of these potions when the time came.

She glanced back to look for Samson, but he was standing just outside the tent, talking with a couple of young men. They were evidently delighted to see him and Samson was laughing with them, gesturing with his hands.

'I expect they're talking about a pair of chacidhah birds that have come to nest on the river,' said Azubah, 'just beyond the village. When Samson was a boy, he had a fascination with them because of their great wingspan, and I remember him running along the river bank many times, his arms stretched out as though he would fly up into the sky after them.'

'Is this the bird the Philistines call ba-sheq?

The one that carries the soul of a newborn baby?'

'It is indeed. It's also known for its loyalty. When a chacidhah mates, it does so for life.' Azubah smiled gently and scraped some honey into a large flat bowl. 'It must be very difficult for you to know some of the traditions of both your cultures, but not enough of either.'

Delilah nodded. 'I feel I have come too late to understand my heritage.'

'You have the best teacher of all, though,' replied Azubah, looking past Delilah towards the tent opening. 'I was crossing this river at a shallow place further up the valley when the time came to give birth to Samson. My mother urged me to move to land, but I felt myself rooted to the spot. I lay down in the water for many hours and when he finally came, I felt the water flow right through my body and carry the pain away. Since that day, I've marvelled many times at how naturally Samson understands our people, where we have come from, what matters to us, how we live. He knows the surface of this land as well as he knows the palm of his hand, but he knows its history too, how our peoples divided themselves and yet what keeps them together.'

'He inspires great confidence among the Israelites in Ashdod,' said Delilah.

'I fear you may not see much of him while you are here. There is a dispute in the next village which he's been called upon to judge, and I think even Samson will find it difficult to knock any sense into them.'

'I've seen a certain amount of the knocking

too,' said Delilah, smiling.

'And he was such a small boy to begin with!' Azubah poured some water from a jug into the bowl of honey, then began foraging in a box on one of the benches.

'Can I help you prepare something?' asked Delilah.

'Do you know how to make his favourite drink?'

'I know the ingredients, but the recipe is a mystery.'

'Samson always claims no one makes it like I do, but that's the sort of flattery a mother is accustomed to from her son.'

'Then I'd be honoured if you would share the details. I wouldn't mind such a compliment myself.'

Azubah laughed quietly. 'I shall be happy to explain the precise preparation. But from the way he looks at you, my dear Delilah, I don't imagine you need any other enchantments to gain his heart.'

★ ★ ★

With Samson's reunions completed, they ate together in the tent, just the three of them. The meal was nothing like the complex arrangements favoured at Philistine feasts.

'I had hoped that you might enjoy some rest while we are here,' said Delilah, putting her spoon into her bowl. 'But your mother tells me you are called upon to judge a dispute.'

Samson smiled affectionately at Azubah, and

sliced a piece of meat from the freshly roasted lamb before laying it gently on her plate. 'I presume she's not told you that she is perfectly capable of judging the dispute herself.'

'Then she is the source of your wisdom?' Delilah winced, embarrassed by how thoughtlessly she'd spoken. She was so accustomed to teasing Samson and she felt so comfortable here, that she'd forgotten her place as the guest.

Samson raised an eyebrow. 'If that becomes known, then all my influence in these lands will fall away.'

Azubah smiled and patted her son on the arm. 'What he means is that because I hold the village medicines, people tell me their troubles. So I often know more about the dispute than the contesting parties will admit to Samson. I'd never interfere, of course. The ruling of a Judge finds its way into the customs of our people.'

'Which is why so many of the villagers seek my mother's opinion. I'd be far busier if she weren't here to sort out troubles before they start.'

Azubah looked at Delilah. 'That's exactly the sort of flattery I was speaking of earlier.'

Samson's mother began to gather the empty dishes together, refusing Delilah's offer of help, and carried them out of the tent. They were left alone together.

'You seem to belong here,' he said quietly.

'So do you.' She glanced up at him. 'I never want to leave.'

'Then don't hate me for having already made plans for our journey back. I must leave for the other village early, but will return in time so that

291

we can make it back to Ashkelon before nightfall. You will be home before you are missed.'

'I wish my mother could have come with us. It would be a different life for her here.'

And I have the money to make it possible, she thought. Her mind was suddenly filled with plans. Perhaps she should mention it when she got home, arrange for her mother to travel here. She caught herself: what sort of vain dreams were these? As if Phicol would let her take her ill-gotten payment and run away without delivering up the goods in return.

Samson interrupted her thoughts. 'I have a request.'

She glanced up quickly. 'Of course. What is it?'

'My father is buried a short distance from the village. I'd like to — '

Delilah leaned forward and took his hand. 'But as a Nazirite, you aren't able to visit his grave.'

Samson's face cracked with relief. 'You know about this.'

Delilah's heart swelled with pleasure at the way he smiled. 'I'll do whatever you need me to.'

Samson seemed about to say something, but instead he reached for her, sliding his fingers around the nape of her neck and looking deep into her eyes. 'A simple libation is all I ask — my father didn't take the same vows as me, and he loved the taste of honeyed wine.'

'I'll go in the morning while you are away in the other village.'

'It's where I wish to be buried also.'

She shook her head quickly. 'It will not come to that.'

Delilah crawled quickly across the blankets and tucked herself into his lap, encircling as much of him as she could in her arms. She wanted to hold on to him forever here in the comfortable, safe tent, so far from Ashkelon, so far from Phicol and Ekron and all the troubles the Philistines brought.

'It will not come to that,' she said again, more firmly, breathing the words into his chest as if they might somehow enter his heart and strengthen him too.

31

Delilah barely stirred when Samson left the tent before dawn, but the quiet rustle of the fire roused her some time later and she disentangled herself from the soft blankets. The morning clung chill and dank to her skin, and she wondered if unseasonal rain had come in the night. She pulled her dress on quickly, gazing down at the hollow in the bed where Samson had lain beside her. She reached for it, trying to find some memory of him in the cradle of their craving for each other.

Outside, Azubah was crouched beside the fire, poking at the embers with a stick. It had not rained, but the sky was cast seamlessly grey. Where Samson's mother had glowed in the delight of his return the previous sunny afternoon, this morning she seemed small and tucked in on herself beneath the weight of the cloud above her. Delilah hesitated by the tent, but she knew that Azubah had already sensed her presence, and instead she waited until the older woman turned towards her.

'I'm sorry we have to leave so soon,' said Delilah quietly. 'I'd like to stay longer.'

'I wish you would,' replied Azubah.

Delilah came closer. Azubah's face seemed to have aged too, as though she'd learned something in the night that had troubled her deeply. As Delilah searched her face for a clue to the burden she carried, Azubah reached for her hand.

'These are difficult times for our people, Delilah. They will not become any easier.'

'I know. Life in Ashkelon is very tense.'

'I don't believe that we'll be able to stay in the valley for much longer.'

'Will the Philistines try to claim this land again?'

Azubah tilted her head to one side, but didn't answer.

'Have you heard something?' Delilah gazed at the fire, seeking heat in the flames to warm her soul. 'Do you know of something that will help Samson in the struggle with the Philistines?'

'It has not been easy for you,' said Azubah. 'It's dangerous to be between two sides in a war.'

The older woman's gaze was so intense, Delilah wondered if she'd allowed her troubled thoughts to escape her lips in the night.

'What matters is that you have found the right path now,' continued the old woman. 'You were born to choose, just like your father, yet you have found the strength to make the right choice for yourself and your people.'

Delilah's mouth was dry, yet she couldn't take her eyes off Azubah. 'You fear for Samson,' she heard herself say.

'It's natural for a mother to do so.'

'No, there's something more — '

But Azubah stood up from the fire and went into the tent, returning a moment later with two small pouches, one of white cloth, the other of black.

'I know you are going to my husband's grave this morning, so I'll give you these before I forget. The white contains the goldflower, to ease Hemin's misery. Pour bubbling water over it and stew it until the water colours. The black pouch contains the poppy-blood. It's a powder so you can simply stir it into a drink. There are two doses here, so divide the powder in half and mix it with wine. She should need only one dose, but the second will help if the delivery is very long.'

Delilah stood up and. took the pouches from Azubah, tucking them into her purse. 'Is there something I should know about Samson, something that will help him if he is in danger?'

'Do you not trust him to be safe?'

Delilah's chest tightened as the memory of Phicol's fat face swam unbidden into her head.

'You said these are difficult times,' answered Delilah slowly. 'I know enough of the Philistines to be sure that their arrogance will only drive them harder. Lord Phicol is not as stupid as he seems.'

'Then pray for Samson,' said Azubah. 'That is what he'll do for himself. He trusts in God to show him the way, and you will have to learn to put all your trust in one God instead of in many.'

'Then I should begin at your husband's grave,' said Delilah quietly.

'Come,' said Azubah, holding out her hand. 'I'll show you the way.'

*   *   *

The ride back to Ashkelon lacked all the pleasure of the journey to the valley lands, and Delilah felt stiff and tired, her body jolted by every stride of the horse. Their departure from the village had been quick — the negotiation had taken longer than Samson had thought, and they had not lingered over their goodbyes. Azubah had kissed Delilah on the cheek, then held her son tightly in her arms. She made a mark on his forehead with her fingers, then turned away to her tent and Samson had not looked back either. As they cantered towards the city, Delilah felt his embrace was even stronger than before and though she felt safe in his arms, she couldn't stop thinking about how she was going to get around Phicol's demands. Despite Ekron's warning, she couldn't make the final deception that had been asked of her. She'd just have to return the money, find a way to earn back the silver she'd already spent, and —

'Delilah, I need your help,' said Samson, interrupting her thoughts. He hadn't spoken since leaving the settlement.

Delilah twisted in Samson's embrace to see his face. He slowed the horse and she saw they weren't far from where Joshua had left her the previous day. He was probably already waiting for her there. 'What is it?'

'I didn't speak of it before we left, but you should know of it now that we are returning. I suspect that someone among my followers is being threatened by the Philistines in order to turn their allegiance against me.'

'I'm surprised that hasn't happened before,'

she said, trying to keep the lurch of anxiety out of her voice.

'In these times of hardship,' he said, 'bribes are much harder to resist.'

Delilah tried to still her thudding heart. 'It would have to be quite a price to turn someone against you.'

'Treasure alone might not convince,' said Samson, 'but Phicol is clever enough to guarantee that a disloyal Israelite would be immune from execution also. For some, that might be enough.'

Delilah suppressed the memory of the shimmering pile of silver she had counted on Joshua's bed, fearing that its shine would show in her eyes. Samson was right: there were more powerful incentives than money; the silver had bought her services, but he'd steadily bought back her loyalty with different coin.

'So what do you need me to do?' she asked.

'Watch out for me. You don't know the men around me as well as I do, so you have none of the blindness of familiarity. Also, women have a tendency to observe the smaller details of a man's behaviour.'

Under other circumstances, Samson's words might have been humorous, but his need was clear. 'Do you suspect anyone in particular?'

'Everyone — '

Delilah swallowed her guilt silently.

' — and no one. That's the difficulty for me. I've known most of these men since they were children. I believe I know them as I would brothers. But in every basket there is a piece of

rotten fruit which can spoil the others. Surely those who have followed you so loyally wouldn't let hatred grow so quickly?'

'I hope you are right. But you have taught me a great deal about trust, and I wonder whether I've given it too willingly.'

Delilah swallowed down the bitter taste of fear. She'd definitely return the money to Phicol as soon as she got back, and deal with the consequences later. She'd move to the valley lands, bring Beulah with her, live with Azubah —

She squeezed his arm, so big in her tiny palm. 'I'll do what I can.'

'I worry for you too,' he said, studying her affectionately. 'What excuse did you give to Achish and your mother for coming away with me?'

'I didn't, I told them I was going to Ashdod.'

'To see Jered?'

'Not exactly. I said I wanted to see it for myself, alone, so that I could judge if I wanted to live there. I cruelly raised their hopes again, but — '

'So your family don't approve of your relationship with me.'

'They don't know about it,' she said quickly.

'Truly?'

'I come and go from the vineyard a lot anyway, there are always people coming in and out, so my movements are not noticed.'

'And what of Ekron? He watches you as a bird of prey hovers above a mouse in the sand.'

'Well — '

'Don't make excuses for him, Delilah. He is

not in control of his passion for you and such a man is a danger to everyone around him.'

Samson shook the reins to hasten the horse, and Delilah twisted forward again. She felt like the rope in the Charioteers' Cup, pulled taut between Ekron and Samson, but there was nothing to be done about it. She'd simply have to take the strain herself.

★ ★ ★

Joshua was waiting patiently by the cart when Samson dropped Delilah at a distance and galloped off. She made her way to the cart and climbed up.

'How was Ashdod?' he said sarcastically.

'Very pleasant,' she smiled back.

'I hope he's worth it,' said Joshua. He tutted to the mules and they moved off.

Delilah was weary and the jolt of the cart was soon rocking her to sleep. Joshua was good enough to travel in silence. But as they neared Ashkelon, he roused Delilah from her rest with a nudge in the ribs. 'I don't want to get caught up in that,' he said, nodding towards a large crowd funneling through the city gates. 'I'll cut across the fields towards the vineyard.'

Delilah's sleepiness was chased away by a feeling of unease. 'No,' said Delilah, leaning forward. 'I want to know what's going on.'

A ripple of shouting rose up from the crowd and as they drew nearer, they could see a cluster of Philistines hurling rotten fruit at a couple of Israelite farmers who had a cart of wares beside the wall. 'It's not safe,' said Joshua, turning the reins. 'Look at them.'

'I need to know,' said Delilah putting her hands over his and stopping the horses.

Joshua gave her a pleading look, but she didn't relent. 'Well,' he said, 'you're not going in there alone. There isn't a person in the household who would forgive me if anything happened to you.' He turned the cart along the walls and tied up the donkeys at a post, then Delilah let him help her down.

She pushed impatiently through the throng at the gates, for the crowd was big and yet no one seemed to know where they were all heading.

'Look at their faces,' whispered Joshua once they were through. 'It's like the Festival all over again.'

Delilah nodded. It reminded her too of the brawl that Samson's presence had caused, and the crowd was growing more raucous as they moved through the narrowing streets. There was a rhythmic chanting up ahead, but she couldn't make out what was being shouted, and the noise only echoed off the buildings like the swirl of the sea from deep inside a shell. Delilah glanced at Joshua, relieved he was wearing the uniform of a Philistine slave. He looked conspicuously Israelite, particularly because of his dark curly hair, but the Philistine skirt would show he belonged to her.

Suddenly the crowd stopped; its mass too great to move any further. They were near the temple. As Delilah looked around her for a different route, the bell began to toll, a single chime, over and over.

'Isn't that the sacrifice bell?' said Joshua. 'But the Festival is long over — '

Delilah pushed through the crowd, into a narrow alley and took a looping route to the south. She realised that Joshua was following, and asking her to slow down, but the sense of unease was growing with every step and driving her on. The streets that didn't lead directly to the gates were less busy and the bell tolled on, one chime for every five steps, as though it was pacing her journey. She took the narrow alley behind the Priests' House, opposite the temple. Here the crowd was at its most dense, and attention was focused in the direction of the temple steps. She managed to squeeze her way through near the front of the crowd.

'Like a bit of blood, do you?' asked one man as she nudged her way past. 'You're going to get an eyeful now. His Highness, the Great El, will feast well tonight.'

She saw the bloodied backs and arms first. Two young men, their wrists bound behind them, their ankles chained, were bent double on their knees, facing the temple in a metal cage. In front of them, the leaders of Philistine society so gaudily dressed in their finery on the temple steps. The contrast was shocking, the white shifts and glittering capes and headdresses against the raw torn flesh of the prisoners.

The bell stopped. Delilah gulped down the bile that was rising in her throat. What was happening here?

She was about to ask the person next to her, when one of the prisoners turned his head towards his companion as if to speak. Curly hair matted with blood, face puffed and scratched — such curly hair — the distinctive jaw —

Abidan.

Jubal.

They were to be the sacrifice.

32

Delilah traversed the edges of the crowd until she was alongside the temple steps, threading her way behind the cordon of soldiers who were standing in battle pose in front of the crowd, their weapons pointed in threat at the prisoners behind the bars. Her frantic thoughts snagged on every little detail. *There's nowhere for them to run to.*

Phicol stood at the centre of the gathering of lords, his tall headdress and ceremonial staff distinguishing him as their leader. Ekron stood in the row behind, his eyes bright, his tongue flickering against his lips. His thirst for blood was clear, but Delilah was more shocked to see Hemin in the party. She was nearest, propped up against a column, her belly distended beneath a yellow dress hemmed with black. She looked pale and tired, but her mouth was fixed in a smile and she smirked when she saw Delilah.

A guard stood in front of her.

'Let me pass,' she said.

The guard looked back, and Ekron nodded. He moved aside.

Delilah could almost taste the stench of sweat and blood that hung over the temple steps, and had to steady herself before she climbed them. She took a deep breath and squeezed along the back of the steps behind the dignitaries. One of the priests was reciting the sacrificial incantation, and she knew she didn't have much time. She grabbed Ekron's arm and pulled him round to face her.

'What have you done?' she shouted. 'These men are nothing to you.'

'Do you know them?' snapped Hemin from behind her. 'Are these your nightly suitors, so rigid with desire?'

'They're followers of Samson,' said Ekron, ignoring his sister. 'That's enough.'

'But they're nothing to you — '

'It's no good pleading their case with me, Delilah,' said Ekron coldly. 'His Lordship ordered their capture.'

At the sound of his name, Lord Phicol turned towards Delilah, his hands clasped at his waist, his fat face as cold as she'd ever known it.

'I thought you might turn up when you heard what was happening.'

'Let them go,' cried Delilah. 'They are good men, good young men, it's not them you want — '

'It's no good begging me for their lives, Delilah. If anyone is to do that, it should be Samson. But where is he?'

'You can take me — as his emissary.'

'Ah,' said Phicol. 'I've been waiting a long time to hear that.'

Delilah felt something wet on her cheek and she turned as Hemin spat again, her chin now unpleasantly wet and warm with her stepsister's venom.

'Israelite slut,' hissed Hemin.

'My dear,' cautioned Phicol. 'Try to find more

elegant language to use among our friends. I applaud the sentiment, but you need a more diplomatic turn of phrase.'

Delilah wiped her face with the end of her stole. Ekron was staring at her, then at Abidan and Jubal, back and forth as though he couldn't believe his eyes.

'You would defend them?' he asked, astonished. '*Did* you sleep with them as well?'

Delilah threw him an angry look and tried to move towards the boys, but Ekron grabbed her.

Phicol nodded. 'My dear, you can't help them now.'

Delilah shook off Ekron's grip and crouched quickly, peering through the row of lords to the prisoners. 'Abidan, it's me, Delilah — '

Both boys lifted their heads towards her, and she fixed on their eyes, trying to ignore the appalling mess of blood and bruises. 'I'll do what I can for you,' she cried desperately in Hebrew over the rising shouts of the crowd.

'And what exactly can you do?' asked Phicol in Hebrew, dragging her to her feet. He switched back to Philistine, smiling smugly at Delilah's surprise. 'You are not the only one to speak in many tongues. So my dear, will you throw yourself to your knees over these two villains?'

''But they're just boys — '

'They may be boys to you, but they have Philistine blood on their hands.'

'It's Samson you want,' she said desperately.

'But you won't bring him to me, will you? You created this, my dear, by refusing to do as I asked. This way, I know I have his attention.'

'But he won't bend to your threats and intimidation. Every one of the Israelites would give up their lives before they gave in to you.'

'All but one of them,' said Phicol steadily.

It was a moment before Delilah grasped his meaning, but eventually, reluctantly, she let him draw her attention through the Philistine guards to a man who stood in the shadow of the temple entrance. Caleb.

'It only took one, Delilah,' said Phicol in her ear. 'Just the right one.' He laughed, his breath brushing her cheek. 'I wasted my money on you, I admit it. I should have guessed that one of them could be turned.'

She shivered beneath Caleb's gaze, for where she'd expected malice, guilt, or even triumph on his face, she saw only the burning heat of lust.

'What did you promise him?' she made herself ask Phicol.

'Can you not guess?' he answered. 'The one thing he's desired all along. Jealousy is such a powerful intoxicant. Apparently he noticed you at Hemin's betrothal, and has been unable to get you out of his mind ever since.'

Delilah swallowed, her mouth dry. Yes, he had been there, hadn't he? The spokesman who disputed the dowry on Samson's behalf . . .

'And as I already own you too,' continued Phicol, 'his will be an easy fee to pay.'

Delilah shook her head in disbelief, but became very still as the pieces from the more recent past fell into place. Caleb's shyness around her, the way he looked at her — that first time in the tavern, on the way to the roof terrace, in the orchard, across the crowd at the festival. How had she missed it?

'Well, now that you are here, Delilah, you can join us,' said Phicol. He gestured to the balcony and his private guard formed a cordon to the steps. Delilah backed away but Ekron gripped her arm.

'Let me go!' she shouted, wrestling against him, but Ekron's grasp was firm and it was pointless to struggle.

'My dear,' said Phicol. 'You are practically the guest of honour.'

He led the way through the cordon, followed by the other lords, then by Hemin. Ekron kept his hand tight on Delilah's elbow until they had passed, then he led her past Caleb and up the stairs. As they climbed, a rush of cool air flooded around them. Delilah wanted to ask Ekron what was happening, but she refused to show him her uncertainty.

But as she reached the balcony Ekron thrust her forward in front of Lord Phicol. 'You will witness the consequences of your actions,' he said. 'If you'd done what you were paid for, only one man would have died.'

Delilah lurched back from the edge, but Ekron dragged her upright next to Phicol and stood behind her, his hands forcing her arms against her sides.

She looked down at the boys. She knew Abidan was on the left, but the violence of their capture had levelled their looks, and they were distinguishable only by their build. Tears welled in her eyes, and Delilah desperately tried to picture Abidan's beautiful untroubled smile, and the way Jubal's crooked nose would wrinkle when he was thinking.

With an ominous metal clanging, the discordant torrent of jeers suddenly grew into a long high holler, the Philistine cry for sacrificial blood. Delilah waited for the executioner to appear on the steps, but suddenly the crowd's cry was swollen to dreadful depths, angry and low, and the temple vibrated beneath her feet. The noise fell away leaving a terrible sound. The roar of a creature, rising up around them all. Now Delilah understood the cage.

She swallowed hard against the fear that was threatening to choke her.

'Not this,' she whimpered. 'Please.'

Ekron's hands tightened their grip, and his breath was sour on her neck.

A Philistine soldier used a rope to lift the doorway to the cage. Abidan and Jubal must have known what awaited them, for they struggled upright together, their hands clasped in that familiar way Delilah had seen so many times before.

Delilah turned to Ekron behind her, his face unreadable.

'Is this what you have become?' she said.

But his answer was lost in another terrifying roar and Delilah glanced down to see a lion walking calmly between four handlers. They each held long catchpoles with the nooses secured around the beast's neck. They steered the lion towards the open gate.

The crowd remained silent.

As the nooses released in turn, the lion stepped inside, and the gate fell closed. The beast paused for a moment a pace or two from the boys, as if suspecting some sort of trick. Delilah found a prayer on her lips. *Spare them, God. Spare them.*

But someone broke the silence of the crowd with a howl, and the others took up the cry. The lion leapt at Abidan, raking with its paws. Though Jubal swung his bound fists at its face, he couldn't keep it off his friend. The lion knocked him back with its claw, tearing deep into his chest, and Jubal cried out in agony. Abidan had sagged to his knees, and in the blur of golden fur and blood, she saw the lion take his arm in its teeth and tear it from the shoulder like breaking bread. The limb swung uselessly from the wrist binding. A final clamp of its teeth at his throat and Abidan was dead.

Jubal was lying back on the ground, his chest rising and falling under a slick of blood. He turned away, shielding his eyes as the lion came at him. His screams died quickly as the lion shook his life away too.

Delilah snatched at the end of her stole and shoved it into her mouth to stifle her retching, but she couldn't stop the tears that were pouring down her face. She blinked and blinked to keep her eyes clear, but the temple steps were soon awash with blood and broken bone and it became impossible to discern two lifeless bodies among the torn flesh that so fascinated the lion. Phicol suddenly threw his staff onto the top of the cage and the lion, momentarily distracted, looked up. Its face was matted dark with the blood of its victims, and Delilah had seen enough. She jerked herself free of Ekron's grasp and ran down the stairs. Two soldiers caught her up, but she heard Phicol tell them to let her go.

Delilah tried to run back to the city gates, but her tears made her choke. She staggered and stumbled along, too blind to notice Joshua until he'd grabbed her arm.

'Come with me,' he said.

Delilah tried to answer but she couldn't get the words out and she let Joshua lead her to the cart. The crowds could still be heard baying behind, and they met no resistance leaving by the city gate.

They rode away in silence, Delilah racked by a sobbing she couldn't control. In time, she ran out of tears, then, as they turned onto the vine-yard road, she became aware of something moving in the cart behind her. She turned to see Ariel peering out from beneath a bundle of awnings.

She reached for him, so alive when the boys were now so horribly dead. 'How — '

Ariel pushed back the awnings a bit further. 'I was outside the gates, trying to find out what was going on, and I spotted your driver. I hid in the cart when he went back into the city to get you.'

Joshua pulled the cart up beside a tree and hopped down beside the donkeys, fiddling with their harnesses so as to be out of earshot.

Delilah glanced back at Ariel, but the pain in his eyes was so fierce she had to look away. 'You know it was Abidan and Jubal.'

'I knew they'd been taken. They were captured

at Onan's orchard. I got there too late to help.'

Delilah swallowed and looked up again. 'It's meant as a message.'

'I'll tell Samson myself.'

'Take me with you. I can tell him what Phicol told me.' She sighed. 'And I can tell him which of his followers is responsible.'

'This wasn't just a lucky arrest?'

'Caleb gave them up. Phicol has bought his loyalty.'

'Caleb?' Ariel shook his head. 'Are you sure?'

Delilah nodded. There was nothing more she could add without revealing her own part in the dreadful corruption. She could only hope now that the truth would stay hidden with Caleb, well out of Samson's reach.

Ariel jumped swiftly out of the cart. 'Go home. I'll come and find you in a few days.'

'Tell Samson — '

But Ariel had gone down an alleyway and was already out of sight. Joshua hesitated for a moment, then climbed back on the driver's bench, urging the donkeys on again.

'Is he with Samson?' he asked.

Delilah couldn't bring herself to answer, but Joshua nodded to himself. 'If I had to give you up to someone, it would only be Samson,' he said quietly.

Delilah knew she should acknowledge him somehow, but she barely had the energy to sit upright in the cart. And she still had to face her family, face their questions about the imaginary trip to Ashdod, and the rumours that would swell up quickly from the town. She had to find

312

composure she didn't feel and strength she thought she'd never know again.

★ ★ ★

Sleep wouldn't save her from the misery of memory, and in the light of early morning Delilah fetched her own water for a bath, sponging herself over and over so that the smell of blood might leave her skin. But even in clean clothes, she couldn't rid herself of it, and she took her blue dress and stole to the kitchen and threw them in the fire. They were the same clothes in which Samson had held her only yesterday, but she couldn't bear to see them ever again.

Beulah found her down by her father's grave a short while later. She kneeled down beside Delilah, twisting her daughter's hair gently in her hands until Delilah leaned into her shoulder. There were no tears left, only the dreadful dullness of loss. Beulah stroked her hair and waited, and eventually Delilah spoke.

'I want you to come with me to the valley lands.'

'Our lives are here, Delilah, with Achish.'

'This is no kind of life for us. You know how Phicol treats the Israelites.'

Beulah's hand stopped against Delilah's shoulder. 'We have to trust Achish to look after us.'

'I trust no one any more. Phicol is capable of anything.' She sat up and looked at her mother. 'Please. Come with me. There is somewhere safe

313

in the valley lands that we can go. Think of it as going home, for Father.'

For a moment, Delilah thought she would agree, but the flash of surprise hinting at a long-imagined possibility, quickly dissolved into that old cautiousness that had been her mother's habit since her father had died. It would take a more reasoned argument to convince her, but as she tried to form it into words, she saw Joshua hovering at the edge of the vineyard, clearly waiting for her. Beulah noticed him too, and politely left them alone.

'Your friend,' said Joshua, 'the one you saw yesterday — '

Delilah nodded. It was better if he didn't know Ariel's name.

'He asked me to tell you. The lion is dead.'

'By Samson's hand?'

Joshua nodded. 'Your friend didn't see it happen, but rumour is flying all over the city. The lion was found at dawn outside the temple, its throat cut with a sharpened jawbone from a donkey.'

Delilah winced. She feared for his state of mind. How had he managed to even get close to the beast?

'There's more. A message was written in Hebrew in the lion's blood across the temple altar.'

Delilah gasped. Such an insult was hard to fathom. 'What did it say?'

''This lion died at the Hands of God, this jawbone is the Weapon of God. You will be vanquished by the Spirit of God.''

33

Delilah hardly left her room for three days. She was tortured by images from the temple steps, and with her fears for Samson, who was surely either paralysed or rendered reckless by his rage. The timing of the events at the temple meant that Achish had no interest in questioning her about the trip to Ashdod, so she'd escaped that inquisition, but that trivial lie seemed insignificant beside the appalling truth she was now facing. Though the streets of Ashkelon would be full of jubilant Philistines, energised by the execution, the vineyard was contrastingly subdued. Even from the safety of her room, Delilah could tell that Achish was disturbed by what had taken place.

Beulah tried to explain his thoughts to Delilah the evening after the execution, when Delilah had stayed in her room instead of coming down for dinner.

'He understands the political reason,' Beulah said, 'but not the inhumanity of it. Why make such a public spectacle of these two men?'

'They were hardly more than boys,' murmured Delilah from beneath a mound of blankets. The weather had turned hot again but she couldn't get warm.

Beulah reached for her daughter's hand. 'Achish couldn't possibly understand the burden you carry,' she said carefully, 'but he'd want you

315

to know that he is thoroughly distressed by the way the city is changing. He's always treated the Israelites with fairness and equality — '

'He didn't stand up to Phicol when he should have done,' said Delilah angrily. 'No one has. Phicol bears the responsibility for Abidan and Jubal's deaths, but every Philistine is responsible for the reasons.'

'You know their names,' said Beulah quietly.

Delilah turned over in bed, dragging the blankets around her head. 'I knew them and I loved them.'

'Delilah — '

She suddenly pushed herself upright. 'And what of you, Mother? If you won't leave the vineyard, what will happen to you when the Israelites are driven from these lands?'

'It will not come to that.'

'I don't know how you can be so sure.'

Beulah left her alone after that, and Delilah was guiltily glad of it. But over the days that followed, her desire to confess it all to her mother was replaced by agonising over what Caleb's next move would be. Surely Philistine soldiers would be scouring every hiding place Caleb had told them about.

And there was still a tiny, selfish thought that shamed her: with Caleb in Phicol's hands, would Samson learn of her own treachery? Not for the first time, she felt utterly powerless, trapped in a web of her own making. However much she wanted another confidante, she couldn't bring herself to tell her mother; the shame — the details of the tawdry bribe, the betrayal of a

316

Judge of the People — it would be too great.

It was no use to sit in the vineyard house and fret over it. She had to do something.

She was pacing irritably up and down the vineyard rows on the third evening, trying to work out the possibilities, when Joshua ran to join her.

'Your friend has sent a message.'

'Ariel?'

Joshua nodded. 'He asks you to come to the slums southeast of the city, at once.'

Samson had asked for her. At last.

Delilah turned quickly for the house, Joshua trailing behind her.

'There are some bags in the eaves,' she said. 'They contain money.'

'The bags I'm not supposed to know about?'

'Take some for yourself, a hundred say.'

'Delilah — '

'I mean it. Get it to your brother or hide it somewhere, whatever you want. Just take it. Bring me a hundred too.'

'Very well. I'll find you at the olive tree.'

Delilah dressed quickly in her room in a plain flax-coloured shift and stole, then ran down the backstairs to the courtyard behind the servants' quarters. Joshua gave her a small fat pouch, which she tucked into her purse, then she kissed him quickly on the cheek and ran through the vineyard and onto the city road. After a short while, she veered off onto open ground, crossing towards the sprawling Israelite settlement that had grown outside the city walls. Instinctively she glanced over her shoulder from time to time.

317

Your conscience is trailing you.

She slowed as she reached the outermost shacks and tents, and made her way cautiously between the clogged, makeshift houses. How would she find Samson in here?

Ariel suddenly stepped out ahead of her, and clasped her hands between his.

'Thank you for coming,' he said. 'It cannot have been easy.'

Delilah felt her tears well up again unbidden and reached for the purse. 'I have some money I want you to distribute where the boys lived,' she said.

Ariel looked inside.

'There's so much here, how did you — '

'It doesn't matter. Just see it does some good.'

Ariel tied the pouch onto a belt under his tunic, then nodded further into the settlement.

'Follow me.'

It was unfamiliar, and she felt uneasy among the ramshackle alleys. In the dusk, it was hard to tell where they were, but Delilah could smell baked bread, and the sourness of a laundry. She squeezed after Ariel through a narrow channel between walls, and found herself in a small square space crowded with men, most of whom she recognised from the tavern. Samson stood across the room, his arms folded, and though he made no outward gesture of recognition, Delilah felt a sudden rush of relief flood between them as his eyes briefly met hers. Had he doubted seeing her again, as she'd doubted it herself? Ariel led her to Samson's side, and settled her on a stool. Samson didn't look down again at her,

318

but she knew immediate comfort at being with him again, even in such circumstances as these.

The mood was oppressive with grief and anger, and in the light of a single rush lamp, Delilah could see that several faces were wet with tears. She realised this must be the first time they had met since the deaths of their friends, and more so, that they had been waiting for her. For a while no one spoke but eventually Ariel cleared his throat and spoke.

'Did you decide what is to be done about Caleb?'

'Nothing,' said Samson.

'But he knows so much about us, about you — '

'There is nothing to be done.'

'You should at least find a new place to hide out in the north.'

'What would be the point?' asked Samson, his voice bereft of its usual richness. 'If he knows me so well, he could easily guess where I am.'

'Then let me kill him now. That way he can't be of any use to them.'

'And how will you do that?' Samson stood up, dominating the crowded space. 'No. Our only choice is to fight on, and assume our enemy knows us better than he did before. Caleb is nothing now.'

'But he lives!' said Ariel.

Samson turned to him. 'None of you are to risk your life for his. I absolutely forbid it. I won't lose any more men for his one damned soul.'

Shortly afterwards, the meeting broke up.

Samson's orders were for all to lie low for the immediate future, and to await his instructions. The room emptied with the men clasping each other, then leaving in grim silence. After they had gone, Delilah saw that this square space between four shacks was a makeshift home, with a bed and a small hearth in the corner, ventilated by a tiny hole in the roof.

'Have you been living here?' she asked quietly.

Samson shook his head. 'I'll stay here tonight. Tomorrow I will move on.'

Delilah crossed to where Samson stood, gazing up through the hole at the sky. She slid her hands up over his back, then down his arms. She could feel the tension in his body, and there were bandages on both his arms.

'You killed the lion.'

'My God possessed me with his rage,' said Samson.

He put his arms around her, as if to hide the sight from her eyes. She gave herself to his embrace.

'You feel trapped here,' she said.

'I feel trapped by my own stupidity.'

'You knew someone was going to betray you, you told me so yourself.'

'But I should have known it would be Caleb.'

She swallowed. *I could tell him now*, she thought. *We're alone.* Instead she simply said, 'Why?'

But Samson only stepped away and unbuttoned his tunic, letting it fall to the ground. His body was as strong and proud as she'd ever seen it, but something in him seemed broken, like the

320

dying trunk of a vine that still carries fruit. Delilah unfastened her stole, then drew her dress off over her head, moving quickly to press her bare skin against him.

They stood for a long time, kissing in the shadowy room, the murmurs of the settlement falling like dead leaves around them, rediscovering each other's bodies after what felt to Delilah like several months apart.

As he entered her, he shuddered and she closed her eyes, only opening them again when she felt wetness across her skin. He wept silently, but with no shame, letting his tears fall on her face, her neck, her breasts, his quickening breaths catching on his grief. Delilah concentrated all her attention on lifting him from his misery into the solace that intimacy brings. She wanted to cry herself, but she knew to do so would leave her a dry husk of guilt. If only she had the words to make him understand what she'd done, the awful path she'd trodden. But there were no words, and even as she tried to form them, she realised they'd never be uttered.

She'd care for him tonight, attend to his desires and his needs, allow him to possess her as though she were the strong one, the one who had managed to escape the horrors at the temple. But as the welcome surge took her as well, she understood. He was trying to erase her memories as much as his own, as if their shared passion brought some absolution, temporary at least, for the sacrifice made by Abidan and Jubal.

★ ★ ★

Some time later, Delilah got up from the bed to pour water into a drinking bowl, and found a pouch resting against the ewer.

'What's this?' she asked quietly.

Samson raised himself up on one arm on the bed, and lifted his hand to his head. He pulled off the leather band that held back his plaits then, one by one, released the small leather straps that tied the ends. The ritual of the unravelling held Delilah transfixed in the shadows. He ran his fingers through the unbound plaits, loosing the great mane against his shoulders.

Delilah knew his wordless actions invited her to approach and touch his hair for herself, but she still hesitated before crossing the room. He'd barely touched the plaits in her company before, yet now he laid his hair out before her. Finally she went to him, standing between his legs as he sat on the edge of the bed, drawing his hair over his shoulders. She trailed it over her arms, feeling its weight, its richness on her skin, pushing her fingers through it from his scalp right down to the tips. It felt so alive she wanted to wrap herself in it, feel its embrace, yet she hesitated to do so. For all the luxuriousness, the intimacy, she knew this moment was more than bodily seduction; his untethering was a sacred act.

She went to the ewer and emptied it into a large deep bowl, then brought it back to the bed. Samson lowered himself to the floor, kneeling in front of the bowl and Delilah silently drew the hair into the water, running through it with her fingers, cupping the water over it until slowly it grew heavy and wet. He was so vulnerable, bent over like this, his sacred plaits unbound and sodden. He was blind to the world, trusting her completely. She felt the weight of the responsibility as though his wet hair lay on her own shoulders. And then, slowly, he slid his hand beneath the hair and swept it back over his head, water coursing down his body in rivers, the hair snaking against his flesh.

She handed him the pouch and he poured a soft, sweet-smelling oil from a silver vial into her cupped hands. She began to draw it through his hair, pushing her fingers through again and again, rhythmically stroking it, left and right, until the water began to seep down into the bed and the hair began to soften beneath her touch. She was reaching around his neck to draw the hair over his shoulder when she felt him grow tense against her.

He snapped his finger to his lips and stood up, but Delilah could already hear the rattling of the walls, and in a moment the room was flooded with light. She darted for her clothes but before she knew it she'd been lifted onto the bed and was standing behind Samson.

'Have I interrupted something?'

Delilah peered at the voice. Lord Phicol was standing in the centre of the room, his face illuminated by the glare from a rush torch, held by Caleb.

34

There were soldiers too. At least ten, clustering around Phicol.

There's no way out of here, thought Delilah desperately.

The crackling of the torch was the only sound in the room. Samson hadn't moved since Phicol and Caleb had burst in. His eyes were fixed on his betrayer.

But Caleb was staring at Delilah, as was Phicol, their eyes sparkling in the torchlight. Phicol didn't bother to restrain his curiosity at the sight of her naked body, his tongue flickering over his lips. Caleb's eyes swam over her, drinking her in.

Samson held out his arms. 'Well?'

'No!' said Delilah. She threaded her arms over Samson's shoulders, to pull him back. 'You can't!'

Phicol gave a wheezing chuckle.

'Will you submit to me, Samson?' he said. 'If you do, I'll let her go unharmed.'

Samson took a deep breath. 'Your promises are like dandelion blossom. They will disappear in a breath of wind.'

'Take them!' said Phicol.

The men didn't move.

Samson crossed the floor quickly, and snatched the torch from Caleb, dousing it in the water bowl. The room plunged into moonlit shadow.

Then, with a great cry, the walls seemed to be torn away, and suddenly the night air was all over Delilah's skin.

Samson's men swarmed in and fell upon the Philistines. They carried makeshift weapons in their hands: cooking pots and wooden posts.

Delilah leapt away off the bed and grabbed her dress from the floor. She pulled it on and jumped aside as one of the Israelites collapsed beside her, his face covered with blood. There were writhing, kicking bodies everywhere, and the air was filled with screams and furious cries. But the fight was turning against the Philistines. Their swords were snatched and plunged into them, their legs were knocked out from under them. Howls echoed as they were dragged out into the darkness of the settlement.

Delilah saw Caleb crawling along the floor towards her, oblivious. She stepped quickly forward and kicked him hard in the side of the neck with her bare foot. She grimaced with the pain of it, but Caleb turned over onto his back, groaning.

Phicol was backing away, but he was easily surrounded by Ariel and two of Samson's other followers, the brothers Micah and Tomer. The remaining Philistines were finished off on the floor or fled.

Samson came to Delilah's side.

'Are you all right?'

She looked at the ground, awash with blood and a carpet of dead or dying men.

'Are you hurt?' he said.

The others were tying Phicol to the pole that

325

held up the canvas roof.

'We should kill him now,' said Tomer, drawing his knife. Phicol's face wobbled with fear.

'No,' said Samson. 'Leave him here.'

Micah's face was aghast. 'What?'

'It's this one I want,' said Samson.

Beside him, Ariel was hauling Caleb to his feet.

There was a burst of noise from some distance away. Men shouting, and someone asking, 'Where is he?'

Ariel grabbed a sheet from the bed and threw it at Samson. 'We have to leave now!'

Samson tied the sheet around his waist, and took Delilah's arm. She saw her purse on the ground. There was hardly any money in it now, and she knew Phicol was watching her. With the reprieve from Samson's own lips, his colour had recovered a little.

'If you go with him now, you can never come back,' he said.

'I wouldn't come back anyway. How could I pretend to be a Philistine when you are one? You are tearing these lands apart — '

'These are our lands.'

'They have never been your lands.'

'If you cross me, you will regret it.'

'I'm no stranger to regret.'

Delilah followed Samson from the wreckage of the hut.

★   ★   ★

Delilah hadn't known there were caves anywhere near Ashkelon. As they clambered over a hilly

326

rise she smelled the sweetness of wet seaweed, and saw the shimmering sea spread out below.

'He must have followed you,' said Samson. 'We should have been more careful.'

Delilah let herself be pulled along. Her mind turned over the situation, leaving her stomach hollow. It wasn't herself she feared for now, but her family. Beulah, Achish, even Ekron. Surely Phicol's threats to them were empty — they were Hemin's family too, and respected members of the community.

Samson led her down a steep path towards the beach, where the air grew damp and still. A vaulted cave opened up into the rock, its depths only hinted at by a couple of rush torches. The place looked empty at first but then Delilah saw Micah and Tomer at the rear of the cave, and between them Caleb, sitting completely still on a rock. As they drew closer, Delilah caught the glint of metal and realised that a blade was resting against his throat. It was held by Ariel, a still and ghostly executioner.

Delilah hesitated behind Samson in the mouth of the cave. She'd thought Caleb would pay for his betrayal elsewhere, out of sight, not in a safe Israelite hideaway. But here he was, shattered by his capture but very much alive. Samson would surely want to know the depth of his treachery. Suddenly she wanted to run away. Faced with certain death, Caleb would be quick to give up anyone who could share the blame. She drew her stole tightly around her but the shivering came from deep inside her.

'We waited for you,' said Ariel from the shadows.

'Does anyone else know he's here?' asked Samson quietly.

'No. I thought it better this way.'

Samson stood in the centre of the cave, his head almost touching the stone ceiling. That broken man Delilah had tried to heal just a short while earlier had rebuilt himself in the wake of the fight. He stood unchallenged at the centre of his court. The ghosts of Abidan and Jubal stood beside him. Caleb had no allies in this place.

'What happened to your faith?' said Samson to Caleb. His voice was low but it filled the whole cave. Caleb looked up, but didn't speak.

'When did you stop being an Israelite?' said Samson.

'I couldn't go on.' Caleb choked on the words.

'You knew this was a fight to the death.'

'I couldn't go on.'

'What changed you?' demanded Samson. 'You grew up in this fight.'

Caleb dragged his eyes from Samson, and Delilah felt them fall on her just as they had in the settlement.

Dear God. He's going to give me away.

'The Philistines are going to win,' said Caleb flatly. 'There are more of them, they are better equipped, and they have the money to feed their campaign. They will not stop until they have won.'

Samson leaned over Caleb. 'I thought you believed as I do that we are fighting for the will of God — '

'They don't care for our God,' snapped Caleb. He pressed his neck into the knife blade as though he was willing it to do its work. But Ariel turned it flat. 'Look at their gods, all so earthbound. Fertility and crops, fire, war, water. They believe in the land and the sea, in what they pillage and harvest to feed their people. But we aren't feeding our people, and you're demanding our faith in someone who doesn't listen to our prayers!'

Delilah swallowed hard on her fear as Caleb's eyes locked briefly onto hers. 'I've insulted everything you believe in, Samson,' he continued, 'yet still you let me live.'

Ariel twisted the blade onto its edge and Delilah shuddered. Caleb stared at Delilah, but she could only look at Ariel, waiting for the knife to move. And Ariel watched only for a sign from his leader.

'Let him go,' said Samson suddenly.

'You can't mean that,' snapped Ariel. 'After what he did to Abidan and Jubal?'

'Ariel, those are my orders.'

Ariel paused a moment longer, then threw the knife with a clatter onto the rocks.

Caleb hesitated, stunned, between them, then staggered through his former friends towards the mouth of the cave. As he passed Delilah she stared deliberately at Samson.

They listened to his feet scuffing up the cliff path. When he was out of earshot, Ariel slumped onto the floor. 'He betrayed us all.'

'He is no use to the Philistines now,' said Samson.

'But he'll go right back to them and tell them about the cave.'

'He won't.'

'How can you be sure of him? He fooled you once already.'

Samson crouched down in front of Ariel. 'We all feel his duplicity; we all mourn for Abidan and for Jubal. But Phicol can no longer use Caleb, and Caleb has lost everything that ever mattered to him. God will judge him.'

Delilah held her breath, searching Samson's face. Was there some part of him he daren't admit — some sliver of his heart that understood her betrayal too, in spite of Caleb's words?

Samson lifted Ariel to his feet and laid his hand on his comrade's shoulders. 'Tonight Caleb led Phicol into a disaster from which they were the only ones left alive. Even if Caleb goes straight back to him, he'll be the Israelite traitor who shouldn't have been trusted.'

Ariel held his leader's gaze for a moment, then picked up his knife and tucked it into his belt. Delilah exhaled silently.

'We should have killed Phicol,' said Micah.

'I considered it,' said Samson. 'We have humiliated him, and there will be consequences. But they would have been much worse had we killed him.'

Delilah walked slowly to the mouth of the cave to look out over the sea. She dreaded the form those consequences would take, far more than she feared his personal threats to her. It would do no good to dwell on what she couldn't know. She had chosen her path.

She felt Samson's arms wrap around her waist and his chin rest against her head. Whatever path she took now, someone would get hurt. Delilah wanted to remain in the moment for as long as possible, and she was grateful for the silence. It spared her the need to lie further.

For Caleb could have destroyed her with a few words, but he hadn't. In the desolation of his understanding, some fragment of longing for her had remained. And she knew it had been just enough to spare her the justice she deserved.

'I'm afraid,' she said at last.

His arms pressed her more tightly. 'So am I,' he said.

35

Though the night passed peacefully, Delilah was aware that her safety on the shore was only a temporary reprieve. When she clambered to the top of the cliff the next afternoon to collect clean sea grass for their beds in the cave, she saw a pall of smoke lingering above the city. Large fires must be burning somewhere. Phicol's vengeance had begun swiftly.

Samson had left early that morning leaving Delilah in the custody of Tomer, who tolerated his nursemaid role with good grace. He led her down to the water with nets and tried to show her the rudiments of fishing. After a few failed tosses of the net, she sat on the sand and watched the experts. It was hard not to be reminded of Abidan and Jubal when she watched Micah and Tomer together: the brothers did not resemble their dead friends physically, but only in their strong companionship. She thought of her own family, and she wondered if Ariel had managed to get her message to Joshua, letting them all know that she was safe.

Samson returned late that evening with Micah, and Delilah followed him down to the sea while he bathed. He was tense and quiet and floated alone in the water for a long time before he came back to the beach.

As he dried himself on the sand next to her, Delilah said, 'Are things very bad in the city?'

Samson shrugged back into his tunic. 'It's carnage. There has been fighting in the settlements throughout the day, Philistine citizens attacking Israelite traders and their families. Seventeen Israelites were murdered today alone. A new curfew has been imposed, banning all Israelites from the centre of the city at all times.'

'Including the market?'

'Yes.'

'How are they supposed to earn a living?'

'They aren't. And I'm sorry to tell you that Onan's orchard, his barns, his house, were burned to the ground.'

'Dear God. Is he safe?'

Samson was quiet for a moment, and when he spoke his voice was hoarse.

'He is, but his wife and daughters died in the blaze.'

Delilah's hands went to her mouth. 'No.'

'Apparently Phicol carried the torch to set the blaze himself.'

She turned away, her thoughts filled with the pretty faces of Onan's family. Phicol had mentioned the orchard to her; he was moving through Samson's allies. She couldn't say it of course, and reached for him.

'I must move our people from the city,' he said after a while. 'Where Phicol can't reach them. The roads are already clogged with families scattering in all directions, but there is no strength if we become separated from each other. Closer to the border with Judah, the lords will be less inclined to follow.'

333

Delilah lay alone in their cave bed that night, for Samson was too restless to settle for long and went back to the city soon after he'd bathed. But she couldn't sleep for the chaos of images in her head. At one point she dreamt that she could smell the burning fruit of Onan's orchard all around her. She must have dozed off eventually, though, for she was woken by Tomer gently shaking her arm, and the cave was light.

'I have to leave you alone here today. Samson needs me to help gather our people together to move inland. Will you be all right? We'll come back for you later.'

'Any word from Ariel?'

Tomer shook his head. 'He didn't come back last night.'

Delilah watched him go, then quickly gathered her possessions. She'd hoped that Ariel would bring her a message from the vineyard, and she couldn't wait any longer. She had to know that Achish and her mother were safe, not to mention Joshua. With Tomer gone there was no one to keep her there.

* * *

Delilah was relieved to see the vineyard just as she'd left it, and it wasn't until she climbed over the fence at the bottom of the slope that she admitted her darkest fear. Since she heard about Onan's orchard she had constantly heard Ekron's warning from Phicol in her head.

If you don't do as he asks, we'll lose everything.

Her heart was still banging as she ran up the rows towards the house, and she almost cried to see her mother sitting in the courtyard twisting the fine strings for tying the vines from a basket of grasses. She hesitated for a moment near the well, watching her mother sitting so peacefully alone, happy in her work, while Ashkelon was falling to pieces around her.

Beulah turned at the sound of Delilah's approach, and jumped up from her chair. Delilah gathered her tightly in her arms.

'Delilah! At last! We had no idea where you were.'

Delilah squeezed her. 'I tried to send a message.' She pulled back from her mother's embrace and studied her face. 'I caused you sleepless nights. Please forgive me.'

'You're here now. I'm not letting you out of my sight.'

Delilah took her hands. 'Mother, you must pack some of your things and leave with me right now. It's not safe for you to stay here. Phicol is singling out Israelites — '

'You are not to worry. I've heard all the rumours,' said Beulah. 'Ekron is in the house right now, explaining it to Achish.'

'You don't understand,' she said. 'Our people are being killed. I have somewhere for us, somewhere safe.'

'No, Delilah, my place is here. Achish has been so good to us, to me. I can't leave him just because of a rumour.'

'It's not a rumour, Mother. Phicol has suffered a great humiliation and he does not care who

335

suffers now. If he arrests you, he won't care for Achish's feelings.'

'He'll do no such thing.'

'He will. I know it.'

But Beulah shook her head again and Delilah felt powerless. There was no way to explain why Phicol had threatened her personally. There wasn't time.

Beulah put her hands around her daughter's face. 'I know that you trust Samson and that he means well for the Israelite people — '

'Samson doesn't even know I'm here — '

'But Phicol is family.'

Beulah smiled, sure of her convictions, then turned back to the bench, picking up the string she'd been working on. Delilah followed her, trying to think of another line of reasoning, but Joshua came running into the courtyard.

'I heard you were back, but you have to leave. Right now! Phicol is on his way here with his personal guard.'

Delilah went to her mother's side. 'I told you he'd come for you.'

'If he's bringing his guard, it's only to protect himself from trouble on the streets,' said Beulah.

'I don't think it's your mother he's come for,' said Joshua.

'Is it me?'

'He's turned the city upside down looking for you these last two days,' said Joshua. 'He's been telling every Israelite that he means to make you pay.'

Beulah suddenly had fear in her eyes. 'You must go. To Samson. Quickly.'

336

'Please, Mother — '

'Go. I'll be safe.'

Delilah looked frantically around, trying to think. What would Ekron do when Phicol turned up looking for her? How would he explain it to Achish?

'Mother, you have to be ready to leave as soon as I come back. I have to fetch something then I'll return for you.'

She ran out of the courtyard without waiting for an answer, heading round the back of the house to the servants' quarters, Joshua close behind her. 'Is the money still in the roof?'

'Yes. Are you taking it with you?'

'I'm certainly not leaving it here for its rightful owner.'

Joshua grabbed her arm. 'Is that silver Phicol's? Did you steal it?'

'Sort of,' panted Delilah, climbing up the ladder to Joshua's room. 'Help me get this down to the olive tree. We can hide it up there.' She tugged hard at the rushes and the bags dropped heavily by her feet. As they climbed down, she heard the rhythmic tread of soldiers on the march.

They were just creeping round the side of the house towards the well when Delilah heard Achish's voice cut through the courtyard. 'My Lord. What brings you to the vineyard this morning?'

Delilah peered into the courtyard. 'Mother!' she hissed.

Beulah glanced at her, then fluttered her fingers in a gesture of silence and got up from

337

the bench. Delilah grimaced. There was no way to get her mother out without being seen herself.

'Let's get you out of here,' said Joshua. 'I can go back for her later.'

They ran as quietly as they could down the slope, but the bags of silver were heavy and Delilah's legs felt weak as they reached the tree. Joshua clambered up onto the first branch then reached down and Delilah hoisted the bags of silver up to him. She tried to climb up after him, but her strength was failing her and she slumped back.

Joshua had begun to climb further up. 'Come on, Delilah. You've got to get out of — '

A dreadful scream rang out across the vineyard.

'Mother!' Delilah paused with a hand on the branch.

Joshua seized her wrist and pulled her up. 'Delilah! Hide!'

'I have to do something!'

'No! Delilah! There's nothing — '

More screams began to peal from the house, dreadful sounds tearing into the morning. Then as suddenly as they had begun, they died away and silence fell over the vineyard.

Joshua's eyes were wide at the horror, his mouth mechanically repeating the same words. 'There's nothing you can do. There's nothing you can do.'

He clung onto her. Tears stung Delilah's eyes and she stared at him rather than out at the house. *This can't be happening. Not in Achish's house. Not my mother.*

When she dared to look again through the branches, smoke was pouring out of the windows of the house into the courtyard, and Phicol was coming down the vineyard road, leading his troops. There was no sign of Ekron with him.

Delilah tried to yank her hand free of Joshua's, but he held on tightly.

'Don't! It's a trap to lure you out,' he hissed. 'If Phicol sees you, he'll kill you.'

'Let go of me!' She pulled free, and jumped from the tree. She stumbled up and ran.

Joshua caught her after a few paces, and with his hands around her waist, tackled her to the ground. 'Please, Delilah, don't!'

She tried to claw free, digging her nails into the soil. Joshua wouldn't release her, and she collapsed sobbing.

As soon as the soldiers disappeared, she crawled from Joshua's grasp and ran as fast as she could towards the burning building.

Smoke was billowing out of all the windows now, the air bittersweet with all the burning wood and fabric. Delilah dropped to her knees where the smoke was thinner and scrambled across the courtyard. She crawled through the door to the hallway. She had to keep her eyes half-closed against the stinging smoke. Her fingers touched something wet.

Blood.

A dark stain pooled around her hand, and just beyond it two vine-workers lay together, their throats slashed. Beyond them three of the housegirls and the cook, their clothes bloodied

339

around their stomachs. Delilah's head spun with nausea.

He's killed them all.

She gagged, coughing on the smoke and the sickness that wouldn't stay down. She looked around desperately, trying to work out which way to crawl. To the study or the library, or —

At the edge of the hall she saw a hand, shadowy in the thick haze, reaching out towards her. Delilah crawled across the floor, grabbing at it as soon as it was in reach. It was so heavy; a hand shouldn't be that heavy or that cold —

The body slid down in front of her, the head rolling awkwardly, and Delilah screamed. Her mother's face was clear and pale, but her throat was a river of blood and the front of her dress was dark with it.

Delilah howled, but the smoke choked down her grief. Her mother's hand now still and dead where so recently it had been warm and loving.

There's nothing you can do.

Delilah pressed the fingers to her mouth, kissing them, then she let her mother's hand drop and crawled back towards the courtyard. The smoke was becoming so dense around her that she could hardly breathe. She saw movement, a heap of brown cloth twitching. Someone had survived! She jumped up and ran to the body, a dark lump in the smoke, grabbing it and pulling with all her might. She found strength that she couldn't imagine, and in the fresher air she saw who it was.

'Achish!'

He began to cough, his violent shaking making

it even more difficult to move him, but she hooked her arms beneath his and dragged until they reached the well. She propped him up against the stone, then plunged her hands into a pail of water, cupping some for him to drink.

'Achish!'

'Delilah — '

'Yes. It's me. Don't talk, just drink.'

Achish shook his head. 'You — have to — go,' he coughed.

'I'm not leaving you.'

'You must.' Achish patted vaguely at his chest and Delilah noticed his tunic was sodden with blood, three deep wounds fusing flesh and fabric. She struggled to keep her grip.

'I'll get you out of here,' she said.

'But Ekron — Ekron — '

'It's all right. I'll find him, don't worry.'

'Ekron — '

And then he gave an odd gurgle and a whimper and his body grew heavier still.

Delilah stared down at him. He was dead. They were all dead.

In front of her something sounded like thunder and a wall shifted. The house was falling in on itself. Ekron was still inside. A raft of slates slid off the roof and scattered sparks around her. Some hit Delilah but she barely felt them. She had to move.

There was nothing left for her here.

36

'I had to go back,' she said. 'You understand that, don't you?'

Samson had been waiting anxiously when Delilah brought Joshua over the cliff to the cave. His men stood around him, ready to go off in search parties. He pulled her close and embraced her for a long time, until finally he asked:

'And who is this?'

Delilah's head was so full of plans for revenge and for survival, that it wasn't until Joshua stood in front of Samson in the mouth of the cave, his beautiful but slender body dwarfed by the warrior, that she realised how hard this moment was for him. He'd lost her as a lover long ago, but now he handed over custody of her safety too. She hovered awkwardly between them.

'It's Joshua. He helped me escape.'

Samson listened as she described in halting sentences what had happened to her family.

'He's attacked you to get to me.'

Delilah bit down a reply. She couldn't see how to disagree without revealing what she'd tried so hard to conceal. *He attacked me because I betrayed him. Because I made a fool of him.*

'In the name of God!' Samson shouted. 'This will not go unanswered.'

'No,' she said, stroking his hand while her mind made frantic turns. 'This proves that Phicol will stop at nothing. Don't rise to the bait,

Samson. Don't let his threat to me destroy you too.'

'It's too late for that,' he said, more quietly.

She looked at his grim expression. 'What do you mean? What have you done?'

'It's what Phicol has done which cannot be undone. Vengeance always begins with the deed itself.'

Delilah shook her head in frustration. 'No. Absolutely not. I forbid you.'

'You wouldn't see him pay?' asked Samson.

'I wouldn't see you die!' said Delilah. 'You are my family now. I'm the one who should have seen the threat sooner, instead of blissfully hiding away here with you, pretending the rest of the world wasn't really there. I should have gone straight to the vineyard the night after Phicol found us, and taken my mother from Ashkelon then.'

'She wouldn't have gone,' said Samson.

Delilah flinched. 'How do you know?'

'For the same reason she had stayed all this time. Because she loved Achish. It was never easy, she must have known it was becoming more dangerous, and yet she stayed nonetheless. Rather like you. And me.'

Delilah flinched. How could he see so clearly into the hearts of others, but not have realised the black core that had poisoned her for so long? No, she wasn't like her mother. Her mother was good and sweet and loyal and her heart was always open.

But I've allowed myself to be bought; I've wavered and hidden behind indecision. I've tried to pretend that loving you will make all my mistakes go away. I'm not like her at all.

She placed a hand on his cheek and pulled his face to look at her. 'I want us to leave Ashkelon, now, while we still can.'

'We cannot.'

'Phicol will not stop until he's killed you, killed Ariel and Micah and Tomer and every Israelite in these lands. The other lords in the other cities will hear what he's begun here and it will give them the courage to do the same, spilling out of their fortresses. Then we'll have nothing, not even the land between the cities — '

'I won't leave until we have won this battle. My loyalty is to my God and to my people.'

'But you can't win — '

'You doubt me?'

'I realise now just how far Phicol will go.'

'And I thought you already knew him so well.'

Delilah took a deep breath and lifted her gaze. Samson's deep blue eyes were studying her intently. And then they registered the fear in hers and he took a half step away from her.

You are bracing yourself for the worst, she thought. *And you are right to.*

She squeezed his hands, such futile compassion in view of what she was about to say. The little speech had never been rehearsed, but now it was unexpectedly ready, and she rushed to spit it out.

'Some months ago, Phicol employed me to help bring you down. He believed that despite your refusal to marry me, you were interested in me after all, and he wanted to use me to weaken you. I was sceptical that I could achieve such a thing on my own, but I agreed because I thought that the conflict between Philistines and Israelites was doing only harm to both peoples, and because I lived between them, I was somehow better placed than anyone else to judge that.'

She paused, scanning his face for a reaction. But it was still and empty. He snatched his hands away from her like she was a fire and he was afraid of being burned.

Her tongue flickered over her dry lips. 'I learned before long that I was wrong. Not just about Phicol's plan, but about everything. The Philistines and the Israelites. You taught me — *you* taught me that I couldn't live without care for one side or the other.'

Samson shook his head, and staggered backwards, falling heavily on the sand. 'Not you.'

'Please,' she said. 'Please, my love. You asked me on the way back from the valley lands to help you, and now I'm doing just that. You have lost Abidan and Jubal and Caleb too, and your trust has been shattered. That's why I'm telling you this. I love you. I love you with every part of me. You have won me over with your honesty and your resolve and your belief.'

The reasoning sounded twisted now, and she knew she didn't have the eloquence to state her case. She suddenly thought of Ekron standing over her on the road to the vineyard. Then too he had tried with weasel words to excuse himself. He too had shed tears on the road, begging for forgiveness, and she hadn't given it to him. So

345

why should Samson understand her? She smiled weakly at him.

'Phicol knows that I love you, and that's why you must go. He'll kill you now, just as he's killed the others.' She reached for him again, and found his hand, but it was as limp and heavy as Beulah's had been. 'And I couldn't bear that.'

Delilah had run out of words and she stared pleadingly at him. His only answer came as he released his hands from hers. His expression had altered just a little, his sky-blue eyes turned from hot summer to cool winter, but she felt as though he was seeing her for the first time, assessing her anew.

'Please say something,' begged Delilah. 'It would have been easy enough to continue to lie to you.'

He brushed past her towards the mouth of the cave and she snatched at his arm as he passed, but he pulled it away.

'Please, Samson. You must leave Ashkelon, you must.'

'No.' He stood with his back to her at the mouth of the cave, filling the opening, his arms folded across his chest. 'If you were able to see the reason in the Israelite cause, then you must also understand why I stand by it. I've devoted my life to it.'

'Samson — '

'Why would I take your advice now?' he shouted. 'Answer me that!'

'Because I love you!'

He turned on her and raised his hand. She braced herself, but the blow never came. When she opened her eyes again, he stood there, and tears were falling from his eyes. She wanted nothing more than to hold him, but it seemed as impossible then as turning back the tide.

'I love you,' she said again, barely a whisper.

Samson began to walk away down the beach, leaving Delilah alone in the cave. She wanted more than anything to run after him, but she forced herself to remain calm. That was what she'd done over and over today. Been forced to sit and wait and watch as the consequences of her actions formed in front of her. Now Samson was slipping away from her, as inexorably as a boat drifting out to sea. And she felt so terribly alone.

I can't lose him as well.

But she hadn't, yet. Her word must have touched him somewhere. He'd trusted her once, absolutely. Perhaps he could again. He hadn't struck her down, or sent her away.

She began pacing back and forth in the cave, afraid to go out onto the beach after him. Yet the gloom swamped her, casting impenetrable shadows over the tangle of her love and her fear. She crawled to the front of the cave, hoping that the sun might shed light on what she should do now, how she might make him see that the only way to live was to flee. It was no good trying to concoct some sort of story. He wouldn't listen to her now. If she was to make him leave, it would have to be against his will, that strong will —

* * *

Through the long afternoon, Delilah watched them from the mouth of the cave with an aching heart. Samson stayed by the water with Joshua, casting and recasting the nets with Tomer. Though he was there, just a stone's throw away and up to his knees in the water, it might as well have been across the sea in another land. Often she caught him looking towards her, deliberating, and she became more certain as the hours passed that he'd stride up the beach and dismiss her.

But this wasn't about her any longer. The harm she had done could not be taken back. She must pay that price. She'd betrayed him twice, and he'd escaped. Of course he couldn't forgive her. She would betray him again, but this time it would be for his own good.

As the men picked fish from the nets, Delilah set a bowl on the fire and began to heat water, stirring in honey as it warmed. Samson had grown used to a blander drink without his favourite spices, but Delilah remembered that Azubah had given her a small clutch of cinnamon sticks before they left the valley lands. She went to the back of the cave and dug around in her purse for the bundle. Her thumb caught on something and she pulled out one of the pouches of medicinal herbs that Azubah had given her. It was the white pouch, of goldflower —

Delilah dropped it, stung afresh by the idea that had been forming in her head. It hardly bore consideration, yet it was a painless, simple way to get Samson out of the city.

She picked up the purse again, found the black pouch of poppy-blood and without further thought she took it quickly to the fire and poured the whole lot into the bowl of honey drink. She cracked a couple of the cinnamon sticks and crumbled them in, then stirred it with a twig. There was little time to waste. Tomer would arrive shortly with fish for Delilah to gut for dinner, and somehow she had to make sure that he and Samson drank the honey drink but Joshua did not.

The men came to the mouth of the cave and Joshua greeted her happily. Samson had obviously not told anyone of their conversation. He hesitated at the mouth of the cave, sniffing the air, and studying Delilah with curiosity. Her heart leapt into her throat. Did poppy-blood smell when you heated it? But then he crossed swiftly to the fire and sat a few paces away. She couldn't read his expression, and realised the forced normality must be for the benefit of the others.

He sniffed again, and she realised it was only the cinnamon he'd smelled. 'Your mother gave me the recipe,' she said.

Samson moved closer to her, but still did not touch her. 'I wouldn't mind a rind of lemon.'

'That I don't have.' She reached across and slapped Tomer's hand as he reached for the bowl. 'Not yet. A little while longer.'

She looked up at Joshua. 'Could you get me some fresh water to rinse the fish in?'

'I'll go,' said Tomer.

'Let Joshua. He has to find his way if he is

349

going to live here for a while,' said Delilah.

Tomer shrugged and sat down opposite her, and as soon as Joshua was out of sight, Delilah filled two drinking bowls and offered them to the men.

Both men drank deeply, and Delilah placed her fingers in Samson's. When he didn't pull away, she felt hope blossom in her heart. Was it possible that he was already treading the path to forgiveness? He rolled the drink around in his mouth, then swallowed it, and she nodded.

'Good?'

'It tastes different.'

'It's the cloves. Cinnamon without cloves — '

'I'll have another,' said Tomer, and Delilah refilled the bowls, watching as both men downed the second drink. She had no idea how quickly the poppy-blood would act, but she didn't have to wait longer. Tomer was talking about his father, who'd taught him to fish, when he suddenly started to slur.

'Are you all right?' asked Samson.

Tomer suddenly keeled over.

Samson tried to get up, but he wobbled unsteadily beside Delilah. She stood, feigning concern.

'What's wrong?'

'I feel — What did you do? What was in the drink?'

Joshua came into the cave, lugging a jar of water, as Samson tried to stand up.

'What's going on?'

'What did you do to me?' cried Samson to Delilah, struggling to hold himself up against the cave wall.

Delilah's composure dissolved into tears and she clung to him. 'I'm sorry, forgive me, I'm trying to help you.'

'What — ' Samson staggered, then his knees gave way. He fell onto his hands, but he couldn't hold himself. His head sank to the floor beside Joshua's feet.

Joshua stared at Delilah. 'What did you do?'

Delilah tried to wipe the tears from her face but they just wouldn't stop. She crouched down beside Samson, gently stroking his cheek. 'It's the only way.'

37

She explained to Joshua about the drugged drink. He listened without a word, but nodded.

Delilah gulped for air and wiped her face with the back of her hands. If the idea was to work, she had to pull herself together.

'There's an Israelite farmer up the coast,' she said. 'Give him some silver and bring his cart and horse to the top of the cliff.'

'What are you going to do?'

'Just go. I'll be ready when you get back.'

Joshua headed up the cliff path, leaving Delilah in the cave. Tomer was snoring, flat on his back, and Delilah rolled him onto his side, so he wouldn't choke when he woke up. Samson had fallen heavily onto his front, and she crept around him, still not sure he was fully asleep. His eyes were closed though, and his face was creased with a miserable confusion of anger and disbelief. Delilah touched his hair. There was one more thing she needed to do.

'Forgive me, God,' she said, 'Please help him understand.'

She reached for Tomer's knife, then she kissed the blade and took a deep breath. Samson was facing her, and she gingerly lifted his head and took the knife to it, easing it against his beard. Tomer kept it razor-sharp. A handful of hair came off in the first pass, and though she'd never shaved a man before in her life, she moved the blade quickly and carefully over his skin, removing the layer of hair as easily as she would have skinned the fish.

She completed one side of his face, then got to her feet and stood astride him, leaning over his head. She was thankful his hair was in braids, for it made her job much easier. She felt murderous, laying them out, neat and dead in a row. When all seven were gone, she set about neatening the uneven stubs of hair, carefully taking the blade closer to his scalp, and chin.

Laying his head back down as if it was a bowl of the most delicate clay, she studied him quickly. How young he looked. How vulnerable. As she had hoped, his hair defined him, and now he resembled any other Israelite, his face oddly pale where the beard had shielded his skin from the sun, his head smaller against his massive shoulders.

She crouched and cradled it in her lap, delicately fingering his eyelashes, his breaths slow and steady against the hairs of her arm.

Until he coughed, she didn't realise Joshua was standing in the entrance to the cave.

'Oh Delilah, no — ' he whispered as he came closer.

'You don't have to say anything. I know what I've done.'

'Do you?' he said, chewing on his knuckles, his face pale with fear. 'Pray mighty God has not seen.'

'But would you recognise him now?' said Delilah.

Joshua hesitated, then crouched beside her. He

shook his head, as much in bewilderment it seemed, as in answer to her question. 'But how will we move him? He weighs at least twice what I do.'

Delilah stood up. 'Let's use a fishing net to drag him.'

'He's the leader of our people and you would haul him like a bucket of dead fish?'

'There's no other way. We are going to drive him to the valley lands, back to his mother. He'll be safe there and then we can cross the border to Judah.'

'So be it,' said Joshua.

He grabbed a net and shook the remaining fish free. They laid the net beside Samson but it was a struggle to roll his body into it, and they were both grunting by the time they heaved him out of the cave and onto the path. The sun had set and Delilah sank to the ground exhausted.

'You were right,' she said. 'We can't do this.'

'I have an idea. Wait there.'

Joshua disappeared up the cliff into the dark. Soon after Delilah heard the soft clop of hooves and he returned leading two horses by their harnesses. In his other hand he held a rope. 'Tie this to the net; I'll get the horses to pull him up.'

Delilah looped the rope round the net, using a knot that Tomer had shown her. Then Joshua began to guide the horses slowly. Thankfully, the track was smooth and stoneless, and she cushioned Samson's head as the body slowly slid up the path on the thick net. Their progress was painfully slow, but in time the horses had tugged him to the foot of the wagon. Getting him in took all Delilah's remaining strength, and Joshua groaned as he hooked his hands beneath Samson and heaved him the final few feet into the cart. He was soaked with sweat from the effort, and lay down on the bench to cool off while Delilah ran back to the cave to get blankets and a few belongings. She cast a quick look around, then poured water on the fire to extinguish it. Tomer had not moved.

'I'm sorry,' she whispered.

Joshua reined the horses and the cart jerked forward. Delilah covered Samson with blankets, and stroked the rough stubble of his cheek. He looked so fragile now, like a child. *I'll keep you safe*, she promised.

They drove the cart towards the city, then turned north. The road was deserted, but through the steady creaking of the cart wheels and the rattling of the cicadas came less comforting night-time sounds. Delilah twisted back and forth in the cart, nervous of the distant shouts and the calls of wild dogs. They were travelling without a torch, but there was enough moonlight to light the way and before long, Delilah picked out the terraces of the abandoned vineyard, and the blackened splash of the burned house at the top of the slope.

'We must fetch the money,' said Delilah, with more resolve than she was feeling.

'My God, you like to live dangerously,' replied Joshua.

'Once we leave Ashkelon, we have nothing. This is — '

'I know,' said Joshua. He shook the reins. 'I'll

go further north, then cut back in, avoiding the settlements.'

Delilah nodded and dug around in the bottom of the cart for her purse. She pulled out the knife, then twisted her own hair together and sliced through it, flinging the cut hair onto the road. If they were to get round the city unrecognised, she'd have to make a sacrifice too, though it was nothing compared to Samson's. She rubbed the bare nape of her neck, shivering in the unfamiliar breeze.

'Oh no,' said Joshua.

Up ahead, the bright lights of torches shone around a roadblock of chariots and soldiers. They would certainly be stopped. The question was, what could she say?

'Should I turn around?' whispered Joshua.

'No,' she said. 'Keep going.'

Delilah's heart rate sped up as they closed. *I can get us through this.*

A soldier stepped forward from the others and held up a hand. Joshua brought the horses to a halt, and Delilah saw him straighten his back. She pulled a blanket over her legs as the soldiers closed in around them, their torches held high over the side of the cart. Their eyes glittered like molten coins as they studied her, like the wolves that sometimes hovered at a distance in the desert. Delilah blinked into the light, clinging on to her nerve.

'This is my brother,' she said in Philistine. 'He is very sick with marsh fever. Stay back if you want to be well.'

'Where are you taking him?' asked the soldier.

'Far out of the city, where he cannot harm anyone.'

'Good riddance,' replied the soldier and waved them through.

A short distance later, Joshua eased the cart off the track. Samson stirred vaguely beside her. They had unwrapped him from the fishing net, but he was bound by blankets, and in his sleep he was fumbling to free himself.

Delilah shushed him by gently caressing his forehead, but she felt nervous. 'Where are we?'

'Not far from the vineyard.'

Delilah considered the choice. Leave Samson in the wagon and make a run for it to get the heavy bags of silver, or drive closer and risk being seen. 'I think we should try to get as close as we can, those bags are — '

'What's that?'

Delilah followed Joshua's gaze to the right, from where a cluster of lights was rapidly approaching.

'Oh Se't,' hissed Delilah. 'Go, just go!'

But Joshua couldn't get the horses to turn quickly and they reared at the blaze of torches swarming around them. He tugged at the reins but by the time he'd settled them, the cart was surrounded by soldiers, several with swords drawn.

'Can we help you?' asked Delilah.

'What are you doing here, so far off the road?' asked one of the soldiers.

Delilah repeated her excuse about her brother's illness.

One of the soldiers held his torch closer to

357

Samson's shorn head. He obviously didn't recognise him.

'You're on private property,' said the soldier. 'Return to the gates and get a permit for travel.'

'Private property?'

'This belongs to the Lord Phicol.'

Delilah cursed inwardly and felt her anger rise. Of course it did. He'd always wanted the vineyard for himself.

'I'm sorry,' she said. 'We must have lost our way. But my brother is very sick as you've seen — '

'Let me see.'

Delilah froze. She'd not heard the approach of another horse, but the voice was unmistakeable. Lord Phicol rode into view, his ceremonial armour gleaming in the torchlight. He peered at her with rude delight from astride a stocky horse.

'Pull back the blanket. Let us see this beloved brother,' said Phicol.

The soldier snatched off the blanket. Samson stirred and rolled his head slowly. Phicol steered his horse close to the side of the cart. 'Unless Ekron has grown overnight, I believe that is Samson.'

'Are you sure, My Lord?'

Phicol reached into the cart and grabbed unsuccessfully at Delilah's arm. 'Look at him. Shorn like a lamb for sacrifice. Ekron! Come here!'

Delilah couldn't help looking past the torches for her stepbrother. He wasn't dead! The soldiers seized on her movement and hoisted her out of

358

the cart. She screamed and kicked, but was dumped on the ground in front of Ekron. She struggled to her feet, reaching for him to steady herself, but he stepped back out of reach as though she truly was contagious.

'You're alive,' said Delilah. 'Your father was so worried — '

'Of course I am,' snapped Ekron.

'I'm disappointed in you,' said Phicol to Delilah. 'You shouldn't have been caught so easily. I wonder why on earth you allowed yourself to come so close to the vineyard, unless — Unless of course you had left something precious behind, perhaps some silver?'

Delilah was stalling for time when the cart shuddered behind her. The soldiers slid into line, drawing swords as one.

'Don't!' she cried. 'Don't touch him!'

The cart rocked and Samson slowly raised himself up to sitting. He blinked at the glare of torchlight shining on blades, staring around him in confusion, his hands flailing as he sought the nature of his confinement. Then his hands moved to his head, his forehead creasing into deep dark lines.

'What have you done to me?' he cried out. 'In the name of God, what have you done?!'

'I believe your beloved has cut it all off,' said Phicol.

Delilah's eyes filled with tears. It had seemed so right when he was asleep, but now he looked broken, damaged, unable to protect himself. And she had done this to him.

Instinctively she reached for Samson. Ekron

grabbed her hands and held them fast behind her.

'Leave her alone,' shouted Joshua from the driver's seat.

'And what kind of man are you?' sneered Ekron at him. 'Hiring out your lover to another man; did she give you a share in the fee?'

Samson was trying to stand up in the cart, but he was still groggy and it wobbled, felling him against the side of the cart. He sank back, running his hands over his head again and again, searching for his hair. It was as though he barely noticed the blades brandished around him.

'Let him go,' cried Delilah to Phicol. 'Look at him. What harm can he possibly do the Philistines now? You have won, so let him go.'

'Your game is at an end, Delilah,' said Phicol coldly. 'There are no more trades, no more chances. It's over.'

'Delilah?' cried Samson. 'You do this to me?'

He tried to stand again, but this time he was too near the side and the cart rocked dangerously to the right. Joshua jumped clear, but Samson fell through the side, wood splintering around him as he slumped into the dirt.

'I was trying to protect you,' she said, leaning towards him, but Ekron yanked her arms back so hard that she cried out.

'Get him away from here!' Phicol barked at his soldiers. 'I want him out of reach before anyone comes for him.'

Ekron dragged Delilah further back and she could only watch as the soldiers swarmed over

Samson. He swung an arm groggily, but they had ropes around him. She willed him to break them, as he had before, but now to expect such strength from him seemed foolish. The net was dragged from the cart and thrown over him and he barely struggled as they wrapped him up in it. His limbs squirmed like some huge wounded beast from the sea.

Delilah's legs gave way beneath her, and Ekron let her fall to the ground in front of Samson. Through the tangle of ropes and net she sought out his face, but though his eyes met hers, their beautiful blue had gone cold grey in the dark. He was already lost to her.

Six men took a grip of the bundle and heaved it back into the cart.

'You made it so easy in the end,' said Phicol. 'I'm almost disappointed in you.'

'Take me instead of him,' begged Delilah from the dirt. 'Take me, please.'

'You're spoiled goods, as far as I'm concerned,' said Phicol. 'But Ekron can have you. I believe he still harbours a desire for your sordid charms.'

Ekron looked shaken by his employer's words, and he hovered awkwardly over Delilah. As he hesitated, Delilah felt something brush against her, and she saw Joshua leap on Ekron, his hand glittering in the torchlight. He'd found Tomer's knife, the knife that had already caused so much grief. He pushed its tip to Ekron's throat.

'Let her go,' shouted Joshua. 'Let her go or I'll kill you.'

'Stupid child,' said Phicol, nodding. There was

361

a movement behind Joshua, and his mouth abruptly gaped like a landed fish. He dropped the knife and looked down at his chest. A silver blade protruded from it, and a dark stain was swelling swiftly from it.

Delilah screamed. Joshua stared dumbly at the blade, then his eyes fell on Delilah's. His lips and chin darkened as blood gathered in his mouth and spilled out. The blade was withdrawn and with a whimper he sagged in on himself and fell sideways onto the sand.

Ekron shrank away from Joshua's dying body in disgust.

'Take Samson away,' said Phicol. 'Leave the whore.'

Delilah crawled towards the cart, trying to drag herself up on it, but two soldiers hauled her back and the cart shuddered into motion.

'Fight them, Samson!' shouted Delilah, clutching at the cart. 'Remember what you believe in! Don't give up!'

But he only lay in the cart, staring past her.

'I should congratulate you, Ekron,' said Phicol, walking his horse on. 'Her seduction of Samson was a clumsy arrangement and at times I doubted you. But it had the right conclusion.'

He jerked the reins and trotted off with his guards into the night, leaving Ekron alone with Delilah. She crawled towards Joshua, feeling for him in the dark, but his breaths were faint and fast, and his chest sodden. She turned his face into the moonlight. His eyelids were half-closed and his mouth bubbled with spit and blood.

'Joshua?'

He turned his gaze on her weakly, and she ran her finger across his forehead, seeking the boy she'd been so fond of. His skin was already cool.

'Thank you, my friend, thank you.'

The life left him with a long, hoarse breath. She lowered his head gently.

Ekron stood over her. 'You brought all this on yourself,' he said.

'No,' said Delilah bitterly. 'You brought this hell on us all. On Samson, on me. On my mother. On your own father — '

Ekron snorted. 'He got what he deserved as well.'

'What is wrong with you?' asked Delilah, struggling to her feet. She wouldn't crawl at his feet any longer. 'Your father died with your name on his lips.'

A strange look crossed Ekron's face, but it soon passed and he gripped Delilah's elbow hard. 'He should have stayed out of the way. Then he wouldn't have been hurt. I tried to explain it, but he would never listen to me.'

But Ekron — Ekron — Delilah remembered Achish at the well. Then understanding spread over her like a sickness.

'Dear Gods, you killed him,' she said.

Ekron's stillness was all the answer she needed.

'You killed your father,' she continued. 'Ekron, no — '

'He tried to stop us,' said Ekron, his mouth a cruel twist. 'Your mother was easier.'

Delilah's body began to shake, and she lashed out with her fists, pounding at Ekron. He caught

363

the first blow, and scrabbled for her wrists. She scratched and lunged with her teeth, but suddenly her legs were taken away and he was on top of her, pinning her with his knees either side of her waist.

The stony dirt dug painfully into her back but Delilah tried to resist as Ekron leaned in, his face right over hers. His hot breath stank of wine and meat. Still, though, she held his gaze.

'The gods would be ashamed to look at you!'

'My father was weak,' said Ekron, breathing hard as he tried to restrain her, 'and his loyalties were torn. There is no place for that in these times. You will learn to be loyal now, to me.'

Delilah wrestled against him, but there was no escape. He had her, for now.

But she could still lift her head, and she looked deep into his eyes, anger filling her heart. 'I will learn nothing from you.'

38

Two months later

Ekron shuddered, a thin groan escaping his lips. His hair was plastered over his forehead and his eyes bulged. Then he sank down, panting.

Delilah turned her head to the side and tried not to suck in her stepbrother's odour. On the wall, their shadows intertwined. She closed her eyes. Waited.

When his breathing had slowed, Ekron lifted himself off her.

She lay still, his sweat cooling on her skin.

'Clean yourself up,' he said, on his way out. 'You're serving dinner tonight at His Lordship's table.'

Delilah rolled off the couch, and pulled her dress down over her body. She walked unsteadily to the mirror stone, and tucked her hair behind her ears. In the month since her capture, it had barely grown. Certainly not enough to cover the bruise beside her left eye. Ekron had taken to wearing a heavy gold ring on his right hand.

The room smelled particularly sour to her, not just of the daily indignity she suffered in there, but the reek of the gaudy paints he'd chosen for its decoration. But the whole house was like that, built hurriedly on a plot adjacent to Lord Phicol's, still creaking as it settled on its foundations and its plaster dried in the autumn sun.

Delilah knew the house well; she'd scrubbed every square of its stone floors. She worked hard, seeking in fatigue to hide from her thoughts, from what she had become. Ekron had wasted no time making her understand her new role, calling on her at all hours of the day and night to cook for him, clean his quarters, change the silk sheets on his bed, and sate his desire for her that now bubbled over like a jar of wine left to ferment for too long.

Samson was dead.

That first morning after the capture she'd woken on a hard bench in an empty room, when Ekron had come to her early and calmly broken the news that he had been executed overnight, strangled by three Philistine soldiers who had all lost brothers to the Israelite rebels. She'd held off the miserable wail that had surged through her soul until Ekron left. Then she slumped, sobbing, in a corner, unable to imagine Samson's last moments. Had he tried to defend himself when the moment came? Had he justified his cause to these soldiers? He'd been so broken when Phicol captured him, that she dreaded how mutely he might have accepted his fate. They would have tortured him, surely, in their quest for revenge.

She had curled up in a stupor for the rest of the day, uncaring of the passage of the sun over the house. With night Ekron had returned and tried to force himself on her. She'd kicked and clawed and bitten until he backed away, bloodied and moaning. She'd cursed his name, called him a bastard child of Mot, the God of Death. She'd denounced him as a coward and a murderer. She said that she had always known these things and seen his rotten soul even as a boy. Unnerved by her fury, he'd left her without a word.

But the reprieve had been short. He came again, as she slept. This time he brought a switch of elm, and he'd drawn courage from strong drink. His face was bandaged where she'd raked his skin away and she tore at the cloth, but the drink gave him a brutal edge she couldn't overcome. He lashed her over and over until she was groping blindly against the cane with her arms. She'd cried bitterly, shouting for anyone to help her, even Samson. He'd laughed then and pushed her legs apart. She had no strength left to stop him.

Afterwards, he'd dragged her, still wet from his pleasure, down into the kitchen where he'd thrown her into the pantry and demanded she make him a meal. And from that moment on he'd inflicted on her a cruelty she could never have imagined of him. After so many years of believing him quite different from Hemin, Delilah saw that he was infinitely worse. She saw now that this Ekron had never been far from the surface, and that the little kindnesses that had marked the habit of their childhood had stemmed from his desire, nothing more.

In the beginning, she had tried to convince him to let her work at the vineyard at least. He'd inherited the land and had deliberately instructed the servants in the harvesting in front

367

of her, betraying both his ignorance of the process and his insistence on depriving her of an activity that might console her. But one afternoon when a servant had come running to the house to say that the grapes were rotting before they could be pressed, Delilah had snapped.

'You care nothing for your father's legacy,' she'd shouted at him, in front of the vine-worker. 'He worked his entire life to provide a comfortable existence for you and Hemin, and now you are destroying that, just so you can prove that you are better than him. Except you are too stupid to do even that properly — '

Ekron had given her such a beating there and then that she'd wondered afterwards whether he'd been thrashing away the memory of his father too.

* * *

Delilah went through to the dormitory she shared with the other servants, women whom she'd once ignored during her visits to Phicol's home. Now they averted their eyes as she passed. She took off her soiled clothing and sponged herself down with cold water, sloughing at her flesh as she did daily to try to rid herself of any trace of Ekron.

It wasn't as obvious when she was prone on Ekron's couch, but standing here, naked, Delilah knew it wouldn't be long before the gentle swell of her stomach and breasts would become impossible to hide. The black tunics they wore for work were loose and shapeless, and Ekron was too concerned with his own body to pay much attention to Delilah's, but the signs would only grow clearer.

A second moon had recently come and gone without the passing of blood, and she'd woken most mornings feeling sick. She had wondered once, that morning in the valley lands, whether she was pregnant, for Azubah's careful study of her had reflected her own suspicions. But it had been too early to tell, and she'd comforted herself with the knowledge that Samson would be with her when she learned for sure.

But now, with only Ekron to notice, there was simply dread. He'd certainly kill the baby, perhaps kill her too, for there would be no clearer proof that she'd never belong to him. Delilah clasped her hands over her abdomen.

Dear God, please let me be mistaken. Don't make our suffering worse. Take this child from me before Ekron does.

★ ★ ★

The opulence of Lord Phicol's dinner table made Delilah feel sick again — roasted fowls swimming in oil, pickled fish, a sweet stew with figs and lamb. Hemin was only weeks from giving birth, and sat like the legendary Nile hippopotamus on a pile of cushions on the floor, her head level with the low table. She hadn't expected sympathy, but if anything her stepsister's enmity had grown. She took great pleasure in sending Delilah back and forth to the kitchen

369

for individual servings of cold food that she stuffed into her mouth with both hands.

'You haven't trained her very well,' Hemin sniped at Ekron, waving her fistful of roast goat at Delilah, who was standing at her post by the wall. 'She was always a lazy dog.'

Ekron didn't answer.

'I can't quite believe you've made the same mistake as Father. Having them in your bed doesn't improve them.'

Ekron blushed. 'Be quiet, will you?'

'You *are* having her, aren't you?' said Hemin, giving her brother a filthy smile over her drinking bowl. 'I believe it's the done thing, though Ba'al knows why. At least you know her place now. As my husband likes to say, those who get above themselves, always fall the furthest.'

Ekron grunted, and Phicol gave a chuckle. He was sitting on his couch, his legs spread, folds of ample belly hanging over the belt of his skirt. He picked idly at his dinner. Hemin's shrill voice only added to the dizzying atmosphere in the room. The heat of the night, the muddle of colours and smells of the food pressed around her, and Delilah was relieved when Hemin sent her to the kitchen yet again. On the way back, she loitered for just a few moments in the corridor, balancing a bowl of apricots in her arms as she leant against the cold stone wall. From the dining room, she heard Phicol barking at Ekron, banging his spoon irritably on the arm of the couch.

' — refuses to give up the location of the northern coastal hideout.'

'We don't need to know it.'

'We do, Ekron, we have to know that there are no more places for those dirty runts to hide. I want this land razed to the ground, I want to know every single hole and hut between the coast and the Sorek Valley, and from Gaza to the river at Tel Qasilah. The Israelites must not be able to hide out in our Philistine lands.'

Delilah peered through a gap in the door curtain as Ekron put his drinking bowl on the table and leaned forward to pick up a grape. 'He's not been shaken by his ordeals thus far, but even Samson will not be able to resist the pain of fire.'

Dear God, he's alive.

Delilah swayed, grabbing onto the curtain to steady herself. The bowl of apricots spilled from her arms and smashed on the floor, the sweet shatter of pottery piercing her stupor. But her legs gave way and she fell forward, pulling the curtain down on her.

'Get her out of here,' she heard Phicol shout.

Delilah was shaking violently as two male servants enfolded her in their strong arms. She was carried back through the kitchen and out to the yard.

They're keeping you alive. Dear God. Dear God what have I done?

They took her back to an empty chamber and left her there. She sank against the wall and the tears came, spilling over her cheeks.

They're hurting you, my darling. How they must be hurting you.

She cried until her body ached, and she was

nothing but a dry husk of grief. Then gradually she became aware of the gentle caress of a cold damp cloth against her forehead.

'There, there. Are you feeling better?'

Delilah opened her eyes a little to see the parched knees of an elderly woman sitting on the ground next to her.

'Thank — ' She coughed. 'Thank you.'

'It won't do the baby any good if you cry like that.'

Delilah looked around frantically. They were alone. The woman's eyes were kind.

'Don't tell. Please don't tell.'

'It's not your master's, is it?'

Delilah shook her head, but the movement made her feel sick and she spat out the bitter taste in her mouth.

'We know who you are,' said the old woman, 'and who has been taken from you.'

'Please don't tell anyone about the baby,' whispered Delilah.

The old woman shook her head. 'And have the hopes of Israel die with you? Of course not.'

Delilah swallowed a sob and tried to sit up.

'Master says I'm to take you home.'

Delilah nodded weakly and took the woman's wrinkled arm. She climbed to her feet. The walk to Ekron's house was short, but Delilah's legs felt like they weren't her own and she needed the support of this woman three times her age. She accepted a dry kiss on the forehead, and slipped quietly through the gates to the rear of the house, heading for the dormitory. At least she might rest quietly until Ekron got home and —

Ekron stepped out of the shadows in front of her.

'You have to see it from my point of view,' he said smiling. 'You were easier to break without the hope of Samson's survival to keep you going.' He leaned towards her, his breath thick with wine.

'Go to bed,' said Delilah. 'Please.'

'Is that an invitation?'

'I will never lie down with you again.'

Ekron grabbed at her neck and pulled her to him, his lips full and wet and almost on hers. 'Oh yes you will, my little darling.'

Delilah wriggled free. Not tonight. She was weary, but she'd fight him tonight, even if it meant more bruises. 'You disgust me,' she hissed.

Ekron slapped her hard against the cheek, but the pain only fanned the flames of her anger.

'Without Phicol, you would be nothing.'

Ekron snorted and reached down for a small wine jar that was resting against the wall. 'Let's drink to that. Let's drink to the riches he's brought me. Let's drink to my persistence.' He uncorked the jar with his teeth and spat the stopper across the yard. He drank deeply, then offered the jar to Delilah.

Delilah made a fist and tried to hit him, but he jerked back. The wine jar fell and smashed at his feet. He grabbed at it pointlessly, then lunged at her with outstretched arms.

She moved out of the way, and he fell against the wall to steady himself.

'I'll always be Samson's,' she said. 'No matter

how many times you force yourself on me.'

Ekron grabbed her, clumsily ripping at her tunic. He shoved his forearm against her throat, trapping her against the wall. As he loosened his belt, she grabbed at his wrist and twisted his arm into his shoulder as she'd seen Samson do so many times. Ekron yelled, and she slipped from his grip. But she couldn't get out of reach quickly enough. Something snagged her ankle, and before she knew it she was face down in the dirt.

He was on her quickly, tearing at her tunic, pressing her into the ground. She tasted wine-soaked dirt on her lips. The wet shards of the broken jar were dangerously close to her face.

Ekron lifted a fraction, to push his hand up the outside of her thigh, and Delilah wriggled forward. He crawled over her. She felt a blow to the back of her head and her nose was slammed into the ground, bringing a shock of white pain.

She blinked hard to see clearly again. One long shard glistened beside her. She slid her fingers through the dirt towards it.

'Still fighting, sister?' Ekron panted.

Delilah twisted beneath him. His teeth were bared, his face livid. She grabbed the shard and drove it at his neck. The tip broke the skin and met little resistance. She shoved it in deep and hard. Ekron's eyes widened.

Hot blood drained over her knuckles.

'Lilah?' The word was high-pitched, and he sounded just as he had as a boy, trying to master his voice.

Ekron rocked back, scraping at his throat for the object that silenced him. Delilah kicked herself free, scampering back through the dirt.

Ekron tried to speak again, but it was just a gurgle. A dark stain was spilling down his front, draining the colour from his face. Delilah looked around to see if there was anyone who would rush to his aid. Three servants were gathered in the doorway, gawping in silence.

'Go now,' Delilah shouted, 'while you can!'

They glanced nervously at each other, then disappeared into the dormitory. Ekron was making an odd hissing noise, his lips moving like a fish's over bloodied teeth. He reached for her, but he clasped at air. Then he collapsed sideways, his body twisting awkwardly.

Delilah watched as his breathing became slower, and his feet nudged each other gently in the dirt. Her heart was thudding in her ears and she was only dimly aware of the servants scuttling past with their small sacks of belongings until they were out of the gate.

She waited until Ekron's body was completely still, then she wrapped her tunic across her and turned for the gate. There should be time to reach the vineyard and collect the silver — if it was still there — before Ekron was discovered, and by sunrise she'd be well on her way to the valley lands.

39

Four months later

Ariel reined in the donkeys and the wagon halted.

'Are you quite sure you want to do this?' he said. 'I can just as easily go into the city myself.'

Delilah shook her head. She felt huge and conspicuous. There was no hiding it any longer, but the tented dress and cape was traditionally Philistine, so there was no reason it should draw unwanted attention.

'I should go with you, though,' said Azubah. Samson's mother, clothed in the long belted robe and shawl of a midwife, sat opposite. 'If the baby comes early — '

'It won't,' said Delilah. 'Besides, I need you to stay safe for when it does.'

Azubah squeezed Delilah's hand in her own. Her skin was soft and warm like old leather. 'Tell my son that I'm proud of him.'

Delilah let Ariel help her down and she set off towards the city gates. With the hood of the cape lifted up over her head, and a garish quantity of jewellery around her neck, Delilah knew she could pass for a Philistine visiting from Gath. Her heart jolted with anxiety as she reached the sentries, but she met no interrogation and was waved through.

She walked through the once familiar streets.

The other Philistines kept a respectful distance, and she received the smiles of the other women with her own. There were hardly any Israelites to be seen, just the occasional boy running an errand or woman weighed down with food from the market, clearly on her way to her employer rather than her own home. Phicol had apparently taken to calling Ashkelon the cleanest of the Philistine cities, and no Israelite traders remained in the market. Instead the square was filled with neat rows of Philistine stalls. And there was Sarai with her bowls of beads, chatting happily with a customer, the ring on her middle finger suggesting that perhaps she'd settled her heart on someone since Ekron's death.

Delilah walked away as quickly as the weight of the baby would allow her. Though she'd promised Azubah that the baby wasn't ready yet, she'd felt its kick and roll within her for many days. Perhaps it sensed that it was returning to its father. Delilah turned south, taking the long straight road to the jail. The temple loomed fat and golden to her right and she glanced at the steps, offering a silent prayer for Abidan and Jubal. On the balcony, two men were hanging the last few traditional boughs of juniper for the end-of-winter festival. She shook off the incipient gloom and increased her pace.

Delilah was prepared to weave an excuse for entry at the gates of the jail, but on a whim she simply passed two silver coins through the window hole, and she was admitted without question.

'I wish to see the Israelite, Samson. He was

implicated in the death of my brother,' she said.

The gatekeeper studied her, taking in every detail of the elaborate outfit. His eyes lingered longest on the mound at her waist. 'It's foul down there, m'lady.'

'I've come a long way for this opportunity.' She offered another pair of coins, and the gatekeeper reluctantly led her into the noisy heart of the jail, boiling with trapped sunshine and the frustrations of confinement.

A second guard was less easily convinced by the silver and more concerned for the wellbeing of a heavily pregnant noble.

'It's on my neck, ma'am, if anything happens to you down there. His Lordship — '

'And His Lordship will have fear from the High Priest of the temple in Gath if I'm not permitted to see the prisoner.'

'You have come all the way from the border lands?'

'Then you understand the seriousness of my journey.'

Delilah held out four silver pieces, but the guard shook his head. 'If you must go, then I take no fee for it. The underworld of this prison is the god Melqart's domain. You'll need your money for his altar, if you are to survive this journey.'

Delilah nodded. 'It's what that devil deserves.'

The jail grew quieter and cooler as they descended the four flights of stairs deep into the cellars. Delilah shivered as the sweat dried beneath her clothes. The darkness was lit at intervals by glowing torches, and punctuated with the occasional whimpers of the desperate. The air was filled with the unmistakeable stench of sweat and festering wounds.

'He's in the end cell.' The guard sketched a mark of blessing above her head then retired to his post at the head of the corridor, leaving Delilah to walk the last stretch alone.

The rotten air clung to her as she passed cells which looked empty, but she couldn't be sure. In the gloom she could make out the remnants of lives stolen here, fragments of clothing, a broken pot, the scurrying feet of rats. She struggled to breathe as her feet carried her on.

She reached the last cell. Beyond the solid iron grille was a narrow stone square, pitched in shadow. Her first thought was that the guard had sent her the wrong way, and there was no one here.

'Samson?'

No answer, but something shifted in the gloom.

She'd promised herself that she wouldn't cry. That she would be strong for him. But this was too much.

'Samson?'

The shape moved again, and her eyes strained to make out his limbs. He was slumped in a corner, completely naked, his chin resting on his chest.

'It's me,' she said. 'Samson, it's your Delilah . . .'

His head lifted weakly. Delilah listened and between the steady drips of water behind her she heard a faint mewling from his mouth and the shallow breaths of one who still clung to life.

'My darling . . . ' She clung to the grille to steady herself. The man in the cage was so far from the picture she'd held in her heart that the collision of hope and reality crippled her. What had she expected?

'Oh, Samson,' she whispered. 'My love . . . '

Her voice broke on her words, but he showed no sign of having heard her. She put her hand on her belly and carefully crouched down to level her head with his. 'I've brought you something to drink, some food . . . '

She reached beneath her cape and brought out a narrow silver flask filled with honey drink brewed over the fire far away in Sorek, and a flatbread she'd baked herself, rolled around sliced meats and fruit. She unwrapped it, offering it towards the grille.

As her eyes adjusted, she saw that his were still closed. His hair had grown back a little and his face was unevenly dark with straggling wisps of beard. His shoulders, though bowed, were still broad. He must have lost half of his weight in captivity, but the man she loved was still recognisable from this shadow.

A sob burst from her and she rested her head against the grille. 'Samson,' she cried. 'Samson!'

'You betrayed me.' His voice was so quiet and hollow, it barely reached her across the tiny cell, But it sparked the guilt within her and she seized at the grille.

'I was trying to save you!'

For a long moment he didn't move, then he

turned towards her, his face contorted as though it hurt him deeply even to look at her. Delilah instinctively lowered her gaze. When she dared look again, and saw what they had done to him, she wailed.

'Oh — Oh God, no!'

They had taken his eyes. Those beautiful blue eyes were gone. Bloodied hollows stared back at her.

She gulped back the sickness that heaved up within her, swallowing hard to steady her voice. 'What have they done to you?'

But Samson only shook his head. 'I should have seen it.' He laughed quietly, bitterly. 'But I was too much in love with you.'

Delilah breathed deep and hard, trying to control herself. 'There was nothing to see,' she said through tears. 'Not in the end. I couldn't bear to lose you as well. If I had got you out of the city, you would've had time to calm down, form a new plan, keep on fighting. It's what you would have done had your head not been clouded with thoughts of revenge.'

'What do you know of me?' he said, his voice warming with anger.

'I know that your fight was too important to give up on account of me.'

Samson turned his face away from hers again and didn't reply.

I'm losing him, she thought desperately.

Delilah dragged herself up against the grille and reached for him through it. 'I love you. Please . . .'

'You know nothing of love.'

381

'I know you,' she said. 'That's what I know of love.'

He didn't move, and with his rejection the last of her energy flooded out of her. She gulped down the words but she could no longer stifle them. 'I came here with your mother, Samson. With Ariel too. We heard — We heard that they are going to kill you.'

Samson unfurled slowly and rolled onto his knees. He crawled across the cell, feeling his way. The muscles of his arms had wasted, and his legs were so thin, she wondered if he'd eaten at all. His cheekbones, below the sunken lids of his eyes, threw deep shadows across his face. She wanted only to hold him, to cradle him again.

He stopped before he reached the grille and leaned against the wall. It was close enough. Delilah pressed her arm further and found his hand. She linked her fingers into his. For a moment his hand tightened and she felt his power stirring, but he softened his grip. Beneath the stench of his imprisonment, the rich smells of memory lurked.

'Why have you come?'

Delilah pulled his hand tenderly towards her through the grille. His arm unfurled like the weak tendril of a vine, so pale under the torchlight. She opened her dress, resting his palm on the bare swollen flesh of her stomach.

The creases on his brow lifted, his features smoothing like sand shifting under a desert breeze.

'It's yours,' she said.

His fingers spread over her belly in a gentle

382

caress, and his other hand reached for her face. He stroked away her tears, and she forced herself to look where his passion, his love for her had once looked back. His eyelids were closed, shrunken and wrinkled.

'You are still beautiful,' he said.

Delilah chewed her lip and swallowed silently to suppress a fresh flood of grief. She collected herself, and said, 'Ariel has been gathering men in the mountains. He plans to storm the jail before the sacrifices for the festival.'

'I forbid it,' said Samson, suddenly finding sharpness. 'Dagon desires a sacrifice to mark the end of winter.'

'But Dagon is not your God — '

'Then no other Israelite should be sacrificed in his name. Ariel should know that.'

'I'll go to plead with Phicol — '

'You will not.' His fingers trailed over her lips, and he smiled. 'I will soon join my God and your only duty will be to our child. He must survive. You and Azubah are to see to that.'

'They will kill you — '

'Then I shall die.'

Samson struggled to his knees and drew himself up against the grille. He pressed his head to it and Delilah kissed his forehead, his cheeks, his nose, breathing words of love into his skin. He accepted them like the sprinklings of holy libations on an altar.

Then he retreated from the grille.

'Now go, Delilah.'

She pushed the food and the flask of drink

into the cell. 'I can stay as long as you need me — '

'Delilah.'

'We will pray for you,' she said.

'And I for you.'

She fastened her dress again, and walked away, drying her tears as she went. Each step away from him wrenched her heart.

At the gates, the gaoler nodded to her.

'I hope you got what you came for.'

40

The sky was heavy with low-lying clouds that lingered but wouldn't drop their rain. Two days had passed since Delilah's visit to the prison and the day of the festival was upon them. Azubah couldn't bear to make the journey, and Ariel had agreed to call off his suicidal plan once Samson's wishes had been made clear.

Delilah defied her clinging exhaustion and returned once more to Ashkelon. She wanted to go back to the vineyard one last time, but she didn't dare, for with Ekron's death Phicol would surely have taken responsibility for it. With Samson's execution imminent, his troops would certainly be on the alert. But Ariel drove the wagon within sight of the western edge of the vineyard slopes and she could see that the burned house had now been completely demolished. The vines were brown and tidy against the slope. Perhaps someone was caring for the land in their own way.

Wandering within the walls, Delilah saw that much here had also changed. Where Onan's orchard had been a green oasis within the city walls, now a pair of tidy white houses were being built. The festival attracted wealthy Philistines from all over the region, so the city was alive with colour and babbling voices. Soldiers had gathered everywhere.

Delilah's feet followed the old tracks, so full of

memories: the entire street where the tavern was had been knocked down and the land stood empty; and the granary was now in the hands of Philistine farmers, the dust of milled grain coating every surface of the yard. She didn't dare go near the jail.

But as the light began to fail in the late afternoon, Delilah returned to the temple she'd so carefully avoided all day, and mingled with the crowds, wrapped snugly in their cloaks, stamping their feet to keep warm. She took up a position near the doorway of the Priests' House, opposite the steps on which Abidan and Jubal had died, and watched from beneath her hood as the three processions came to the temple.

First, the priests in their flowing white robes left their house in silent single file, forming a respectful channel on the temple steps to welcome the second procession. Riding on a small chariot pulled by four of his personal guard, came Phicol and Hemin and their new daughter, swaddled in a shawl of red and gold. They stopped in the square before the temple steps, and behind them walked all thirty of the Ashkelon lords, heavy with their robes and headdresses. The crowd cheered, but there was a tension in their mood that couldn't be ignored. The end-of-winter festival was always one of hope rather than celebration, given the uncertainty of the seasons to come.

The lords climbed up onto the balcony to the accompaniment of wooden pipes, and as the priests formed the ceremonial arc on the steps, the sacred executioner stepped forward with his double-edged axe. There was still no sign of Samson. Delilah felt the baby kick within her again and around her the crowd parted to look down the road to the jail. They fell quiet at first, and she could hear the grumbling of a cart as it ground slowly towards the temple. Like the rush of distant winds, the jeers of the crowd soon spread to the congregation.

Philistine spectators waved their boughs of juniper, ready to hurl them into the cart as it passed, and the air was awash with the heady sweetness she'd be glad never to smell again. The shouts and taunts redoubled, and Delilah was jostled as the crowd strained to get a better look at the prisoner. She shrank back against the Priests' House, fearful that Samson would spot her, remembering too late that without his eyes, he could only feel the rage of the crowd, not see it.

The cart came into view. Samson was on his knees, his hands tied behind his back. The crowd, inexplicably, became quiet, and the last of the shouts was carried away on a light breeze. Samson's feet were unbound. Dressed only in a loincloth — they had spared him that indignity — he looked starved, but no longer wretched; his head was raised. He seemed passive, resigned. Looking at the twine that cut into the skin of his wrists, Delilah remembered a time when he could have broken them as easily as he could breathe.

Up above his people, Phicol waved his own juniper branch. He tore off a tiny twig and pressed it into his baby's hand.

The priests, sensing the shift in the crowd's mood, quickly parted to let the cart through. Soldiers pulled Samson off the back and dragged him to the ground. He landed in a heap and the spectators gave a unified gasp of something close to sympathy. Rolling on his elbow, he pushed himself to his feet.

Someone threw a stone that landed at his feet. Then came another, hitting his stomach and bouncing off. He flinched, but didn't shy away.

Under the hail that followed, a soldier wasted no time in driving Samson up the temple steps, and the lords began to file down from their balcony. The crowd roared, suddenly emboldened, as Samson reached the gateway.

Delilah leaned back against the wall and clasped her hands over her swollen stomach, as though she could shield the baby from what was to come. Night was closing in and the grey clouds now hung fat and dark above the ominous toll of the temple bell. She heard the single shout from the Priests, 'Dagon!' and the reply from the lords, 'Hear us!' and she gazed through her tears up to the sky.

The breeze stiffened suddenly into a wind. Waves of cold, sand-scattered air whipped through the crowd, making everyone turn and shield their eyes at once. It was as if the desert had exhaled.

The wind strengthened into a gale, setting dogs barking in various parts of the city. The horse that had pulled Samson's cart snorted and reared.

When the wind finally stilled, the soldier

leading Samson surveyed the sky with an air of trepidation, then shoved Samson into the temple recesses. Delilah had always avoided the sacrificial ceremonies, but she knew what happened from Ekron's bloodthirsty descriptions in the days of his apprenticeship to Phicol. Samson would be made to kneel at the altar, where the executioner would take a side stance and bring down the axe across his neck. His body would be held to drain over the sacred gully, and his blood would trickle down to the feet of the statue of Dagon.

Please God, she murmured, *don't let him suffer, don't let —*

The ground shook beneath Delilah's feet and the crowd cried out. Delilah stumbled, but managed to keep her balance. On the temple steps, people had dropped to their knees. There was a thunderous crash, and a fat black crack splintered the face of the temple. People turned to grip each other. Some tried to run, but there was chaos. Spectators were crumpled and fell beneath each other's feet. In front of the temple, the crowd became a writhing maelstrom of bodies. Shouts of warning and alarm vied with bloodcurdling screams.

Delilah took a few involuntary steps towards the temple — where was Samson? With a crunch of scraping stone, the balcony of the temple convulsed and tipped. Delilah drew back with a gasp as a huge chunk of masonry crashed from one end. Phicol appeared on the balcony, his headdress askew. With one hand he supported himself, with the other he clutched a screaming Hemin.

Then the whole structure toppled and both she and Phicol vanished within it. The air exploded with dust, billowing through the crowd, carrying their desperate shrieks of pain and fear like surf on the waves.

'The Priests' House will be next!' yelled a man, seizing Delilah's arm.

Roof tiles tumbled around her, smashing at her feet. She followed the man, weaving round the edge of the square, pausing only for one last look back. The ground shook again, and the temple gave a dreadful shudder. The outer walls leaned in as one, and it collapsed on itself with a roar of destruction, exhaling rubble over those unlucky enough to be nearby. People surged around her, running for the gates as though chased by God's anger.

Delilah stood motionless by a well, as they streamed past her. The ground had stilled and the dust was beginning to settle. Only half of the rear wall remained. Somewhere under the rubble, Samson's body lay broken along with all the others.

But it was over.

★   ★   ★

They held Samson's funeral in the valley of Sorek. It had taken several days for the Philistines to dig through the wreckage of the temple, manoeuvring huge sections of stone to reveal the unrecongisable, pulverised remains of the unfortunate spectators. For night after night,

390

the sky above the city echoed with the keening wails of grieving families.

Of Samson's body there was no sign, but Ariel opened the ground where Samson's father had been buried, and they laid in it the robes that Samson had worn for the Charioteers' Cup. Azubah spoke a simple prayer asking God to accept Samson into the afterlife, and to watch over them all.

A survivor from the temple collapse, who had managed to live for three days before succumbing to his injuries, spoke of God's wrath being visited on them. His memories were dismissed by many as the delusions of a dying man, but for Delilah, who heard them third or fourth-hand, they provided a shiver of triumph. According to the injured man, a tailor who'd made the journey from Ashdod, Samson, on being left in the vestibule to the temple, had asked one of the ushers to lead him to the centre. The boy had complied, and the sight of the Israelite giant being pulled along by a slight young man half his size had produced roars of laughter in the assembled crowd. Over the commotion Samson had dismissed the boy, bracing his legs apart between the two wide columns in the middle of the temple floor. Reaching with his hands, he'd flattened his palms against the supports, as if the stone itself gave him strength, and dipped his head. The ailing Philistine's recollection lost its cohesion as he slipped into delirium. He spoke of hearing Samson's prayers even though he himself was seated far away. He remembered the ground shaking, and the executioner running for cover as the statue of Dagon began to topple.

Delilah had no tears left. In the days that followed the earthquake, she'd cried them all so many times. Alone, and in groups, tribesmen had come from the land around to offer their respects to Samson's mother. Among them rumours were already spreading of what had happened in Ashkelon.

Some said God was angered by the sacrifice of his chosen son, others that Dagon himself was sickened by the Philistine thirst for human blood. The children chose to believe the fanciful tale of the dying witness — that Samson himself had brought the temple down around his captors, his strength restored by his great faith. Perhaps, in a way, he had.

* * *

They're all dead now, Delilah thought, as the grave was filled in. *Achish, my mother, Ekron, Hemin, Phicol, Abidan, Jubal, Joshua, Samson. All gone.*

She felt the kick of the baby within her, and she looked past Azubah's head towards the east. Nothing remained to keep her in Ashkelon now, so she would travel to a place where no one knew her name. Perhaps there was a patch of land somewhere that she could tend to as her child grew older. She would take what she had learned of humanity, of cruelty, of guilt, of jealousy and death, and turn over the soil, burying the past. Away from here, she would remember only the finer things — loyalty, charity, love.

In her hand she stroked the lock of golden hair. A few rows of vines would be a start. She could watch the grapes swell under the sun, and press their juice. She could savour the sweetness of the past.

THE END

We do hope that you have enjoyed reading
this large print book.

Did you know that all of our titles
are available for purchase?

We publish a wide range of high quality
large print books including:
Romances, Mysteries, Classics
General Fiction
Non Fiction and Westerns

Special interest titles available in
large print are:
The Little Oxford Dictionary
Music Book
Song Book
Hymn Book
Service Book

Also available from us courtesy of Oxford
University Press:
Young Readers' Dictionary
(large print edition)
Young Readers' Thesaurus
(large print edition)

For further information or a free
brochure, please contact us at:
Ulverscroft Large Print Books Ltd.,
The Green, Bradgate Road, Anstey,
Leicester, LE7 7FU, England.
Tel: (00 44) 0116 236 4325
Fax: (00 44) 0116 234 0205

Other titles published by
The House of Ulverscroft:

THE GHOST OF LILY PAINTER

Caitlin Davies

It's the summer of 2007, and when Annie Sweet sees 43 Stanley Road, the Victorian house is so perfect she longs to move in. But with her husband increasingly distant, and her daughter absorbed with friends and a new school, Annie is left alone to mull over the past. Soon she becomes consumed by the house and everyone who has ever lived there, especially young Lily Painter, a rising star of the music hall. Then Annie uncovers a dark episode from Edwardian London, in which two notorious baby farmers lured young unmarried mothers with the promise of a better life for their babies. Until Annie solves the mystery at the heart of the scandal, the ghost of Lily Painter will never be able to rest.

WHAT YOU DON'T KNOW

Lizzie Enfield

With a lovely husband, two gorgeous children, and a job in the real world, some would think that Helen Collins has it all. So when plain, bald Graham Parks walks into her office, ready to be cross-questioned about his book, Helen isn't expecting to fall for him. He's the exact opposite of her good-looking husband Alex, who woos women daily in his role as a TV character. But after fifteen years together, Helen wonders what it would be like to sleep with someone else. What begins as harmless flirtation quickly develops into something far more threatening, pulling Helen to the edge of something that may just turn her world upside down. It's exciting, alluring, all-consuming. But is it worth the risk?

SWAMPLANDIA!

Karen Russell

The Bigtree alligator wrestling dynasty is in decline. And Swamplandia!, the family's island home and theme park, in the Florida Everglades, has sophisticated competition — The World of Darkness. Ava, is a resourceful, but terrified twelve-year-old, who must manage seventy gators, and the vast landscape of her grief. Her mother, Swamplandia!'s star attraction, has just died; her sister is having an affair with a ghost called the Dredgeman; her Grandpa has been sent to an old folk's home; her brother has defected to The World of Darkness to keep the family afloat; and her father is AWOL. To save them, Ava must journey on her own to a perilous part of the swamp called the Underworld, a harrowing odyssey from which she emerges a true heroine.

WRECKER

Summer Wood

It's June, 1965, while a war rages in Vietnam, San Francisco is tripping towards flower power and Wrecker is born. Lisa Fay — a young innocent from a family farm down south — is knocked sideways by life as a single mother in a city she could barely navigate on her own. Three years later, she's alone again. Kids aren't allowed in prison. And Wrecker is scared silent, furious, hell-bent on breaking everything in his path. When he's sent to live with relatives in the wilds of Humboldt County, life for Melody, Len, Willow, Ruth, Meg and Johnny Appleseed will never be the same again. And for Lisa Fay, one thought keeps her alive through fifteen hard years. One day? She'll find her son and bring him home.

JAMRACH'S MENAGERIE

Carol Birch

1857. Jaffy Brown is running along a street in London's East End when he comes face to face with an escaped circus animal. Plucked from the jaws of death by Mr Jamrach — explorer, entrepreneur and collector of the world's strangest creatures — the two strike up a friendship. Before he knows it, Jaffy finds himself on board a ship bound for the Dutch East Indies, on an unusual commission for Mr Jamrach. His journey — if he survives it — will push faith, love and friendship to their utmost limits.

THE TUDOR SECRET

Christopher Gortner

It is the summer of 1553, a time of danger and deceit. Brendan Prescott, an orphan, is reared in the household of the powerful Dudley family. He is brought to court and finds that he is to be sent on an illicit mission to the King's brilliant but enigmatic sister, Princess Elizabeth. But soon Brendan is compelled to work as a double agent by Elizabeth's protector, William Cecil — who promises in exchange to help him unravel the secret of his own mysterious past. A dark plot swirls around Elizabeth's quest to unravel the truth about the ominous disappearance of her seriously ill brother, King Edward VI. With Elizabeth's lady-in-waiting at his side, Brendan plunges into a ruthless gambit of half-truths, lies and murder.